ALSO BY R. A. SALVATORE

FORGOTTEN REALMS

TIMELESS

R. A. Salvatore

HARPER Voyager
An Imprint of HarperCollinsPublishers

TIMELESS. Copyright © 2018 by Wizards of the Coast LLC. All rights reserved. Printed in the United States of America. No part of this book may be used or reproduced in any manner whatsoever without written permission except in the case of brief quotations embodied in critical articles and reviews. For information, address HarperCollins Publishers, 195 Broadway, New York, NY 10007.

HarperCollins books may be purchased for educational, business, or sales promotional use. For information, please e-mail the Special Markets Department at SPsales@harpercollins.com.

Harper Voyager and design are trademarks of HarperCollins Publishers LLC.

FIRST EDITION

Designed by Paula Russell Szafranski

Frontispiece and opener art © Aleks Melnik / Shutterstock

Cover art by: Aleski Briclot

Library of Congress Cataloging-in-Publication Data has been applied for.

ISBN 978-0-06-268859-0

18 19 20 21 22   LSC   10 9 8 7 6 5 4 3 2

To Diane and to my family.

The rest of this doesn't matter so much, you know?

CONTENTS

DRAMATIS PERSONAE

In the past . . . all of them drow.

HOUSE DO'URDEN

Matron Malice Do'Urden: The young and ferocious drow leader of House Do'Urden. Ambitious and insatiable, she is determined to climb the hierarchy of Menzoberranzan's nearly eighty houses to one day gain a seat on the Ruling Council reserved for the top eight houses.

Patron Rizzen Do'Urden: Malice's open consort, father of Nalfein, he is considered an incredibly mediocre companion by the ambitious Malice.

Nalfein Do'Urden: Malice's oldest son, elderboy of the house, Nalfein is everything one might expect from the loins of Patron Rizzen.

Briza Do'Urden: Malice's eldest daughter. Huge and formidable.

Matron Vartha Do'Urden: Malice's mother, who died a century earlier.

HOUSE XORLARRIN

Matron Zeerith Xorlarrin: Powerful leader of the city's fourth-ranked house.

Horoodissomoth Xorlarrin: House wizard and former master of Sorcere, the drow academy for practitioners of the arcane magic.

Kiriy Xorlarrin: Priestess of Lolth, daughter of Zeerith and Horoodissomoth.

HOUSE SIMFRAY

Matron Divine Simfray: Ruler of the minor house.

Zaknafein Simfray: Young and powerful champion of House Simfray, with a growing reputation putting him among the greatest warriors in the city. Coveted by ambitious Matron Malice, both for the growth of her house and her personal desires.

HOUSE TR'ARACH

Matron Hauzz Tr'arach: Ruler of the minor house.

Duvon Tr'arach: Son of Matron Hauzz, weapon master of the house, determined to prove himself.

Daungelina Tr'arach: Eldest daughter of Matron Hauzz and first priestess of the minor house.

Dab'nay Tr'arach: Daughter of Matron Hauzz, currently studying at Arach-Tinilith, the drow academy for Lolthian priestesses.

HOUSE BAENRE

Matron Mother Yvonnel Baenre: Also known as Yvonnel the Eternal, Matron Mother Baenre is the undisputed leader of not only the First House, but the entire city. While other families might refer to their matron as "matron mother," all in the city use that title for Yvonnel Baenre. She is the oldest living drow, and has been in a position of great power longer than the longest memory of anyone in the city.

Gromph Baenre: Matron Mother Baenre's eldest child, archmage of Menzoberranzan, the highest-ranking male in the city, and most formidable wizard in the entire Underdark, by many estimations.

Dantrag Baenre: Son of Matron Mother Baenre, weapon master of the great house, considered one of the greatest warriors in the city.

Triel, Quenthel, and Sos'Umptu Baenre: Three of Matron Mother Baenre's daughters, priestesses of Lolth.

OTHER NOTABLES

K'yorl Odran: Matron of House Oblodra, notable for its use of the strange mind magics called psionics.

Jarlaxle: A houseless rogue who began Bregan D'aerthe, a mercenary band quietly serving the needs of many drow houses, but mostly serving its own needs.

Arathis Hune: Lieutenant to Jarlaxle and assassin extraordinaire. Taken into Bregan D'aerthe after the fall of his house, like many of the members.

◆ ◆ ◆

In the present . . . many races.

Drizzt Do'Urden: Born in Menzoberranzan and fled the evil ways of the city. Drow warrior, hero of the north, and Companion of the Hall, along with his four dear friends.

Catti-brie: Human wife of Drizzt, Chosen of the goddess Mielikki, skilled in both arcane and divine magic. Companion of the Hall.

Regis, aka Spider Parrafin: Halfling husband of Donnola Topolino. Companion of the Hall.

King Bruenor Battlehammer: Eighth king of Mithral Hall, tenth king of Mithral Hall, thirteenth king of Mithral Hall, now king of Gauntlgrym, an ancient dwarven city he reclaimed with his dwarven kin. Companion of the Hall. Adoptive father of Wulfgar and Catti-brie.

Wulfgar: Born to the Tribe of the Elk in Icewind Dale, the giant human was captured by Bruenor in battle and became the adopted son of the dwarf king. Companion of the Hall.

Artemis Entreri: Drizzt's former nemesis, the human assassin may be the drow warrior's equal in battle. Now he runs with Jarlaxle's Bregan D'aerthe band, and considers Drizzt and the other Companions of the Hall friends.

Guenhwyvar: Magical panther, Drizzt's companion, summoned to his side from the Astral Plane.

Lord Dagult Neverember: Open lord of Waterdeep and lord protector of Neverwinter. A dashing and ambitious human.

Penelope Harpell: The leader of the eccentric wizards known as the Harpells, who oversee the town of Longsaddle from their estate, the Ivy Mansion. Penelope is a powerful wizard, mentoring Catti-brie, and has dated Wulfgar on occasion.

Donnola Topolino: Halfling wife of Regis, leader of the halfling town of Bleeding Vines. She came from Aglarond, in the distant east, where she once headed a thieves' guild.

Lady Inkeri Margaster: A noblewoman of Waterdeep, she is considered the leader of the Waterdhavian house of Margaster.

Alvilda Margaster: Close associate and cousin of Inkeri. Also a noble lady of Waterdeep.

Brevindon Margaster: Inkeri's brother, another Waterdhavian noble.

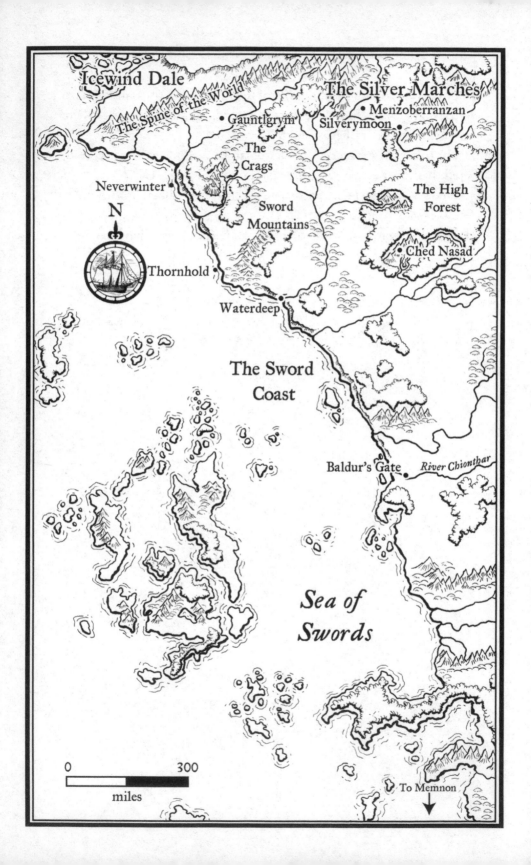

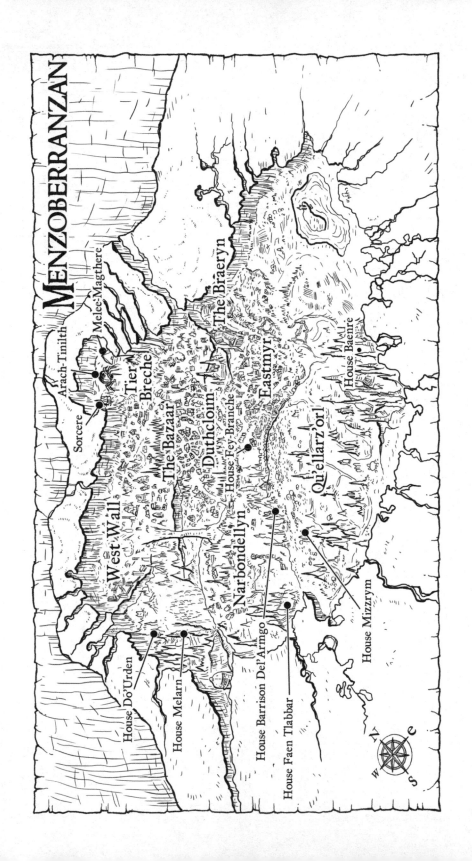

PROLOGUE

THE YEAR OF DWARVENKIND REBORN
DALERECKONING 1488

My lady Zhindia," the demon said, leaving a trail of bubbling sludge as she slid from the summoning pentagram of House Melarn, the Eighth House of the drow city of Menzoberranzan. The handmaiden Eskavidne was in her natural form now, a misshapen lump of sludge that looked somewhat like a half-burned candle, but with waving tendrils sticking out like leafless branches dancing in a gale. Every word the grotesque creature spoke bubbled with muddy plopping sounds.

Already battered by recent events, Matron Zhindia Melarn could not hide her surprise and trepidation as a second handmaiden appeared within the summoning circle, this one in the form of a beautiful drow woman, scantily dressed and grinning wickedly. They were always grinning wickedly, Zhindia knew. That was part of the reason she liked these yochlol demons.

"Yiccardaria?" Zhindia asked. "Why are you here?"

"You summoned," the demon in drow disguise replied.

"I summoned Eskavidne," Matron Zhindia insisted. "Why would you—"

"You have no doubt heard of Yiccardaria's . . . misadventure," Eskavidne answered for her sister yochlol. These were two of the Handmaidens of Lolth, the Demon Queen of Spiders, the goddess of the drow.

Zhindia nodded tentatively—she had heard some rumors of Yiccardaria being defeated on the surface world.

But if that was true, then how was she here? And why had two answered her summons for just one, Zhindia had to wonder—and worry. Particularly in light of her own misadventures, Matron Zhindia and her house had to be wary of . . . everything. They had lost standing, and Zhindia had become a bit of a mockery, something that simmered within the prideful woman's entire body, leading her to fits of rage-filled trembling. She knew that she was clinging to a very slippery ledge here. The matrons of the eight highest-ranked houses—and *only* eight—sat on Menzoberranzan's Ruling Council, and now, because of her own disastrous miscalculations and failure against the sinister workings of the matron mother of the city, her house had been demoted to the least of those ruling eight, with other ambitious houses right behind and looking for ways they might usurp her in this time of Melarni vulnerability. For all the matrons of Menzoberranzan's dozens of houses, the goal was singular: to sit on the Ruling Council.

It was a position Matron Zhindia did not intend to relinquish.

And now not one but two powerful demons stood before her in her summoning chambers, one of them unbidden, and she had to wonder if she would have a choice in maintaining her position.

"Pray tell, what have you heard, Matron Zhindia?" Yiccardaria asked.

As her sister spoke, Eskavidne waved her tentacles, black light of demonic magic flashing, and changed into drow form, sending abyssal mud flying about the chamber.

Zhindia spun away, thinking she had been attacked, but then wiped the dots of mud from her face and regarded the mischievous yochlol, standing quite naked and unabashed with a hand on one hip.

"What is this about?" Zhindia dared demand.

"What have you heard of my sister's troubles?" Eskavidne asked again.

"Yes, I am saddened that you did not summon me directly," Yiccardaria said, moving to stand beside the other and draping her hand on Eskavidne's wonderfully delicate shoulder.

"I had heard that you were defeated and so banished to the Abyss for a century," Zhindia replied.

Yiccardaria sighed, just a hint of that gurgling mud in her exhale.

Eskavidne giggled. "Defeated," she said. "Pummeled. Pounded into a pile of excrement by the fists of a mere human."

Yiccardaria sighed again and slapped her sister demon on the shoulder. "No mere human," she insisted. "A monk, the celebrated Grandmaster of Flowers of the Monastery of the Yellow Rose in a land called Damara. Mere human? This man, Kane, has transcended the mortal coil that marked him once as human. He is now—"

"Oh, you know all about him . . . now," Eskavidne teased.

"Because I intend to pay him back, with great care and patience."

"This does not concern me," Matron Zhindia declared, taking back control of the situation. She reminded herself repeatedly that the key to dealing with demons, even the very handmaidens of her goddess, was to maintain confidence. "Why are you here?"

"Does not concern you?" Yiccardaria replied with a huff. "The circumstances of Drizzt Do'Urden do not concern you?"

The flash in Matron Zhindia's eyes betrayed her calm visage at the mere mention of the heretic drow, the same one who had led the attack on her house that had killed her daughter. Zhindia, too, had almost fallen to the blades of Drizzt, only to have been humbled, slapped and thrown about by one of his allies.

And this very same Yiccardaria had been there, in her room, when she had been humiliated. Watched . . . and did nothing.

"Why are you here?" Zhindia asked for the third time, her stare hateful and fixed on Yiccardaria as she recalled that terrible day.

"Because you summoned me," Eskavidne explained. "The barrier between the Underdark and the Abyss has thinned, and so our Spider

Queen determined that my sister could subvert the century of banishment, but only by first accompanying another handmaiden to this place."

"In summoning Eskavidne, you freed me," Yiccardaria added, and she bowed gracefully. "And thus, I am in your debt."

"As you were in my debt when you allowed that abomination to beat me in my own chambers?" Zhindia said impulsively, before she could think better of it. She was referring, after all, to Yvonnel, a drow woman whom many believed to be the avatar of Lolth herself on the world of Toril.

"You are versed well enough in the ways of Lolth to understand my place in that moment" was all that Yiccardaria bothered to say in reply. "I was merely observing, as the goddess wished, and protecting . . . you."

"You stood by Yvonnel," Zhindia insisted.

"I tempered her."

"She—"

"—is none of your concern," Eskavidne interjected, ending the argument.

Matron Zhindia licked her suddenly dry lips. Who was this creature, Yvonnel Baenre, after all? She knew Yvonnel was the daughter of Gromph Baenre, the former archmage of Menzoberranzan, and a worthless fool named Minolin Fey, and there had been great fanfare and wild rumors that Lolth herself had gone to the pregnant Minolin and blessed the child.

Yet Zhindia didn't believe a word of it, though she could not deny the unusualness of Yvonnel Baenre. Named after the greatest matron mother Menzoberranzan had ever known, this child—and she was just a child, barely four years old—had somehow grown into a full adult woman, and with undeniable sophistication and magical powers.

Certainly, Zhindia's curiosity had been piqued—no more so than her hatred for Yvonnel, but she didn't dare press the issue at that time.

"I summoned you to speak with you about my daughter," Zhindia told Eskavidne.

◆ ◆ ◆

"YOU ARE CERTAIN OF THIS?" MATRON MOTHER QUENTHEL
Baenre asked for the third time.

Her brother Gromph didn't bother to answer this time, and instead just huffed indignantly.

"Zaknafein Do'Urden, the father of Drizzt, has been stolen from
the grave and returned to life," Quenthel said, her gaze down, for she
was speaking more to herself than to her brother. "If it was Lolth who
freed Zaknafein Do'Urden from death, then why? And if not Lolth,
then who?" She looked up at Gromph and asked, "The false goddess
Mielikki?"

Gromph could barely contain his chuckle at the way his sister had
felt the need to include the word "false." Mielikki was no less a deity
than Lolth, of course, and these little bits of servile delusion always
amused Gromph, who considered himself above all the squabbling
about which god was bigger than which.

"I have found no indication either way," he finally replied. "Though
I really didn't look very hard. In the end, it seems such a minor thing."

"Yet you felt the need to come to my throne room and inform
me," Quenthel replied, her lips curling into a snarl.

"You asked me about the goings-on on the surface. That is a going-
on. Fourth in a list of four, you will note, behind the construction of
the Hosttower, the empowered teleportation gates of the dwarven cities, and the progress of the halfling village and its connection to the
dwarf fortress of Gauntlgrym. I would not have placed the news of
Zaknafein's return last if I thought it of great importance."

"Yet of the four, that piece of news is the one most important to
Lolth," the matron mother scolded. "That is the one offering us clues as
to Lolth's will, likely, and to what she will expect of us in this matter."

Gromph shrugged as if it hardly mattered . . . because to him,
it did not. On the surface, he was witnessing a godlike creation in
the rebirth of the Hosttower of the Arcane, but it didn't involve the
Demon Queen of Spiders or any other deity. Using the fire primordial
trapped in the pit of Gauntlgrym, Gromph and others were growing
a living tower, a magical hollow stone tree of enormous dimensions

and supernatural beauty that resonated with the eldritch powers of a beast that was as old as, and in many ways as formidable as, any god.

He would lead the research and study at the Hosttower, expanding his mind and his power. Once, he had believed that being the archmage of Menzoberranzan would be the pinnacle of his achievements, but now he had discovered farther horizons.

What did he care, really, for a mere swordsman named Zaknafein Do'Urden?

"It is good that Tsabrak Xorlarrin is archmage of Menzoberranzan now," Quenthel was saying as all that went through his mind.

Apparently to sting him.

But Gromph silently agreed with that assessment. The less time he spent here, the better for him. In truth, he wouldn't come here at all, except that he knew if he didn't studiously report to Matron Mother Quenthel, she'd likely cause trouble for him and his growing Hosttower.

The grand doors of the Baenre throne room swung open then, and from the far side of the long and narrow chamber entered three drow women, all fabulously attired in garb signaling their high stations within the city.

"Well?" an impatient Quenthel demanded as the trio approached.

The middle drow, who looked very much like a taller version of the matron mother, snorted and shook her head. "Nothing," she said. "There is no explanation for the return of Zaknafein Do'Urden to be spoken by the handmaidens or any other demon we have contacted. It simply is, with no hint of why that might be."

Matron Mother Quenthel's arched eyebrow showed the perceptive Gromph that she had not missed the slight in their sister Sos'Umptu's chortle, or the failure to properly address her by her title. Gromph thought it so very typical of the ever-arrogant Sos'Umptu never to show fealty to anyone who was not Lolth. He hated her the most of all his siblings.

"Or of who did it?" the matron mother asked.

"Or that," Sos'Umptu replied. "The only emotion behind the answers I could garner from the many demons I interrogated was that of indifference. Even from the handmaidens, which means the yochlol either were instructed to not care, or in truth simply don't."

"So the resurrection of Zaknafein was not Lolth's doing," Quenthel mused.

"That is not what she said," Gromph felt obliged, and quite pleased, to point out.

The matron mother snapped a threatening glare over at him, but twitched and backed off her stern gaze as she more fully digested Sos'Umptu's exact wording—and the implications of Gromph's accurate response.

"The Spider Queen ever gives us puzzles to solve," Quenthel said.

"Or perhaps it truly does not matter, Matron Mother," said Matron Zeerith, the oldest of the trio, who sat on a comfortable pillow atop a magical floating disk. She fashioned a seated half bow when Quenthel regarded her.

"We've other matters requiring our more immediate attention," Zeerith explained. "The name of Drizzt will soon enough be forgotten, or will be appropriately sullied by those of us who have witnessed him siding with dwarves and elves against his own people. He is no hero to Menzoberranzan, despite the best efforts of that strange young creature you named Yvonnel."

Quenthel fashioned a resigned look, then glanced from Gromph to the third of the trio, Minolin Fey, as Zeerith finished. These were the parents of Yvonnel, though Quenthel (and most others, Gromph knew) couldn't understand why a dullard like Minolin Fey had been granted so special a child. Gromph could only nod to his powerful sister in reply, for in truth, he couldn't understand it, either. Minolin had been a plaything to him, nothing more. The idea that a being as extraordinary as Yvonnel had come from that play had him as flabbergasted as anyone else, though of course he considered it proof of his own superiority.

"Drizzt was a conduit to great power, that of the hive mind of the illithids, nothing more," Matron Mother Quenthel finished, in a tone that told all that she wanted the last word on this particularly troublesome subject. "A pity it did not consume him along with the other heretic, who stood beside him and channeled the illithid power."

Gromph nodded, but privately disagreed with the assessment. Zeerith Xorlarrin was known as a great friend to the males of Menzoberranzan, as she and her house were the most liberal of all with regard to the station of the drow men. But even she did not fully appreciate the power of the idea of Drizzt, or that his name was being whispered in the taverns of the Stenchstreets and along the outer walls of the houses, where drow males paced in servitude to the female hierarchy.

Or maybe she did know and understand, Gromph thought then, when Zeerith flashed him a little smirk, and perhaps her claims of Drizzt being soon enough forgotten were just for show to Quenthel and particularly to Sos'Umptu, that zealot Lolthian nightmare of a sister.

"To those other and more important matters, then," said old Zeerith. "House Do'Urden will be formally renamed to House Xorlarrin at the next council?"

"It will, Matron Zeerith Xorlarrin," Matron Mother Quenthel agreed. "It is your house now, soldiered by your family, and so it should openly bear your name, a name that strikes fear in the hearts of our common enemies. And will you stay in the West Wall, or go back to your former compound?"

"Both, if it pleases you."

"Take the old compound as your home," Quenthel decided, surprising all in attendance. "Keep House Do'Urden as yours for now, but it will make a fine reward to a house I choose to elevate."

"And regarding elevation . . ." said Zeerith.

"Matron Byrtyn Fey will not challenge your ascent to a higher seat on the Ruling Council," Minolin Fey interrupted, speaking for her mother.

That drew a scowl from Zeerith—Gromph didn't miss that it was one mired in incredulity and disrespect. Minolin had spoken as if there was a choice in the matter. If House Fey-Branche *did* refuse, wholly removing the nobles of that house would prove no difficult task for House Xorlarrin.

"And so I will lead the *Fifth* House of Menzoberranzan, where before we of Xorlarrin were third in line," Zeerith said.

Before you stupidly tried to conquer Gauntlgrym and begin your own city, Gromph thought, but wasn't quite arrogant enough to say aloud.

"You will ascend, I am sure," said the matron mother. "But for now, I need the stability and the alliance of the two houses above you."

"Yes, you have the strength and alliance of five of the top six ruling houses," said Zeerith. "But I beg you to take care, for many others have turned to Matron Mez'Barris of the Second House."

"The city is split," the matron mother agreed.

"And ripe for civil war," said Zeerith.

"It will not be," Sos'Umptu interjected. "The many demons remain, and serve Lolth above all else. House Baenre remains strongly in the favor of Lolth."

"There will be no unity," warned Zeerith.

"I am possessed of the memories of the greatest Matron Mother Baenre, Yvonnel the Eternal," Quenthel reminded her coolly, and it was no act, Gromph noted. His sister was in control here, and feeling quite confident in her decisions.

"I remember the founding of this city," Quenthel went on. "Keenly so. Never has there been unity, nor will there ever be. And yes, we need to be careful in our plotting here, but so, too, does Matron Mez'Barris. More so, I say, because those houses immediately behind her are not insignificant."

"Including my own," said Zeerith, and Quenthel nodded and smiled, and it seemed to Gromph almost an invitation for Zeerith to go to war.

Almost.

"Then you have heard of the call for the restoration of House Oblodra?" Zeerith remarked, somewhat offhandedly, but she had clearly saved the biggest revelation for last, and this one did make Quenthel squirm. "After the salvation of the hive mind against Demogorgon, could you not anticipate such a thing?" Zeerith continued, obviously savoring every word.

"The great Matron Mother Yvonnel Baenre—my mother, *your* ally—dropped House Oblodra into the Clawrift by the power of Lolth," said Gromph, who most certainly didn't want House Oblodra restored. He was learning the Oblodran magic from the one known surviving member of that house, and he rather liked the advantage of having a skill so rare among his kin. "Or have you forgotten?"

"Surely, I have not!" Zeerith exclaimed. "But there are many who either have forgotten, or never knew, or who hardly care now in this time of uncertainty and danger. For all of their heresy, House Oblodra was possessed of a strange magical power that served Menzoberranzan well in the fight with Demogorgon. It is undeniable."

"I have heard the whispers," Quenthel said, and in such a command- ing tone that even Gromph bit back his forthcoming retort to Zeerith. "And they are denied. The illithid hive aided us in our struggle against Demogorgon, indeed, but there will be no invitation for remnants of House Oblodra to return to a place of power in Menzoberranzan."

Matron Zeerith turned her wary eye upon Gromph, and he un- derstood her suspicions here. He had been with the illithids in their action against Demogorgon. He had felt—indeed, had helped channel and add to—the power of that psionic enchantment. So had Jarlaxle's powerful psionic lieutenant, Kimmuriel Oblodra of the aforemen- tioned, now-destroyed Menzoberranzan house. Gromph was allied with House Baenre, of course, and so was Jarlaxle, effectively giving Matron Mother Quenthel the most prominent and powerful access in all of Menzoberranzan to the strange magic of the mind called psionics.

Quenthel wasn't about to surrender that advantage. Zeerith under- stood that, Gromph could see, and despite his affinity for Zeerith, the champion of mere males, he couldn't help but be pleasantly surprised that his sister was handling this one so well.

That was the moment when Gromph realized that he was still tied to his homeland, to Menzoberranzan, and most importantly and intimately, to House Baenre. For all his protestations and complaints and near heretical histrionics, deep in his heart, Gromph remained the elderboy of House Baenre.

It had not occurred to him in recent years, not until this very moment, that he cared whether House Baenre remained the First House of Menzoberranzan.

"Pray go, Matron Zeerith," Matron Mother Quenthel said suddenly and unexpectedly. "Let us each plot the best ways to move House Xorlarrin back to its rightful place without invoking war or losing the alliance of the Third or Fourth Houses."

"And of this resurrected champion, since the topic has come up?" Zeerith asked rather sharply.

"Nothing," said Quenthel. "Lady Lolth has not demanded that we catch Zaknafein, and so we will give him no more attention than a minor noble in a destroyed house deserves. And the same for his son, this heretic, Drizzt. When we were done with him here in the battle with Demogorgon, Yvonnel decided to let him go, so we, too, will let him go. She is gone, as well, and likely near to him. If she decides to kill him in the end, so be it. If not, he is nothing to us. He was a spear, and that spear was hurled and made its kill."

Matron Zeerith sat there imperiously for a few heartbeats, not blinking, not letting her gaze stray at all from Matron Mother Quenthel. She was clearly, Gromph thought, sizing up the unexpectedly formidable matron mother that Quenthel had become.

"I think you have chosen well, Matron Mother," Zeerith said with another half bow. "Your course cannot anger the Spider Queen. If you change your mind, or need anything from House Xorlarrin, know that we will be ready to heed that call."

"I would expect no less. Nor would Lady Lolth."

Zeerith bowed again and sent her magical disk into motion, gliding for the exit.

Gromph suppressed his desire to clap for his sister, and tried to hide as well his happiness that Matron Mother Quenthel had chosen not to go to war for the sake of Drizzt or Zaknafein. Gromph didn't want a messy conflict between Gauntlgrym and Menzoberranzan. Not then. Not when the Hosttower was growing grand and enchanting and there was so much for him to explore in the ways of magic and psionics!

◆ ◆ ◆

ACROSS THE CITY, MATRON ZHINDIA MELARN STEWED IN helpless rage.

"There is nothing," explained Eskavidne. "Your daughter is forever removed. There is no soul to resurrect."

The matron winced. She had recovered most of her priestesses, but not her only daughter, the heir to the Melarni throne. For Yazhin Melarn had been killed by the same weapon that had taken Jerlys Horlbar, Zhindia's mother: a cruel and vicious dagger wielded by the human friend of Drizzt Do'Urden.

And Eskavidne merely confirmed what was already known: a person killed by the blade of Artemis Entreri had no soul left to resurrect.

"You are glad to hear this, no doubt," Zhindia said to the priestess she had called to her side, the first priestess of House Melarn, Kyrnill. The accusation hung there, for Kyrnill had once been the matron of House Kenafin, agreeing to serve Zhindia upon the merger of their houses (but only, both knew, because she hadn't expected Zhindia to survive for long).

"Why would you think such a thing, Matron?" Kyrnill said.

"Play no ignorance with me," Zhindia retorted.

Kyrnill looked to the two yochlols, who laughed and nodded.

"Very well," Kyrnill said. "You intended to elevate Yahzin above me, that she would soon become first priestess and so succeed you to the throne of House Melarn."

"And did this trouble you?" Eskavidne asked Kyrnill.

The former matron laughed. "No. In the end, the choice wouldn't have been mine, or Matron Zhindia's. As Lolth wills, so we follow."

"That was a wise answer," said the ever-burning Zhindia.

"Matron, I have served you well," Kyrnill replied. "When our houses merged, of course I wished to become Matron Melarn. But Lolth chose otherwise, and so I accept my place."

"It is a place that brings great favor from the Spider Queen," Eskavidne assured her. "For both of you."

"Such great favor that we were overrun by the heretic and his ribald friends," Zhindia groused. "Such great favor that I am childless again, and after all the effort I put into grooming Yahzin as a proper Melarni matron."

"Everything for a reason," Eskavidne said.

"A curious comment for a handmaiden of the Lady of Chaos," Zhindia observed.

"Chaos *is* the reason," the handmaiden replied immediately. "And now your house is weakened and you have lost ground, while Matron Mother Quenthel tightens her grip on the city."

"Matron Zeerith Xorlarrin," Zhindia spat. Of all the many drow she loathed, Zeerith Xorlarrin was at the top of the list. And now House Xorlarrin had returned, or soon would, replacing House Do'Urden, against whom Zhindia had waged war, and lost.

"Are you ready to surrender?" Eskavidne asked, words that struck like lightning bolts against the two powerful priestesses standing before her, both of whom looked at her with abject shock.

"In this dark hour for House Melarn, are you ready to abandon that which brought you greatness?" Eskavidne went on. "You are the purest of Lolth's followers upon Toril. Does that no longer matter to you?"

"What are you saying?" Kyrnill asked.

"What are you offering?" Matron Zhindia properly rephrased the question.

"Some information has come to us," Yiccardaria explained. "The father of Drizzt has been stolen from his eternal rest and restored to his son's side. He who was once raised in the slavery of Zin-carla has somehow found great reward. Many claim that it is an affront to Lolth, and that blessed will be she who rectifies this abominable heresy."

Zhindia and Kyrnill exchanged intrigued glances.

"Many claim?" Zhindia asked.

"It is not our place to say more," replied Yiccardaria. "The mysteries of the world are how the Spider Queen determines her most loyal and valuable followers."

"Lady Lolth requires intelligence, not mere obedience," Eskavidne added. "Some might look at this happening as a clear sign that they must intervene, but others will perhaps accept that this is not a pressing matter."

"Does the matron mother know of this?" Zhindia asked.

"Of course," said Yiccardaria. "As she knows that Lolth herself confronted the heretic Drizzt on the surface world, and that Lolth did not destroy him."

"Why?" The deep surprise resonated in Zhindia's almost frantic question.

Both handmaidens giggled.

"Fine. Then who returned to Drizzt his father?"

"Mysteries," cooed Yiccardaria.

"A web of them," Eskavidne added.

Kyrnill moved as if to speak, but Zhindia, deep in thought, waved her hand to silence the fool.

"A web, yes," the matron of House Melarn said. "Blessed are we because Lolth has given to us this great web of intrigue, that we might unravel the divine mysteries and bring to her great pleasure." Her smile widened and she nodded.

"The web of Drizzt, the heretic, who brings chaos, glorious chaos, simply by being," she continued. "And when that chaos subsided, Matron Mother Quenthel took a strand of that web and weaved a war in the Silver Marches, and sent House Xorlarrin to conquer the ancient ruin of Gauntlgrym."

Zhindia looked to the yochlols, but they remained impassive, letting the matron unwind the story herself. "Those failures threatened the order of Menzoberranzan," she reasoned. "Thus did Matron Mother Quenthel take a strand of that second web and weave a third."

"By filling the streets of Menzoberranzan with demons," Kyrnill said, and Zhindia nodded eagerly. "More glorious chaos, yes, but which led to the matron mother tightening her grasp on the city."

"And brought the great Demogorgon to the gates of Menzoberranzan," Yiccardaria reminded them.

"And thus did Yvonnel take a strand of Matron Mother Quenthel's web and weave yet another," said Zhindia, her eyes glowing with excitement. "To use Drizzt the heretic and the illithids—the illithids!—to strike down Demogorgon, which greatly pleased Lolth, his greatest rival, of course. Oh, but the Spider Queen must have enjoyed the spectacle of her people turning the great Demogorgon into a pile of quivering sludge."

"Perhaps that is why she allowed Drizzt to live," Yiccardaria remarked.

"Is this her word?"

The handmaiden giggled again. "Were it her word, I'd not have qualified my statement."

"Was it a hint, then?" asked Kyrnill.

"No," Zhindia answered, and with resolve. "What joy would that have brought to Lolth? This heretic is not worth the breath of her single word to snuff out his life. No, she has given us a web, one with strands to pull, if only we are wise enough to see how."

"That is always her way, Matron Zhindia," said Yiccardaria.

"That is her beauty," added Eskavidne.

"So, to be clear, the Spider Queen has issued no edict regarding the heretic Drizzt or his resurrected father?" Zhindia asked. "She offers no guidance on this?"

"What good is a web that is easy to navigate?" Yiccardaria purred.

Zhindia's chest rose with exultation and anticipation. As far as she could understand it, two handmaidens of Lady Lolth, the closest and most trusted advisors of the Spider Queen, the voice of Lolth to her devout priestesses, had just given her their permission to strike back at the very rogue drow who had so stabbed at the power of House Melarn and left Zhindia childless.

She would find this new web of intrigue, and a strand to pull.

And then she'd weave one of her own.

PART I

Echoes
of the
Past

You can't see webs in the Underdark. You'll feel them, too late, tickling and teasing, and perhaps you'll cry out in fear or disgust before you die.

But you won't see them.

Not those of spiders, or of other creatures laying traps for wayward fools who have ventured where they do not belong.

And few do. Few belong in the Underdark, and those who live there see the darkness as an ally in their own treachery.

Here the duergar dwarves chop and gnash the stone, swinging picks with the strength of hate. Ever growling, ever cursing, any spark from metal on stone revealing grizzled faces locked in a perpetual and threatening scowl.

Here the monstrous cave fishers lay their long lines, ready to snatch an unwary visitor and drag him, flailing helplessly and pitifully, up the cliff to a waiting maw.

Here the huge umber hulks burrow, through stone, through flesh—it does not matter.

Here the giant mushrooms gather and plot catastrophe.

Here the living, sentient shadows flitter and fly, cold fingers ready to throttle anything possessed of the warmth of life.

Here the lurkers pose as floors. Here the piercers hang among stalactites. Any who are found by either would think that the Underdark itself had risen to devour them.

In so many ways, they would not be wrong.

And then they, like so many before, would die, would be eaten by the shadow.

For this is the Underdark, where shadows huddle too closely to be called shadows, where light marks the bearer more than it marks the way before him, where every hunting ground is bordered by another hunting ground, where most are lucky to simply choose the manner of their own deaths, to stick their own swords into their own hearts before the tentacles of the displacer beast pull them from the ledge, or before the spider has finished sucking out the life juices, so slowly, in an inescapable cocoon.

Here the demons often roam, insatiably angry, masters of murder.

Here the quiet, odorless, invisible gases of distant tumult make sleep eternal, or make a flash of flint and steel into a fireball to humble the archmage of Menzoberranzan.

Here is the ominous heartbeat of distant, dripping water, a single sound dancing from stone to stone, amplified by the profound stillness.

Here are the rattles of the bones of unshriven dead, tickled to movement by the dark magic of the dark place, raised in undeath to claw and chew.

Aye, this is the Underdark, and here lies Menzoberranzan, the City of Spiders, the city of those who worship the demon goddess who calls herself the Spider Queen.

Only a fool would come here unbidden.

Only a fool would come here bidden.

For here are the drow, the dark elves, masters of magic divine and arcane, masters of weapons edged in the cruel enchantments of the Faerzress, the magical boundary that gives life to the Underdark and that connects it, so fittingly, to the lands of demons and devils.

Yes, here are the drow, and they will stop killing one another just long enough to kill you.

"What should I bring, Father?" asks the young man about to set off on an adventure into the Underdark, in a fable common throughout Faerun.

"Two coins."

"Waterdhavian gold? Cormyr silver?"

"It does not matter," says the father.

"How much food shall I pack?"

"It does not matter. Two coins."

"Water, then, surely, Father. How much water shall I carry?"

"It does not matter. Two coins."

"I will buy all I need with only two coins? What weapon is best, then? A sword? A bow?"

"Two coins. Only two coins."

"To buy all that I need?" the confused son asks.

"No," answers the father. "To cover your eyes when you are dead. Nothing else that you bring will stop that."

This is the Underdark, the land of murderers.

The land of the drow.

—Drizzt Do'Urden

CHAPTER 1

The Matron's Web

A hundred years," Patron Rizzen said to Matron Malice Do'Urden, the two in the small chamber that served as a throne room in the minor house of Daermon N'a'shezbaernon, more commonly known as House Do'Urden. Despite the limitations of the room—such chambers in most Menzoberranzan houses were far larger—Malice had done her typically brilliant job in designing and decorating the place to make it a true tribute to Lolth, the Spider Queen. Her throne, upon a raised dais, was upholstered in black silk emblazoned with red spiders. Behind it hung great draperies of heavy black material, and they swayed constantly in a magical wind, making them shimmer and seem alive.

Attached to these were webs, of course, actual spiderwebs crawling with actual spiders, most larger than a drow's closed fist, all venomous, and all trained through an assortment of magical spells to leave Malice alone.

To the sides of the throne stood two jade statues, the pride of House Do'Urden. Many drow houses kept animated jade spiders, but

Malice had taken that accepted practice one step further in a bold move that had risked angering the Spider Queen. The jade statues of this lesser Menzoberranzan house animated as half-drow, half-spider driders. It was a cosmetic difference from the normal golems of Menzoberranzan, nothing more, but the willingness of Matron Malice to do such a thing spoke of great audacity—and the favor Lolth still showed her.

Malice's small face tightened as she stared at Rizzen, her consort, though it wasn't clear whether her disgust was aimed at his statement of fact or more particularly at him.

"Few matrons have served for a full century," the often-oblivious male added. "This is a great day. A great day for you and a great day for House Do'Urden."

"House Do'Urden," Malice echoed with a derisive snort. She had taken control one hundred years before to the day, the day her first child, Briza, was born, the day her mother and matron, Vartha Do'Urden, died. Malice Do'Urden had imagined great things on that long-ago day. She knew that she had been flush with the favor of Lolth, for she had given birth to a girl, and the magic spell of poisoning she had enacted during the birth had worked beautifully. Never had she heard a suspicious word uttered about the death of Matron Vartha Do'Urden.

So, she had full control of her house, and though it was but a minor house, it was one with great potential and—importantly—a solid, defensible compound in the West Wall section of Menzoberranzan. Indeed, House Do'Urden had been built right into the impregnable western wall of the great cavern, reducing its critical defensive points considerably. And Malice had her daughter, now a high priestess, and one of formidable size and strength.

But the crawl from obscurity in Menzoberranzan was not an easy one, and Matron Malice was never one to be regarded as a particularly patient woman. Yes, House Do'Urden had climbed many places in the hierarchy of the city, but that was mostly because of interhouse wars depleting the ranks above them, or other houses disbanding for lack of nobles or being absorbed by the greater ruling houses. Indeed, Malice knew that House Do'Urden's best weapon in its ascent had thus far been nothing more than its obscurity.

They hadn't been important enough for any greater houses to care.

Now, though, as they neared the ranking of the top dozen houses, that was surely changing. Obscurity could take the Do'Urden clan only so far. They were dangerously thin of nobles, for Malice had lost two sisters and a brother in the last three decades. They had no accomplished house wizard to boast of, and their weapon master, Malice's oldest brother, Dreveseer, had not waged a decent fight in half a century.

The noble blood had not been replaced, and now House Do'Urden was close enough to mattering for other houses to take note, just as she was least prepared to do much about it.

"When I consider where we have come . . ." Rizzen said dramatically, heaving a great sigh. "And it is all because of Matron Malice's webs. Your quiet alliance with two of the great houses, a bond built solely through your charismatic—"

"Shut up," Matron Malice told him, and meant it, not just because she was sick of his voice. Everything Rizzen was saying was true enough, for Malice maintained relationships with two of the most powerful matrons in Menzoberranzan. But those two matrons hated each other, and so such webs were better kept unilluminated.

The room's door opened and Malice's other child, Nalfein, entered. He was a handsome drow, small like Malice and only a few years younger than Briza. Unlike his sister, though, Nalfein was mediocre in every way. Though undistinguished at Melee-Magthere, the drow academy for warriors, Nalfein should have demanded open combat so that he could claim his place as weapon master of House Do'Urden. But he couldn't bring himself to do it, likely fearing that he could not win, and Malice simply didn't want to give the important title to him, fearing that any notoriety at all would put him in a position to defend himself against challengers.

And there just weren't many Nalfein would defeat.

She looked from the approaching man back to Rizzen, barely suppressing her scowl. Nalfein was his child—Rizzen claimed Briza as his as well, but only because he was told to, for he knew the truth of her conception, and it did not involve him. He truly had given Malice her mediocre son, but no others. Just another in a long list of his disappointing traits. As she looked upon Rizzen now, the thought occurred to her, and not for the first time, that perhaps she should have long ago sacrificed him to the Spider Queen.

But Malice just sighed when she turned back to Nalfein. Rizzen was loyal enough, never questioned her, and always slobbered all over her every decision. He was a satisfactory lover, she supposed, and it wasn't like she kept her amorous activities exclusive to him. And while Matron Malice didn't want to admit it—wanted to take the easy excuse and blame Rizzen—given the sheer number of lovers she had taken, her lack of any more children in the last ninety-five years almost certainly had more to do with her than with him.

"She has left the compound," Nalfein informed his matron.

"She went alone?"

"On a Xorlarrin disk. She will not be bothered."

"You told her the answer?"

Nalfein nodded. "She inquired about the question."

"That is none of her concern," Malice replied. "All she needed to know was the answer."

Malice felt the curious looks of the two males upon her, but she cared not at all. House Do'Urden had been stagnant for far too long. The days of hiding while the houses above them destroyed one another were over now. It was time for Matron Malice to make a statement and to strengthen her house to make it worthy of its current station. To make those ambitious houses behind Do'Urden know they could not fight her, and to make those houses above know that attacking Do'Urden would wound them too greatly to be worth the gain.

Lolth had shown her an opportunity here. She would not miss the chance.

HIGH PRIESTESS BRIZA DO'URDEN SHIFTED UNCOMFORT-
ably on the floating disk as it glided through the twisting streets of

Menzoberranzan. Every stalagmite mound in the great cavern had been worked and hollowed to serve as an anchoring tower for a drow house. Curving stairways and balconies swept the lengths of the natural structures, highlighted with glowing, harmless faerie fires of varying hues, from purple to red and every shade in between.

Moving near to the established houses didn't make Briza nervous—she was on a magical disk that carried the identification of House Xorlarrin, and thus the imprimatur of Matron Zeerith, who led Xorlarrin, the fourth-ranked house in the city but in close alliance with House Baenre, the unquestionable rulers of Menzoberranzan. Established houses of Menzoberranzan would not trouble Briza when she was upon such a disk, surely, but the city was also full of unpredictable rogues, and her path to the raised region of the cavern that housed the greatest houses would take her near to the Braeryn— the Stenchstreets—where opportunists with little to lose huddled in gangs.

Still, she reminded herself that she was a high priestess of Lolth, no minor title and accomplishment, and so instead of fretting, she called upon her goddess and placed protections and wards upon herself.

They were not needed. Gliding up the ramp of the Qu'ellarz'orl, that raised area of the cavern, Briza relaxed her fears of being assaulted, but tightened in the face of certain judgment. Before her lay the great houses of the city, including most of the eight whose matrons sat on the Ruling Council. They would all take note, no doubt, of her passing, and so the tryst between House Do'Urden and House Xorlarrin would be no secret—if it ever had been.

That's why Briza had been surprised to learn that Matron Zeerith Xorlarrin had sent a disk to carry her to their meeting in the first place. Matron Zeerith was flaunting this, not because House Do'Urden was of any importance to the ruling houses, but because of the rumors, resurfacing again as Malice celebrated her hundredth year as matron, that House Do'Urden had done some very dark dealings with House Xorlarrin's principal adversary, a lower-ranking house but one with a formidable reputation, House Barrison Del'Armgo. Matron Zeerith surely wanted Matron Soulez Armgo to see Briza float up the ramp to the Qu'ellarz'orl.

Which meant that Briza was a pawn in the great game between the houses.

That thought weighed heavily on her strong shoulders as she passed the impressive compound of Barrison Del'Armgo—a compound too large and fortified for a house of its rank, surely. This family was far down the ladder of hierarchy, far lower than House Do'Urden, even, but Briza understood quite well that if House Do'Urden went to war with House Barrison Del'Armgo, it would result in a swift and catastrophic defeat for her family.

Within the latticework of the fencing of the Del'Armgo compound, all designed as intricate spiderwebs, the Del'Armgo soldiers marched in perfect cadence and tight formations. They were always marching, always drilling, always training, and no house—no two houses together—could boast a stronger contingent of male warriors. To cap that off, the Barrison Del'Armgo soldiers were led by a young weapon master named Uthegentel who was quickly becoming a legend in the drow city.

Many eyes turned to regard Briza as she drifted past.

She stared straight ahead, pretending not to notice or care, and then, very soon after, she really *didn't* care, for the disk climbed the ramp to the noble section and soon rounded a bend, bringing her in view of the city's Fourth House.

Of all the drow families, none was stronger in arcane magic than House Xorlarrin. Unusually for their race, Matron Zeerith afforded her males great latitude and station, and almost all of them, even those whose claim to noble birth was thin at best, attended Sorcere, the drow academy for arts arcane. And Matron Zeerith had put those wizards to work decorating the curving walls of her compound, which were painted in a permanent shifting wave of faerie fire colors, a mesmerizing dance through the spectrum of normal visible light.

Battlements floated above the wall tops and gracefully curving stairways wound about the stalagmites and stalactites within the compound, often bridging great expanses of empty space to connect the many structures.

Centering the whole of the place was a singular, gigantic tower, which somehow appeared taller than the ceiling of the great cavern. Similar magical tricks exaggerated length to the walls, so that they seemed to go on for hundreds and hundreds of yards. It all gave off a sense of scale at odds with the house's station . . . which was exactly the point.

Briza fought hard to calm herself as the disk floated right before the large central gates of House Xorlarrin, which swung open to admit her. She jumped in surprise as she started to float between them, realizing that each gate was anchored not by a carved metal post, as she had believed, but by a small iron golem.

Briza paused there, basking in the view and noting the irony of the vicious rivalry between Matrons Zeerith and Soulez, for among all the houses of Menzoberranzan, these two were the ones most reliant on mere males—Zeerith for wizards, Soulez for warriors.

Giving an exasperated sigh, Briza willed the disk to move up to the sweeping stairway that led to the decorated front door of the grand central tower, and there its back end lifted, unceremoniously dropping her to a standing position before the entrance. Her biggest mistake was in keeping one hand on the disk for support as she tried to steady her balance, for the disk then blinked out of existence and poor Briza stumbled and nearly fell to the ground.

She gathered herself and her dignity, knowing that many eyes were upon her—and knowing that in this particular house, many of those daring to laugh at her were likely males.

Angered at the thought, she quickly composed both her posture and her expression. She moved up to the door, which opened before she arrived at it. There stood a man in opulent purple robes splotched with designs of spiders and starbursts. His unusual haircut, long and hanging past his shoulders in the front but short to the base of his skull in the back, marked him as Horroodissomoth, the Xorlarrin house wizard and a master of Sorcere who had nearly upended the great Gromph Baenre himself in the contest to be named as the city's archmage.

"Well met, Priestess Do'Urden," he greeted her, giving a low bow. "Do come along, for you are expected, of course."

"Of course," she replied, in a tone meant to remind the wizard that for all his accolades, he was a mere male and she a high priestess of Lolth. He was two hundred years her senior, at least, but in Menzoberranzan, he had been right to bow before her.

The large Do'Urden priestess squared her broad shoulders and tightened her chin as she made her way beside Horroodissomoth to the fancy throne room of House Xorlarrin.

"My great matron," he said when they at last came to the walk before the throne, which was another floating disk, but one with ornate armrests and a high back, covered in runes that magically scrolled, spelling out prayers to Lady Lolth. If she concentrated on them, Briza thought she could hear the spelled words magically whispered.

"Great Matron Xorlarrin," Briza said, and she gave a little bow.

"I am reminded that today is your birthday, Priestess Briza," Matron Zeerith replied. "Indeed, I remember that day those hundred years ago when your grandmother so suddenly took ill and died."

There was more than a little sinister suspicion in her words, Briza realized, which caught her by surprise, for what could anything that might have happened a hundred years before have to do with the deal that was being consummated this day?

With no further explanation, though, Zeerith continued, "You have brought the alteration of the jade spider dweomer?" She added sourly, "I expected your matron to personally deliver it."

"I . . . have," Briza sputtered, casting aside the disparagement. "And the salve you requested. There is no better alchemist—"

"Do not speak of your matron's skills in this place," Matron Zeerith cut her short. "We of House Xorlarrin are not without the finest implements and practitioners of alchemy in all the city. There are simply many potions and salves too mundane for us to bother with. Better to barter, especially when the bartering is so one-sided that the other house remains in our debt."

Proud and angry Briza did well to bite back her retort.

Matron Zeerith waved to one of the priestesses at her side—her daughter, High Priestess Kiriy, Briza believed—and the woman rushed forth to take the scroll tube and the salve jar.

"House Tr'arach will march soon?" Briza asked.

"I know nothing of that which you speak."

Briza stared hard at Matron Zeerith, who glared back at her. Drow houses sometimes went to war with each other, and sometimes other houses knew of the coming battle. But they didn't speak of it, *ever*, Zeerith's look coldly reminded her.

"When will House Do'Urden be compensated for our efforts?" Briza tried instead.

"When payment is secured," Zeerith replied. "You would not do well to doubt House Xorlarrin."

"I do not."

"Good, then finish the payment," said Zeerith.

Briza looked at her curiously, for Kiriy had taken the two items.

"What is my answer?" Matron Zeerith clarified.

Briza thought back to her strange conversation with her brother, right before she had climbed upon the Xorlarrin disk. He had given her a word, a single word, for Matron Zeerith, though she had no idea what it might be all about.

"Child?" Zeerith prompted when she had hesitated too long.

"Yes," said Briza. "The answer is yes."

Zeerith Xorlarrin cackled and snorted. "Ah, it was ever so obvious!" she said. "Your mother, dear child, she is such a lure."

A lure.

The label stung Briza, mostly because she knew that it was true. Matron Malice was indeed a lure, to any who would be lured. Her sexual appetite and exploits had become quite the subject of gossip throughout Menzoberranzan. To this day, Briza hadn't decided whether Malice used sex to gain confidences and advantage or she was simply insatiable. Nobles, commoners, men, women, many—even driders, claimed one set of rumors—it did not matter. Many of those whispers were accompanied by titters, of course, and more than a few by scorn and judgment that Malice was acting beneath the dignity of her station.

Perhaps that was true, Briza had often mused, but what seemed truer to her was that her mother was continually advancing House Do'Urden. In the City of Spiders, in the religion of Lolth, little else mattered, and certainly not anything as unimportant as carnal pleasures.

"Yes," Matron Zeerith said, mulling it over and laughing a bit more before fixing her stare upon Briza. "You do not even know what your answer means, do you?"

Briza spent a long while returning the stare before shaking her head.

"The implications it carries for you, I mean?" Zeerith clarified.

"Perhaps if you told me the question," Briza replied, but Zeerith was laughing wildly before she ever finished the request.

"Go, child, go," Matron Zeerith said, waving Briza away. "Tell Matron Malice that House Xorlarrin will deliver her prize when it is secured."

Briza continued to stare at the Xorlarrin leader as she backed away from the throne. Near the entrance of the room, she was collected by a pair of young wizards and escorted out, informed on the way that there would be no disk to carry her home.

When the gates of the Xorlarrin compound closed behind her, it occurred to Briza that perhaps she should not have come out here alone after all.

"OF COURSE THE ANSWER WAS YES," MATRON ZEERITH TOLD Kiriy and Horroodissomoth back in the throne room. "The resemblance is unmistakable, as well as the size of that one! I am surprised that ogreish creature didn't split tiny Malice in half when she was born!"

Horroodissomoth, who was also Kiriy's father, laughed heartily.

"Did you ever bed her?" Matron Zeerith demanded suddenly, stealing his mirth. He cleared his throat a few times before stuttering, "N-no, of course not, no."

"I would think you curious," Zeerith said, seeming rather disappointed. "I know I am. This Malice has made quite a name for herself."

"Well . . ." Horroodissomoth dared to say.

"You did!" Matron Zeerith accused, but she was laughing more than showing any jealousy or anger.

"What is this about?" High Priestess Kiriy interrupted in frustration. When the two turned to her incredulously, she sheepishly asked, "What are you talking about?"

"The answer was yes," Zeerith explained.

"To what?"

"Patron Rizzen Do'Urden claims paternity of Priestess Briza, but any who know the two, and view tiny Malice as well, would doubt such a claim."

"Then what is the answer supposed to mean?"

"That Briza's father is the brutish warrior Uthegentel, of House Barrison Del'Armgo," Horroodissomoth answered after Matron Zeerith nodded for him to proceed.

That had Kiriy's jaw hanging open. Although of a minor house, Uthegentel Armgo was considered by many to be the most formidable weapon master in all the city. A giant of a drow, he was known to fight with a terrible trident, and scores of victims indeed had been hoisted into the air on its murdering tines, displayed like a trophy.

"And it was no accident," Matron Zeerith said, her voice becoming suddenly serious. "It was done as half of a trade."

"For dark magic," the wizard said. "Birthing magic, which should not be."

Kiriy stared at him blankly.

"Using the power of creation, the act of giving birth, as a means to greater destruction," Horroodissomoth explained. "It is an old technique of potentially great power, but one that has been shunned, and is not sanctioned by the Ruling Council."

"But would that power not be Lolth-given?" the confused woman pressed.

"It should not be" was all that Horroodissomoth replied, and coldly.

"Matron Vartha Do'Urden would agree with you," said Matron Zeerith. "But if we are correct in our suspicions, then we must be extra vigilant whenever Matron Soulez Armgo or any of her wretched daughters is fat with child. Particularly that loathsome Mez'Barris creature."

"You think they have unlocked the secret of birthing magic?" asked Horroodissomoth.

"They gave Malice something in return for allowing Uthegentel to infiltrate their house as a sire. The timely death of Matron Vartha is too perfect to be simple coincidence."

"Too perfect?" Kiriy echoed, trying to follow. "Are you saying that Matron Malice allowed herself to be impregnated by Uthegentel Armgo in exchange for some dark magic that rid her of her mother?"

"So it would seem," answered Zeerith.

"I have never heard of this birthing magic," said Kiriy.

"To take the power of creation and reverse it to destruction," Horroodissomoth explained. "It is demonic and dark."

"So is Lolth," Kiriy reminded them, and the wizard could only shrug.

"Perhaps the birthing magic is Lolth-given, perhaps not," said Matron Zeerith. "But it is a secret few have unlocked, and one of great power, it would seem. Matron Vartha Do'Urden was no minor priestess. She withered and died in a matter of hours. And so House Barrison Del'Armgo is no doubt thrilled by the ascent of House Do'Urden. They have a hold over Matron Malice now, and will likely absorb her house if ever it benefits them."

"Absorb?" Kiriy asked skeptically. "House Do'Urden is the greater house! Why are we even discussing this Barrison Del'Armgo family? More than half the houses of Menzoberranzan are more highly considered and ranked."

Both Horroodissomoth and Matron Zeerith laughed at that remark. "Unless you meet an untimely end, you will come to see more clearly in time, my child," Matron Zeerith predicted. "Matron Soulez or her daughter will sit upon the Ruling Council soon enough. Would that Matron Mother Baenre could see it, and be rid of the troublesome Armgos now, before they grow too strong for an easy eradication."

"Matron Soulez has the great favor of Lolth," Horroodissomoth reminded.

"Then perhaps this birthing magic is not frowned upon by the Spider Queen," Kiriy suggested, and her mother's face spoke volumes. As she thought on it more herself, the young high priestess started to see what her matron saw: that the main reason so many matrons considered birthing magic profane was because they hadn't figured out how to do it themselves. Or even more likely, because it was so powerful that it *threatened* the matrons, as Vartha Do'Urden had apparently learned.

"And now Matron Malice comes to us for help in securing her desired treasure?" Horroodissomoth asked with a shake of his head and a disgusted look on his face, appearing to very much want to change the subject.

"Because Matron Soulez Armgo cannot yet project the power to help in Malice's quest. Worse, Soulez Armgo would keep the treasure for herself. Or feed him to Uthegentel to keep that vain brute satisfied."

Horroodissomoth shrugged, seeming unconvinced. "I hear that this one might defeat Uthegentel. Both he and Dantrag Baenre have watched the progress of the young warrior from afar. By all accounts, he is extraordinary."

"That will be Matron Malice's problem, not mine."

"But will we not be helping Matron Soulez as we help Matron Malice?" a still-confused Kiriy interjected.

"It is a good question," Zeerith told her daughter. "But I think not. Malice's acquisition will anger Uthegentel, who cannot stand any to be compared to him, that foolish half ogre. But it will intrigue Matron Baenre's favored son. House Baenre's eyes will be squarely upon House Do'Urden in short order, and so whatever advantage Matron Soulez might have over Matron Malice, she will be unable to act without alerting House Baenre. House Barrison Del'Armgo will not risk that."

"We should take care to never underestimate Matron Malice Do'Urden," Horroodissomoth remarked. "She knows she is vulnerable now, with her weak house and her uninitiated climb to where she can hear the echoes of the Ruling Council. In one move, she will ward off those lesser houses who think to take her down—the cost will be too high if this one is all that his reputation claims—and she will also put off any plans of Barrison Del'Armgo to absorb her."

"And she gains a deal with Matron Soulez's most hated rival," Kiriy added. Matron Zeerith nodded approvingly at her daughter's perceptiveness.

Many matrons had rivals and enemies among their peers, but no two hated each other more than Zeerith and Soulez. Few would have guessed such a thing, for the two houses' relative distance in their rankings made them such disparate enemies on the surface. But Zeerith knew the truth, and understood that Soulez was gaining power exactly as she had, by using drow males in more prominent roles. Yes, House Barrison Del'Armgo would climb fast, and while others looked on in shock, Zeerith would hardly be surprised when her earlier prediction to Kiriy came true: when Matron Soulez, or more likely her daughter, took her seat upon the Ruling Council.

It was not out of the question, to Zeerith's thinking, that Mez'Barris Armgo would one day become the matron mother of Menzoberranzan, displacing the great Baenre.

But Horroodissomoth's warning did not ring hollow, for now Matron Malice Do'Urden, also of no house of significance, had managed to weave impressive deals with both Xorlarrin *and* Barrison Del'Armgo.

And this deal would include another shadowy force as well, one growing stronger under the tutelage of House Baenre, and one from which, soon enough, no house in Menzoberranzan would desire enmity.

"Take the gold and the bartered commoner warriors to Jarlaxle," Zeerith instructed Horroodissomoth.

The wizard crinkled his nose, having little taste for the leader of that shadowy force. "Must I? He is insufferable."

"Which is why you must. I want nothing to do with him," Matron Zeerith said, though it was a lie, for she had already had much to do with the rake called Jarlaxle.

But her husband didn't need to know that.

CHAPTER 2

The Too-Quiet Charge
of House Tr'arach

From the shadows of an alleyway beside the gates of House Baenre, a dandy-looking young drow watched Briza Do'Urden run from House Xorlarrin. He lifted his eyepatch—a recent magical acquisition, enchanted to show him things his eyes could not and to prevent him from being seen by things other than eyes—to better survey the woman. She wasn't much younger than he, and he thought that, yes, he could indeed note the resemblance to her rumored father.

He smiled knowingly as the priestess from House Do'Urden moved cautiously and kept glancing all around, as if she expected a host of murderers to rush out and throttle her. He was particularly curious, and entertained, as she hustled past the Barrison Del'Armgo compound.

Jarlaxle had heard those rumors from a very reliable source, so of course he had searched for corroborating evidence. He made it a point to try to know the truth about everything. It was particularly important to him to be so informed because he had no house to protect him, not formally, anyway.

Knowledge was how he stayed alive.

Well, that and his obvious charms—or at least, that was what he would insist to any who asked, usually while running one hand through his short white hair, which he had teased and styled with the goo of destroyed gelatinous cubes so that it stood straight up atop his beautifully curving skull, like a crown of white fire.

He was of noble birth—among the highest of noble births any male in Menzoberranzan could ever achieve—but he was not wealthy. *Yet.* He surely intended to be. Simply because he had not yet reached that lofty goal didn't mean he couldn't *act* as though he had substantial means. He ran a fledgling organization mostly on promises and grand visions, and spent more coin than he kept on the finest of clothes and a few other useful baubles he could not manage to steal—like the eyepatch.

And in the land of shadows, Jarlaxle seemed a walking lamp. His clothes were always brightly colored—a fashionable combination of a bright blue shirt, a tight-fitting and tailored red vest, and a gaudy belt woven of giant feathers, one of which was rumored to be quite magical.

He carried only one weapon, a rapier, openly, but those who knew him knew that he could bring another to his hand in an eyeblink, whether a dagger for throwing, a multitined dirk for parrying, or another rapier.

Of course, with this rogue, the weapons, whatever they might be, were more distracting than lethal. For the kill, Jarlaxle usually found other, more creative means.

He wasn't here to kill, though. Not at this particular moment.

"It is good that you have come," he said, still facing the now-empty avenue, though he knew his contact from House Xorlarrin was standing behind him.

"Perhaps Jarlaxle is not as clever as he believes," Horroodissomoth remarked.

"You only found me because I wanted you to find me," Jarlaxle replied. It was a lie, mostly to cover up his obvious blunder of lifting that eyepatch to view Briza Do'Urden, for that item would have stopped the Xorlarrin wizard from magically determining his location.

But he never conceded a truth that would diminish his mystique, and so pressed on. "Our time is short, if Matron Zeerith truly wants this done."

"What do you know?" Horroodissomoth asked. "What news of Houses Simfray and Tr'arach?"

"Nothing definitive. But the streets around them are unusually quiet this day."

"You understand your task?"

"I understand my payment," Jarlaxle answered, turning to face the wizard.

"It is a hefty sum."

"As agreed." The dandy held out his hand, but the wizard did not produce the sack of coins and jewels.

"He must be delivered and he must be alive."

Jarlaxle sighed impatiently and did not retract his hand. "Matron Zeerith's contacts have spoken to me at length. The deal was agreed."

"I am simply—"

"And that deal included my payment up front," Jarlaxle reminded him.

"Do you know who I am?" demanded the haughty Xorlarrin wizard, who was indeed among the greatest of mages in the city.

"Enough so that the crossbows and spells and murderers trained upon you right now would be sufficient if needed," Jarlaxle answered. "And enough to wisely let you find me here, in this place, right beside the compound of Matron Baenre, dear friend to your Matron Zeerith."

Horroodissomoth straightened and eyed the mercenary slyly.

"And dear friend to me," Jarlaxle added.

"Half now," the wizard offered.

"And I will deliver you half of this warrior who has so caught your attention."

"Not mine."

"Your matron's, then," Jarlaxle bluffed, feigning ignorance of the true transaction here.

"Matron Do'Urden," Horroodissomoth was compelled to correct.

"Oh, of course, when Zeerith is done with him. This one is a fine prize, by all accounts. Many noble women have watched him from afar. The grace of his fighting movements is simply breathtaking, I have been told."

"You pretend that you do not know of him personally."

"My dear Horroodissomoth Xorlarrin, I know of *every* drow in Menzoberranzan personally."

"And this one?"

"He is magnificent. He was too good at Melee-Magthere, you know? The masters kept him muted in his practices and sparring. They didn't want him to embarrass the sons of noble drow houses, since his is a house so lowly that the coming battle between it and House Tr'arach would not even be discussed on the Qu'ellarz'orl, except for the presence of this one."

"It is not discussed anyway."

"We are talking about it."

"Only because a bounty was paid for him . . . for him alive."

Jarlaxle shrugged. It did not matter. "Give me that bounty, then, and I will go about my work. Delay any longer and explain to Matron Zeerith that the warrior in question might be dead or might be in the hands of Jarlaxle, who has raised the price."

Somewhere in the shadows behind him, Horroodissomoth heard the cranks click on a dozen crossbows, a whisper of an arcane word—perhaps a trigger for a wand—and the chant of a divine prayer.

And before him, Jarlaxle stood calmly, holding forth his hand.

Horroodissomoth gave him the bag of treasure.

"And do remind Matron Zeerith that any other survivors I take from this fight belong to me, legally and with the blessings of her and her allies on the Ruling Council. That was our deal, and the treasure I most wanted in exchange for my services."

"Are you building an army, Jarlaxle?" the wizard asked. "An army of houseless rogues? That might get a male killed, you know."

"Might get a lot of drow killed," Jarlaxle answered. "More than you can imagine, I expect."

The wizard snorted. "Be quick, Jarlaxle, for Tr'arach marches this very night."

"How do you know?"

The wizard laughed and snapped his fingers, disappearing in the blink of an eye.

Jarlaxle closed one eye and peered all about solely through the eyepatch, its magic assuring him that yes, Horroodissomoth was truly gone.

The young mercenary breathed a sigh of relief, reached down, and tapped his belt buckle, which silenced the illusory sounds of his non-existent surrounding army. He quietly tucked his bag of treasure into a belt pouch, one that looked small but would hold a dragon's hoard of pretty things.

Now all he had to do was figure out how in the Nine Hells he was going to extract this reportedly magnificent young warrior from the upcoming interhouse war without losing half of his still-meager mercenary band.

Or his own head.

"IT IS EXAGGERATED," DUVON TR'ARACH ASSURED HIS mother, Matron Hauzz. "I was with him in the academy. He is a fine swordsman, yes, but to speak of this upstart in the same sentence as the greater weapon masters is folly."

"There are whispers that even Uthegentel Armgo wishes nothing to do with this Simfray creature," said Daungelina, the eldest daughter and first priestess of the minor house. She had just passed a century of life, and so it had become clear that she would never become a high priestess. But a matron?

Duvon scoffed. "More likely, Uthegentel would not waste his time with that one. Why would he? What would be his gain?"

"Reputation?"

"The great Uthegentel has killed a dozen drow warriors in a single fight. Reputation?" He shook his head in disgust at what he considered an idiotic suggestion. "In even agreeing to fight this minor Simfray brat, Uthegentel would diminish his reputation."

"Be at ease, my son," Matron Hauzz ordered. "This one's reputation

is formidable, whatever your impressions of him from your time together in Melee-Magthere. I wonder, though, how you can be so certain
all these decades removed? I wonder, too: why are you so eager for this
fight?"

"The glory of House Tr'arach!" the young warrior said without
the slightest hesitation. "And I can assure you, Matron, that if Uthegentel Armgo, or Dantrag Baenre for that matter, was now serving
as weapon master of House Simfray, I would beg you to forgo this
battle. But for this pathetic imposter? No. I will kill him with my own
blades."

"Take care, little brother," Daungelina said with a derisive snort.

"I have seen him. I know how to beat him."

Daungelina rolled her eyes but turned back to their mother, for
it was clear that none in the room wanted to pursue this argument
further. If Duvon's high opinion of himself got him killed in the van-
quishing of House Simfray, it would be an annoyance, nothing more.
Matron Hauzz had grand plans indeed, and alliances ready to enact as
soon as House Tr'arach proved itself in this battle, and her son's grand-
standing didn't overly concern her.

A mere fifty years hence, House Tr'arach would rank among the
top twenty of Menzoberranzan's hierarchy, she was confident. And
while Matron Hauzz would almost certainly never sit on the Ruling
Council, she intended for Daungelina to hold one of those seats.

"The wizards are prepared?" Matron Hauzz asked. "Those we have
hired to commence the barrage will be ready?"

"Xorlarrin wizards come at a high price, but they have ever proved
worth the gold," Daungelina replied, and it filled her with pride to even
speak of the fact that she had made a deal with the powerful Fourth
House. She, mere Daungelina Tr'arach, had stood before the throne of
Matron Zeerith and treated with the formidable matron as someone
who commanded her attention.

"And your priestesses?"

"We will throw fire down upon them!" Daungelina assured her
mother. "We will freeze them in their boots, leave them paralyzed and
unable to defend when Duvon's murderers come upon them."

"It must be done quickly," Matron Hauzz explained. "We must move without warning and with all speed."

"Only say when, my matron," said Duvon.

"She just did, you fool," Daungelina answered, and Duvon glanced at her sidelong, seeming quite confused. "The Xorlarrin wizards are in position," the first priestess continued.

"I was not told."

"You are a male. You are told now," said Daungelina.

From the throne, Matron Hauzz laughed and waved them away to action.

Out from the walls of House Tr'arach, out into the darkness between the faerie fire glows of the minor houses in the lower section of Menzoberranzan went the soldiers and priestesses.

All about them remained quiet, save the whispers of onlookers spreading the word that a drow house was on the march.

JUST THE GATES, HORROODISSOMOTH SIGNED TO HIS MIN- ion wizards in the intricate silent hand code of the drow. The group of six was levitating across the avenue from House Simfray, cloaked in a field of mass invisibility, though each wizard had also been granted an enchantment to counter that dweomer so that they could still see one another. A tricky bit of magic, but one that was no problem for the most powerful mage of House Xorlarrin. *All lightning, all fire. On the gates only.*

One lightning bolt will suffice, one of the Xorlarrin wizards signed back.

"All," Horroodissomoth said aloud, even though he had put a ban on all vocalizations other than the soft chanting needed for some spells. He wanted to impart on those beneath him that he had a plan . . . and that he did not like being questioned.

In rapid succession, he added with his fingers. *We open the gates and our job is done here, unless I instruct differently.*

He closed his eyes briefly to recall the words for another spell, then looked back down the avenue when his lieutenant tapped him on the shoulder. Not only was Horroodissomoth's sight enhanced to counter the invisibility, but other enchantments gave him sharper vision than any normal drow might know. As soon as he turned, he noted the frontline advance of the Tr'arach warriors, creeping along the compound wall of another minor house.

Count ten, he signed to his wizards, and he began his spellcasting, a dweomer that would take longer to enact than a simple fireball or lightning bolt.

He closed his eyes and concentrated on his spell with such focus that he didn't even register the sudden and furious magical barrage that reached down from the floating group to rain destruction upon the gates of House Simfray. Lightning rattled the bars, fireballs melted the hinge pins. Other spells joined the barrage, these designed to set off any glyphs or wards the Simfrays had put upon their entryway.

A flash of ice froze everything solid, until the next fireball turned it to steamy fog.

And more lightning rang out to slam the metal, to bend and twist and ultimately open the gates.

With those attacks, the Xorlarrin wizards became visible once more, but only for an eyeblink, until Horroodissomoth re-created their camouflage.

Now it was up to the Tr'arach warriors, charging in, hand crossbows clicking whenever a Simfray guard was spotted and pointed out. Flanking the running fighters came Matron Hauzz's noble son, Duvon, and his elite guard, riding great lizards with sticky paws that allowed them to go right up a wall or over a fence with ease.

Second servings! Horroodissomoth signed, and his wizards began preparing their next round of magical fun, this time involving spells for more specific and situational tasks, like webbing to block an alleyway or enchantments to slow the movements of or steal the magic from an enemy.

On Horroodissomoth's signal, the Xorlarrin wizards all joined hands, arranging themselves in a V-shaped formation as the house wizard, at the point, flew off, dragging his weightless minions behind.

Across the street they went, up near the curving stairway of one of the two forward towers flanking the front walk and courtyard of House Simfray.

There they waited and watched as the combat began between Simfray and Tr'arach.

FROM BACK ON THE AVENUE, JARLAXLE, WHOSE EYEPATCH defeated invisibility, watched the floating wizard formation with some mixture of trepidation (he did *not* wish to tangle with Xorlarrin wizards), hope (had they been sent to help him nab the warrior?), and admiration (for he suspected that this was nothing more than Horroodissomoth extracting coin from all sides of the conflict).

He will likely fight along the higher terraces, he signed to his principal lieutenant, Arathis Hune. Jarlaxle nodded, then both pulled their magical *piwafwi* cloaks tight about them and Jarlaxle let the skilled assassin lead the way. They moved from shadow to shadow, across the street, sliding just behind the line of Tr'arach warriors and just before the second attack group, the one including the priestesses of Matron Hauzz's court.

The pair came up quickly on the Simfray wall far to the right of the blasted gates. Arathis Hune slipped aside and Jarlaxle moved past him, producing what seemed to be an oblong cloth of black velvet. Jarlaxle flicked it out before him, spinning it as it flew, and in that rotation, it elongated, doubling in size, then tripling beyond that new perimeter. It hit the Simfray wall flat, and there it stuck, or rather, melded.

For the cloth became a hole in the previously substantial wall, and through that hole went Jarlaxle, with Arathis close behind. Inside the gate, Jarlaxle pulled at the edge, removing the hole, reverting it once more to a simple oblong cloth, and then looping it fast on his belt.

The pair surveyed the compound before them. Fighting had already begun along the lowest level of the right-hand tower, not far from them.

Jarlaxle pointed to the left tower and bade Arathis to go.

And if I find him? the assassin's fingers asked. *Am I to reason with a deadly warrior in the heat of combat?*

In response, Jarlaxle produced a bolt for a hand crossbow, one that seemed a bit larger than typical, and thicker.

Thick with poison.

This will stop him? Arathis signaled.

Jarlaxle shrugged. Arathis heaved a sigh, one Jarlaxle had seen before. He was more than aware that they were a new mercenary band, taking great risks to try to solidify their numbers and power before some other gang, or some drow house, absorbed or slaughtered them. But while both Jarlaxle and Arathis understood that they would likely get in over their heads, this was the kind of risk on which reputations—and further business—could be secured. It didn't make the job any easier, especially as the fighting intensified in both towers and the priestesses of both warring houses arrived on the scene, lighting the darkness with flame strikes, animating magical hammers that attacked on their own, and holding opponents fast with mind-numbing paralysis.

This might well be one of those "over their heads" moments.

Pray for me, Arathis signed. *But not to Lolth!*

Despite the tense situation, Jarlaxle managed a smile at that, a saying that was becoming litany for his band of mercenaries, all of them outcasts from the matriarchal society of Menzoberranzan and the misandry of the Spider Queen.

Off went Arathis Hune to the left and off went Jarlaxle to the right tower, and while the assassin simply used his practiced skills to ascend, Jarlaxle put on a pair of extraordinary gloves that allowed him the sticking properties of a spider leg, and enacted one of several dweomers on his fabulous boots to grant him levitation.

It's all about style, he thought.

On he went, hand over hand, verily running up the sheer tower wall.

◆ ◆ ◆

THERE IS YOUR FRIEND, ONE OF THE XORLARRINS SIGNED TO Horroodissomoth, who nodded, even though he hardly considered the rogue Jarlaxle a friend.

And there the prize, signed another, directing them all to a series of bridges between the towers where battle was only then being joined.

The advance warriors of House Tr'arach, a pair of lizard riders among them, swept out from the right tower, while a small contingent of defenders came forth from the left tower's door. Sorely outnumbered, the Simfray contingent slowed—all but one.

That seemingly fearless warrior came out eagerly, red eyes flashing, a sword in each hand, both spinning at his sides, then one in front, one over his head, then across and back out again.

A volley of hand crossbow darts shot out from the Tr'arach group, flying down the narrow bridge, but that lead Simfray warrior spun and ducked, his *piwafwi* flying wide, collecting in its thick protective folds all the missiles that would have struck him.

He came out of that spin just as a lizard rider leaped upon him—or tried to, for one sword caught the creature's descending maw, the other slashed in at the side of the mount's left leg, and under that leg went the warrior in a roll, just ahead of a stab by the skilled Tr'arach rider.

As he went under on his back, in the same fluid movement the Simfray fighter tucked his legs and caught the descending lizard, not fully, but enough to redirect it out to the right, where he kicked out with all his strength, sending lizard and rider over the low rail.

The lizard caught that rail and held fast, the rider jerking back but holding his seat, for the propensity of these mounts to run along the walls and ceilings required that he be tied into the saddle. Lizard and rider struggled to regain their footing on even ground, but the Simfray warrior was already there, one sword stabbing and slashing at the lizard's face, bloodying its maw once more and retracting too fast for the beast to clamp its teeth upon the blade, while the other sword performed a clever parry against a stab from the rider, catching the blade along the side and sliding it down fast—*quite* fast—fast enough to cut through the saddle's stirrup tie, and the lizard's skin, as well.

The mount lurched and snapped at its own rider reflexively, and while the hanging drow was agile enough to avoid that, the tangle gave the Simfray warrior all the opening he needed.

He jumped into the air, flattened out straight, and double-kicked the lizard in the chin and throat, driving it back, expelling it from the bridge except for a single foot catching hold on the bottom rung of the rail.

The Simfray warrior had no time to finish the task. He hit the bridge and bounced right to his feet, charging ahead, the whole exchange having taken no more than a few heartbeats. "Kill it!" he called to his heartened comrades, who were coming quick behind once more, and on he leaped to meet the Tr'arach footmen charging at him two abreast, with the first pair lowering long multibladed polearms.

Left went the Simfray champion, then back to the right just one step, then back left to the bridge rail. His cuts and dodges forced the Tr'arach footmen to angle their unwieldy weapons, but these were skilled drow fighters and they kept up with his movements, offering no apparent opening.

They were surprised, however, when he suddenly darted straight at them, more surprised when he threw his right-hand sword straight up into the air, and fully off guard when he pulled a long whip from his belt, snapped it across right to left, rolled his wrist to wrap it down around the polearms, and yanked it back the other way. Before they could extract their weapons—one wisely just dropped his polearm and tried to draw his sword—the Simfray champion was upon them, driving both enemies to his right with a series of stinging stabs, a barrage that doubled when he clamped his whip back against its magical hold on his hip and regained his second sword, plucking it from the air with practiced perfection as it dropped from his throw.

Then he was past them, cutting back to the middle of the bridge, spinning as he drove between the next two in line, then the two after that, his blades working in a magnificent blur, each sword taking on two of the opponents to that side, parrying, riposting, knocking the Tr'arach fighters off balance.

Fatally so.

For behind the champion came his minions, following his lead, and every pair of Tr'arach fighters he passed was immediately too hard-pressed to consider going in pursuit.

The integrity of the Tr'arach formation on the bridge buckled.

It had barely had a chance to form in the first place.

STILL FLOATING WITH HIS XORLARRIN FELLOWS UP BY THE tower, Horroodissomoth glanced all about. Since he could see them anyway, he had no idea which, if any, had cast another spell to become visible.

"Who cast the slow spell?" he asked, for looking down at the bridge, at the scrambled Tr'arach fighters, their movements surely seemed magically slowed when compared with the dizzying blur that was the Simfray champion!

The wizard beside Horroodissomoth chuckled and shook his head. "Matron Zeerith should have extracted a larger payment from Malice Do'Urden," he remarked.

Horroodissomoth stared at the magnificent warrior, who had by now passed through the line, leaving the invaders wounded, tangled, and disorganized as the Simfray house guards came upon them. The champion didn't hesitate, and didn't enter the other tower. Instead, he leaped from the bridge to the rail of the stairway encircling the tower, slid just a bit lower, then leaped again out from the tower to catch the bridge support. Then back to the stair, then back to the tower, dropping ten to fifteen feet with each bounce back and forth, until he sprang out on the ground, angling his legs perfectly as he touched down to throw him into an absorbing roll, once, twice, and back to his feet in a dead run toward the main Tr'arach battle group, which was mostly composed of some very surprised priestesses.

Horroodissomoth was happy he wasn't standing there with them.

PERCHED ON THE SIDE OF THE TOWER, JARLAXLE HELD HIS breath with both trepidation and awe as the Simfray champion came bounding down, leaping from rail, to bridge support, to the tower's side, and back again with such ease and grace that it seemed as if he had been practicing this amazing and speedy descent every hour of every day.

"Hmm," the clever mercenary said as his prey sprang past and far below. Just "hmm," because for one of the rare times in his eventful life, Jarlaxle found himself without proper words.

Across the way he saw a flash, a signal from Arathis Hune, and he gave a nod, indicating that he would get the champion while Hune could attend to other matters, as they had arranged.

Although, looking down, Jarlaxle had no idea of how he might get anywhere near the dervish below.

There the intended prey was, down on the field between the Sim-fray towers, rushing and rolling past flame strikes, javelins, and flying poisonous darts. He came upon a priestess waving a snake-headed scourge, but a minor one, sporting only two venomous heads . . .

. . . then sporting none, as the champion's sword slashed across.

And behind that cut, his whip snapped right into the face of the Tr'arach female. Jarlaxle expected the warrior to run past, as he had up on the bridge, but no, he went in hard and finished the priestess with a great cut of his one drawn sword, neck high.

She was enhanced with defensive enchantments, Jarlaxle noted as he spotted the sparks and flashes of various colors from her magical protection barriers.

They didn't help.

Her head fell free.

Now a Tr'arach foot soldier came on fiercely, his swords dancing and weaving as he quickly closed the gap.

But the Simfray champion drew his second blade and matched that flurry with brilliant ease, every strike of the invader's neatly fended off and driven wide, again and again, until finally the Tr'arach warrior was forced off balance, just a bit.

Just a tiny bit.

But too much against this champion, who pressed past and cut the invader in the back of the leg, dropping him helpless to the ground.

"I should have charged Zeerith more," Jarlaxle lamented. Now almost to the ground, he paused, still on the side of the tower, and noted that the champion did not finish this kill as he had done with the priestess.

The mercenary didn't have time to ponder it, though, and suddenly all his efforts to procure this living prize seemed for naught, for the Simfray champion stopped suddenly, so suddenly, dead in his tracks, moving not at all, as if he had simply frozen in place.

And there beyond him on the field stood First Priestess Daungelina Tr'arach, grinning wickedly and waving a lizard rider—her brother, Duvon, Jarlaxle realized—in for the kill on the clearly helpless champion held paralyzed by her powerful dweomer.

Jarlaxle looked to the other tower, hoping to see Arathis Hune close enough to offer some help. But his partner was nowhere to be found . . . and he himself was nowhere close enough to help the soon-to-be-dead champion.

"DEAR SISTER, YOU TAKE THE FUN OUT OF IT!" DUVON Tr'arach said, pacing his lizard mount past Daungelina, who stood staring at the Simfray champion, grinning wickedly at the success of her spell of holding.

"Just claim the kill, you fool," she replied. "Your reputation will gain greatly, and we will tell them all that you defeated this Simfray coward so quickly that it appeared as if he was frozen in fear."

"The best lies are truths told with double-sided meanings," Duvon recited, and though he might have a slight bit of regret for killing this defenseless male, he kicked his lizard into a charge anyway, chuckling as he did so.

"Of course," First Priestess Daungelina called after him, "your newfound reputation will put you in the notice of Dantrag Baenre and Uthegentel Armgo—that one always desires a worthy challenge."

Duvon slowed his mount and looked back to glare at his sister, who was grinning ever wider now.

But no, he shook aside those warnings. He wanted this kill,

whatever the risks, and he set his mount into a charge once more, left hand grasping the reins, right taking his fine sword out wide, neck height to the perfectly immobile victim.

Drow priestesses endured years of rigorous training, more than the minions of any other god on Faerun. From their earliest days, almost all girls in Menzoberranzan, particularly those of noble birth, were taught the semantic, somatic, and material components for the divine magical cantrips and minor spells given by the grace of Lolth. When they arrived at Arach-Tinilith, the drow academy for priestesses, they learned ever more intricate and powerful spells and trained their bodies to channel the magic without personal harm.

But all of that was only part of the training. They also were immersed in studies of martial arts and recognition—recognition of wounds needing to be healed, of demonic powers that might be too great to control, and of victims of their spells, such as the champion caught on the field before the charging Duvon.

Daungelina had not taken her eyes from him since casting the enchantment, her skilled gaze looking for any movement, an eyeblink even, that would reveal a weakness in her dweomer.

But no, he was frozen, fully frozen.

At least, that's how he appeared to her.

For this champion, too, had trained from his earliest days, and as he grew to know the world around him, he had trained specifically to fool priestesses of Lolth like this one, who was so typically overconfident in her powers that she'd never believe someone could fight through one of her spells. Yet he had done just that, resisting her spell—and reversing her own training *back*, having recognized it fully, and so reacting with complete, perfect control.

He didn't move, but it had nothing to do with her spell.

So it was a shock to Daungelina when, as her brother neared, in the split instant before his decapitating kill, the Simfray champion exploded into motion, diving to his knees and spinning forth his sword underhand, like a spear, to bore into Duvon's lizard's face.

The lizard screeched and lurched, Duvon's blade cut high above the dropping warrior, and even as Duvon tried to halt his mount, yanking the reins with both hands to begin its turn, the Simfray champion's whip cracked in his face.

Reflexively, Duvon fell back, over the outer shoulder of his turning mount, his weight going far out and flipping the injured lizard right on top of him. In a frenzy from the pain of the stuck sword and the confusion of the fall, the lizard flailed and clawed, and poor Duvon could do no more than cover and cower and hope the mount didn't tear out any irreplaceable organs.

Or, even worse, could do little to correct his helplessness against the deadly warrior that should have been felled by his sword just seconds ago.

But no, he noted with some surprise . . . and relief. The champion was running on, fearlessly, recklessly, charging for his sister and her guards.

JARLAXLE LEAPED DOWN FROM THE TOWER AND FIRED HIS hand crossbow at the fallen Tr'arach noble son, thinking it would be good to salvage that one. He hoped his sleeping poison would do the trick.

But as he did, a pair of Tr'arach warriors came around the curve of the tower behind him, rushing in pursuit of the Simfray champion. The lead fighter stopped and ducked, and the second flipped right over his companion's back, turning as he went, so that both were quickly facing Jarlaxle and now charging his way.

That didn't work . . .

Purely on reflex, the mercenary tugged his rope belt through the loops on his pants, his pouches, magical and normal, falling to the ground as the cord pulled free. He flung the belt on the ground ahead of the charging enemies. One of them smiled wickedly, as if at the absurd notion such a mundane object could distract them, let alone trip them up.

But then the rope became a living serpent, long and thick, and the smile quickly disappeared from the warrior's face. A two-headed constrictor, which attacked immediately from either end, wrapped the ankles of the Tr'arach warriors and tangled them together. They did well to keep their feet, and even managed to turn their blades toward the serpent, until Jarlaxle, quicker on the draw, produced a wand from a loop in his *piwafwi* cloak and spoke a command, launching a glob of syrupy goo that plowed into the pair and threw them over backward and to the ground.

Now they were truly entangled, the snake tightening, the goo holding them fast.

"Your house has failed!" he told them, running off the other way. "But I have a place for you!"

He hoped that would prove true, of course, but it seemed a minor thing as he turned his focus back to the Simfray champion and the Tr'arach nobles, to see the area before his prize become a blur of translucent, magically summoned spinning blades. The air around the weapon master filled with floating, sticking webs—as well as another Tr'arach warrior leaping in at him from behind.

Jarlaxle's wince quickly became a look of sheer incredulity, for the Simfray champion exploded into motion, spinning all about and slashing with his one sword to fend the webs away. Across came his blade at the last moment, and with such speed and power to take aside the Tr'arach warrior's swords. Down went the champion, into a roll to trip up his pursuer.

And as the warrior tumbled over him, he planted his whip hand on the ground and pressed upward, inverted, to double-kick the Tr'arach warrior in the back, sending him stumbling forward right into the blade barrier enacted by the first priestess.

The Tr'arach male screamed, but only for half a heartbeat, and then his body was cut apart, his momentum and the movement of the blades creating a mist of red liquid and pieces of brain and bone and flesh.

And behind that gory confusion came the Simfray champion, for now the blades were clearly marked with blood. He called upon his innate drow abilities and created a globe of impenetrable darkness in the air before him, covering the blade barrier, then darted into it as if to round the defensive shield.

The first priestess began another spell while her personal guards rushed for the spot, expecting the champion to burst forth around the side.

But no, the Simfray warrior had called upon another magic common to drow nobles, that of levitation, and instead of crossing through the globe of darkness, he leaped *up* out of it, climbing high above the blade barrier at just the right angle to bring him clear. He dropped his levitation dweomer as he went over, landing agilely on the ground right before the surprised Daungelina.

And for all her guards and wards, a host of magic granted by the Spider Queen to this devoted cleric, the first priestess of House Tr'arach was dead, just like that.

CHAPTER 3

No Winners

Jarlaxle winced at the gruesome kill, but still almost laughed out loud at the precision and efficiency the Simfray champion displayed in cutting the throat out of Daungelina Tr'arach. And the brutality, which gave him pause, for this one truly seemed to enjoy that kill. Jarlaxle couldn't help but note the stark contrast to the way the champion had pulled his blows against the common warriors of the invading house, or even against Duvon Tr'arach, yet utterly destroyed the priestess.

When the vicious Simfray warrior turned on Daungelina's guards, Jarlaxle almost yelled out for him to show mercy, for every male drow saved might prove an addition to the mercenary's fledgling band, after all. But he was pretty sure the Simfray champion didn't *care* about Jarlaxle's venture. He needn't have worried, though, for the pair of guards apparently recognized that this single warrior had them sorely outmatched, and so, with their own champion down and the first priestess dead on the field, they turned and fled.

Jarlaxle's relief over potential new recruits proved short-lived, for the blade barrier died away and the Simfray champion was looking back the way he had come, toward Duvon, who was groaning and thrashing in his poisoned sleep under his flailing lizard, and toward Jarlaxle, someone the mighty swordsman knew did not belong to House Simfray.

On he came in a wild charge, whip cracking, sword spinning.

Jarlaxle turned and fled for the tower. He got to the wall but heard the weapon master closing fast behind. So Jarlaxle leaped and called upon his own powers of levitation, climbing up the wall as quickly as possible.

Behind him leaped the warrior, to the wall, then up again, reaching with his whip and just missing Jarlaxle's foot, at the same time deftly dodging the small and spinning black cloth Jarlaxle threw down at him.

Growling at his miss, the warrior dropped to the ground—then dropped ten feet farther than he had expected as that thrown cloth spun down and widened and became a gaping hole in the dirt below him.

Jarlaxle floated down the tower quickly, touching down just beside the magical pit he had created, feeling altogether quite pleased with himself.

"We must speak," he called to the warrior in the darkness below, hoping the brilliant Simfray champion hadn't been hurt too badly in the fall.

He got his answer, to both his remark and his fears, when a whip cracked up from the darkness of the hole, catching him fast about the ankle, and the surprised Jarlaxle was unceremoniously yanked from his feet and tugged into the blackness.

FLOATING UP ABOVE THE BATTLE, HORROODISSOMOTH XOR-larrin was thoroughly enjoying the play, and laughed out loud when the always-cocky Jarlaxle was taken down. He saw the mercenary hit the ground hard and go sliding in, clawing futilely at the dirt as he went.

Instead of finding purchase, though, apparently Jarlaxle caught the edge of his own magical hole and pulled it in with him, for the whole of the thing folded in on itself suddenly when Jarlaxle disappeared from view A heartbeat later, where the hole had been there was only the unremarkable ground once more, with no sign of the mercenary or the Simfray champion.

"Jarlaxle was carrying a bag of holding," another wizard remarked to Horroodissomoth. "That belt pouch of his held a pocket dimension."

The Xorlarrin house wizard grimaced at that information. Bringing an extradimensional item into the effects of another extradimensional item could open rifts through the planes of existence, and would most often send the bearer and anyone caught in his proximity untethered to the Astral Plane, floating lost and helpless for eternity.

And that was the best possible outcome of such a deadly and devastating action. One simply did not merge extradimensional magic items!

Horroodissomoth felt a twinge of regret, and even wondered if he might find some way to launch a rescue mission to try to retrieve Jarlaxle once he returned to House Xorlarrin.

Retrieve Jarlaxle and the Simfray champion, the one Matron Zeerith had paid Jarlaxle to collect.

But more for Jarlaxle, Horroodissomoth had to admit to himself, even if he would never tell anyone else, and certainly would never tell Jarlaxle. He rather liked the strange mercenary, and found him quite entertaining and sometimes even useful.

And yet, that champion of course was a sight to behold—such grace and cleverness.

Yes, it would be marvelous to rescue that one, too.

"Ah well," Horroodissomoth lamented to his fellow wizards. "They were merely fighters, after all."

"Are we finished here?" another wizard asked.

Horroodissomoth looked to the bridge, then to the field below. The invading house was on the run, one noble down and wounded, the other dead on the field. Despite the efforts of the Xorlarrins, intentionally meager as they were, House Simfray had seemingly withstood the assault. By Matron Zeerith's command, that was not supposed to happen—the bought champion couldn't be extricated in that outcome!

But now the champion was gone, in any event, and so the outcome no longer mattered.

"Yes," he told his floating entourage, and he heaved a great sigh. "It is time to go home."

ANOTHER OUTSIDER CREEPING ABOUT THE SIMFRAY COM-pound had no idea of the events that had transpired out on the field between the towers, and this intruder, too, understood the necessities of a Tr'arach win—or at least, of a Simfray loss.

Arathis Hune moved with the sound of a shadow, nothing more, flowing from room to room to hallway to stairway within the main tower of House Simfray. Most of the house guard were out on the bridge and fighting through the levels of the other tower, for this structure's defenses, bolstered by the magic of the priestesses of House Simfray—and that whirlwind who called himself weapon master—had kept the Tr'arach invaders at bay thus far.

The main doors at ground level, and those coming in from the bridge, had not been breached, and no Tr'arach invaders had entered the throne tower, as far as Arathis could tell.

But *he* had entered, using a magical potion to turn his corporeal form into a gaseous cloud. He had avoided any glyphs and wards set on the windows because he had gone through no window, rather flowing in through a crack in the curving stone wall.

He wasn't sure how much longer his enchantment would hold—potions were such unreliable things in that regard—and so he was careful to keep close to nooks and alcoves and other areas or furniture that would offer him some concealment should the dweomer dissipate.

He heard voices when he came into a curving hallway, above the bridge level and near the tower's top, he believed. He floated up to the ceiling and stretched along the high corner, and there held still as a trio of priestesses came rushing by, talking excitedly about the victory on the bridge and the field below.

"Matron Divine will organize a counterattack and House Tr'arach will be fully destroyed!" one said with obvious glee.

"But only if we can save enough of our warriors," another pointed out, and on they ran, heading for the bridge, no doubt.

Because of the extensive study Jarlaxle had demanded of him before their little adventure here, Arathis Hune had recognized one of the priestesses as Matron Divine's daughter, who no doubt had a seat at her war table.

Which meant that the war table was no longer full, though his target would certainly still be there.

Arathis Hune knew he was close, and now knew, too, that in their confidence of victory, the Simfray priestesses had broken their defensive prayer formation, the standard practice for drow houses that found themselves under attack.

The attack had failed, and so, they believed, the coordinated prayers of power would no longer be needed.

And thus, Matron Divine would not be well guarded.

"BUT THEY ARE REPELLED!" A YOUNG PRIESTESS PLEADED.

"But at what *cost?*" Matron Divine Simfray hissed back. She had just been told of the loss of her weapon master and consort, the young warrior she had intended as sire for a host of Simfray children.

"We do not know the full—" the young priestess started to reply.

"Find him! Find out!" Matron Divine yelled in her face. "If he is dead, *you* are dead." She swept her glare off to the side, to the third priestess remaining in the room, who stood before her pushed-back chair at the edge of the round table, staring blankly Divine's way.

"Both of you!" Divine shouted at them.

The priestess didn't blink, didn't react at all, which made Matron Divine even more agitated. "Did you *hear* me?" she shrieked. "Find him! I will know what happened to him."

"He just disappeared, they said," the young priestess standing beside Divine tried to explain, but Divine didn't even turn her way, still staring at the third in the room, at the young woman's inexplicable lack of reaction.

"Find a finger, find a hair, find anything of him that I can use to beg of Lady Lolth a resurrection," Matron Divine said with a low growl, and still she stared at the priestess across the room.

She did look back at the younger one, then, just for a moment, just long enough to yell, "Go!" before turning back to the other and repeating the command.

The young priestess broke into a run for the door.

The other one simply fell over, unblinking even when her face slammed into the floor.

The young priestess skidded to a stop, looking back in blank amazement, which only deepened when she saw the killer, crouched under the most sacred table in House Simfray, a place where he could not be. It wasn't possible . . .

Her mind could not comprehend it, because she had not seen the low cloud creeping under the door and across the stone floor like the fog on a surface lake in autumn.

She hesitated again, shaking her head in helpless denial.

She should have kept running.

A spinning disk—like a dinner plate, she thought, but sparkling with lightning energy—reached out at her from under the table. She got her arm up to block, but the disk's fine edge dug in deep and the crackling arcs of stinging lightning held it there, stabbing at her flesh and demanding her attention.

And taking her attention—too much of it!—when Arathis Hune rushed in behind his throw. Normally he fought with a short sword and a dagger, but now he held his sword in one hand and an aspergillum in the other, which he pumped back and forth as he approached. Except, instead of spraying holy water, Arathis Hune's instrument sprayed oil of disenchantment, which fell over the wounded young priestess and stole her personal spells of defense, and even, for a few heartbeats, the defensive enchantments on her vestments.

This one was pretty, Arathis Hune thought, and surely it was a pity that he had met her in this particular situation.

But the orders were clear: no priestesses of House Simfray were to survive this night.

Arathis Hune's poison-coated short sword slipped into the woman's belly.

The assassin spun away immediately, tearing his serrated-edged sword roughly from his doomed victim. Without even considering the view before him, he went right back under the table—and wisely, for Matron Divine had created a ball of flame in the air above him, her Lolth-given fires roaring down from on high.

The table blocked them and Arathis Hune came out the other side, closing fast on the Matron, his aspergillum flashing once more.

Horrified, recognizing the disenchantment, Divine Simfray fell back. She lifted her snake-headed scourge, but that, too, failed her, the magic refusing to come at her call to animate the three serpents.

"My lady," Arathis Hune said, lifting his hands to a less-threatening posture. "You need not die here."

Matron Divine glared at him.

"I am Arathis Hune of Bregan D'aerthe."

"Then you are a houseless rogue, for House Hune was defeated many years ago." She tried her scourge again, just a bit, and noticed that one of the snakes was beginning to stir.

"No, and yes, for I am now with Bregan D'aerthe."

"A house I do not know."

"No house, Matron," Arathis Hune explained. "We are a band of mercenaries, growing strong in the Braeryn—"

"Stenchstreets!" she scoffed, using the more common name for the lowliest section of Menzoberranzan. "Then you are nothing!"

"House Baenre knows us, and approves," Arathis Hune countered. "And House Xorlarrin paid us to be here."

"On behalf of Tr'arach?" All three snakes on her scourge were writhing now, she noted.

"No. No." He paused and winced as the young priestess across the room began to cry out in agony, gurgling and spitting blood, he knew without even looking. "No, and it need not end badly for you. We are men, mostly, but not exclusively. I am granted permission by Jarlaxle, who leads us, to offer you a position of comfort and great power. Your house is lost, Matron."

She laughed. "You are wrong. The Tr'arach nobles lie dead on the field. We still control our house."

"But you do so without your champion. And your control is not quite as solid as you were led to believe—your tower is breached. You have one way out, and that is to come with me, else I'll leave now and let the Tr'arach horde take you and do with you what they will."

Matron Divine lifted her three-headed scourge, a formidable weapon, and even more so in her skilled hands. She stared hard at this assassin, but the male didn't even flinch.

"We must go," he said instead, and then, when she gave him a doubting look, he added, "I could have struck immediately, when your scourge was disenchanted. This you know."

Matron Divine licked her lips and glanced about. She was hoping one of her priestesses would return to her, something Arathis Hune feared himself. But he kept his mien calm, and that discomfited the matron.

"The Xorlarrin wizards breached your gate," he said. "Surely you know this, for House Tr'arach could never have mustered the magical power to execute such a grand entrance. Lady, we must go at once."

Matron Divine looked around again, knew no one was coming, then nodded and lowered her scourge. It was barely to her side when Arathis Hune came ahead swifter than Divine's serpents, his sudden, practiced thrust planting his sword in her belly.

She staggered back, stumbling, trying pitifully to lift her limp scourge against another attack, but the assassin had already backed out of range.

"As I said, I could have struck when first I stood before you," he said honestly, "but alas, it took my blade a few moments to coat itself once more with that most exquisite poison."

Matron Divine stared at him hatefully, but already she was coughing, her lips reddening with her vomited blood. She sank down to her knees, then dropped her scourge and rolled facedown to the floor.

Arathis Hune wasn't about to let a treasure like this pass him by. He pulled a sack from his belt and tossed it over the scourge, then waited just a moment until the snakes, now separated from their wielder, settled.

Some priestess of a lesser house would pay well for such an item, he knew. Very well.

He gathered up his treasure sack and whispered, "Jarlaxle need not know."

CHAPTER 4

Tying Up the Web

Jarlaxle understood what he had done—by pulling the edges of the hole in on itself, he had created an extradimensional pocket, a cube of extra space untethered to the Material Plane of existence, untethered to anything but itself. Still, he was more than a little disoriented, for it wasn't so much that the pocket of extra space was turning as that its center of gravity kept shifting. One instant he was standing on the floor; the next, on the wall.

He took solace in the belief that the dangerous man he had caged with him was likely fully off balance—at least, until he heard the cut of a sword not far from his face, then caught the crack of a whip on his backside as he scrambled away in the absolute darkness.

And then it was light, brilliant light, by Jarlaxle's design, as he threw a ceramic pellet against the wall, or ceiling, or whatever it was, smashing it and releasing the blinding dweomer.

He saw the Simfray champion diving aside, rolling his *piwafwi* cloak up over his stung eyes.

"I am not who you think I am!" Jarlaxle proclaimed.

"I think you are nobody," came the angry answer.

"Not so," he said, just a bit hurt. He shook off his pride, though, and added, "I can help you if you let me."

"Treachery!" the Simfray champion replied, and rushed ahead suddenly, sword leading, whip up high to crack at his adversary's face.

Good fortune was with Jarlaxle, as was usually the case, when the gravitational orientation of the room again shifted, sending both him and his opponent flying down hard to the side.

The reprieve would last only a few heartbeats, Jarlaxle knew, as the champion began his correction—such magnificent reflexes!—even before he landed.

"I am not Tr'arach," he said. "I came for you."

"And so you shall have me!" said the champion, coming forward with a thrust, slash, and cracking whip.

No novice to battle, Jarlaxle had his swords in hand to parry, block, and duck the attacks. But being a skilled warrior and fighting this brilliant swordsman were two different things, and it was taking much of his concentration to keep the swirling weapons at bay. Still, he had enough presence of mind to attempt to clarify his position.

"I only want to help you!"

The champion came on again, but with less enthusiasm, and this time Jarlaxle easily avoided the attacks.

Stepping a bit more out of reach, he said, "A noble house paid well."

"For my head?"

Jarlaxle rolled his eyes. "Only if still connected to your body! Listen to me—I'm trying to *help* you. No one is going to kill you."

"I'm absolutely positive of that."

"Fine. Bravado. Yes, you're an amazing warrior. No one is disputing that. But let me ask you something: for all your skill with your weapons, can you get us out of here?"

The champion straightened and stared at him.

"Exactly. Nobody of any station cares about House Simfray, or House Tr'arach," Jarlaxle bluntly stated. "And neither will much exist after this day, in any event. Idiot minor houses who can ill afford the loss of a single drow doing battle." He shook his head in disgust. "And over what? For what gain? Does Matron Hauzz Tr'arach think she will one day sit upon the Ruling Council? It is preposterous, and you know it."

"Perhaps you should have told that to her."

"And to your own Matron Divine?"

The champion caught Jarlaxle by surprise when he spat on the floor.

"Your mother?" Jarlaxle asked him, and the warrior laughed.

"Your *lover?*"

He laughed louder.

"But you *are* Simfray . . ." Jarlaxle reasoned.

"Only because they gave me that name," he answered. "But then, like all of *this,* it hardly matters."

Fortunately, Jarlaxle properly read the inflections in the man's voice, and so when the champion reached into his innate drow magic and produced a globe of absolute darkness, Jarlaxle wasn't surprised. And in that darkness, Jarlaxle rightly surmised that the fighter would no longer count upon good fortune in the shifting room, and so, like the champion, Jarlaxle called upon his own innate magical abilities and enacted another spell of levitation. Floating up from the floor, which then became the wall, he met the champion in the middle of the blackened cube of nowhere space, and he matched him, thrust for thrust and slash for slash, through a sudden and violent melee.

Jarlaxle couldn't believe how many cuts were coming at him in the darkness—it was as if the champion were wielding two swords and not just the one. And so he had to stay too close for the stinging whip to be effective, working his own blades in a series of crosses and sweeps to cover as many defensive angles as he could manage.

"Who are you?" the Simfray champion demanded. Jarlaxle almost smiled at the frustration in the warrior's voice.

"A mere houseless rogue."

"Trained as a noble son!"

"Self-taught."

"Liar!" On came a ferocious barrage, and Jarlaxle had to spin away and throw another pellet of magical light, which he did not want to do—such enchanted globes didn't come cheap, after all.

The champion shied for just a moment.

"Why do you persist?" Jarlaxle asked.

"You attacked House Simfray!"

"There *is* no House Simfray, fool!"

"The Tr'arach priestesses—"

"Lie dead, yes, I know," Jarlaxle interrupted. "I watched you kill them. I have to say, you seemed to take a great deal of pleasure in the deed."

"Because they deserved it," said the champion.

"But the Tr'arach males did not?"

That caught the champion off his guard just as he floated against the far wall—and seemed prepared to shove off it to renew the melee. But he didn't, not immediately.

So Jarlaxle took advantage of this momentary respite and pressed further. "You could have killed a dozen, including the noble son of Matron Hauzz himself, but you did not," he said "Because they did not choose the fight, correct?"

The champion just stared at him.

"House Simfray is dead," Jarlaxle reiterated.

"You cannot know this."

"I make it my duty to know such things. But if that doesn't convince you, know that the wizards who came against you were *Xorlarrins.* So yes, friend, I can know it, unless you believe that Divine Simfray could withstand the power of House Xorlarrin."

There was a brief silence. Finally, "Who sent you here?"

"Xorlarrins."

The champion growled.

"Not to fight!" Jarlaxle explained quickly. "Simply to make sure that you were not killed."

"A prisoner, then?"

"No!" Jarlaxle cried immediately, expecting the champion to fly out at him. "There is an opportunity opened to you, a great one. One that will afford you comfort and status, coin and enchanted gear beyond anything you now carry. Powerful matrons greatly desire the services of Zaknafein Simfray." Jarlaxle paused, and before the champion could respond, added, "Who desires only to kill them, I am sure."

That gave the man pause once more.

"Trust me, my friend—"

"I am not your friend."

"But you *should* be, to both our gain. Trust me anyway, though, if for no better reason than that you have no other options. When I say that I, above most, understand, you should believe me. I am not a houseless rogue by choice, or because of a drow war."

"Then how?"

"It is too long a story for us here, though one that I hope I can share with you over some lovely Feywine one day soon."

"So . . . now what would we do?"

"Leave," Jarlaxle answered. "The air in this place won't last forever, and I've little desire to see which of us falls first."

"And when we leave, what does that even mean? Where will we appear?"

"Right back where we entered . . . I hope. The longer we wait, the less the chance of that."

"Right back into the fight," Zaknafein said.

"The fight is over. I expect that, by now, Matron Divine is dead and House Tr'arach has fled."

Zaknafein stared at him hard, seeming none too pleased.

"Your house is gone, and that is a good thing," Jarlaxle said. "For you, at least. Maybe not so much for Matron Divine and her priestesses. And it will be good for many of your associates, and for many males of House Tr'arach, as well."

Jarlaxle saw the flash of intrigue on the weapon master's face and knew that his instincts had led him well. This one hated the Lolthian priestesses, hated the whole matriarchy of Menzoberranzan and the wicked demon queen who granted to her worshipers the power to enforce it.

"I have agents set all about House Simfray, beyond the perimeter of the battle, to collect surviving men from both sides, to join my band if they desire," Jarlaxle allowed.

"And who are you?"

"I am Jarlaxle, who leads Bregan D'aerthe."

The champion put on a curious expression. "Assassins for hire?" he asked, using one of the possible translations of the drow name.

"Much more than that. Information for payment, mostly, and a band of collectors useful for procuring valuable goods—why, like you!"

"Never heard of you or your troupe."

"Well, you've now heard of both."

"And remain unimpressed."

"He said, standing against the wall of a prison from which he cannot possibly escape."

"He said, wondering whether or not to kill the pretentious fool standing before him."

"The pretentious fool who can leave," Jarlaxle corrected, and he pulled out a wand and pointed it at himself.

But Zaknafein's whip took it from him, an expert snap that sent the wand flying across the room to the waiting hand of Zaknafein, who caught it, turned it upon himself, and let the command word come to his thoughts.

"You really should not—" Jarlaxle started to say.

"I will tell them of your unfortunate fate," Zaknafein answered, and he spoke the command word, expecting to be teleported far from that extradimensional prison.

Instead, he caught a glob of viscid goo in the face, the force of it sending him spinning into the wall—or floor, or ceiling, or whatever it was—right behind him, and was there stuck fast.

"I *tried* to warn you" was all the apology Jarlaxle would offer. He shook his head, ran his hand through his styled shock of white hair, and got his bearings, then stepped over and took the wand from the hand of the flailing captive.

"We will speak again very soon," Jarlaxle said, helping the poor Zaknafein get the glob away from his mouth enough that he could breathe. The magical goo wouldn't last forever, but more than long enough to suffocate a victim if left to its own devices.

With that done, Jarlaxle located the seam in his portable hole and opened it wide enough to crawl back out onto the now-quiet battlefield—and he was relieved indeed to see that his extradimensional space remained there. Portable holes were useful items, indeed, but they were tricky and often unpredictable. Closing one fully while inside, as Jarlaxle had done, could lead to catastrophe.

Back outside, the risk was gone, so Jarlaxle closed his toy once more, then picked it up, no more than an unremarkable piece of black cloth, and tucked it, and its contents, into his pocket.

The bridge above him, the field around him, and the tower behind him were thick with the dead, male and female, Tr'arach and Simfray. But many were gone, including Duvon Tr'arach, he noted, and so he was confident that Arathis Hune had completed his task and that his other minions had efficiently begun the extraction of potential recruits.

His confidence became surety when he went to the spot where he had entangled and then entombed the two Tr'arach soldiers with his wand, to find his belt set upon the ground in the shape of a letter J alongside his fallen pouches, and one in particular, which would have seemed, along with its contents, unremarkable to any who did not know the command words to open its deeper, extradimensional pockets.

Jarlaxle sighed in relief when he picked that up, considering that he had incidentally dropped it in the fight when he had pulled off his living rope belt. It dawned on him that if he had taken that pouch into the extradimensional hole, the conflicting magic would have torn rifts in the barriers between the planes.

Even Jarlaxle, who lived for adventure, didn't think that would be a very good thing.

"JARLAXLE HAS HIM," ARATHIS HUNE REPORTED TO MAtron Zeerith Xorlarrin.

She seemed surprised, the assassin noted, though not as much so as her house wizard, Horroodissomoth, standing beside her.

"And where *is* Jarlaxle?" Matron Zeerith asked.

"Secure and awaiting your instructions."

"In the Clawrift?" she asked, referring to the great and deep chasm that ran through the huge Underdark cavern housing the city of Menzoberranzan. The Clawrift, endlessly deep, crawled with kobold slaves, but was also rumored to be the base for Jarlaxle's secretive Bregan D'aerthe band—by those who had even noticed the mercenary group thus far.

"He is *secure.*"

"Is he even on the Material Plane?" Horroodissomoth interjected, drawing a scowl from Matron Zeerith.

Arathis Hune arched a white eyebrow at the wizard. "Where else would he be?"

"Does one ever know with Jarlaxle?" Matron Zeerith answered.

Arathis Hune conceded that with a shrug.

"My wizard here was convinced that Jarlaxle had fatally erred, taking an extradimensional bag into an extradimensional hole."

The assassin laughed aloud. "Jarlaxle would never be that careless."

"I watched it," Horroodissomoth insisted.

Again the assassin shrugged. "I know nothing of that. I know that I just left Jarlaxle, who has the Simfray champion at his side . . . in a way."

Now it was Matron Zeerith's turn to arch her eyebrow.

"We have him and he is unharmed," Arathis Hune assured her.

"And his loyalty to House Simfray?"

"There is no House Simfray," the assassin asserted.

Zeerith again seemed a bit confused. "The Tr'arach attackers were driven from the field, with nobles killed."

"Through no small effort of Zaknafein, yes," the assassin answered. "But Matron Divine is dead, as are all of her children and relatives. There is no House Simfray."

"Then House Tr'arach won?"

Arathis Hune shrugged and laughed this time. "Few of their force returned to the house. Many, including all of the priestesses who went to House Simfray, were killed. Others have turned to a different path."

"A differ—" Matron Zeerith paused. "Jarlaxle *took* them? Or rather, *you* took them, for your little band of troublemakers?"

"I cannot speak to that."

"You just did."

She knew, of course, Arathis Hune understood; and she knew, too, that he had wanted her to know. He hadn't agreed with Jarlaxle's decision to use this moment to raise the visibility of Bregan D'aerthe—they had absorbed nearly twoscore warriors, a pair of wizards, and a priestess from the fallout of the Tr'arach-Simfray war, an amazing haul, depending on how many survived their wounds—but still remained a fledgling band, and obviously couldn't even be certain of the loyalties of the newcomers. Of course, Arathis Hune knew that he didn't know what Jarlaxle knew. There were other influences behind the scenes, most likely with First House Baenre, guiding Jarlaxle's choices here, and Arathis Hune had been beside Jarlaxle long enough to trust the strange fellow's judgment.

"Would you have us deliver the prize to you or to Matron Malice Do'Urden?" the assassin asked, changing the subject.

"Our part in this is never to be mentioned. Take him to Matron Malice."

Arathis Hune bowed and turned to go, but paused to ask one more question. "Does House Xorlarrin hold any bond with House Tr'arach beyond the hiring of your wizards to open the way to House Simfray?"

"What do you imply?" Horroodissomoth demanded.

"He wants to know if we care whether or not Matron Hauzz falls," Matron Zeerith answered the wizard, and her tone told Arathis Hune that they did not. He smiled and turned again to leave.

"Tell Jarlaxle that I wish to speak with him when he disposes of his current affairs," Matron Zeerith ordered him as he went, and he smiled at her appropriate choice of verb.

◆ ◆ ◆

HORROODISSOMOTH SNORTED DERISIVELY WHEN THE AS-
sassin was gone.

"Let go of your anger," Matron Zeerith told him.

"They are houseless upstarts," the wizard argued. "That is a dangerous combination and one that should not be tolerated in the order
of Menzoberranzan."

"Order?" Zeerith echoed. "Have you ever met a handmaiden of
Lolth?"

"There is necessary order within the chaos," the wizard replied
stubbornly.

"And Jarlaxle's fledgling band is now part of that order."

Horroodissomoth snorted again.

"Do you think they exist without the blessing of Matron Mother
Baenre?" Matron Zeerith said, chuckling at him.

Horroodissomoth seemed as if he was about to respond, but rocked
back on his heels instead.

"You are putting far too much thought into all of this," Matron Zeerith
scolded him. "It was a minor transaction made for our gain. We learned
an important secret about the potential relationship between Uthegentel
Armgo and Matron Malice. Matron Mother Baenre has asked of her allies that they keep a close watch on Matron Soulez Armgo and her
family. She will reward me for this information. And this day, we have
begun a relationship with a band of mercenaries who may prove valuable
to us. Finally, we now have good standing with House Do'Urden."

"Why would we care for House Do'Urden?"

"Because I do not underestimate them, particularly now that they
will claim Zaknafein Simfray in their ranks, and you would be wise not
to, either. Matron Malice is cunning, loyal enough, and wise enough to
allow her house to be easily manipulated by her betters. She may one
day sit on the Ruling Council, but even if not, it is quite possible that
someday in the future she will prove a useful ally for House Xorlarrin.
Or foil—which is not always a bad thing. At the very least, we have
leveled the loyalty of Malice between us and the ascendant House
Barrison Del'Armgo.

"Regardless, it is done, and requires no more thought and effort," she told her wizard. "Now it is time for us to consider our other duties. We will watch, from afar, as the play continues."

Horroodissomoth bowed in acceptance, and that was the last time anyone of note in House Xorlarrin paid any heed at all to the goings-on of the minor house called Do'Urden for decades to come.

Hindsight would prove this unwise.

CHAPTER 5

Bartering with Bartered Goods

The empty black chamber opened suddenly and a surprised Zaknafein tumbled out, falling a dozen feet to land upon a mound of piled blankets. He was back on the Prime Material Plane of existence, at least, but now in a pit, lichen-lit, in a deep cave. He rolled around to free himself of the blanket break-fall and looked up to see his captors staring down at him from above.

"I apologize for the insult in dumping you so unceremoniously," said Jarlaxle. "But you still have your weapons, and I have seen you put them to use quite effectively. You understand my caution, I am sure."

"Didn't I earn your trust in your black hole?" Zaknafein called up.

Jarlaxle grinned, appreciating the sarcasm—an art that seemed so often lost upon his otherwise intelligent race. Perhaps it was because everything involving Lady Lolth was so serious, he had often mused. An uncareful word or a misread joke could get one killed. Or worse.

"I trust that you got all of the goo out of your nose," the mercenary said in reply. "That is all the trust I offer at this point in our inevitably long and friendly relationship."

"Your confidence is inspiring," said the captured weapon master.

"Because it is always backed by cleverness."

Down in the pit, Zaknafein chuckled and admitted, "Well played, rogue."

"If you would care to put your weapons—all of them—in the basket to the side, we will get you out of there," Jarlaxle explained. "You are not a prisoner here, but I'll not have you walking around with a whip and sword, or those daggers you have hidden away. I must protect my associates, you see."

"Yourself, you mean," came the reply from the pit. "You and I have unresolved business."

"Balance the scales on our friendship, Zaknafein. Understand that what I have done has saved your life . . ."

"Whoever told you that I would wish that?"

The simmering anger behind that response—clearly not aimed at this particular incident, but a more general sense of growling rage—caught Jarlaxle off guard.

"Well, in any case, it was not your choice to make," Jarlaxle answered. "Not then. And perhaps you will find a more palatable life now that you are free of House Simfray, and more importantly Matron Divine."

The warrior in the pit glared up at him, to which Jarlaxle only shrugged and said, "Your weapons, and you walk free. Else remain there until hunger compels you."

The mercenary nodded to his henchmen, then turned and walked away. He gave a little smile just a couple of steps later when he heard the clang of a sword hitting the floor in the pit behind him.

A SMOOTH CASCADE OF WATER RAN DOWN THE WALL, DIS-appearing into a crack cut at the base. Lichen glowed on the wall at the sides of the waterfall, but not behind, the strange lighting effectively turning the falling sheet of water into a mirror.

They were in a natural cave, but the accoutrements made it appear to be anything but. In addition to the strange waterfall, the chamber sported magnificent bookshelves of carved giant mushroom stalks, with every other shelf holding some marvelous figurine of various monsters, while the shelves between were thick with books—more books than Zaknafein had seen since his time at the academy, when he had visited Sorcere, the school of wizards.

White stone chairs set with thick purple cushions framed a decorated hearth lined with swords and other fabulous, if inefficient, ornamental weapons. Orange and red flames danced about a pile of crystals in that grand fireplace, but this wasn't an actual fire, for no heat spilled forth into the chamber, and none was needed. Rather, it was faerie fire, like that limning the many structures of the city, and created for atmosphere only.

And that effect, Zaknafein had to admit, seemed to be incredibly sanguine and disarming—too much so, perhaps.

He made a mental note to remember that, and his guard remained up.

"Do relax," Jarlaxle said to him, as if reading his every thought. The mercenary motioned to a table at the side of the room heaped with good food and bottles of wine. "You must be famished, so please, eat to your fill."

Zaknafein stared at him suspiciously, but did move to take a seat.

"Oh, now you fear I will poison you?" Jarlaxle said, feigning hurt feelings. "After all we have been through together?"

The warrior never took his gaze off Jarlaxle as he did indeed make his way to the table. He had only barely begun to eat when he heard the mercenary say something to another drow, a wizard, judging by his robes, who immediately launched into spellcasting.

Zaknafein followed the casters gaze to the waterfall, which shimmered as if with inner light, then formed within its smooth flow an image, crystal clear, of a female drow—judging by her attire, one of great stature. A high priestess or perhaps even a matron.

"She is alluring, is she not?" Jarlaxle asked.

Zaknafein shrugged noncommittally.

"Alluring and clever and quite skilled in the art of lovemaking," Jarlaxle explained.

"And you are her consort," Zaknafein surmised, acting quite unimpressed.

Jarlaxle surprised him with a laugh. "I have never met her, in any way. Perhaps I shall someday."

"In her bed, no doubt."

Jarlaxle sucked in his breath. "I do not know," he said doubtfully. "I know her intended husband, and he is a drow of formidable martial skills. Indeed, formidable enough that I don't wish to fight him again."

"Is that why I am here?" Zaknafein asked in all seriousness. "To kill him?"

The wizard beside Jarlaxle burst out in laughter.

"Suicide is unbecoming," Jarlaxle said, and Zaknafein's frown became an angry scowl as he sorted out the riddle.

"Matron Malice Do'Urden," Jarlaxle explained, indicating the woman shown in the waterfall. "By her cunning, her house has steadily climbed."

"I have heard of House Do'Urden," Zaknafein admitted.

"And they of you," Jarlaxle explained. "Matron Malice paid a powerful house well to make sure that you survived the war when House Simfray did not. She desires you, openly, as weapon master of House Do'Urden, and privately, as consort."

Zaknafein knew that he looked very much like he wanted to murder Jarlaxle at that moment, and he didn't try to hide it.

But the mercenary simply snorted at him, as if his attitude was preposterous. "There are worse fates, my friend."

"I am not your friend."

"We've been over this. You will be," Jarlaxle said. "And take heart, for you have just leaped to more power than even you could have imagined. You will thrive in House Do'Urden, and House Do'Urden will thrive with you."

"In ways in which I hardly care."

"Don't be so obtuse. For one thing, you care for adventure and battle. That much I know."

"Some battles," he conceded.

"Well, House Do'Urden will know many battles in the coming decades," Jarlaxle assured him. "The ambitions of Matron Malice in war are second only to her ambitions in lovemaking. You will get to experience both. I am rarely jealous, but—"

"Shut up."

"As you wish. But you should understand—"

"You are still talking."

Jarlaxle paused and sat back in his chair, giving Zaknafein a long while to stare at the image in the waterfall and come to terms with the sudden change of events.

"I must deliver you to her," Jarlaxle explained after a long delay.

"And if I refuse?"

"You cannot refuse. It is that simple. You will be given to Matron Malice and House Do'Urden, there to make a new life."

"Or I will kill every one of them."

"In that, you do have a choice, though I see no gain for Zaknafein in that event."

Zaknafein glared at him.

"Matron Malice played no part in the fall of House Simfray," Jarlaxle assured him. "Everyone knew that Tr'arach would march against you, and she merely wanted to ensure that the most valuable asset of House Simfray was preserved and put to good use."

"And now I am to be her plaything?"

"Or she yours," said Jarlaxle. "It is all in the perception, yes? You will get a warm bed—quite often very warm, if the rumors are remotely accurate—finer food than you have ever known, better weapons and armor than you have ever known, and a cohort of powerful drow about you greater than you have ever known. Surely House Do'Urden will prove a more worthy home for the great Zaknafein than House Simfray ever could."

"Take care with your words."

Jarlaxle laughed at him. "Oh, do not even pretend that you gave a single curse of Lolth for Matron Divine or the others you once called family. Haven't we already discussed this in our intimate time together? Do you think you are the only refugee of House Simfray who I have taken into my home? I have extracted a score of your colleagues, Zaknafein, and they now serve Bregan D'aerthe, and willingly. I know all about you, and how much you hated Divine and the other priestesses of that miserable house. Now you are called to a greater station, one that will give you opportunity more fitting for one of your extraordinary skill.

"So please, quit hiding behind your frown. You need not thank me now, but one day, you will."

His blunt talk surprised Zaknafein and put him back on his heels. For so many years, he had hidden successfully behind a dour face, but he suddenly thought it a ridiculous facade against the truth of this strange mercenary's words.

"If I agree . . ."

"You cannot disagree," Jarlaxle reminded him.

Zaknafein paused and considered the truth of that. "Better for you if I agree," he said.

"It matters not at all to me," Jarlaxle assured him.

The two stared at each other long and hard, and Zaknafein believed that Jarlaxle was lying about whether the outcome mattered to him. Yet, it was just as clear that one way or another, he was being delivered to House Do'Urden.

"My payment is secured," Jarlaxle said. "All I need do is drop you, alive, at Matron Malice's door. What happens after that is not my affair."

"If I agree," Zaknafein stubbornly repeated anyway, "I would ask of you just one favor."

Jarlaxle's stern face softened as the moments passed. "I will grant it if I can, but only in exchange for your assurance that you will not kill me if one day I bed your future wife."

Zaknafein just sighed and helplessly shook his head.

◆ ◆ ◆

"I PAID YOU WELL!" MATRON HAUZZ YELLED INTO HER DI-
vining bowl at the smug face of Horroodissomoth Xorlarrin, who was
on the other end of her magical communication.

"And the Simfray gate was destroyed, as we agreed," the wizard
replied.

"You watched my forces slaughtered on the field! You watched my
daughter murdered on the field!"

"Surely you did not expect House Xorlarrin to engage in the actual
fighting of a war that didn't happen."

His strange wording served as a cold reminder to Matron Hauzz that
drow house wars were not to be discussed. They never happened if no one
talked about them, but as soon as one did, as soon as the truth of an attack became too widespread and openly spoken of for the Ruling Council to ignore, the aggressor house would almost certainly be punished.

Or, put more precisely, it would almost certainly be wiped out.

"Yes, of course," a shaken Matron Hauzz replied.

"Gather yourself and your minions and take the time to reassess,"
Horroodissomoth advised. "Matron Simfray and all of her priestesses
are dead. Your losses were great, but House Tr'arach may still recover,
and do so with your most hated rival gone."

"My children—" she started to say.

"You still have Dab'nay, who fares well at Arach-Tinilith. And
take heart, for Duvon is not dead."

"What do you know?"

"He will return to you shortly," Horroodissomoth replied, and he
waved his hand and cut off the communication, the water in Matron
Hauzz's scrying bowl going dark.

The drow matron put her hands on the edges of that bowl for
support and heaved a great sigh. She hadn't won, that much was
clear. More than half of her fifty foot soldiers, her three strongest
priestesses—including Daungelina, the only high priestess of the
house besides Hauzz herself—and the two feeble wizards who called
Tr'arach home were all dead or missing. House Simfray had been hurt
even more, yes, but not so much as to consider this a victory.

"It is true," Dab'nay said from behind her. "I do fare well at Arach-Tinilith. I will become a high priestess, Matron, to properly serve House Tr'arach as first priestess."

The matron managed a halfhearted nod but didn't look back at her youngest child, who was still a child indeed, barely forty. Dab'nay had entered the academy quite young, and had now spent more than five years at the school. She had been so dedicated to her studies that Matron Hauzz had not seen her much in that half decade, and had therefore been surprised to find her returned to the house this day. Now, of course, it seemed a fortunate coincidence.

"I have heard the same whispers as Horroodissomoth Xorlarrin, Matron," Dab'nay went on. "My brother, Duvon, lives, but the same cannot be said for any of the priestesses of House Simfray. And their much-heralded weapon master is not to be found. Some say that he was sent flying through a rift to the Astral Plane, untethered, and if that is true, well, then he is no more."

"Small comfort," muttered the miserable Hauzz.

"Not so, my matron!" replied the grinning Dab'nay. "If Zaknafein Simfray is never to be found again, then we will let it be known that Duvon killed him. None can dispute it. That is no minor gain to your reputation or to that of House Tr'arach."

Perhaps it was so, Matron Hauzz dared muse. Perhaps House Tr'arach would recover soon enough. If they could enhance Duvon's reputation to great heights, Matron Hauzz could tempt soldiers to her side. She did turn to regard her child then, and nodded.

"Perhaps," she whispered. "Perhaps."

OF COURSE DUVON WAS ALIVE, AND IN FACT WAS EVEN THEN approaching the front door of House Tr'arach.

"Weapon master!" the two guards greeted him. "Good news, then! We had feared—"

"Shut up," the young noble said, his mood dour and defeated, though his wounds had been fully mended by magical spells and salves. "You had feared that House Tr'arach would not survive, and rightly so."

"But Matron Simfray is dead," said one. "They all are."

Duvon shrugged as if it meant nothing. "Gather all the forward guards," he commanded. "I would speak with you all right now, right here, to offer you another course, and one that you might find most profitable."

They both looked at him skeptically.

"Now!" he barked and they rushed off.

Duvon signaled behind him, back to the small entry corridor and the street beyond, and two shadowy forms slipped into the Tr'arach compound, moving to the side of the entry door.

A few moments later, the guards returned, along with several other sentries who had been posted in the forward guard rooms.

"You may go to the Clawrift, if you choose," the young noble told them. "And beg of the drow who wait you there to join their ranks. Some will be accepted. For the rest, I can only wish you well, wherever you go."

"Your matron awaits you," one of the guards said sternly, while others stared hard at the surprising young noble.

He had their attention. That was his task. He thought it unlikely that any would accept his offer. But it didn't matter.

Because they didn't notice when Arathis Hune placed Jarlaxle's portable hole against the wall to the side of the door, or when a second shadowy figure slipped into the structure, silent as death.

"MATRON HAUZZ, YOUR SON WILL SEE YOU," HE WHISPERED into the ear of the Tr'arach sentry.

The woman stared at him hatefully for a few heartbeats, but looked past him to her two dead companions, both cut down so quickly that she hadn't even known the intruder was there until she was the last one standing—and standing with a blade pressed against her neck.

"Matron Hauzz!" she called, and knocked on the heavy door of the throne room. "Your son will see you!"

They heard a cry inside, of glee, it seemed, and then heard locks being sprung and bars tossed aside, along with some whispered chants to dispel the many guards and wards that had been placed upon this most important portal.

The intruder heard it all and shook his head, amazed at how beautifully that strange Jarlaxle creature had arranged this. Normally, no matron in the midst of a conflict would open her door without magically scrying the hallway, but Jarlaxle had assured him that Duvon would be expected and so the entry would be expedited.

He eased the third sentry, now impaled upon his blade and quite dead, down to the floor and set his feet to spring. As soon as the great door budged, he shouldered through, throwing aside the young drow priestess who had turned the handle.

He fell over her at once, hitting her with a barrage of slaps from his twin swords, a flurry that appeared far more violent than it truly was, though he surely wanted to inflict mortal wounds upon her simply because of her station.

Down went the young priestess, crumpling upon the floor.

"Who are you?" Matron Hauzz demanded from across the room, her snake-headed scourge in one hand, a magical wand in the other.

"You know," he said, stalking toward her.

"Who?" she demanded.

"I am Zaknafein, of course."

"And you are dead."

She shot a lightning bolt from her wand, but he was already out of the way. She tried to strike with her scourge, but his swords were too fast, and a snake head fell to the floor.

He struck and turned a complete circuit, moving around her with blinding fury, his blades slashing and stabbing in a continuous dance, every strike hitting her personal wards and sending a shower of magical sparks into the air. She thought him in a blind frenzy, but it was not so. For while his movements seemed too furious, haphazard even, they remained coordinated, and he in perfect control.

Soon the heads of her other two scourge snakes followed the first to the floor, and in the intervening time, none of her strikes had gotten near to hitting him.

She tried to retreat, but he was too fast.

She tried to call upon her divine magics, but his relentless assault had worn down her magical guards, and her vestments, for all their defensive powers, could not save her.

He struck her once, twice, a dozen times, red lines of blood pouring forth. He was behind her somehow, but she didn't know it, except in the very last flicker of life, the last image that came to her eyes and registered in her dying brain as her head spun down to the floor.

"So be it," said Priestess Dab'nay, rising to her feet across the room. She looked down at a large welt on her forearm. "Did you have to hit me so hard?"

"Were it my choice, you'd be dead," Zaknafein told her.

She leaned back cautiously. "Jarlaxle gave me his word," she reminded him.

Zaknafein wiped his bloody swords on Matron Hauzz's vestments, then slid them away. "Return to Arach-Tinilith with all haste and gather your things," he instructed. "Then go to the Clawrift, across the way from the south tower of House Oblodra."

The young priestess stared at him with her jaw hanging open. "Who told you I should do this?"

"Jarlaxle," Zaknafein answered.

"No, it cannot be. I am to remain here, as Matron Dab'nay of House Tr'arach."

"Things have changed, my lady," Zaknafein informed her. "There is no House Tr'arach."

"And if I refuse?"

Zaknafein smiled wickedly, looked down, and kicked Matron Hauzz's severed head across the floor toward her. "In that case," he replied, smiling even wider, "there is no shadow deep enough to conceal you."

He walked across the room, moving very near to her, and whispered, "But fear not, for Jarlaxle thinks you impressive, and Bregan D'aerthe is in need of priestesses."

Her scowl did not diminish.

"If you did not wish such a fate, perhaps you should have convinced your foolish mother not to attack my family," Zaknafein answered that look, and when he made it personal, the blood drained from Dab'nay Tr'arach's face.

He left her, then, and left the ruins of House Tr'arach. Jarlaxle had granted him his wish, that he be allowed to kill Matron Hauzz, and so Dab'nay wasn't the only one who had to accept a new life this eventful day.

CHAPTER 6

Careful Cultivation

I t is not a perfect technique," Jarlaxle argued. "Would Matron Zeerith have me risk the masterpiece that is Zaknafein?"

"You were supposed to deliver him to Matron Malice cleansed of his memories," High Priestess Kiriy replied.

"Of *some* memories," Jarlaxle corrected. "Would you have him forget his training?"

"You are a frustrating one, Jarlaxle."

"Is Matron Malice displeased?"

"No," Kiriy admitted. "Quite the opposite, if the rumors of her nightly screams are to be believed."

Jarlaxle chuckled at that, shaking his head at the reputation of the insatiable Malice Do'Urden. "Another skill that was not erased by the Oblodran psionicists," he said to bolster his point.

"And yet, you were given extra coin to employ a psionicist of that house," Kiriy reminded him.

"And thus I employed one to counsel me, and in that counsel, I reconsidered the wisdom of your choice," Jarlaxle answered.

Kiriy's expression was full of doubt.

"It is not a perfect technique, so I was told," the mercenary reiterated. "All of this might have been to ruin if I had let the psionicist intrude upon the mind of this brilliant warrior. Was it worth that risk?"

"Perhaps not," Kiriy said . . . and held out her hand anyway.

"I had to pay for the counsel."

She motioned with her fingers, wanting the extra gold back.

With a grin and a chuckle, Jarlaxle produced a small purse from his magical belt pouch and handed it over.

"Matron Zeerith fears that we might have dropped a wounded displacer beast into the home of Matron Malice," Kiriy admitted. "If the Simfray champion is thick with angry memories . . ."

"He is not, and any he might harbor would not be directed toward his new matron in any case," Jarlaxle assured her.

Kiriy grinned knowingly. "You have heard that House Tr'arach has fallen? That Matron Hauzz was slain, most brutally?"

"There are whispers, yes" was all the confirmation Jarlaxle would give, along with a sly grin. She knew, he understood. She knew that he had granted Zaknafein revenge. "Please assure Matron Zeerith that Zaknafein did not need to have his mind and memories wiped clean by a psionicist Oblodran or a mind flayer. He will behave."

"Who are you?" Kiriy Xorlarrin asked, unable to hold back a chuckle.

"A houseless rogue."

The high priestess snorted and shook her head.

"I trust that Matron Zeerith was pleased with my performance," he said with a bow.

Kiriy remained laudably impassive. "If we need you again, we will call upon you," she said, and turned to leave.

Jarlaxle was glad that he had gotten through that encounter so easily, and with the Xorlarrins apparently okay with his decision to not wipe Zaknafein's memories. On a strictly personal level, Jarlaxle didn't want that; in their short time together, he had become intrigued by the Simfray—or, rather, *Do'Urden*—champion.

As he moved down to the Braeryn, though, Jarlaxle more than once considered the possibility that allowing Zaknafein to keep all of his memories had not been kind to Zaknafein.

When he entered the Oozing Myconid, a tavern that prided itself on having the foulest beverages in the drow city, and saw Zaknafein sitting at their customary table, head down, shoulders slumped, that unsettling notion was only reinforced.

The mercenary motioned to the bar—like the staff of every tavern in the city, they knew him well and knew what to bring him—and moved to join the weapon master of House Do'Urden.

"Exhausted again?" he asked, pulling up a seat at the table before being asked. "Matron Malice is killing you, my friend."

Zaknafein lifted his gaze upon the mercenary. "You are not my friend."

Jarlaxle motioned to the bar again.

"Why would you say such a thing?" he asked. "Truly, I am wounded."

"You would be, if I could get away with it."

Zaknafein ended by lifting his drink to his lips and scowling at Jarlaxle from over the rim. But the mercenary caught something else in that scowl, something less threatening.

"Is it malaise or exhaustion, then?" Jarlaxle asked with a sly grin.

"You seem very interested," Zaknafein replied. "Why not go and sample Malice's wares yourself, if you have not already?"

"Would that not bother you?"

Zaknafein's snort was sincere, the mercenary knew.

"Is it not at least enjoyable?" Jarlaxle pressed.

Zaknafein shrugged. "Her skill is undeniable, and few practice more diligently." The warrior couldn't suppress a small smile, a crack in his armor of dourness, and Jarlaxle laughed aloud.

"Then what is it, my friend?" Jarlaxle asked. "You are in a superior house to Simfray, by far, and one that has the notice of the great houses, yet enough alliances to ensure that it isn't simply obliterated. Your own star will rise along with House Do'Urden's. Matron Malice is ambitious enough to ensure battles in the near future—she brought you into her house for your sword and your . . . *dagger*," he said with a wiggle of his eyebrows, causing Zaknafein to roll his eyes. "To fight and to sire. So why the malaise? Why is Zaknafein out of House Do'Urden this night and roaming the Stenchstreets, drinking ale and wine inferior to that in Matron Malice's cupboard?"

"You asked me to meet you here," Zaknafein dryly reminded. "As always."

"True, true. But why do you come? You owe me nothing, and deny that we are friends."

"You pay for the drinks."

"Ah, but as we've already discussed, you have finer drinks at House Do'Urden, and I am sure that Matron Malice provides all that you want as long as it does not render you unconscious and unable to please her."

"And Malice makes of me a banner for House Do'Urden," Zaknafein blurted, and Jarlaxle then had his answers.

He noted that this was the second time Zaknafein had referred to Malice without using her title—an offense that could be punished by death in Menzoberranzan, where matrons were supreme, even sacrosanct.

Zaknafein was bored, notwithstanding the excitement he might be offered in Matron Malice's bed. He was a "banner," indeed, walking the outer balconies of House Do'Urden to show off Matron Malice's powerful new acquisition and to remind the other houses—the ambitious lesser families, the fearful equal families, and the efficiently ruthless greater families—that the cost of attacking House Do'Urden could prove great.

But Zaknafein had no interest in protecting House Do'Urden, Jarlaxle understood (and he had understood the same thing with this one regarding House Simfray), other than self-preservation. Zaknafein held no allegiance to Matron Malice or to anyone else, and the lack of purpose and lack of excitement were battering his sensibilities. The fact that he had been taken to a more stable house, where battles with other houses were not common, as they were among the most minor houses like Simfray, was not, to Zaknafein's thinking, a good thing.

Jarlaxle smiled as he studied the warrior, remembering the look on Zaknafein's face in the battle for House Simfray. That version of Zaknafein would never wear such a frown and scowl as were on display here this night.

The barman brought the drinks Jarlaxle had called for and Zaknafein reached for his, but Jarlaxle grabbed the warrior by the forearm and held him back.

"No more for now," he said.

Zaknafein stared at him curiously.

As soon as the barman had moved away, Jarlaxle explained, "I have found a weakness in the defenses of a noteworthy house, Barrison Del'Armgo. If we are clever, we can get in, and there are treasures to be had, ones that a warrior such as yourself would greatly desire."

"You want me to go on a *burglary* with you?" Zaknafein incredulously replied.

"There are potential rewards."

"And potential costs."

"You do not strike me as one filled with fear."

That gave Zaknafein pause. "But why?" he asked.

"For the same reason you come here," Jarlaxle answered. "To keep yourself on the edge of disaster. To keep yourself alive."

"Barrison Del'Armgo?" Zaknafein asked after a short pause. "I have heard of this house."

"Perhaps if we are fortunate, we will find Weapon Master Uthegentel when we are in there," Jarlaxle replied with a smile. "Then I will get to learn if Zaknafein is as mighty as the whispers hint."

Jarlaxle knew what he was doing, and those words soon had the pair leaving the Oozing Myconid side by side. Zaknafein's mood seemed much improved. He walked with a purpose and an eagerness, his hands going to the hilts of the fine swords sheathed on his hips.

He wouldn't need them, though, Jarlaxle knew. Not tonight. For Jarlaxle had paid handsomely for this excursion.

Still, Zaknafein didn't grow disappointed when Jarlaxle's planning proved to be perfect, perhaps too perfect, and the pair slipped into the Barrison Del'Armgo compound and across to a small stalagmite that held a side armory.

No alarms were raised, no guards came against them. In short order, the pair were back out again without being noticed at all, as far as Zaknafein could tell. They weren't laden with loot, and indeed had taken only two items—swords—and had left two behind.

Whatever disappointment Zaknafein might have felt in the lack of battle was surely mitigated by the fact that he now wore finer blades on his hips than those he had abandoned.

"They will never even know," Jarlaxle confidently assured his partner in crime when they crossed the city to the West Wall. Zaknafein's previous blades were not much different in appearance than these, and only a priestess or wizard bothering to try to detect magic on the weapons— and only one very skilled in the divination—would recognize that the enchantments on these two were much stronger than on the swords Zaknafein had left behind in the Barrison Del'Armgo armory.

"That is the best kind of thievery, you know," Jarlaxle offered. "Where the victim remains oblivious."

Zaknafein shrugged. "Seems a great risk for so little reward."

Jarlaxle nodded his agreement, but privately, he most certainly did not agree with that assessment. The reward for him was not the swords Zaknafein now wore, but the bond that he had strengthened between himself and this intriguing and superbly skilled warrior.

Although the swords were pretty spectacular in their own right.

He left Zaknafein before the wall beneath the balcony of House Do'Urden.

"Half a tenday?" Jarlaxle asked, setting their next meeting, and the warrior nodded—eagerly, Jarlaxle thought.

THE PAIR MET A HANDFUL OF TIMES OVER THE NEXT MONTH, mostly drinking and playing bar games and finding enjoyable diversions with lovely companions in the Oozing Myconid's many smaller bedchambers. On one occasion, Zaknafein managed to join a brawl, and another night, Jarlaxle took him on a scouting expedition that very nearly got them caught within a private compound by the priestesses of a ruling house.

Life had become a game for Zaknafein, as it was for him, Jarlaxle recognized, and so he was happy. The rogue eagerly anticipated each new encounter with the weapon master.

Until the next scheduled meeting, that is, when the confident mercenary entered the Oozing Myconid to find Zaknafein's chair empty. The mood of the tavern seemed somber that night, and when Jarlaxle sidled up to the bar, the barman silently handed him a rolled parchment.

"I am not desiring such attention, Master Jarlaxle," the proprietor of the Oozing Myconid said. "None of us are."

Jarlaxle broke the seal—the emblem of House Do'Urden, he noted—and began to unroll the parchment, but stopped quickly, took out a wand, and cast a disenchantment upon it, then paused and called upon the dispelling powers of the wand again for good measure.

With a sidelong glance to his barkeep friend, Jarlaxle moved to the far corner of the room, away from everyone, and very slowly unrolled the parchment.

It had indeed been heavily trapped, the script on the parchment penned in a devious wizard's ink that would explode when read. Jarlaxle's suspicious nature—and an incredibly valuable wand—had dispelled the glyph.

Mostly.

A burst of fire jumped out at him and he tried to duck away. He nearly got under it, but his scalp and hair caught some of the flames. His hair was still burning when he stood back up straight, and then flamed higher when a nearby patron, trying to help, no doubt, threw his drink upon the smoldering hair—a drink perhaps a bit too strong for such heroics, which instead simply puffed into a small fireball over Jarlaxle's head.

But then the barman was there with a pitcher of water and the crisis was averted—except for his singed hair.

Cheers and laughter rose up within the Oozing Myconid, and Jarlaxle took a bow, acting as if the whole thing has been staged for their pleasure, and trying not to grimace at the lines of pain shooting into his head.

He had to blink his eyes hard and repeatedly to focus his vision as he read the parchment. And for all the drama and burning, it simply said:

Appear at the court of Matron Malice Do'Urden immediately!

"Not a good day for you, rogue," the barman noted, reading over his shoulder. "It might be that some things are more trouble than they're worth."

Jarlaxle considered Zaknafein then and shook his head. "And some things are not," he replied. He left the tavern and headed toward House Do'Urden, but veered for the Clawrift. He needed some time. And as he considered his next move, one thing seemed certain: Matron Malice was not happy.

First and most important things first, though: Jarlaxle needed some healing salves and a good mirror—he needed desperately to do something with his half-burned hair! He went right to his private chambers in the maze beneath the Clawright. He sifted through the ruins of his perfectly shaped white forest and sighed heavily when he recognized that it would take a long time to repair the damage—and likely more than a little coin, since the scar would be considerable and spellcasters with such power didn't come cheaply.

Then, on instinct, he took a different route. For many years, Jarlaxle had kept all but the top of his head shaved, both to accentuate his spiked coif and because he simply liked the shape of his head.

So be it—he could like it more.

With a twist of his wrist, he produced a knife from a secret compartment on his belt, and then delicately went about the task of sculpting the remaining white forest, leaving him with an exquisite line of hair along the middle of his head, from his forehead to the base of his skull. A bit of dark makeup from his disguise kits to cover the still raw skin and the mercenary not only could look at himself in the mirror again without wincing, but thought he appeared rather exotic and fine.

"Good enough, then," he congratulated himself, then considered his options for only a brief moment before convincing himself of what he had to do.

He went to House Do'Urden, boldly.

"You are, or were, of House Simfray, then?" Matron Malice Do'Urden asked when Jarlaxle was brought before her.

"Never, good lady," he replied, and he swept a low and graceful bow.

"Then how do you know my weapon master?" she demanded, and around her, several drow bristled, including the huge priestess Briza, even more formidable up close, who looked like she could break Jarlaxle in half with her bare hands.

Jarlaxle offered that one a smirk, and nodded knowingly and teasingly at her before answering, "It was I who took him from the field of battle and brought him to you. On behalf of Matron Zeerith of House Xorlarrin, I should say."

It amused him how much the bluster went out of the gathered Do'Urdens, with all in the room exchanging nervous glances, no doubt wondering if their brash Matron Malice had at last put herself into a pit too deep to escape. Not Malice herself, though, Jarlaxle noted. That one, clearly quite unshakeable, just sat back in her throne comfortably and stared down at the mercenary.

"Fine—you brought him to me. But I did not pay for half of Zaknafein," she said. "Yet you seem to think that we should share him." She tapped her fingers together before her delicate and very pretty face.

"My lady—" Jarlaxle started to respond.

"I did not give you permission to speak," she said.

"I was but answering."

"I asked you no question."

Jarlaxle held up his hands and for once kept his mouth shut.

"Who are you?" she asked.

He didn't answer.

"That was a question," she pointed out.

"I am pondering how best to respond, for the truthful answer is one more complicated than you would think."

"You are Xorlarrin?"

Jarlaxle laughed and shook his head. "I am of no house, and at the same time of all houses who would desire my services. I am Jarl—"

"A houseless mercenary trying to play with the matrons of Menzoberranzan. Disgusting," Briza said.

"Bregan D'aerthe is my house," Jarlaxle clarified. "And it is one that House Do'Urden would do well—"

"What is that?" a seemingly unimpressed Matron Malice demanded. "And who are you, particularly?"

"I am the one who delivered Zaknafein to you, in response to the request and recompense of Matron Zeerith Xorlarrin," Jarlaxle reiterated, and quickly so that he could not be interrupted yet again.

"And you are a mere male," Malice warned. "Never forget that, Jarl . . . ?"

"Jarlaxle," he replied with another sweeping bow. "A humble servant of chaos, doing what I might to make the world a more exciting place."

"You will not much like the excitement I will create about you," the dangerous Matron Malice promised. She nodded to the side, where a curtain was then drawn, revealing a very unhappy Zaknafein. "How do you think you would fare against this marvelous warrior I have taken as a consort? If I tell him to kill you, he will."

Jarlaxle shrugged.

"So confident," Matron Malice mused. "How will you fare against him when he is gigantic and has eight skittering legs?"

"This one?" Jarlaxle asked, indicating Zaknafein. "Nay, you would not do that, and Lolth would not sanction it."

"Beware your words," the large priestess beside the throne growled as Malice's eyes went wide.

"I don't fear my own words," he said flippantly. He pointed to his friend. "He is a magnificent warrior and thus he is Lolth-blessed, I am sure." Jarlaxle took note of Zaknafein's failed attempts to hide his grimace at that remark but continued anyway. "You would not waste him so."

"You would do well to realize that you know nothing of what I would or would not do," Malice warned. "And you and your band of houseless nothings should take note that I am watching now. You will never see Zaknafein Do'Urden again, rogue, unless it is in the last moments of your life."

"Yes, Matron Malice," Jarlaxle said with yet another respectful bow. He thought it was time for him to take his leave, and so he did.

"WHY?" ASKED THE DIMINUTIVE MATRON OF THE STRANGest house in Menzoberranzan, powerful because they were, in truth, an enigma to the others. K'yorl Odran ruled House Oblodra, whose strength rested on the little-known magic of the mind, the same powers practiced by the illithids. If there was a dark elf in Menzoberranzan who could employ that psionic magic who was not of House Oblodra, Jarlaxle didn't know her or him. Which was why he was before Matron K'yorl today.

He shrugged, acting as if he didn't understand the question.

"You are not one to spend favors on such trivial things," the matron clarified. "And what happened to your hair?"

Jarlaxle reflexively ran his hand over his mostly bald pate, but only lightly, not wanting to smudge the makeup covering his most recent scar. "You do not approve?"

"I very much approve," K'yorl replied. "The strange style fits the strange Jarlaxle."

"Many consider House Oblodra to be the strangest of all."

"And we count on that to keep them afraid!" K'yorl said with a laugh.

Jarlaxle laughed along, but was too nervous to allow for the distractions. "Have you found any success?"

"I have to be careful, you understand," she replied. "To invade the home of a drow family is an act of war."

"That is why I asked you. Because your intrusions cannot be discovered."

"Anything can be discovered, Jarlaxle, and you would do very well to remember that. But yes, I have seen inside House Do'Urden, and through the eyes of Zaknafein. And your suspicions of his melancholy were well-founded."

Jarlaxle blew a heavy sigh.

"Even when she beds him, his thoughts are on murder," Matron K'yorl explained. "Every thrust is reimagined as a dagger plunging into the witch."

He thought back to a comment he had made to Zaknafein using the same analogy, and inwardly winced.

"He's trapped," Jarlaxle whispered, speaking more to himself than to K'yorl. "He sees his life as tedious and without purpose." He came out of his contemplation to regard the matron, who was staring at him with an amused and knowing expression.

"And you intend to do something about that," K'yorl remarked. "Take care, for Matron Malice is flush with fire and often acts before she properly understands the implications." She paused and looked at him slyly. "Ah, but you have no intention of arguing with Matron Malice, do you?"

"I know someone who can better make the case," Jarlaxle admitted.

"When you go to Matron Mother Baenre, give her my best wishes," the matron of House Oblodra said insincerely.

Jarlaxle nodded and matched K'yorl's smirk with a wide grin. He knew that this one hated Matron Mother Baenre profoundly, but knew, too, that she would be glad to have Jarlaxle put in a kind word about her to the dangerous Baenre.

Such were the webs of Menzoberranzan, always shifting, always shimmering, always ready to catch one who did not step lightly.

"I will," he said, and K'yorl laughed and nodded.

THE MONTHS ROLLED BY. JARLAXLE DID NOT FORGET, BUT neither would he move impetuously. He wouldn't go to his benefactor with this unbidden, for there was too much at stake here, and he wasn't quite sure how to gauge the dangers of Matron Malice Do'Urden. He couldn't just ask a favor from Matron Mother Baenre, after all. Menzoberranzan didn't work like that. He needed a reason to include his desire in her desire. Finally, he found the opportunity when he was called upon by a representative of House Baenre, instructing him to perform a service for the matron mother. It seemed a fairly simple and straightforward task, and one Jarlaxle and his rogues had performed on previous occasions: he was to go to the drow city of Ched Nasad and assassinate a priestess who had whispered ill rumors of House Baenre into the muddy ear of a handmaiden of Lolth.

His first instinct was to gather Arathis Hune and a few others specializing in such wicked business for the assignment. Matron Mother Baenre had not called upon him in a long while, after all, and it would not do to keep her waiting. The entire future of Bregan D'aerthe rested upon the strong shoulders of Matron Mother Yvonnel, and she was not known for mercy.

But this was his chance to find that which he really wanted, he told himself, and so Jarlaxle instead rushed off to House Baenre. He was known there, and so given audience . . . though with powerful guards, supremely armored and armed, all about him.

"I received your instructions and am prepared for the journey," he explained when he found himself before the throne of the great matron mother of Menzoberranzan.

"Then why are you here?" she asked coldly.

"To beg of you a favor."

"Need I remind you that the favor I bestow upon you is in merely letting you live?"

He swallowed hard and bowed as respectfully as he could manage. As much swagger as he possessed, he could not find his confidence here, standing before Yvonnel the Eternal.

"I l-live to serve you," he stammered.

"You serve Jarlaxle and none other," she replied, but with a laugh, which gave Jarlaxle a bit of hope. "But you are sometimes useful, which is why I let you play with your little band of criminals."

Jarlaxle shuffled from foot to foot. "I would ask for a private audience," he said, hardly expecting his request to be granted.

But Matron Mother Baenre surprised him—and probably everyone else in the room—when she clapped her hands together loudly, dismissing her guards and those Baenre nobles in the audience room, all of whom rushed away without hesitation or question.

Jarlaxle stood before the most powerful drow in the world, and he felt far less at ease than when he had been surrounded by a host of powerful Baenre nobles—priestesses, wizards, even the great Weapon Master Dantrag—and guards wielding cruel weapons.

He looked at her, studying her smug expression, and understood in that instant that she had well anticipated the effect of dismissing all her allies. She was reminding Jarlaxle that she didn't need them, and letting him know in no uncertain terms that she feared him not at all.

The mercenary lowered his gaze and quietly chuckled, and indeed, drew strength from the woman's confidence. If she didn't fear him—and she should not, for he truly did mean to serve her—then perhaps she would listen to him with an honest ear.

"Do tell me of this little favor I'm to do for you . . . and do not bore me," she said.

"I need your assistance in procuring an associate for this task you have requested of me," he said.

Matron Mother Baenre scoffed, rather loudly, her volume and tone giving Jarlaxle the distinct impression that she suddenly believed that torturing him to death might be pleasurable.

He suspected that such dark thoughts had been magically suggested to him. That wasn't supposed to be possible with his eyepatch, of course, but this was the matron mother of Menzoberranzan here.

He could not help but feel naked and defenseless under her withering gaze.

Still, he had a reputation for brazenness to uphold, so he tried to recover with "I only ask because it will allow me to serve you better."

"There are only two people in here," the great Baenre replied. "And neither of them believe what you just said."

"Well put, Matron Mother."

"You're very close to being a waste of my time, Jarlaxle."

He swallowed. "There is a warrior, a champion, I wish to cultivate,"

Jarlaxle said. "I would have him accompany me to Ched Nasad, and serve beside me when he can. He is a brilliant fighter, so much so that he is known to Weapon Master Dantrag, I am sure."

"Take a wizard."

"I prefer a blademaster."

Matron Baenre scoffed at that. "There is a reason that Dantrag holds little power in this house, though he is the finest weapon master in Menzoberranzan."

It occurred to Jarlaxle that a certain hulking warrior of House Barrison Del'Armgo might have something to say about that recounting of hierarchy, but he wisely kept the notion to himself.

"Zaknafein, Malice Do'Urden's new plaything," an exasperated Matron Mother Baenre reasoned. "You are speaking of the former Simfray champion, Zaknafein. You're as transparent as the protections of that ridiculous thing over your eye."

Jarlaxle swallowed hard.

"What is it about that one for you, Jarlaxle?" Matron Mother Baenre asked, leaning forward in her throne and resting her elbow on her knee and her chin in that hand, and seeming very much intrigued.

Jarlaxle, quite flummoxed, found himself without words, and so he simply shrugged.

With a huff, Matron Mother Baenre waved her hand, sending him away, and on some magical cue, no doubt, the chamber began filling with Baenre nobles and guards once more.

Jarlaxle bowed with every step backward until he was out of the hall, and he didn't linger for a heartbeat in the great compound of the city's First House. He would go and prepare his hunting party, suddenly keenly aware that he would do well to not fail in the task Matron Mother Baenre had put before him.

"WHAT BOTHERS YOU?" MATRON MOTHER BAENRE SAID TO her second son, Weapon Master Dantrag, soon after Jarlaxle had departed.

"Nothing, Matron Mother, of course," Dantrag dutifully answered, bowing repeatedly in an obvious effort to eliminate any notion that he was complaining.

"You do not particularly like Jarlaxle," she observed. She looked around at her other children as she spoke and knew that she could have been addressing any of them with that remark. And why should they like the houseless rogue, of course? House Baenre was supreme in their eyes, rightly so, and the idea that such tasks were being contracted out to a mercenary band was bad enough—shouldn't they be the ones going to Ched Nasad to kill the priestess who spoke ill of Yvonnel the Eternal?—but a band composed of mostly males, and *led* by males?

"The good fortune of this band, Bregan D'aerthe, will serve us in ways that allow us to focus our efforts on those things that matter most," she said to Dantrag. To all of them.

"If he ever disappoints you, I will gladly kill him," Dantrag replied with another bow.

That brought a smile to Yvonnel's old face, which Dantrag clearly took as a compliment, particularly when she added, "I am most confident of that."

But that wasn't why she was smiling. None of her children, not Dantrag or the great Gromph, not High Priestesses Triel, Quenthel, or Sos'Umptu . . . none of them knew. Jarlaxle didn't know.

Other than Yvonnel herself, there were perhaps two others in all the city who knew, and if they spoke of it, they would evoke the wrath of Lady Lolth herself.

Jarlaxle was Yvonnel's son, her third-born son, who had been, as custom dictated, sacrificed upon the moment of his birth.

THE VERY NEXT NIGHT, RIGHT BEFORE FINISHING THE PREParations to depart Menzoberranzan, Jarlaxle was summoned to House Do'Urden. He didn't know what to expect, of course, and so he was quite relieved when he discovered that he would not be allowed entry into the house, nor would he find himself before the wicked Matron Malice that day.

Instead, Zaknafein was at the front balcony, and floated down to the street below to meet the approaching mercenary.

"My Matron Malice has discovered a newfound respect for Bregan D'aerthe, it would seem," the weapon master said with an appreciative grin. "Ever since her ogreish daughter returned this day from Arach-Tinilith after a discussion with Matron Mistress Yvarn Baenre."

"I tried to tell her," Jarlaxle said innocently, and started away, Zaknafein beside him.

"And who must I fight this night in exchange for my reprieve?" Zaknafein asked.

"Whomever you choose, I suppose," Jarlaxle said with a snort. "For myself, I am off to the Stenchstreets to drink terrible wine and worse ale, and to bed the ugliest woman I can find."

"Why?"

"The drink is only called terrible because it is not rare and therefore reserved for the haughty fools," Jarlaxle explained. "And the women are only called ugly because they are common. And that is precisely their charm, because their passion is honest and honestly earned, and for the sake of the passion alone."

Zaknafein just shook his head and muttered his desire—nay, his need—for such a drink.

PART 2

For Us!

It is interesting to me to look back upon my writings from many years ago. I often cringe at my conclusions, believing that I know better now and that I've come to a clearer view of whatever situation I must confront, a clearer understanding of the best likely resolution. Oh, I see the same intent, the same hoped-for conclusion in those old writings, but there are little mistakes scattered throughout, and they are now obvious to me.

"Wisdom" is a word often associated with experience—perhaps it should also be spoken of in conjunction with the word "humility," because I now understand that if I look back upon this piece in a decade, or a century, I will likely once again find much to correct.

The other thing that strikes me about these glimpses into the past is the cyclical nature of life. Not just regarding birth and death, but in the many joys and crises that find us, year after year. There is an old drow saying:

Ava'til natha pasaison zhah ques po finnud ebries herm.
"History is a poem where all lines rhyme."

How true! To simply view the conflicts that my friends and I have faced is to see new threats that sound very much like the old. Even the great *tragedies and joys of our companionship follow predictable patterns to one who has lived them, again and again. Paradigms often seem broken, but the nature of reasoning beings will someday reinstate them.*

In this one manner, perhaps Lolth is no fool, or perhaps she is the greatest fool. Chaos brings excitement to her followers—they feel alive! But in the end, they will go right back to where they were before. The rank of a house might change, a nearby foe might be vanquished, a new spell created to darken the skies. But a person traveling to Menzoberranzan today would see a place that rhymes quite closely with the city I first glimpsed from a cradle.

Is it any different with Waterdeep?

For, yes, some civilizations will be wiped away by conquerors. Some will be flattened by volcanoes. Great drought will displace entire cultures and massive ocean waves might sweep others to the silence of the seafloor. But the circle of life continues. The greed and the generosity remain. The love and the hate remain. The mercy and the vengeance remain. All of these countervailing, endlessly competing facets of humans and dwarves and elves and halflings and gnomes and every other reasoning race remain . . . and battle.

And the winner is always in jeopardy and the result is so common, either way, that there is, overall, stasis within the swirl of chaos.

When I told this to Bruenor, he replied that I was dark in more than skin, reached behind his shield, and handed me a drink.

But no, it is not a dispiriting thought, nor one that implies helplessness in the face of fate and predetermination.

Because this, too, I know: while we move in circles, we still move forward. Like my own maturation in looking at my past writing, the cultures mature. To a visitor today, Menzoberranzan would look very much as it did to me when I first peeked out from House Do'Urden, but not exactly the same.

The times grow less dark for all the races, because within the culture, too, is memory, an understanding of what works and what does not. When those lessons are forgotten, the circle winds its way backward, and when they are remembered, society moves forward, and with each cycle, with each affirmation of that which is good and that which is evil, the starting point of the next lesson is a bit closer to goodness.

It is a long roll, this circle, but it is rolling in the direction of justice and goodness, for all of us. It is not hard to look back on history and see atrocities committed on a grand scale that horrify the sensibilities of the folk of this day but were simply accepted or deemed necessary by folk in days more superstitious and unenlightened.

Bruenor wasn't impressed by this claim. He just handed me another drink.

But it seems true to me now, undeniably so, that the life of an individual and the life of a society go in these circles of crisis and peace, and from each, we learn and we become stronger.

We become wiser.

It occurs to me that the beings we on Faerun call gods might be no more than long-living creatures who have heard the rhyme of pasaison, of yesteryear, so many times that their simple experience allows them to know the future. So ingrained is the inevitable result, perhaps, that they can now hear the echoes of the future instead of merely those of the past—they have the foresight of consequence. They have learned great powers, as a swordsman learns a new attack routine.

My own journey nearly ended during this last crisis, not merely because I might have died—that seems a very common condition—but because what I lost most of all was my grounding in reality. The ground on which I stood became shifting sand, and in that sand I nearly disappeared.

And would have, except that now I have learned to tighten the circles of my life, almost to where I have come to hope that my journey from here on out is a straighter road forward, a path to better epiphany and clearer insight.

For the greatest teaching of the monks of the Yellow Rose is the ability to forgive, wholly, your own shortcomings, to accept your physical being as a vessel to a spirit ever seeking perfection. Such true acceptance of oneself, of limitations and weaknesses and failings, allows one to proceed without becoming hindered by guilt and undue hesitance.

To hear the echoes of the past.
To anticipate the notes of the future.
To stride more boldly.
And so, scimitars high, I go, boldly and with a smile.

—Drizzt Do'Urden

CHAPTER 7

Pater

Freezing drizzle and snowflakes were in the air this Luskan winter day, but even so, the open air above Illusk proved too bright for the sensibilities of Zaknafein Do'Urden, a drow who had seen the surface world on only one occasion, hundreds of years before. He huddled beneath the heavy cloak Jarlaxle had given him as the trio of drow—Zaknafein, Jarlaxle, and an exceptional young woman named Yvonnel, the daughter of Gromph, the namesake of the great Matron Mother Baenre. They moved over the bridge to Closeguard Island, and then the next bridge to a second island, upon which sat the gigantic and wondrous structure known as the Hosttower of the Arcane.

It stood like an ancient tree, with huge branches running out from its tower trunk, sweeping upward majestically, each thick enough to hold the private chambers of the wizards within. It was larger now than it had been before its destruction a century past, and it was still growing, with the tip of the trunk and highest branches glowing orange against the gray sky as pulses of lava were fed in through the long underground tendrils that connected this magical structure to the underchambers of the dwarven city of Gauntlgrym far to the south, and more particularly, to the lava pit of the captured primordial that fueled the creation power at play here.

There was no visible door in the base of the Hosttower, but Jarlaxle knew the location of the entrance, and knew, too, the magic words to coerce its opening. The trio passed through the portal and down a hallway to a circular center room lined with a curving staircase that rose up into the great structure and spiraled down below, to the bowels, the caves beneath the surface of Luskan's Bay. As they moved to those stairs to ascend, the drow could clearly hear the sounds below, a great sighing, almost as if the tower itself were inhaling and exhaling like a living being.

Jarlaxle knew just enough about this creation to believe that to be more than coincidence.

The second landing of the stairway offered a door that opened into the largest "branch" of the treelike structure, a narrow, upsloping corridor lined with doors on both sides. Given the breadth of this branch, those doors could have led to fair-sized chambers. But this was a wizard's tower, after all, replete with extradimensional creations— conjured mansions that would seem to occupy a space no larger than a closet on the Material Plane, but would satisfy a vain royal couple beyond the door.

The grandest of these, Jarlaxle knew well, belonged to his brother, the former archmage of Menzoberranzan, Gromph Baenre.

He didn't have to knock, for Gromph's door was magically monitored, and so opened at the expected approach of the mercenary leader.

The trio entered the magical palace, greeted by beautiful, haunting music and a series of softly glowing lines of light, moving through the visible spectrum, seemingly in harmony with the sounds of the unseen instruments.

Beautiful white columns lined the entry hall, delicately carved with lovely sculptures of naked but armed drow women. "Caryatid," Jarlaxle warned his two companions, for these were more than room supports, which were not even needed in the magical construct.

These were guards, and formidable ones.

From an arched opening at the side of the room, Archmage Gromph entered. He seemed more than a little irritated by the intrusion, but obviously he was not surprised, and just as obviously, he could have kept Jarlaxle and the others out of this place had he so desired.

"I trust you enjoyed your journey to House Baenre," Jarlaxle said.

Gromph snorted and walked past the three, motioning for them to follow him back to the entrance.

"Not a meal? Not even a drink to refresh us?" Jarlaxle said.

"I am sure King Bruenor will serve you well," Gromph replied, and Jarlaxle offered a heavy sigh.

Gromph led them right back the way they had come, but down the stairs past the entry foyer, belowground and to another secret door, one that looked very much like the curving wall of the volcanic tunnel they now traversed. Opening this one required more than uttering a series of magical words. The others could feel how heavily guarded with spells and wards and glyphs this door was—more than any other in the tower, including Gromph's own.

And it wasn't just the door that was magically warded. Beyond it lay a sizable room, longer than it was wide, and lined with stone statues that swiveled their heads to regard the intruders. Above them, perched in small alcoves, a host of gargoyles similarly watched, ready to animate and attack.

But only watched, for these were Gromph's pets, and Gromph led this procession.

At the far end of the room stood a pair of stone obelisks. They weren't straight, nor uniform in thickness along their length, nor carved with pretty designs, and truly they seemed out of place in this grand structure of otherwise graceful asymmetry and creative designs. Across the top of these two columns lay a third chunk of gray stone, which seemed as if it had just been dropped there and not carefully placed, creating something resembling a haphazard door frame.

"What is this place?" Zaknafein blurted, clearly overwhelmed by the sun and the surface and the tower and now the many magical and monstrous eyes upon him.

Not turning back to even acknowledge him, Gromph instead

called to the threshold before him, and from a crack in the floor between the jambs, there came a response: a hissing sound.

"Have you ever dealt with dwarves?" Jarlaxle asked Zaknafein.

"Duergar?" he answered, for the evil gray dwarves that lived in the Underdark were well-known to the drow.

"No."

Flames shot up from the crack in the threshold, climbing into the door frame and growing hungrily as if they had found dry kindling to consume.

"Derro?" the warrior asked, indicating another subterranean race of magical dwarves. Zaknafein stared at the door now, at the fires that roiled within that crude frame.

"Just dwarves," Jarlaxle clarified.

"Then no," Zaknafein said, obvious disgust in his voice.

"Your son has a great affinity for them," Jarlaxle replied.

Zaknafein didn't respond, didn't blink or move at all, and on closer examination, both Jarlaxle and Yvonnel realized that he wasn't even breathing. Both turned to Gromph, who stood calmly, a superior look on his angular face.

"You see how easy it is for me to destroy a mere warrior?" he asked, pointing the question at Jarlaxle.

"How easy it is for you to defeat one by surprise, you mean," the mercenary replied.

"When you can strike anywhere, at any time, surprise is the easy part."

"So said the assassin holding the bloody dagger," Jarlaxle quipped.

Yvonnel's heavy sigh ended the exchange, and she stared at the other two and shook her head in disgust, with an expression that was more than a little familiar to both of these old drow, who had known Yvonnel the Eternal.

"Ever have you two pretend rivals been dancing thus," she said.

"You speak like our mother," Jarlaxle said with a laugh, for that was exactly the point, after all. In the womb, the daughter of Gromph, this Yvonnel, had been invaded by the tentacles of a mind flayer, and that creature had given to her the memories of her namesake, Yvonnel the Eternal, the great Matron Mother Baenre. The mind flayer hadn't just recounted those memories to the fetus, but had ingrained them into her as if they were her own.

"'Pretend'?" Gromph asked.

"Your dance is the puffery of a pair of peacocks, though neither of you would soil your fine clothes with the blood of the other, or with your own. You need each other, and that is what fouls the flavor. Just that, so I beg you, enough."

The brothers looked to each other and shrugged.

"It was wise to remove Zaknafein from the conversation before we enter King Bruenor's realm," Yvonnel told Gromph.

"I would never have done it without your approval," the dour mage growled back at her.

"We must know," Yvonnel said, letting the sarcasm pass. "What did you learn on your journey to House Baenre? Is it truly Zaknafein?"

"The handmaidens confirmed it," Gromph answered. "It is Zaknafein, returned from death."

"How?" Jarlaxle asked.

"Why?" Yvonnel asked at the same time.

"Those are the questions, aren't they?" Gromph answered. "And who did it? Zaknafein is returned. Was it Lolth? Mielikki? Some other being of great power?"

"It would have to be, for Zaknafein threw himself into acid," Jarlaxle reminded him. "There was no body to resurrect. He was pulled back to life from another plane of existence, wholly so."

"The handmaidens did not say?" Yvonnel asked.

"I met with Matron Mother Quenthel and High Priestess Sos'Umptu. I spoke with Yiccardaria and Eskavidne, two of Lolth's most favored handmaidens."

"And they deny Lolth's involvement?" Jarlaxle asked.

Gromph shrugged. "They neither confirm nor deny. They say only that it is Zaknafein Do'Urden, truly him, returned from the nether plane, and it seemed to me that they were as curious as you two regarding the who, how, and why of it. I have no reason to doubt them, and less reason to care. Perhaps it was Lolth, and who can know her designs?"

"But you don't believe that?" Jarlaxle prompted.

"No," Gromph replied. "But again, I do not care enough to closely examine the arguments." He turned to the fiery gate. "Mithral Hall has accepted our—*your* call," he said, stepping aside and motioning to the flames.

Jarlaxle looked to Yvonnel and nodded, and the former archmage uttered a chant and dismissed the stasis spell he had placed on Zaknafein.

"How did he come to grow fond of smelly dwarves?" Zaknafein asked, picking up the previous conversation right where it had been cut short, oblivious to the subsequent talk.

"Perhaps we will figure that out together," Jarlaxle offered, and stepped past, taking Zaknafein's arm as he headed for the roiling fires.

Reflexively, and predictably, Zaknafein resisted.

But Yvonnel walked by them and stepped into the flames without slowing, disappearing immediately.

"It is merely a gate, the flames benign," Jarlaxle explained. "Mithral Hall has accepted our call and so the gate has been opened."

He led Zaknafein to the threshold, and went in immediately before the overwhelmed newcomer, who did follow, leaving Gromph alone in the room.

Gromph stayed there, staring, long after the fires had dissipated, the indication the portal had closed. There was so much going on around him now, and the depth of it seemed to hold him in thrall: the Hosttower and its plethora of strange and powerful inhabitants, with more coming in each tenday, it seemed; the mystery of Zaknafein's return, which, though he emphatically claimed not to care, could signal something important; and Jarlaxle, his younger brother, solidifying his hold on the city of Luskan, even gaining acceptance, so it seemed, with some of the surrounding lords, including some from mighty Waterdeep to the south.

The latter was especially vexing—and exciting: drow elves secretly led a major surface city, and were holding it with treaty instead of weapons.

The enormity of that was not lost on Gromph. All he wanted was to continue his studies and growth in this most magnificent living stone tower.

At least, that's what he had been telling himself.

JUST STAY QUIET, JARLAXLE'S FINGERS FLASHED TO ZAKNA-fein when they stepped out on the other side of the fire, into a heavily guarded chamber off to the side of the main level of the dwarven complex.

At the recognition of Yvonnel and Jarlaxle—two drow declared as friends of King Bruenor—several grim-faced dwarves lowered their heavy crossbows. Two artillery teams safety-latched the side-slinger catapults mounted on the walls and sighted in on the magical gate.

"We wish to speak with King Bruenor," Jarlaxle told them.

"Probably in the mines," one dwarf said to another.

"Was with Catti and Wulfgar in the lava pit," that second dwarf informed Jarlaxle.

Still another dwarf, a heavyset fellow with a long yellow beard, walked to the wall, lifted a hinged bit of stone, and whistled through it. A moment later, the whole section of wall cranked upward, like a solid portcullis of thick stone, revealing a corridor beyond. A pair of dwarves in fabulous full mithral armor moved in to greet the visitors.

"We'll take ye," one explained, motioning for the trio of drow to follow.

More than two dozen dwarves accompanied the visitors, with another half dozen following in close order. Jarlaxle and Yvonnel were considered friends of King Bruenor, perhaps, but there were clearly limitations to the trust the dwarves would put in such a title, especially with an unknown third in the mix.

They wound down into the lower levels of Gauntlgrym, coming into the forge room, where the furnaces were powered by the fires of a living primordial, and thus superior to anything that could be created with mundane fuel. Down a short, low tunnel from there, they came into the magical chamber itself, a large and mostly natural cavern. It was steamy in here, for water poured from rootlike tendrils above a pit that dominated the room, and from which came a bright orange glow. The mist didn't obscure vision badly, and from the door, the three visitors to Gauntlgrym could see two human forms: a robed woman, her belly showing her to be in the middle months of pregnancy, and a giant of a human man standing in the center of the landing, overlooking the pit.

"Catti-brie, your son's wife," Jarlaxle said to Zaknafein. "And Wulfgar of Icewind Dale, one of Drizzt's dearest friends."

Zaknafein's face screwed up in confusion at the two non-drow standing before him. He started to respond, but Yvonnel stopped him with an upraised hand and began casting a spell, for it was obvious that Zaknafein would not understand anything said here without some magical assistance.

"And is that . . . ?" Zaknafein asked a moment later, barely able to get the words past his lips as he fully took in this woman, this pregnant human Jarlaxle had just named as his daughter-in-law.

Jarlaxle nodded and smiled. It was indeed Zaknafein's grandchild in Catti-brie's womb.

"Jarlaxle," Catti-brie called, and the mercenary leader tipped his great cap, painted a wide and sincere smile on his face, and moved over to join the two. He noticed then that there had been some recent construction in the chamber, as a tall and decorated metal railing now lined the pit.

For Jarlaxle, who had once gone over the edge of that pit to rescue another dwarven friend and had only barely caught the dwarf before they both plummeted into the living lava far below, the railing seemed a good addition.

"WHAT BRINGS YOU HERE?" CATTI-BRIE ASKED. "I TRUST ALL is well in Luskan."

"Splendid," the drow replied. "The Hosttower is more magnificent by the day—too long has it been since you've seen it, dear lady, particularly given that you were the one who unwound the riddle in reconstructing it."

She smiled at the acknowledgment even as Wulfgar asked, "You have come to see Lady Donnola up above?" He had just taken the short tram ride from the halfling town of Bleeding Vines, which was built in a stony vale around the back door of Gauntlgrym.

"To see Bruenor, actually, to request a portal to Longsaddle," Jarlaxle replied.

"Lady Donnola is returned from Neverwinter," Wulfgar informed him anyway, and a nod between the two confirmed their private dealings and collusion here.

"You were coming to Longsaddle to visit me?" Catti-brie asked, though of course she suspected differently.

"Alas, no," Jarlaxle answered, turning as Yvonnel and the third drow approached. "Although it is grand to see you! I trust you are well?"

"Quite."

"And your baby?"

"All is well," she assured him.

"Then may she or he be born with your grand eyes, Drizzt's warrior brilliance, your wisdom, and the heart of you both," Jarlaxle said with a bow. "What a grand child that would be!"

Catti-brie smiled again and nodded to acknowledge the compliment, but grew a bit confused when Jarlaxle finished by looking to the third member of the group, the unknown drow. That man seemed less than excited at the news. Also, had Jarlaxle played purposely with his choice of words?

"Though if such a child was graced with the color of Drizzt's eyes, I am sure you would not mind," the rogue mercenary leader added with a wink, turning his gaze back to Catti-brie. "But no, dear lady, though I am happy to see you and would surely have sought you out, my journey through here to Longsaddle was to see Drizzt. I have someone he would wish to meet."

The two humans studied the third member of Jarlaxle's group, a drow they did not know, as he pulled back the hood of his magical *piwafwi* cloak.

"I give you the former weapon master of House Do'Urden, once considered the finest weapon master in all of Menzoberranzan," Jarlaxle said, "who trained your husband in the arts martial."

Catti-brie's expression grew more curious. "Trained? Drizzt was trained by . . ."

"Zaknafein," the stranger replied. "I am Zaknafein Do'Urden, come to see my son."

Catti-brie gasped, her blue eyes going so wide they seemed as if they might fall out of her face. "A grand child," she whispered under her breath, echoing Jarlaxle's words.

"Stranger still grows the world," Wulfgar remarked with a chuckle, and he seemed far less surprised and more amused than anything else.

Jarlaxle, too, stared incredulously at Zaknafein, but for a different reason. The weapon master had spoken perfectly the common tongue of Faerun, something he should not know.

"He understands the language for now," Yvonnel explained, guessing the source of Jarlaxle's incredulous expression. "Until my dweomer lapses."

"Zaknafein," Catti-brie murmured, shaking her head.

"Lolth," Wulfgar said, drawing the attention of the other four. "She said she could restore him to Drizzt's side."

"In exchange for his fealty, though," Jarlaxle reminded him, and Zaknafein gasped.

"He didn't . . ." the weapon master asked.

"We're not sure. Did your husband pledge fealty to the Spider Queen, do you think?" Yvonnel asked Catti-brie, to which she and Zaknafein both replied, "No!" emphatically, while Wulfgar laughed at the absurdity of the suggestion.

"But Zaknafein is here," Jarlaxle remarked, though of course he also did not believe that Drizzt would ever pledge fealty to Lolth.

"So you believe," Catti-brie replied, staring hard at the stranger. She resisted the urge to put a hand to her belly, but reminded herself of how much she and her husband had to lose here. And not just them. The events of the past year had seen a dramatic shift in the north for all of their friends, and one favorable to a stable and prosperous environment—a remaking of the lands often and rightly called "the Savage North."

"How do you know?" Wulfgar added, also looking down at the drow they called Zaknafein.

"It is him," Jarlaxle assured them.

"Because he knows things only Zaknafein would know?" Catti-brie asked. "Would not a god—a goddess—be able to discern such things and so imbue them upon a doppelganger?"

"You think us novices in the ways of magic and the gods. Our investigation was more thorough than that," said Yvonnel. Yet she, too, stared at the reborn drow. "If he is not truly Zaknafein Do'Urden, then some deity went to great trouble to accomplish that which could have been done in a more straightforward and easy manner."

"Returning a fake Zaknafein would hurt Drizzt dearly," Catti-brie said, and she added to Zaknafein, simply because she could not help herself, "You look exactly like him." It was true enough. Other than the red hue of his eyes and the fact that he wore his hair short, this man introduced as Zaknafein bore an uncanny resemblance to Drizzt, with the same facial features, less angular than most drow's, and the same physique.

"It would hurt him no more than taking Catti-brie from Drizzt's side," Yvonnel countered. "And that is something far more easily attained."

"Not as easily as some would believe, however," Catti-brie replied, and her blue eyes narrowed as she met the gaze of Yvonnel, who, she had learned, had tried to do just that—indeed, had put a curse upon Drizzt to compel him to murder Catti-brie upon reuniting with her after his battle with Demogorgon. Catti-brie used her own reminder as a warning to herself. She knew the webs of dark elves were deeply layered. At some point, she privately conceded, she would be getting into unjustified suspicions, but that point would run much deeper for drow, particularly one as unusual as this Yvonnel creature, than for other races.

Yvonnel merely shrugged, though, not denying or excusing anything. She had made it clear that Drizzt's inability to do the deed, to strike Catti-brie dead—his strength and the purity of his heart that had allowed him to deny the compelling magic of her curse—had sparked the epiphany that had turned Yvonnel to Drizzt's side. Yvonnel had given up great power—she could have become the matron mother of Menzoberranzan!—to come to the surface, and that price could yet prove steeper still, as agents of Lolth were rumored to now be hunting *her*.

Whatever her past, she was here now, trusted by Jarlaxle *and* by Drizzt, Catti-brie knew, and so she could not hold her stare for long.

Or was that the plan all along? Catti-brie had to wonder. How patiently would they weave their webs to inflict maximum damage on Drizzt?

"Then perhaps the goddess Lolth truly heard the words of Drizzt," Wulfgar reasoned, breaking the tension. "In the tunnel. You were there," he said, indicating Yvonnel. "When Lolth told Drizzt that she could return his father to his side, he made it clear to her that if she was worth following, she would not have taken Zaknafein or so many others in the first place."

"Yes, those were his words," Yvonnel agreed.

"So perhaps Lolth is preempting a play," Jarlaxle offered, looking to Yvonnel, who had long been postulating that the Spider Queen was sensing a change in the mores of her devoted drow children and wanted to stay ahead of that so as not to risk losing her flock.

"I just want to see my son," Zaknafein said, his tone making it quite clear that he had heard enough of these philosophical musings.

"Of course," Catti-brie said, but her stern expression, one then matched by the drow claiming to be Zaknafein, showed all that she wasn't overly enthusiastic about such a reunion. She turned to Wulfgar and bade him, "Go get Bruenor."

The big man nodded and rushed off. Word of the visitors was already spreading fast through the compound, though, and so Wulfgar didn't have far to go to find the dwarf king, and returned with Bruenor, along with an impressive group, including the warrior Athrogate and the unusual Bouldershoulder brothers, in short order.

Catti-brie nodded at her adopted dwarf father's entourage, thinking it quite fitting, given the potential regional implications of this new development. Athrogate had become one of Bruenor's most trusted advisors, and a stone-tough commander in the mold of the legendary Thibbledorf Pwent. But he was also a longtime associate of Jarlaxle, and a member of Bregan D'aerthe, a familiarity and friendship that continued even though he had formally ended that relationship.

The Bouldershoulders, friends of the Companions of the Hall, were new to Gauntlgrym, and were more members of the halfling village up above the dwarven compound than of Gauntlgrym itself. Pikel Bouldershoulder, in particular, with his druidic ways, was serving Lady Donnola as the sommelier of Bleeding Vines. His green touch was already producing promising root stalks, though the growing season of 1488 hadn't yet begun this far north.

Wulfgar must have already informed Bruenor of Jarlaxle's startling companion, because the red-bearded dwarf king hopped right up to examine Zaknafein, shaking his head and barely containing his grin. The two exchanged a greeting, and then Bruenor said something along the lines of "Yer son's to be dancing!"

Catti-brie was hardly listening, her attention following the green-bearded Pikel, who hopped up before Yvonnel and pointed his stump arm at her. The strange and lovable dwarf mumbled some undecipherable words and waggled the fingers of his one hand all about that bobbed limb, which had been lost years before in a battle with giants. A moment later, so befitting the charm of Pikel, a flower grew out of his stump, which he plucked, giggling wildly, and handed to the beautiful drow woman.

"Such a charming little fellow," she said, taking the white rose and bringing it up to her nose to sniff.

And it was more than a charming gift, Catti-brie realized. It was a signal, and she wasn't surprised to catch a glance between Yvonnel and Jarlaxle.

Pikel had just conveyed a message from Donnola Topolino to Jarlaxle through Yvonnel.

There it was again, she realized, a reminder of the great changes in the western realms north of Waterdeep, and an even more poignant reminder of how delicate that situation truly was *if* some of the players—Yvonnel in particular—were not as perceived.

Such an interesting alliance had come together in the north, including Jarlaxle, the halfling, the Harpell family of Longsaddle, and of course, the heart of it all, Gauntlgrym. In reclaiming the ancient homeland of all Delzoun dwarves, Catti-brie's father, King Bruenor, had created a new force in this region.

But he had done so by chasing out a noble drow house, House Xorlarrin, which had been sent there by Matron Mother Baenre to claim it as a sister city to Menzoberranzan.

She looked more closely at Yvonnel—at Yvonnel *Baenre*—with that notion, and reminded herself, too, that Gromph was also of that first family of Menzoberranzan, whatever their current proclamations.

She glanced back to the drow claiming to be Zaknafein and tried hard to hide her trepidation.

"With the dwarven gates, that meeting will be easy enough to arrange, I expect," Yvonnel answered Wulfgar.

Catti-brie winced, both at the thought of how quickly Drizzt might find himself standing before this drow claiming to be his father, and at Yvonnel's interest in the dwarven gates. For those portals bound the alliance—Jarlaxle could come and go from Luskan through the one beneath the Hosttower, covering the hundred miles between the places in a matter of a few steps. Similarly, Catti-brie and Drizzt and the wizard Harpells could come and go from Longsaddle, half again that distance, in a mere heartbeat.

The key, however, was that those gates were controlled by Gauntlgrym—none could enter, or leave, without accepting the call by activating the primordial power on this end of the portal. Longsaddle and Luskan could not be reached directly, but only by going through the dwarven city, impregnable Gauntlgrym.

And that reputation was made even more possible because of the last of the four dwarven gates, the one that led to the tunnels beneath the Silver Marches to the east, from which Bruenor could bring three powerful dwarven armies of his Delzoun kin to his side.

All of that reality gave Catti-brie some measure of confidence here, but also made her determined to verify everything and anything before accepting it as truth. If the drow of Menzoberranzan wanted to retake Gauntlgrym, they would have to find some way to alter or cripple those gates, and she'd be damned if she let Yvonnel or Zaknafein—two drow that she didn't quite trust—help facilitate such sabotage.

Catti-brie rolled the ring on her left hand about her finger, and was glad that she was standing in this chamber in this moment of doubt. No mere bauble, this was a ring of elemental control attuned to the Plane of Fire, and with it Catti-brie could hear the whispers of the god-like creature, the primordial of fire, in the pit below. Those whispers had told her how to reconstruct the Hosttower of the Arcane, and how to rebuild and power the dwarven portals.

The conversation continued around her, mostly with Bruenor talking to Zaknafein, so she tuned it out and fell into the magic of the ring, just to confer with the primordial. This was a being of power to rival Lolth herself, to outdo the Spider Queen, even, and so when she came out of that private communication, the woman stood a bit more comfortably. The gates could not be altered, could not be perverted, the primordial had assured her with its confidence in control over them, and so Gauntlgrym could not be compromised in that manner.

Not even by the powers of Menzoberranzan; not even by Yvonnel, if she was more than she appeared; not even by the Spider Queen herself, unless she wished to wage war with a godly creature of preternatural power.

Could anyone truly threaten King Bruenor's Gauntlgrym, or even Bleeding Vines, with so many allies so close at hand? She thought not.

But, of course, with such power in the disparate alliance also came much responsibility, and much intrigue.

Again she thought of the baby in her belly, for in this regard, it seemed a more personal version of the same thing. Like the alliance of the north her father had built, her family, too, had much to lose.

She sighed, which brought a stop to the conversations around her, and all eyes fell upon her. Catti-brie couldn't help but chuckle at that, and helplessly, for life had seemed much simpler to her when she and her four closest allies had simply been the Companions of the Hall, a band of friends walking the road of adventure, relying only on each other and accountable only to each other.

Now, with Drizzt's father—if it truly *was* his father—making an appearance, life had certainly gotten even more complicated in the past few moments.

Catti-brie shook the dark thoughts away. They were for another day. Today could only be about the momentous return of her husband's long-dead father!

Refocused, she listened more closely to the conversation around her, and realized that she had missed much of it during her contemplations.

"He will know me," Zaknafein said, and it sounded more like a hope than a certainty. "As I would know him."

"He will doubt," Yvonnel warned. "His encounter with the thinned planar barrier between the Underdark and the lower planes hit him particularly hard, and I'd be surprised if such delusions as befell him didn't yet linger. Drizzt walked in great confusion for many tendays, and nothing seemed real to him. His mind was too full of doubt."

"He is past that affliction," Catti-brie said. "My husband's work with Grandmaster Kane has shown him inner peace and guidance."

She didn't miss the flash of a scowl on Zaknafein's face when she referred to Drizzt as her husband. Just a flash. "He is," she added quietly, "much stronger than even we give him credit for."

"It may be as you say. But still, to ask this of him is beyond anything he might have expected," said Yvonnel. "Too great a hope, perhaps."

Catti-brie shrugged, not ready to argue that point, and added, "For just Drizzt, do you suppose?"

Yvonnel locked stares with the woman, then glanced down a bit—to her swollen belly, Catti-brie realized—and offered a conciliatory nod.

"But will Drizzt even recognize you?" Jarlaxle asked Zaknafein. "It was a lifetime ago—"

"*You* recognized me at once," Zaknafein interrupted, somewhat angrily.

"I knew you as an adult, and for centuries," Jarlaxle reminded him. "Drizzt saw you through the eyes of a child, and saw you much less frequently than I, and for a much shorter amount of time. Besides, I am far more used to such anomalies as your return."

"And still, Jarlaxle investigated further, to confirm his hopes," said Yvonnel, and to Zaknafein, Jarlaxle merely shrugged sheepishly.

"Does my son still practice?" Zaknafein asked Catti-brie.

"Every day, of course," Catti-brie replied, and then she began to nod, catching on.

"He will know you then, beyond doubt," Wulfgar put in, and all the others began to chuckle and nod as they came to understand to the plan.

It was true enough, Catti-brie understood. In the arena, doing battle, Drizzt would recognize a long-lost opponent as surely as he would recognize Catti-brie in their lovemaking, even if they had been separated by centuries.

"I would speak with you privately, Jarlaxle," she said. She looked to King Bruenor and added, "And with you, Father; just we three."

"You'd be a fool not to," Jarlaxle replied. "And Catti-brie is no fool."

THE CIRCULAR CHAMBER IN THE BOWELS OF THE IVY MAN-sion in Longsaddle was hot—very hot—and steamy, coaxing the knots out of strong muscles and the sweat from the practicing warrior.

His movements were slower than in years past, but that was not due to age. Rather, it was deliberate. In his daily practice sessions now, Drizzt Do'Urden maintained complete concentration on every bend, every turn, every extension, forcing the most out of his muscles in both length and strength.

When his left arm swept forward, Drizzt's mind turned inward so completely that he could feel the interactions of his muscles, could feel the bend of tendons, and could then angle both elbow and shoulder for perfect balance and speed.

Or at least, *almost* perfect. Drizzt worked now to adapt the mind-body training he had received from Grandmaster Kane to the many hours of work he had put in at Melee-Magthere and in the years subsequent actually fighting. While the techniques were not a perfect match, the skilled veteran drow had found enough similarities to make the whole greater than the two parts. It would be a long process, an unending one, he knew, but one well worth pursuing.

He retracted the arm and kept pulling back that left shoulder, turning about, legs bending to corkscrew him down very low to duck the imagined attack from the rear, and as he came around, he brought his right-hand scimitar, Icingdeath, across in a wide hook. Again, every muscle worked in harmony, Drizzt keeping full balance all the way through the movement, rolling on the balls of his feet at just the right moment to keep maximum strength in his countering slash even while his left-hand blade maintained an absolutely perpendicular aspect before his torso, lifting up to harmlessly raise the incoming spear or sword, or to block with balance and strength any downward chop of an axe or hammer.

Yes, he knew, this strike-and-turn routine would prove superior to anything he had ever before attempted.

All he had to do was create enough memory in his body to execute it effortlessly, swiftly, and always.

Always. That was where perfection lay. It had to be always, without error.

Almost always would get him killed.

He heard the door open behind him and held the pose instead of continuing his movement, not wanting the disruption to cause him to alter any angles or weight distribution. He heard the footsteps of someone entering the room, felt the disturbance, caught a whiff of the scent and a hint of the breathing.

He knew immediately that it was Catti-brie.

He stood up straight and turned to face his wife, his naked chest glistening with sweat in the low magical light.

"You would fight me?" he asked, but stopped, noting that Catti-brie was hardly dressed for sparring, though she was holding a pair of wooden practice scimitars. "Do you think you still can, safely, this far along with child?"

"Not I," she replied seriously, and threw the practice swords across the floor to her husband.

Regarding her with good-natured suspicion—what was she up to this fine morning?—Drizzt moved over and replaced his very real, and very deadly, scimitars on the room's weapon rack, then retrieved the practice weapons. He closed his eyes, lifting them and feeling their balance, which was nowhere near as precise as his own fabulous weapons, of course.

"This is real," Catti-brie said to him softly from across the room. "You are not being deceived."

Drizzt opened his eyes to regard her curiously, then opened them wider indeed when another entered the room, a male drow carrying wooden swords of his own. Like Drizzt, he was dressed in loose-fitting pants and a shirt opened low on his dark-skinned chest.

At first, through the haze, Drizzt didn't catch the significance, but as his opponent approached, Drizzt's eyes went wider still.

"What game is this?" he whispered breathlessly. He tore his gaze away, turning to Catti-brie, but she was already gone, the door closing behind her.

"No game," the newcomer replied.

Drizzt shook his head, dumbfounded, and started to verbally deny the possibility, but his opponent was not going to give him the chance, lifting his wooden swords and leaping forward in attack.

Nor was it a measured, testing routine, for the challenger came on in a furious rush, blades spinning and stabbing up high and down low.

Drizzt had no time for words—his left arm went out to the side, practice sword sliding vertically to pick off a powerful slash. He hopped and drove his right hand down, escaping the incoming sweep of the other blade. He landed lightly and retreated straight back, his breath taken away by the grace and beauty of the pincerlike attack. Few would even attempt such a strike, for any error left the center wide open to a finishing counter.

But he had seen it before, many times, since the drow who had trained him could do it—the drow who greatly resembled this fighter before him, he recalled, though centuries had passed.

Drizzt chased that thought from his mind as his challenger pursued, spinning a full circuit to send both swords across, then cutting short the double slash with a clever twist, retracting them and thrusting both powerfully.

Drizzt pirouetted to his left, his left-hand blade smacking aside the double-thrusting swords. By the time he had turned back, the challenger was there already, stabbing and slashing, up high and down low once more . . .

. . . and Drizzt matched every movement, his practice scimitars rolling and weaving, always in position as he fell into the dance of his opponent. His balance kept him in tune with the swords, and he noted the movements of the man holding them, looking for the time when they would come at him too near to each other.

From a purely defensive posture, Drizzt shifted to one of anticipation, and when the opening came, when his opponent's striking blades moved too near each other and angled properly for Drizzt, a right-hand undercut and back slash took them aside. Into the gap waded Drizzt, left-hand blade stabbing hard.

But the other drow moved beautifully, with grace so unique that it sent Drizzt's thoughts back across the centuries yet again. The drow accepted the success of the clever parry and went with it, throwing himself out to his left with his deflected weapons and falling into a sidelong roll, twisting as he did so that he came right back up to his feet, facing the turning Drizzt.

Now Drizzt had the initiative, though, and on he came with a blazing assault, his mock scimitars going at his opponent so rapidly that an observer might have thought him a frenzied six-armed marilith.

And yet the other drow matched his speed, swords working beautifully to crack against, slide against, or block every strike. On and on
the fight went, rolling back and forth in the circular chamber, wooden
swords banging and clacking so rapidly that someone hearing it from
afar might have thought a flock of a thousand woodpeckers had taken
up residence in the forest behind the Ivy Mansion.

But no, it was just these two magnificent warriors, fighting in such
harmony that they seemed like one man battling himself.

There was a comfortableness to it for Drizzt, a fond sense of a long-
ago day in a faraway place. And for a few moments, he lost himself in
that memory of being in House Do'Urden in Menzoberranzan again.
Only after he recognized that for the reverie it was did he instinctively
rebel against it, and not just because he had to focus to keep himself in
the present battle and wild swordplay, but also because he knew vividly
that falling into a false hope was a painful experience indeed.

With a snarl, Drizzt pressed on, stepping forward, putting more
power behind every swing. His opponent retreated with equal speed
and balance, finally shifting his back foot to the side and turning in
suddenly, looking to regain the offensive advantage—and just barely
ducking a stab for his face.

However, Drizzt would not be deceived by so simple a shift, and his
turn had him even more aggressively pursuing his challenger.

The other drow spun farther and ran, Drizzt right behind. Into a
roll went his enemy, coming up right before the wall, then stepping up
the wall, turning horizontally and flipping backward, spinning—and
striking—as he went.

And Drizzt parried once more, running right past him, running
up the wall as well but halting his backward somersault before it had
begun, springing instead straight back, twisting and turning to land in
a low crouch, legs widespread. He popped immediately upright, stabbing his blades.

But his strike was too high, and was easily ducked and countered,
predictably, with a double thrust low.

It was the correct countering move, normally, but one that
made Drizzt grimace. He had been entertaining some notion here, of

course—how could he not be, given the familiarity with this fighter, the resemblance, and his recent encounter with Lolth? But Zaknafein knew the danger of that counter against this particular opponent—he would not have made such a blunder.

Still feigning desperation, Drizzt did the only thing he could, executing the proper cross-down parry, scimitars coming down in an X to trap the attacking swords down low and keep his challenger bent.

So it was time to end this charade, and now that he had the cross-down, he kicked his foot between his weapon hilts, expecting to break the nose of his enemy.

Only, as his leg lifted, he realized that his opponent was no longer there, and to make such a ghost step, Drizzt knew, that opponent had to have anticipated both the block *and* the counter. ·

Purely on reflex, Drizzt executed the same move he had been practicing before the interruption, rolling on the balls of his feet, fast and balanced, spinning and stabbing into the area where he knew his opponent had to be.

The challenger picked off that thrusting blade, just barely, throwing his hips back and twisting as he did—and that put him in line for the real attack, as Drizzt's right-hand blade swept in from out wide, slapping him hard on the hip.

With a grunt, the challenger tried to retreat, but Drizzt had come around in full balance, and so pursued viciously, ferociously, scimitars stabbing left, then right, then back to the left, where the challenger barely parried, and did so only by turning that way.

Drizzt's right leg came up in a snap kick, hard into the side of the drow's head. Staggering, his opponent tried to backhand the raised leg, so Drizzt released his blade to allow it, but only so that he could follow the swing, rolling under the lifting arm with a sudden dart and turn.

He grabbed as he went under and his opponent had no way to resist as Drizzt turned him under and about, flipping him hard onto his back.

Onto his back, lying on the floor, and with the tip of Drizzt's other practice blade pressing against his throat.

"You have greatly improved, my son," the drow congratulated him.

"Don't call me that!" Drizzt said, pressing his blade.

"Did you think I would fall for your double cross-down trick again?"

"The solution is well known now," Drizzt said. "Likely, it is taught at the academy."

The man on the ground dropped both his swords and eased one hand against the shaft of the pressing weapon, trying to move it a bit to the side, for he was having a hard time drawing breath.

"Who are you?" Drizzt demanded, keeping the blade tight in place.

"You know who I am."

"I saw you fall into the acid. There is no resurrection from that!"

"I did not fall, I leaped." He locked stares with Drizzt and added quietly, and with a familiar inflection, "For us."

Drizzt wavered. His arms began to shake. *For us*, the exact words Zaknafein had said to him right before he had defied the Lolthian curse of Zin-carla, a dweomer that had rendered Zaknafein a zombie slave, an enchantment he should not have been able to deny or defy.

But he *had*, because of his great love for his son.

Drizzt's blades fell to the floor on either side of the prone man. He didn't consciously drop them. He didn't consciously do anything. He just stood there, staring.

"I told you to flee to the ends of the world," Zaknafein said. He lifted his hand and Drizzt clasped wrists with him and pulled him from the floor.

And then Drizzt stumbled away, out of the room, so disoriented and confused that he didn't even retrieve his precious weapons.

Zaknafein moved to follow, but Catti-brie stepped into the doorway through which Drizzt had departed and blocked his way. "Give him time," she advised. Zaknafein stared at her hard and said nothing, but neither did he try to push through.

CHAPTER 8

The Eyes of Topolino

The halfling went about his tasks with apparent diligence, cleaning the great audience chamber of Lord Dagult Neverember in the city of Neverwinter.

His motions were skillfully practiced, though, and his attention was never on removing the cobwebs from a decorative suit of armor or killing the large roaches in the corner skittering through the dusty beams of sunlight streaming in from the room's large window.

He wore an odd-shaped bandage on his head, sloping down from just above his right temple, over his left eye, to cover his left ear. By that ear, the bandage showed a bloodstain—from a bad fall, he had explained a few days earlier, when he had begun his third week of work for the man, Dagult, who was both an open lord of Waterdeep and the lord protector of New Neverwinter.

Like his cleaning skills, things weren't what they seemed there, either. It wasn't a bandage but a magical beret giving the illusion of one, blood included. Nor was his feather duster a cleaning implement but rather a beautiful rapier; and his clothes not rags but finery; and his shoes not wrapped cloth but fine high black boots. His mustache and small beard weren't scraggly, nor his eyes sparkling and strikingly green—in fact, the only thing authentic about the halfling was the dirt he smeared on his face and hands each morning to add to the magical disguise.

The bandage on his head bulged over that left ear, concealing a tiny ear trumpet, cleverly built and magically enhanced to amplify sound. He could hear a whisper from across the hall, even with ambient noise, so long as he turned his left ear toward the targeted speaker.

The target was usually Lord Dagult Neverember, of course, whenever the man was in Neverwinter, although his visits were often mundane—arguments over which parts of the city would be reclaimed from the volcanic rock, or which defenses would be bolstered, or whether this lord or that could lay claim to this house or that—and in those times, the halfling would often turn his ear to the other commoners working in the place to garner the more salacious, and (he had to admit) fun, rumors. Lord Neverember was overseeing the rebuilding of the city, but he clearly hoped to go even beyond that, to make this coastal settlement a worthy sister city to great Waterdeep, the shining jewel of the Sword Coast, a tenday's ride to the south along the Trade Way.

The ambitious man was also obviously trying to strengthen and expand his own position in the greater Sword Coast region, which was something this spy's friends would not much desire. For Lord Neverember was no ally to King Bruenor Battlehammer of Gauntlgrym, and even less liked by Jarlaxle, who secretly controlled the city of Luskan, farther up the coast.

Neverember was dangerous, too, the halfling often prudently reminded himself. The lord wore his pumpkin-colored hair pulled back from his angular face, hanging long behind his shoulders, giving him a severe look that seemed only more intense because of his dark eyes, deep-set so that they almost seemed to be peering out from within a separate bunker. Many of the Waterdhavian lords, living in luxury, had long been fat and soft, but that could not be said of this one, with his broad shoulders and muscled arms. "You are a lion of a man" was a compliment often paid to Neverember by visiting nobles, and one the lord protector of Neverwinter most liked hearing.

This one knew how to use a sword, or a fist, and the halfling had often enough seen evidence that Neverember's temper was quick and sharp.

The lord protector sat upon his Neverwinter throne now, chatting with a lady of some noble standing, judging from her fine gown and jewels. As the conversation between them continued, the halfling spy wished he had been allowed into the chamber earlier to catch the lady's name and title.

"A wise purchase, Lord Dagult," the woman said. "To turn such a handsome profit in so short a time—not even a year!"

"The place has strategic value and was built by the kind of skilled artisans rarely found in the world today," he answered. "I was fortunate to have the gold on hand when the offer was made, and did not hesitate—other than to bargain down the price, of course!"

"*Well* bargained," the woman said. "And Luvidi is not one to be taken so easily."

They both laughed, and the subject turned to whispers of an amorous affair between a lord and lady of Waterdeep. They engaged in that gossip only briefly, though, for then another visitor was escorted into the audience chamber, a dwarf with tight cornrows of thick yellow hair and long braids hanging down all around his large head. Though he obviously paid great attention to his hair, the same could not be said of his beard, which was unkempt and wild enough that the halfling spy expected more than one bird to fly out with every heavy step the fellow took toward the throne.

Behind that dwarf came several others, burly fellows all, pushing and pulling a thick-planked cart creaking under the weight of chests and bags.

"Ah, Bronkyn, good friend!" Neverember greeted, even as the court sergeant introduced the dwarf with "Lord Protector! Commander Bronkyn Stoneshaft!"

Despite himself, the halfling spy turned to survey the scene and stopped his fake cleaning. "Stoneshaft?" he whispered, for it was a name he thought he knew, though one he had not heard in a long time. Since he was often in the court of King Bruenor—the most renowned and powerful dwarf of the north, if not the whole world—there were few dwarves of any importance in the region this spy did not know. Yet he couldn't quite place this one . . .

The halfling's gaze went to the wagon, and he reached up and tweaked the ear trumpet just a bit. He tried hard to keep his expression impassive, then, when he heard a sound very familiar to him, rattling with every turn of the cart's wheels, realized that those chests and sacks were filled with coins—thousands and thousands of coins!

"I put a durned army on yer doorstep getting this here, Lord Protector," Bronkyn Stoneshaft said, bowing before Neverember. "Ye might be wantin' a good place for it!"

Neverember stood and motioned to his sergeant, who called immediately for guards. The Lord Protector then shouted back to another man, one the halfling knew to be the court secretary.

"The deed!" Neverember called. "Let word go far and wide that Clan Stoneshaft once more claims Thornhold as their home!"

"Thornhold," the halfling whispered, for he had heard of the coastal fortress set almost halfway between Waterdeep and Neverwinter along the Sword Coast, just south of the Mere of Dead Men. He had even seen it on occasion in his travels along the Trade Way, though only from afar, and had never bothered to investigate it more closely, for Thornhold was a name from another time, before the Sundering. Was it now anything more than a ruin?

If the coins in the cart were to be believed . . .

The chamber began to fill with soldiers, and while most went to the laden cart, others began hustling all the nonofficial people out of the room: the cleaners and the cooks, and a group of Neverwinter citizens who had come in hopes of garnering a few words with Lord Neverember.

Not wanting any hands touching his disguise, the halfling was quickly out of the room and then the keep proper. From there, he slipped away down the side streets of Neverwinter. He used his magical beret repeatedly, first becoming a dwarf, then a human child, then, finally, when he was far from the court, a normal-looking halfling peasant, wearing ragged clothing and leaning on a cane, his fabulous rapier in disguise.

Looking all about, glancing over his shoulder repeatedly to ensure that he was not being followed, he went to his encounter point, a location predetermined and always watched, where he would soon be met by an associate.

This day, it took almost no time at all, a halfling coming out of the shadows so efficiently that she beat the spy to the low wall, carved from lava stone, that doubled as a bench. She kept the cowl of her traveling cloak up over her head.

The two sat down, side by side.

"What's the word?" she asked.

The spy nearly fell off the wall when he recognized the voice, and he leaned over and peered under the cowl, staring into the eyes of the woman he loved.

"What are you doing here?" he whispered in shock to the lady of Bleeding Vines, the leader of House Topolino . . . and his own wife, Donnola.

"My Spider, did you think I would let you have all the fun for weeks on end?" Donnola answered with that grin that made Regis tingle from head to toe. Impish and innocent and yet, somehow, incredibly sexy and teasing, the smile of Donnola Topolino always brought a great sigh to his lips.

"If this infernal city weren't so full of spies, I would surely kiss you!" Regis said. "How I've missed you!"

"Your disdain for spies is noted, my spy."

Regis laughed, then looked around curiously. "How long have you been here? How did you even know I would come to this place this day?"

"Because I knew you would have something to tell us," Donnola answered.

Regis looked at her curiously.

"We watched the procession of dwarves along the Trade Way,

all the way to Neverwinter," Donnola explained. "Quite a force they placed about that small caravan. If they had bypassed Neverwinter, I might have had to work hard to organize a band to raid the thing."

"Where did they come from?"

Donnola shrugged. "We noted them only a day before they crossed past Bleeding Vines on the Trade Way, coming from the north."

"Luskan?"

"Jarlaxle's contacts knew nothing of them, and nothing moves from, about, or around that city without him knowing it. Somewhere between here and Luskan, I would expect."

"Port Llast?" Regis asked.

Donnola wore a blank expression. She was new to the region, after all, and Port Llast was a minor trading port built inside a quarry.

"A day's ride to the north," Regis explained.

"It's possible."

Regis shook his head, for it didn't make sense. Drizzt knew of Port Llast, certainly, and was considered a hero of the town. There were dwarves there—it was a quarrying village, after all—but nothing this substantial, as far as Regis had ever heard. And certainly the minimal business of the place would not have created such wealth as he had seen in Neverember's chamber this day.

"They came to purchase Thornhold from Lord Neverember," Regis explained.

"Thornhold?"

"A fortress farther down the coast. Jarlaxle will know more of the place."

Donnola nodded. "We should go to him, them. He is expected soon in Gauntlgrym to confer with King Bruenor and the others regarding the primordial's harnessed power in rebuilding the Hosttower of the Arcane. And the magical portals, my love. They are coming active."

Regis hardly heard her, for his thoughts had gone back to Neverember's chamber, back to the noblewoman standing beside the lord protector, in particular. He had seen her in the court of Neverember several times before, along with some other pale-skinned Waterdhavian nobility—at least, the halfling thought them to be from Waterdeep, given their familiarity with Neverember. Only now had the halfling made the connection, that one of the higher-rent taverns near the castle had been exceptionally busy of late, and with orders of fine food and wine flowing in from a line of carts each night.

"Spider?" Donnola asked her distracted lover.

"You go to Jarlaxle," Regis replied. "Tell him of Thornhold and tell him that the dwarves were of Clan Stoneshaft, with treasure to purchase the ruins from Neverember. A treasure worthy of a guarding army."

Donnola sat up straight at that.

"All confirmed," Regis assured her. "So take it to Jarlaxle, and just to him, that we may garner more information before we get Bruenor all riled."

"And you?"

"There's something I want to see here before I return," Regis answered, looking away, down the street toward the tavern he intended to investigate.

He straightened and turned quickly, and so did Donnola, when they heard quite a commotion coming their way, and Regis's jaw fell open as the Stoneshaft contingent came marching into view along the street before them. Line after line, the dwarves marched, heavily armed and armored, the ground shaking under the stamp of their thick boots and disciplined lockstep. They crossed right before the nondescript halfling couple and paid them no heed, marching eight across and forty ranks deep.

At the rear came Bronkyn, riding in the same cart that had delivered the coin to Neverember, and pulled by the same dwarf crew who had hauled it into the lord protector's chamber.

"So many," Regis murmured. "Why so many?"

"To guard a dragonworthy treasure?" Donnola said.

Both halflings gave a bit of a smile at that, and at the possibilities that might follow.

"Go to Jarlaxle with the names," Regis bade her.

"Thornhold and Clan Stoneshaft," Donnola recited once more.

"Aye. And word that the dwarves bought the place from Never-ember."

"I wonder if King Bruenor knew it was for sale," Donnola said. "Or had any word that a large clan of dwarves was planning to set up their fortress so near to Gauntlgrym."

Regis nodded, agreeing with the direction of her thinking. "I will join you presently," he promised. He glanced all around, then, and finding them clear of prying eyes, leaned in and gave his beloved a long-overdue kiss.

"You be careful," she told him breathlessly. "I only let you come out here because you were bored. I had no desire or intention to put you in harm's way."

Regis snorted at that. "We would never send others to do things we would not," he recited and Donnola could only sigh. "That is the credo of House Topolino, is it not?"

"House Topolino is now but one piece of a larger village for which you and I are responsible."

"Bleeding Vines would go on without us," Regis replied. "I'm not about to hide behind a throne." He laughed and grabbed Donnola's ragged peasant smock. "Nor are you!"

"Then I shall go with you," she announced.

But Regis shook his head, his face serious. "You go to Jarlaxle."

"I can send a courier."

"You go," he reiterated. "And make sure that he learns nothing that you don't also learn."

"I thought we could trust him."

"That doesn't mean his purse won't get fatter than those of his trusted and trusting associates."

"What are you onto, my love?" Donnola asked.

Regis shook his head, and truly wasn't sure. This whole thing just struck him as odd, more than even the surprising events would in-dicate. He had been in Neverwinter often of late and had noted no postings of some great fortress for sale, and had seen few dwarves at all within the city other than the long-standing citizens, since it was well known that Lord Protector Neverember and King Bruenor hated each other.

And as unusual as this morning's transaction had seemed, Regis's gut told him that it was even more so, and he had an idea of where he might learn the deeper details.

Regis glanced around, then rolled over the wall in a backward somersault, landing lightly behind it. There he tapped his beret and was rid of his disguise in short order, revealing his beautiful cloak and clothing, magnificent rapier at one hip, three-bladed dagger on the other. His blue-flecked beret, tilted fashionably to one side, replaced the bloody bandage.

He hopped the wall to land back on the street.

"So dashing!" Donnola said, putting her hand across her forehead as if she would swoon.

"Tell our agents that they will need to restock the caches," Regis told her. House Topolino had hidey-holes scattered about Neverwinter City in which they had placed bottles of wine they had brought from Aglarond. Topolino agents knew where to find those bottles to use as barter or cover, instantly becoming wine traders instead of spies.

It helped that the wine was quite good and convincing, the grapes brought from the east to seed the vineyards of Bleeding Vines. Donnola intended to establish a legitimate business out here with the impressive wine, but for now, it served its more clandestine purpose.

"You will try to open a trade partnership with Dagult Neverember?" Donnola asked skeptically. "He knows of our partnership—nay, our kinship—with Bruenor and Gauntlgrym, love."

"No, not with him," Regis replied absently, shaking his head. He hesitated with every word, for he was improvising here, formulating as he went, staring down the avenue where the dwarves continued their march, the same boulevard that held the inn housing the visiting Waterdhavian nobility.

"But there is someone . . ."

◆ ◆ ◆

HE DIDN'T GO STRAIGHT TO THE TAVERN. INSTEAD, REGIS went to a stable just outside of town run by a young elven woman named Aiberdelle Allaley, a widow who lived alone in the adjoining house. There wasn't much business for a stable outside the city walls, and so Aiberdelle's stalls were rarely anywhere near full, but both the Grinning Ponies and the Kneebreakers, halfling patrol bands who had taken up residence in Bleeding Vines, had seen fit to sign a contract with Aiberdelle that ensured her a decent living and more than a little protection, should she need it—although Regis always got the feeling that she wouldn't.

"Ah, Spider Parrafin!" she greeted Regis when he arrived back on her doorstep. "What trouble have you gotten yourself into now?"

"Never that, lady," Regis replied with a bow, sweeping off his fabulous beret.

"Back to Bleeding Vines, are you?"

"Just checking in on Rumblebelly," he said, and he couldn't help but smile at the name of the pinto pony he had recently been gifted by Doregardo, who led the Grinning Ponies.

Aiberdelle returned a sly grin. She knew him too well, he realized, and he thought that a good thing. Truly, Aiberdelle Allaley had become as much a part of the spying network Donnola had created as any halfling from Bleeding Vines.

"Back to Neverwinter, then?" she asked.

"Business to conclude, aye. It is my duty to serve Lady Donnola."

"You could wash her pony, and those of her attendants," Aiberdelle replied. "They are frolicking out in the corral with your own, much like Donnola herself prances whenever her Spider is about."

Regis was certain that he was blushing fiercely, but he giggled nevertheless.

His expression sobered quickly, though. "Did you happen to see the army of dwarves that marched into Neverwinter this day?"

"I heard them. And smelled them."

"But they had no beasts to stable?"

Aiberdelle shook her head, her long silver hair flying freely.

"Any others renting your stalls since I went into Neverwinter?"

"It is midwinter," she reminded him. "Not many on the road, unfortunately. Other than yourself and Donnola's group, I have seen just one paying customer in two tendays."

"Would you keep me in suspense, pretty lady?"

"Little in the world gives me greater pleasure," she flirted back at him.

"If I beg?"

"Are you here to brew?" she asked slyly, for on more than one occasion, Aiberdelle had happened upon Regis when he was hard at work with the portable alchemy lab he kept in his magical bag of holding.

"Daylight oil?" he countered, referring to a concoction he had made for her several times. Dipping a small object into daylight oil made it glow like a bright lantern for quite some time, depending on the quality of ingredients. Better still, the object wouldn't begin to dim until it was used, and could be covered, and so held in reserve, with a simple cloth.

"Well, I do not much enjoy bringing torches or lanterns into the barn . . ."

"Which is why I stable Rumblebelly here," Regis said. "Well, that and the beauty of the groom."

She winked at him.

"Daylight oil, yes," he agreed. "A grand batch, I promise."

"Very well, then. One paying customer, a large man. Seemed like a northerner, with long golden hair. At first, I thought him an Uthgardt, but he was no barbarian. Waterdhavian, and quite cultured, with fine clothes, though he tried to hide them under a weather-beaten cloak."

"A name."

"Yes, I believe he had one of those."

"Please, madam—do tell."

"Brevindon of House Margaster."

"With business in Neverwinter?"

"I do not believe he ever entered the city. Nay, he went north, just a few days ago."

Regis nodded, then took Aiberdelle's delicate hand and gently kissed it. "Might I bother you for some dinner? After I visit with Rumblebelly, I mean."

"And after you brew my daylight oil?"

He nodded.

"And wash the stink off?" she added, drawing a wide grin. "Unless you wish to eat your meal in the barn, I mean."

"I have eaten in worse places, I assure you."

"Why do you assume I am surprised?" she asked, and twirled away, skipping back into her house.

Regis took a few moments to ponder that he always had a smile on his face after meeting with Aiberdelle. What a valuable—and charming—addition to the network of House Topolino.

He didn't go for his pony, then, but straight into the barn, where he pulled from his magical pouch a sack filled with beakers, coils, a cleverly folded table, scales, calibrated spoons, and a large box of herbs and powders. It took him little time to erect his portable alchemy lab, and he began his brewing almost immediately, creating daylight oil on one end of the table and beginning to simmer up a far more complicated and time-consuming purple concoction on the other.

Even while those were brewing, the skilled halfling was hard at work on a potion of his own creation, one he called the gut chaser, which essentially elevated the punch of any drink to that of the fabled dwarven gutbuster—but without the foul taste of the latter.

Using it in concert with the purple potion—a magical delight that would allow him to scan the thoughts of someone with whom he was chatting—had proven quite the effective combination.

All but the purple potion were completed by the time Aiberdelle came into the barn with his dinner, and, surprisingly, with hers. The two shared a meal and a fine conversation, one that veered to the alchemy setup when, halfway through dinner, Regis got up to add a pinkish powder to the purple potion.

"Let me guess," said the elf woman. "A love potion, one that you will use to make me swoon whenever I see you, that you might take advantage."

"Good lady!" Regis said dramatically. "Beautiful lady, you must know that I am espoused to Lady Donnola. Alas, but had we met sooner . . ."

"I mean that you would use my tittering and eye-batting to strike better deals for yourself," Aiberdelle said with a giggle, one that Regis joined.

He went back to sit on the hay bale beside her. "I would not take advantage of you, my friend," he said seriously.

"I would not let you," she replied with a wink. "But others? What might Regis do to those he did not find so charming?"

"Oh, I intend to get some unsuspecting fools to tell me things they should not, of course."

"I would be disappointed in you if you could not."

Regis looked at her curiously.

"I am part of your gang, yes? Your success is my success, and likely my safety," she said.

The words struck Regis profoundly, creating a newfound respect for this elven woman and reminding him that his actions had consequences that went far beyond his own flesh.

"You are. A truly valued member, my lady." He was pleased to see her flush at his words for a change. "It is not a love potion, but rather allows me into the thoughts of another, to see the truth behind their words, often. I have enough ingredients to make several doses. I'll leave you some."

"In case Brevindon Margaster returns?"

"That, and whenever you find need," Regis told her. "And if you ever find need to use it on me, you will find only friendship behind my smile."

"Why would I waste so valuable a potion on that which I already know?" she asked.

THE COMMON ROOM OF THE DRIFTWOOD TAVERN WAS BUSY that night, full of finely dressed nobles of both Neverwinter and Waterdeep, and with a fair contingent of boisterous dwarves as well, led by Bronkyn Stoneshaft, who stood upon a table and sang of his clan's return to the great fortress of Thornhold.

Just outside the door of the collapsed tower that housed the establishment, Regis paused and listened for some hints in that song, but alas, it sounded like every other dwarven ballad, full of dark, cold halls and hard stone, goblins to be vanquished and glittering gems for the taking. When Bronkyn, joined by others, started a second performance, the dapper halfling pushed through the door.

Many eyes turned his way—and why not, with his fine beret and clothing, and wearing such weapons?—and the place quieted for a few heartbeats, but just a few.

Regis heard his name whispered as he walked across the crowded floor toward the bar, and heard, too, quiet voices full of suspicion. Some of the patrons knew very well who he was, and so knew where he was from.

"An unexpected guest," said the tavern's owner, a handsome middle-aged woman with silvery-gray hair, worn up to keep it out of the drinks and food, of course. "Is King Bruenor sending forth his emissaries to the lord protector then, to settle this foolish squabble?"

"Well met, Madame Rosene," Regis replied, taking her hand for a kiss. "I've no business with Lord Neverember, no."

"But ye've come into his city, then, have ye?" asked one man leaning on the bar, his tone and glare hardly welcoming.

"I've heard no declarations of enmity between Neverwinter and Bleeding Vines," said Regis.

"Then ye've not been speaking to yer dwarf friend, Bruenor."

"King Bruenor's business with Lord Neverember is between the two. I represent a separate town, of course, and one that has an interest in bringing fine wine to Neverwinter. From the slump of your shoulders, the gristle on your face, the unkempt hair on your head, and the smell of your breath, I would think you one who would appreciate such an emissary."

It took the inebriated man a moment to digest all of that, but then his eyes popped open wide and he came forward threateningly.

"Oh, sit down," Madame Rosene said to him, holding out her arm to stop his approach. "Or I'll have you clean your own blood from the floor when the little one's done poking a dozen holes in your fat belly!"

Regis paid the drunk no heed at all outwardly, though of course he was ready to stop the man at the point of his fine rapier if Rosene's arm didn't prove enough. The halfling surveyed the scene before him. It wasn't hard to pick out Margasters among the crowd, for they were all large and pale, and there were more than a few in here. Indeed, Aiberdelle's description of them as Uthgardt seemed rather appropriate. Certainly this Waterdhavian noble family could trace its roots, in the not-too-distant past, to some barbarian tribe of the north—it occurred to Regis that he might be able to use the name of Wulfgar, or even the man himself, if any infiltration of this family became necessary. He put that in his back pocket for later.

"You've brought a sample, I'm sure," Rosene said.

From his normal backpack, not the magical pouch on his belt, Regis pulled forth a bottle of red wine.

"Complimentary," he said, handing it over. "I only ask that you make sure your more discerning guests get a chance to sample it."

Madame Rosene stared at his backpack. "And how much more have you brought?"

"Enough to make acquaintances, I hope," Regis replied with a grin. "I've heard that a noble family from Waterdeep is visiting, and that is a market I would truly like to explore."

"Oh? And who's telling ye that?" Rosene said, and her reversion to the brogue of her peasant roots warned Regis that she wasn't pleased about that bit of information being public.

"No one," Regis said. "I see a few flitting about your floor who would fit that background, and you just confirmed it for me, fine lady. Will you introduce me, or should I do so on my own? And do understand that I can discount the wine more generously to a friend of the family."

Madame Rosene gave a helpless little laugh. "Come on, little bug, and I will give you a proper introduction."

Just a few heartbeats later, Regis was sitting at a table across from two formidable-looking black-haired, light-eyed women, uncorking a bottle of Bright Red Shorts, a most delightful blend. Alvilda and Inkeri Margaster watched his every move closely.

He poured a small amount, sloshed it about for a good inhale, and offered it around. Inkeri motioned for him to be the taster, so he did, and then poured three glasses. He had barely put them on the table when Alvilda, the smaller, older, and prettier of the two, pulled a small vial of powder from a hidden compartment in her belt and poured a bit into the wine.

"No!" Regis protested. "Ah, but you will ruin the bouquet."

"Tasteless, odorless, and prudent," Inkeri explained as Alvilda handed her the powder and took a sip of the disinfected wine.

"I already tasted it, right in front of you," Regis reminded them.

"But what spells are upon you, halfling?" asked Alvilda. "Or what potions have you taken right before? Or what tolerance—"

Regis held up his hand to show that he understood. "Are all Waterdhavian nobles as careful as this?"

"All living ones," Inkeri replied.

"Ah. Perhaps I should begin making antivenin instead of wine."

"Perhaps. But I wouldn't give up on the wine just yet. It *is* quite good," Alvilda said.

"Are you prepared to discuss a price?"

"I have only recently come to town," said Regis. "I had thought to spend the night in revelry and save business for another day."

"Yet you came to us with your wares," Inkeri remarked.

"Pretty lady, perhaps the wares were the excuse I needed to meet such fine company this evening."

The two looked at each other with amusement, but at least they didn't roll their eyes openly.

By the end of the second bottle, the three were talking and laughing. Halfway through the third, Regis was dancing with Alvilda while a chorus of dwarves bellowed bawdy songs from atop a large table, a pair of elven bards played a lute and a flute, and another of the Margasters (Regis believed) swept a horsehair bow across a nine-stringed fiddle.

"Should I dance with your sister, too?" Regis asked after one pass through the lines of dancers that soon framed the floor.

"My cousin," Alvilda corrected. "And she has already found her company this night." She motioned to the side of the room, where Inkeri was leaning so far over a table to be near to a finely dressed human, a Neverwinter lord, that she seemed as if she might smother the fellow with her uplifted bosom.

"Knowing Inkeri, her dancing will be prone, and not in this room," Alvilda said, and laughed.

Regis joined in. "Alas, and you are stuck dancing with one whose face barely reaches your waist."

"Which could be all the better," Alvilda replied, and Regis blushed, though after his experiences with House Topolino in the noble courts of faraway Delthuntle, he was hardly surprised. Rarely did the nobility of Faerun hold themselves to the so-called moral standards they demanded of the peasants, as if these pleasures were meant to be theirs alone as a reward for their wealth.

The halfling paused in his dance and winked at his partner, reaching his hand inside his vest to pull forth a pair of small vials filled with a liquid more brown than gold.

Alvilda's expression surprised him for a moment, until he realized that his movement had revealed to her the fabulous hand-crossbow holstered under his vest.

"One can never be too careful," he explained to her, covering the weapon once more. "So many will glance and think me an easy target. Sometimes I must dissuade them."

"I prefer dangerous men," she replied, and at that, Regis motioned to the vials, then to their table.

"An added kick, not unlike that of a mule," he explained, and he brought forth another bottle of wine and filled Alvilda's glass, then appeared to fill his own with the vino, though in truth, he pulled a sleight of hand and replaced his own glass with one containing a similar-looking purplish liquid.

Into each, he emptied one of his vials, mostly water for his own and a gut chaser to Alvilda.

The woman produced her antivenin and sprinkled it in, but of course, it would have no effect on the potent chaser Regis had added, as it was not poison but merely a blast of alcohol so potent that it could cross a dwarf's eyes.

Had Alvilda looked more closely during the toast Regis then offered, she might have noticed a pinkish ovoid floating within his pretend wine.

Halfway through the drink, Alvilda's whispers became slurred.

"Your sister was in with Neverember this day when Clan Stoneshaft arrived with the payment," Regis prompted.

"Cousin!" Alvilda whispered, but much too loudly, and she added, "Shh!" and slapped her hand over her mouth, laughing.

"A fine deal for the lord protector, it seemed."

Alvilda tittered, and Regis got the distinct impression that there was much more going on here than a simple sale, and that led him to focus on the potion he had taken, trying to glance into Alvilda's thoughts.

"This Thornhold must be a beautiful castle," he said.

An image of the place came to him from Alvilda's mind, and far from a magnificent kingly castle, Thornhold looked like the ruin he vaguely remembered, more properly inhabited by wild birds and vermin than gold-drenched kings. And he saw dwarves there—Stoneshaft dwarves! The same Bronkyn he had seen in Neverember's chambers.

Was she imagining the future, he wondered?

More than that image, though, Regis's magical mind reading sent to him a flood of Alvilda's disjointed thoughts: *a ship full of dwarves sailing north . . . chests of coins and jewels, platinum and gold, being unloaded in the dark of night . . . the name Luvidi Margaster signed on a deed, right above that of Lord Dagult Neverember . . .*

"Sold by Margasters?" Regis murmured under his breath. How did that make sense? Why would they sell to Neverember, then watch as the lord protector turned a mighty profit? To Alvilda he said, "It looked like a dragon's hoard on that creaking cart! Not gold, surely!"

Platinum! flashed in drunk Alvilda's thoughts. *A long ton of platinum!*

"Shh!" was all she said, though.

Regis did some quick calculations and tried not to gasp. A long ton, a tonne, of platinum would be more than a hundred thousand coins, valued at ten gold pieces each! No wonder Clan Stoneshaft had come south with an army guarding their carts. The only wonder was why a horde of dragons hadn't sniffed out such a treasure and descended upon them.

And where had a clan of dwarves Regis had only barely heard of come up with that kind of a haul? Bruenor, the most powerful dwarf king in the north—*at least* the north, he acknowledged—would have to empty the treasuries of both Mithral Hall and Gauntlgrym, and likely call in a favor from Citadel Adbar, to approach that fortune. Yet this obscure clan gave it away for ruins with seemingly no concern.

And that concerned Regis.

The halfling's next thought went to Jarlaxle, for who else could manage such funds, but he dismissed it. The drow would never do such a deal with Neverember without informing Bruenor.

He looked to Alvilda, who was staring off into nowhere, her expression wistful, and one last image came to him from her drunken thoughts, a hazy vision of tunnels and vaults of gold and jewels and pieces of platinum piled in chests, and of a secret door in Neverember's throne room that opened to a descending stair.

Regis left Alvilda Margaster passed out in her room some time later, and was quickly out of the Driftwood Tavern, heading back to the streets, where he could don his peasant disguise and report for work in Neverember's palace very early the next day.

First, though, he had to secure this information. But how? Donnola and her party were likely long gone from the city, and he didn't have any readily available contacts that could move the information quickly to Bleeding Vines. He thought of Aiberdelle and nodded decisively. He really did trust that one, and hoped now, as he started for her stables, that his trust was not misplaced.

From his pouch he fished another potion, his most valuable one of all, and one that he had thought to keep for desperate measures only.

But this treasure he could not resist.

If he had truly known what was down that staircase, though, he might have tried harder.

CHAPTER 9

A Most Angry Stomp

Y ou do not understand," Drizzt said.

"Oh, but I do, my love," Catti-brie replied.

Drizzt looked her in the eye.

"Of course you're nervous," she said to him. "This is something you have wanted forever, and now it is here. You are afraid that it isn't real, but it is."

"I know it is, and *that's* what I'm afraid of."

Catti-brie backed away a bit, her face screwing up with confusion.

"I don't know him," Drizzt explained.

"You knew him."

"Did I, though? I knew a grown man, through the lens of one inclined to worship such a figure."

"Originally, yes. But you were no child when you left Menzoberranzan."

"In many ways, I was. I didn't understand the world around me, and had no experience beyond the city, other than battles. When I look at who I am now, at where I've traveled and the horizons I've crossed, I cannot deny that I have come, slowly and sometimes painfully, to see the world very differently than I did when I first walked out of Menzoberranzan. Do you remember? I held a vow to never kill a drow, above all else. For all of my interactions with the other races, for all of my friendship with Montolio, for all of my growing love of Bruenor and Wulfgar, of Regis, and especially of you, I still held dark elves above your races. Such things do not easily resolve."

Catti-brie shrugged, as if that didn't seem so important. "You are here now. You are who you are, *now*. So what do you fear?"

Drizzt looked down the short hall and through the crack of the partly opened and distant dining area door, to see the edge of Zaknafein's shoulder as he waited for them at the dinner table.

"I don't know him," Drizzt said again. "I know what I hoped of him, what I created of his memory. But . . ."

"He was a friend to Jarlaxle," said Catti-brie.

"So? Jarlaxle is no hero to me. I call him friend, yes, and would help him, as I believe he would help me, would help any of us. He is a trusted ally."

"But he is not your father," she said, completing what he'd left unsaid.

"No, and any admiration I hold for him is based on his skills and bravery far more than on his morality. He's a friend . . ."

"But not your hero," Catti-brie finished. "Zaknafein is your hero."

"The thought of him, at least. Often have I asked myself what Zaknafein would do. A useful guidepost, but one, perhaps, that was constructed in my fantasies about a drow who I didn't really know."

"He was pleased that you did not kill that elven child," Catti-brie reminded. "So maybe you don't actually know him, but the fantasy and the reality are not so far apart?"

Drizzt nodded, and Catti-brie gave him a hug. He kept looking past her shoulder, though, to the stranger seated at their table, and he couldn't help but be afraid.

◆ ◆ ◆

THE HUMAN WOMAN WAS DOING MOST OF THE TALKING, and all of it about little things that interested him not at all. After a while, Zaknafein didn't even keep up the pretense of listening to her chatter.

His gaze remained locked on his son. And tellingly, he thought, Drizzt wouldn't meet that stare. He sat at the end of the table, to Zaknafein's left, and seemed to be staring off into nothingness, contributing little to the conversation and nothing at all to the hospitality of this, his home.

Embarrassed? Zaknafein wondered, and a big part of the drow hoped that to be the truth.

"Do you?" Zaknafein heard then, directed at him. He looked up to see Catti-brie hovering nearby—he had not even noticed her rise from the table. She held a bottle in her hand of some wine—Feywine, she had called it.

"Yes, yes," he said, motioning to his empty glass. He looked over to the left, to see Drizzt draining his glass, then motioning to his wife for a refill, too.

Catti-brie filled his glass and took her seat again at the end of the table opposite Drizzt. Zaknafein gave her only a passing glance before turning back to stare at his son.

"What do you remember?" Catti-brie asked then.

"About what?" Zaknafein replied, a bit more harshly than he had intended.

"Does your life in Menzoberranzan seem as if it was only yesterday?" the woman asked. "Are the memories vivid . . . ?"

"Yes."

"And of your time in death," Drizzt interjected. "What do you remember of that?"

"Nothing," he said. "Not even nothingness. Just nothing."

"You were not with Lolth," Drizzt remarked.

"If I was, the pain was not lasting, it would seem."

"You were not," Drizzt insisted. "With the help of some friends, I was able to find you, in the afterlife, and you were at peace—"

"What friends?" Zaknafein interrupted, and he looked to Catti-brie, quite sternly.

"Not her," said Drizzt.

"Dwarves, then?" Zaknafein asked, his tone as sharp as his look.

"Elves," Drizzt answered.

"Drow?"

"No—the elves of the Moonwood, far to the east. With their help, I was able to—"

"You would allow elves to spy on me in my death?" Zaknafein asked, his eyes wide.

"Would it have been better were it me?" Catti-brie interjected.

"No!" Zaknafein cried, and slammed his fist on the table. "You are . . . I mean . . ."

"You do not approve," Catti-brie said, and Zaknafein followed her gaze back the other way, to Drizzt, who was sitting with his hands grasping the table, his breathing labored as if he was fighting to steady himself, perhaps even biting back words.

The room went quiet, then, for a short while.

So, not embarrassed, Zaknafein thought.

Angry.

"Do you?" Drizzt finally asked.

"Do I what?"

"Do you approve?"

"Of?"

"You play coy," said Drizzt. "Your son is married to an *iblith*. Can you even admit that?"

"What is to admit? She sits right here beside us."

"And do you approve?" Drizzt asked more determinedly.

Zaknafein leaned back in his seat. He looked from Drizzt to Catti-brie and back to his son. "This is all very strange to me," he admitted. "And to you, I am sure. But the idea that my son is . . ." He paused and shook his head.

"Say it," Drizzt prompted, and he stood up and walked down the side of the table to stand directly opposite Zaknafein. "Just say it."

"That my grandchild would be . . ." Zaknafein said.

"*Iblith*," Drizzt finished. "Say it."

"I did not say it!" Zaknafein yelled at him, and he, too, was then standing.

"But it is in your mind. It is in your tone, and your stance, and your face."

"I would not use that word, or that sentiment, but yes," he said. "They are not drow. They are . . ."

"Inferior!" Drizzt yelled.

"Yes!" Zaknafein admitted.

"And weak—weaker than drow, right? Yet in my life among them, I have grown. I've learned from humans and dwarves and even half-lings, and put all that to use. Is that weak? Was it weak when I put you down to the floor in our sparring?"

"With toys,' said Zaknafein, and he regretted it the moment the words left his mouth.

Drizzt stepped back and pulled his scimitars off the mantel at the side of the room.

"Drizzt, stop!" Catti-brie implored him.

"These are not toys," Drizzt said. "Nor are the blades belted at your waist—gifts from Jarlaxle, I would presume. So let us learn the truth. To first blood."

"Drizzt!"

Zaknafein slowly stood and drew out his twin swords, rolling them in his hands. "Lead on to the training room," he said.

"Drizzt!" Catti-brie said again, louder and more forcefully.

"Why wait?" Drizzt asked, and he stepped forward and lifted his leg, bringing it up high above his head before slamming it down. The table in Drizzt and Catti-brie's dining hall was no delicate thing, made of thick wood, intricately carved and planed and sealed with a thick coating of clear varnish made from pine sap. A score of fat dwarves could dance upon it without causing so much as a creak from its heavy angled supports.

But Drizzt had been trained by Grandmaster Kane of the Mon-astery of the Yellow Rose—a *mere* human in Zaknafein's eyes—and into this kick he threw all of his life energy, every mote of his inner strength. His foot descended and struck the wood, and cracked it, dropping the table into two halves, all the silverware and goblets and napkins and the centerpiece tumbling into a heap at that center angle.

Catti-brie let out a shout of surprise and fell back, nearly tumbling over.

Zaknafein was less startled, and even as the pieces fell to the floor, he was leaping across the gap as Drizzt sprang toward him, the two passing in midair and stabbing, thrusting, parrying with what seemed a single ring of metal against metal.

They each landed in a turn, facing each other from opposite sides.

Drizzt started, as if to jump again, and Zaknafein mirrored him, but Drizzt stopped short, waiting on his side of the broken table.

So did Zaknafein, something he found quite amusing, and so he laughed aloud.

Drizzt didn't laugh, though, and on he came, no leap, just a stalk, and he set his scimitars to sudden and brutal use, slashing and stabbing alternately, then alternating the other way, and then flipping the sequence hand to hand yet a third time to buy some rhythm.

Zaknafein easily matched that rhythm, executing the parries perfectly, angling his body to set up a riposte that would gain him the initiative to lead the next exchanges. Finally, he thought he had it, so he called upon his innate drow magic to summon a globe of darkness, then rolled his hand under in a backhand parry to move aside a thrusting scimitar. And instead of lifting his second blade to block the coming slash, he went low and forward, thrusting his sword with the expectation of scoring first blood—his son had been too eager, too angry, he believed, and this would soon be over.

So his surprise was great when Drizzt's blade, the same one that had just executed the thrust, came across in the correct angle to turn Zaknafein's stab harmlessly aside, and then it was Zaknafein who scrambled, falling to his left and crossing his left-hand blade up and over to catch the downward slash of Drizzt's other scimitar.

Zaknafein had to give ground and roll under the weight of that strike, but he did so gracefully, keeping away from any tangle with the broken table and coming right back to one knee just outside the globe of darkness.

The globe of darkness that then winked out of existence, revealing a surprised Drizzt, though no less surprised than Zaknafein himself.

"How dare you?" Catti-brie yelled from the back of the room, from behind Zaknafein. "Both of you! This is my home."

Drizzt stood straighter, lowering his blades.

Zaknafein leaped at him.

Across came a scimitar, picking off the thrust, and down went Drizzt, falling into a crouch so low that his butt scraped the ground as Zaknafein's second sword swept above his head.

Drizzt spun, extending a leg, which Zaknafein hopped over. "Ha!" he shouted as he jumped, certain once more that victory was his.

But as Drizzt's leg crossed under, the ranger reversed the sweep and angled his foot for a higher kick, which Zaknafein hardly noticed or cared about.

Because Zaknafein didn't understand the power Drizzt could produce with such a short kick, a kick that moved his foot no more than the breadth of a delicate drow forearm. But the impact was such that it jarred the weapon master and sent him backward, stumbling as he landed from his jump, his hip bruised and pained.

He tried not to favor it—hadn't the time to favor it!—for Drizzt was there, right before him, bending him backward under a barrage of blows.

Zaknafein growled against the pain and matched his son strike for strike, rolling his swords horizontally, one over the other, in a defensive routine predicated on the need to keep his opponent back on his heels, forcing Drizzt to engage the spinning blades or open up clear avenues for counterstrikes.

Drizzt's blades were always there, scimitar clipping sword, again and again, a long and ringing meeting of fine metal expertly engaged.

Zaknafein was standing steadier now, the pain in his hip having subsided, and sought the opportunity to reverse the flow and disengage, that he could come right back in with a more dedicated offensive routine and so put Drizzt back on his heels.

And finally he saw a break. For his rolling sword clipped Drizzt's scimitar and somehow took it from Drizzt's hand, the blade spinning suddenly in response to the strike.

Zaknafein brushed it aside and went forward for the win.

Except Drizzt wasn't there.

Zaknafein felt the flat of a scimitar against the side of his neck, just under his ear, his son standing behind him.

He hadn't even seen Drizzt move, a ghost step executed more beautifully and completely than anything he had ever witnessed or imagined. In that split instant when he had turned his focus to the freed scimitar, bouncing in the air before him, Drizzt had somehow, impossibly, moved behind him!

He gave a helpless chuckle and lowered his blades, then winced at the sting as Drizzt nicked his ear.

"Weak?" Drizzt asked, his voice dripping sarcasm. Drizzt's other scimitar hit the floor beside Zaknafein, and his son stalked out of the room.

Zaknafein turned slowly to view Catti-brie, who stood against the back wall, arms crossed, scowling.

"Good lady," he said with a sheepish shrug. "I am sorry that you had to witness—"

"Just learn from this," she said coldly. "Both of you."

"Summon Jarlaxle," Zaknafein told her. "I will go."

"No," she replied without hesitation, which caught Zaknafein a bit by surprise. "No, that is too easy, and too cowardly."

"Cowardly?" He tried not to put too much anger in his words—he and his son had just destroyed the woman's dining room, after all.

"Drizzt would tell you to go, as you would like to," Catti-brie explained. "But that would resolve nothing, and leave you both with questions unanswered."

"Better than this," Zaknafein said.

"With questions unanswered because you both fear the answers?" Catti-brie said sharply. "Cowardly."

"This is all strange to me," Zaknafein said.

"I know."

"I don't know if I—"

"Neither do I," Catti-brie interrupted. "Perhaps instead of searching for answers so"—she looked around at the ruined room—"forcefully, you would both do well to sit back and allow the context of those answers to surround you, that the answers themselves make sense, and there can be no doubt."

"It is not so easy."

"No," said Catti-brie. "Not for a coward who must hide behind his swords." With that, she walked out of the room.

Zaknafein wasn't mad about that, but neither did he agree. It was more than strange to him that his son was cavorting with dwarves, with elves, even. To Zaknafein's sensibilities, it was offensive. No matter how hard he tried to deny that, there it was, ever present.

The notion that his son, his brilliant drow son, had married a human woman, and had mixed his seed with the blood of a human woman . . .

How would he ever look upon his grandson or granddaughter with anything but pity?

CHAPTER 10

A Chain of Whispers

They are still at the Ivy Mansion in Longsaddle," Jarlaxle told Donnola.

"And Drizzt's reaction?"

The mercenary shrugged. "He will be greatly pleased in time, I would imagine."

Donnola considered that rather ambiguous answer for just a moment before replying, "It is nice when good people win."

The two went quiet as a trio of halflings rambled past, laughing and conversing. They were on their way to the vineyards, it seemed, for one carried a basket, another a hoe, and the third already had her shoes off for some grape stomping, for though the harvest was months away, Pikel Bouldershoulder had woven some druidic magic to coax samples from many vines.

"What do we know?" Jarlaxle asked when the trio was safely beyond hearing.

"Not much, but it is a bit of intrigue," said Donnola. "It would seem that Lord Neverember has sold a most magnificent castle here in the north."

Jarlaxle furrowed his brow. "In Waterdeep?"

"No, not so far down the coast. A place along the shore called Thornhold, bought from Lord Neverember by a clan of dwarves known as the Stoneshafts." She looked as if she wanted to continue, but Jarlaxle's doubting expression gave her pause.

"Not so magnificent," he explained. "I know this place. It is a ruin, unused for decades. Every wall, particularly that facing the sea, is in dire need of extensive repointing at the very least, and the grounds now are no more than brush and stones—and not cobblestones, for most of those were long ago stolen away, those that were not buried under the lava flow and falling boulders from the volcano's explosion those decades ago. I am surprised that any would pay a silver, when simply inhabiting the place would likely suffice for claiming ownership."

"Definitely not a silver. A rather handsome price, I would expect, since the wagons were escorted by a small army of Stoneshaft dwarves," Donnola said.

"Wagons. So curious. And . . . Stoneshaft? I know this name as well," Jarlaxle mused, but after a moment, he shook his head, unable to recall the exact reference. Finally, though, he whispered, "Stoneshaft," more to himself than to Donnola. "The name was associated with this Thornhold, I believe. A clan returning to their ancestral home?"

"If it was theirs in the first place, where did Lord Neverember score this deed?" Donnola asked.

A good point. "You have spies in Waterdeep?"

Donnola stared at him blankly, not willing to surrender any particulars of her network beyond what Jarlaxle already knew.

"Good lady, this may prove important," the drow said.

"Indeed, and that is why I will take what I know and all else I gather to King Bruenor."

"And to me, I pray."

"I am happy to share with you, Jarlaxle, but only if it does not undermine King Bruenor."

"Happy?"

"Pleased for the business," she clarified.

"Ah, just business. Then you should come to me first. I pay better."

"No doubt, but my dear Regis is loyal to the dwarf."

"And you?"

"I love Regis."

"And prefer dwarves to drow," Jarlaxle said, and heaved a great sigh as if truly wounded.

"I prefer neither. Or rather, prefer you equally." She grinned. "I prefer *your* gold and *their* defenses."

It took Jarlaxle a moment for that to fully register, and that cleverness alone charmed him—for it was rare that one could give Jarlaxle pause—and heightened his returned laughter, for indeed, he did love bantering with this most talented halfling.

"How long will you need, do you think?" he asked.

Donnola tapped her chin and looked past him, saying "Hmm" a few times, and Jarlaxle smiled all the wider, for that, of course, was her way of telling him that speed was expensive.

"If the information is readily available, it could well be on its way to me from Waterdeep as we speak," she admitted. "If not . . . well, I will let you know, and perhaps ask for some assistance."

"My contacts in Waterdeep are thin," he said.

"Artemis Entreri is there, though. And the woman named Dahlia, too."

"And you have but one spy placed in the greatest city of the Sword Coast, no doubt," came the mercenary leader's sarcastic reply.

Donnola Topolino merely shrugged . . . and offered a sheepish grin.

"I have business with Amber and Athrogate," Jarlaxle said, tipping his cap and starting for the tram that would descend to the gates of Gauntlgrym.

"I should think your road south."

Still walking away, Jarlaxle looked back at her. "Their road will indeed be in that direction. Who better to look in on a dwarven castle? And who better to collect information that King Bruenor might well need? Other than Lady Donnola Topolino, I mean, of course!"

"Of course," she whispered. She looked past the cottages and house-holes of Bleeding Vines to the new road running south from the village. She could see the small market plaza just outside of town where it forked, southwest to Neverwinter, and due south to the Trade Way and Waterdeep, and to this place called Thornhold. Her gaze went first to that more southern road, but was inevitably drawn to the other, searching for Regis, her beloved Spider. She trusted him, and was glad that he had taken it upon himself to be an active member in the spying network of Bleeding Vines.

But still, Regis was getting himself entangled with some very dangerous people here, she feared, and with the lord protector himself, a man quick to anger and slow to forgive.

And more than that, he was far away, and that was a condition of which she most certainly did not approve.

HE HAD PROPERLY REPORTED HIS FINDINGS TO AIBERDELLE, and carefully scouted the section of Lord Neverember's audience hall wherein lay the secret stairway.

Getting to that door and through it, however, would prove to be a monumental task, one that might force him to consume the very valuable potion he kept at the ready. And without that potion, could he hope to escape?

Regis the castle servant made a point to linger near that door this day, dusting and dusting some more, and all the while noting the outlines of the portal and searching for traps that might be set against intruders. It was a cursory inspection, of course, for the room around him was not empty of guards, and even if he had been alone, he couldn't rightly find any way to note traps of the magical type—glyphs and wards and such.

But he had enough experience to notice anything obvious. And in the meantime he looked, too, for a place where he might hide within the room, stowing away until Neverember and his host of handlers and guards had retired to other quarters.

His hopes diminished with every idea, however, for he could see no way he might easily do so. He would have to leave with the rest of the servants and sneak back in, perhaps, and that seemed a daunting task. Lord Neverember was well aware that he had many enemies, and although he was a proven and formidable warrior, he was not a man to take risks regarding subterfuge.

The halfling resigned himself to the idea of making another of his valuable potions, but could he even procure the ingredients out here on the Sword Coast? The ones he had garnered for the first dose had come from Aglarond, after all, and at great cost.

"Be done with it, fool!" a gruff voice barked behind him, and he nearly jumped out of his boots—which were still boots, although his magical beret made them look like rags wrapped around his hairy feet.

Regis held his breath, half expecting a halberd to poke him in the back.

"You'll rub the glass right off that pane, doddler," the guard grumbled.

The complaint made Regis consider the present circumstances and get his mind off any future plans, and in doing so, he saw that he had indeed done a fine job cleaning this particular pane of the hundred-paned great window behind the lord's seat, although the rest of the window remained quite streaked and dirty. He paused for just a moment to glance out at the late-afternoon sky, the sun nearly dipping below the cold waters of the sea. His gaze moved down to the coast, then inland across the city to the base of the lord's castle . . .

. . . and to a canal, mostly frozen but disappearing under the wall right below this window, and very near the stairwell door.

Was it possible?

A RIDER DID COME UP THAT SOUTHERN ROAD BEFORE DON-nola turned back to her house. Too tall for Regis, and on a horse, not a pony. She thought it curious at first, but then, as she realized the woman's identity, it seemed downright alarming.

She stood there in the middle of the road and felt as if the world

were bending around her, her fears making all but that one approaching rider indistinct.

Aiberdelle Allaley, who should not be here.

The elven woman galloped her horse up to Donnola, skidding it
to a stop, and dismounted before the sweating creature had even fully
halted.

"Milady Topolino," she said with a quick curtsy.

"We just spoke," Donnola said, fumbling for the words. "Just yesterday at sunset." It was true enough. Donnola and her attendants
had arrived for their ponies at Aiberdelle's stable soon after Regis had
prepared his potions and departed on his return to Neverwinter.

"Events move quickly," the elf replied. "I thought you should know."

"News of Re—of Spider?" Donnola asked, hardly able to get the
question out, fearing the answer.

"Aye, lady, he returned to me very late last night, long after you
had set out for home."

"And he is safe?"

"Back in Neverwinter," Aiberdelle answered, and she sucked in
her breath and shrugged. "He was safe when he left me, to be sure,
but he had that look in his eye."

"That look?"

"Adventure."

"He often has that look, and often finds excitement. Why would
you . . . ?"

"I thought the information too important to wait for another of
your . . . associates to hire my services."

Donnola motioned for her to continue.

"There is something great afoot, lady. Dwarves sailing north and
marching south, laden with a dragon's hoard worth of coin."

"Indeed, I already—"

"And Margasters of Waterdeep all about, twined with the dwarves,
I would guess."

"Margasters?"

"House Margaster of Waterdeep. Brevindon Margaster stopped
at my stables, then went north, just before the dwarves came south.

Lady Inkeri Margaster stood with Lord Neverember when the dwarves purchased Thornhold. And the Driftwood Tavern is thick with Margasters."

"Is this unusual?"

"There's more," Aiberdelle promised, lowering her voice.

REGIS CREPT AROUND THE BACK OF THE CASTLE, SLIDING from shadow to shadow.

He came up on the levee of the canal, which directed it under the structure. The current was not strong and small patches of ice were scattered here and there, with the occasional floe moving past. This was the sewer serving Lord Neverember's castle, and only this castle, at least upstream.

Regis could only hope he'd find a way out of the flow before the waste channels found their way in!

He glanced around, pulled off his heavy cloak, and tossed it behind a bush near the castle wall. He had already stripped off his vest, shirt, socks, and boots, wearing only breeches, his sword and dagger belt, his beret, and the hand crossbow hanging around his neck. He closed his eyes and tried to summon his courage, reminding himself that he had gone to the cold depths of the Sea of Fallen Stars in search of oysters and their valuable pink pearls. This water before him was colder than that, surely, but it was not deep, and he would not be in it for long.

"The genasi protect me," he whispered, and he slipped down the side of the levee, disappearing under the dark water without a sound even as his mind screamed in protest at the frigid cold. Under the castle wall he went, swimming with the current right up to a closed grate.

Regis stayed under the water, his genasi heritage granting him the ability to hold his breath for a long, long time. He could see nothing, but his nimble fingers walked all about the grate, finally coming to the lock—and he was relieved to discern that this was not a portcullis but a simple swinging gate.

He brought his hand to his lips and spat forth a pair of lock picks, then went to work, trying to put aside the possibility that the thing could be devilishly trapped.

He simply hadn't the time for that.

In short order—though it seemed an eternity to poor cold Regis—the gate popped open, and he wasted no time in pushing through, then gliding effortlessly along the canal. When he rounded a bend, he noted a light above, shining through the pattern of small floes drifting about.

Slowly, the halfling's head emerged. He was in an underground chamber, a torch burning somewhere beyond his limited vision, for he was facing a ledge of stone. Above and beyond it, he heard talking, a human voice, speaking in the common tongue and with the strong accents of peasant folk.

"Bah, but for all their gold, theys can't pay me more'n a finger o' copper," the man grumbled.

Regis heard some scraping, like a metal rake on stone. He sank back under the water, then came out like a sleek fish, contorting his body perfectly to climb free to his waist and beyond, enough for him to grab the lip. Slowly he pulled himself up, until he was peering over the edge.

Relief flooded through him as he realized that the peasant was talking to himself. The bent man shambled about the small dock room, raking hay from the stone floor—likely the spillover from some chamber buckets, given the smell.

Regis slipped back into the water, treading easily. One hand went to the chain around his neck, pulling forth a small bolt, taking extra care when he extracted the dart from the cork. One scrape from the dart could have him floating back along the canal, snorting and gurgling.

He set the dart to his hand crossbow and very slowly and quietly drew it and locked the bent bowstring. Down he went under the water, except for one hand holding the weapon, then out he came again like a fish, springing up and catching the top of the ledge once more with his free hand.

"Eh, who's that splashing then?" he heard the man ask.

Regis quickly tapped his beret, thinking of a frog, of a lizard man—anything that would make him unrecognizable. Then he came up fast, and just in time, for the laborer was right there before him, rake held high and ready to strike.

But Regis kept his calm and shot first, nailing the poor fellow in the chest, right near his heart. The quarrel barely penetrated, and Regis was glad of that, for a heavier weapon would have killed the man on the spot.

He didn't need the dart to do much damage, though. That's what the drow sleeping poison was for.

The laborer staggered backward, grabbing at the wound, wailing, "I am killed to death!"

Regis almost rolled his eye at the melodramatics. "You're not dead," he murmured. "Just going to take a little nap." The larger man tumbled over onto the floor, upsetting several chamber buckets, and was snoring before he hit the stone.

It wasn't until he extricated himself from the canal that Regis realized how close to the edge of disaster he had been in the freezing water. He found that he could barely stand on his feet, and couldn't feel them at all!

He moved to the torch and began rubbing himself briskly with his hands. At one point, he even pulled the torch from its sconce and ran it all about his shivering form, near enough that he occasionally felt the sting of a stray spark.

He dropped his weapon belt and stripped out of his breeches, pulling open his magical belt pouch to retrieve another pair and the rest of his clothing.

Soon he was the dapper Spider Parrafin again, and he could even feel his warming toes wiggling in his fabulous black boots.

He moved to a door at the back of the chamber, listened carefully, checked it for tripwires or pressure levers, then cracked it open. He knew at once that his guess had been correct, fortunately, and that he was within a larger complex of tunnels. The ones outside this small hidden canal-side chamber moved directly under the main castle, as well. If there was a staircase behind that secret door in Lord

Neverember's audience hall, it almost surely would intersect with the tunnels now before the halfling.

So he used some of his daylight oil to brighten a small board, and out he went, creeping along. The floors were not smooth here, as within the entry chamber, and the walls not square, and indeed more rounded. These were lava tubes, remnants of the volcano that had buried Neverwinter City a few decades before.

The tunnel wound around a bend, then straightened, and Regis sighed, wondering if it would take him beyond the complex altogether, if perhaps this was not the way in after all.

Except, he then noted, this long, straight stretch of lava tube had four distinct alcoves cut into it, two on each side, with a tight-fitting door set in each.

Tight-fitting, heavy, and locked, Regis realized as he moved quickly from one to the next, listening only briefly. He figured that he wouldn't hear any sounds behind the heavy portals unless he happened upon a clan of ogres bowling with dwarves or some other such ruckus.

"Inky, stinky, get some gold," he whispered, with every uttered beat pointing emphatically at a different door in line, first to last then back again, one by one—it seemed as good a way as any to determine which he would first enter. "Never let an orc grow old. Give its scrawny neck a feel. Twist it tight and make it squeal, and put it through this door when cold."

He moved to the second door, the first on the right-hand wall, and again stopped to listen.

Nothing. How could there be?

With a sigh and a glance around, the halfling put down his glowing board and went to work on the lock. He set the tension bar in firmly, telling himself, "There is no trap, there is no trap," repeatedly as he tried to build confidence. For any doubt would slow him and he didn't want to be in this place any longer than necessary.

The pick went in easily but didn't move so readily once in the mechanism, which was extraordinarily crowded. Again Regis swallowed hard and recited his mantra about traps.

He worked and quieted his entire body, every sense focusing on the task before him. He had practiced these arts since his birth in this reincarnated existence, determined not just to be good at his craft, but to be the very best.

He found a reward for those many years of practice. One pin, two pins.

Three, four, five . . .

Regis fell back and stared at the lock in surprise. In went the pick once more, until three more pins had been thrown, and finally, the extraordinary lock clicked fully open.

"*Eight* pins?" Regis whispered, marveling at the magnificent contraption—and at his own skill, for he suspected that there weren't five burglars on the Sword Coast who could have picked this lock.

Well, not counting Calimpost, of course, where thievery was the city's celebrated pastime.

Don't get sidetracked, he told himself. He stared at the lock a few moments longer, thinking that if he came up empty in the rest of his searching, maybe he'd just find a way to take that.

The door opened into the room or tunnel beyond, so he eased it just a bit, then checked the threshold and jamb for any pressure plates. He eased it a tiny bit more and checked again—and a good thing he did!

He pulled his full pack of thieves' tools from his pouch and found a hair-thin strip of metal and a small jar of glue. Treating one side of the metal strip, he slipped it in between the door and the revealed pressure plate, pressing the sticky side as tightly as he could to the jamb.

He eased the door a bit more and checked again, and indeed found yet another trap of some sort, similarly designed. Once more he went to his pack and disarmed the mechanism with a second sticky plate.

Finally, the edge of the door moved past the jamb altogether. Regis suspected there were more dangers in his path, but any further traps were likely in the room just beyond the portal, and so out of his ability to discern.

He stepped back, looked left and right, then kicked the door and leaped back and to the side. And just in time, for as the door opened

in, right to left, it released a heavy bladed pendulum swinging perpendicular to the threshold. It swung right out into the hall, with a
blade so long that it would have creased Regis from crotch to forehead!

Back into the room it went, then back across the threshold, and
a third time, showing little indication of slowing. His patience lost,
Regis timed the next swing, and as the pendulum went back into the
room, so did he, tossing his magical torch ahead, leaping across the
threshold, and diving into a roll off to the right side of the doorway.

Both of his melee weapons, rapier and three-bladed dirk, were in
the halfling's hands when he came up from that roll—to find himself
alone in a small square chamber with a raised wooden floor, stacked
with barrels and chests.

He glanced back toward the hallway and the still-swinging pendulum. He wanted to close the door, of course, but that would not be possible, for there seemed no way to reset the trap and get the pendulum
out of the way, although now its swing was lessening noticeably with
each reversal. Even when it stopped, though, Regis figured he had little
chance of closing the door, for he could tell that the pendulum was
simply too heavy for him to push it back enough to get the door shut
in front of it. He had to be quick, because his entry *would* be noticed.
Blades away, he went for the stacked barrels and chests, but his smile
disappeared when he found them filled with mundane items to run a
large household, such as candles, wine and water, and foodstuffs.

After perusing only a few, he snorted aloud and shook his head—
why would they go to such trouble to triple-trap and hard-lock such
a door? No, it didn't make sense, so he pressed on, rolling some barrels out of the way and discovering, at last, something curious: a
decorated basin of white stone, a singular carving of basin, pedestal,
and base that brought its lip as high as Regis's hairline. The halfling
tested its weight, then grabbed on to the side and slowly pulled himself up to his tiptoes, trying to get a peek inside the bowl.

So heavy and balanced was the basin that it didn't even jiggle as
he put more of his weight against it. That gave him the courage to lift

a bit higher when he noted that the bowl was full of a crystal-clear and odorless liquid, like pure water.

Holy water, perhaps? Some other ceremonial liquid? A magical potion?

He brought his arm to the edge of the bowl for leverage and pulled up higher, trying to see what might be inside at the bottom of the bowl, and he felt himself rewarded when he noted a glitter there, like a diamond.

Or a bubbling flow, he thought when the water extended up into the air above the basin. An enchanted fountain!

But no, Regis realized almost immediately. The water did not splash apart and fall back in like a fountain, for no, it was not being propelled by any flow.

It was lifting itself up, and with definitive form.

A living creature!

Regis flung himself backward, or tried to, but the water monster proved faster and slapped a wet tendril around his head, catching him and yanking him forward, pulling his head over the side of the bowl and pressing it down into the water that this magical being considered its home.

And there it held him, face pressed against the bottom of the bowl, and all Regis could do was take some minor solace in his genasi heritage once more.

CHAPTER 11

His Father's Father

They weren't at the Ivy Mansion, but out in the forest behind it. Drizzt led the way through the door of a small cottage, set within a small lea bordered by pines. Everything about the cottage—the construction, the furniture, the fire pit under a hole in the ceiling—spoke of economy and utility, which brought a curious look and a "Hmm" from Zaknafein when he entered.

"This," Drizzt explained, "is where I do my work."

Zaknafein looked to Catti-brie, who merely nodded, then turned back to Drizzt, even as a howl drifted in from the open window. "Your work?" he asked.

"There are cursed beings in the forest," Drizzt explained. "Werewolves. We call them the Bidderdoos, named after the unfortunate Bidderdoo Harpell, a wizard who began this brood, first with magic, and then because, once he had cursed himself, poor fellow, he wasn't able to control his appetite."

"You kill wolfs?" Zaknafein asked, his language a bit stilted and hesitating. To this point, Catti-brie had been following up Yvonnel's work by casting dweomers upon the resurrected drow to allow him to understand the common language. Repeated use of those dweomers was known to have the side effect of actually teaching the language to the recipient, however, and so it was with Zaknafein already.

"Werewolves," Drizzt repeated, but Zaknafein shook his head in frustration—and both of them looked to Catti-brie.

The woman waved her hands and issued a chant, calling upon her divine Mielikki to grant Zaknafein once more the gift of comprehending their language.

"Werewolves," Drizzt explained when she was done.

"Lycanthropes? You kill lycanthropes?" Zaknafein asked, his command of the language obvious once more. He considered it a moment, then added, "Mercifully, I expect."

"I don't kill them," Drizzt replied. "I catch them and take them to the Ivy Mansion."

"We've a dozen in cells beneath the mansion," Catti-brie explained. "And some of our newer treatments and dweomers seem to be helping, if just a bit."

"Helping? You think to cure them? There is no cure for lycanthropy!"

"And there never will be, if no one tries," Catti-brie retorted, somewhat harshly.

Zaknafein stared at her then, long and hard, and his facial features softened as he did, just a bit, as if he was trying to find a different way of looking at not the lycanthropy issue, but his daughter-in-law.

"And we hunt this night?" he asked Drizzt, though he kept staring at Catti-brie.

"Only if Guenhwyvar finds an opportunity," Drizzt replied. "And not we, but I, alone."

That surprising exclusion turned Zaknafein away from Catti-brie to regard his son. He started to respond to Drizzt, not happy about being left out, but he stopped even as the first words left his mouth, for the name had registered, and instead he asked, "Guenhwyvar?"

"Your son's oldest friend, who has been with him since he left Menzoberranzan," said Catti-brie.

Zaknafein held up his hand to silence her. "The cat?" he asked Drizzt.

Drizzt took the onyx figurine out of his pouch and held it up before Zaknafein's staring eyes.

"The Hun'ett wizard's cat . . ."

"She has been with me through it all," said Drizzt.

"Through it all . . . I should know some of this." Zaknafein shook his head, frustrated. His resurrection had been successful, and most of his previous memories were as fresh as if he had not been gone for more than a century, but there were parts of his previous existence that seemed as if in a distant fog to him. He stepped back and Drizzt called to the panther. Zaknafein remembered enough of the ways of magical figurines, even this one in particular, to remain at ease as the gray mist appeared in the small room, took the shape of a huge panther, and then became exactly that: a giant black panther, all muscle and claws and teeth.

But one controlled, wholly, by the possessor of the statue, Zaknafein remembered, and a good thing, too, for in those small quarters, neither Zaknafein, nor Drizzt, nor Catti-brie would have had a chance to fend off the powerful beast, and they all knew it.

"Guenhwyvar, we have a new friend!" Catti-brie said hopefully when Guen appeared. Guenhwyvar turned to Zaknafein and sniffed.

Zaknafein gave her an easy pat on the head, but he was watching Catti-brie, realizing that she was trying hard here with the feigned excitement in her words to the panther.

"Perhaps an old friend," Drizzt added. "From another time."

Zaknafein didn't miss that, either, the particular emphasis Drizzt had placed upon the last two words. Indeed, Zaknafein felt as if he was from a time and place far, far removed from this.

Guenhwyvar nuzzled Drizzt, then moved over to sniff at Catti-brie in particular, as had become the norm for the panther. She gave a low growl, more of a purr, it seemed, and licked the woman's bulging belly.

"The moon is almost full this night," Drizzt told Guen, and when she looked his way, he motioned his chin toward the door.

Guenhwyvar understood, and out into the night she went.

"There will likely be none about," Drizzt explained as the panther disappeared into the shadows, and Catti-brie moved to shut the door. "The moon is not quite full."

"Then why bring her in?" Zaknafein asked. "Such items are limited in their use, yes?"

"We are working on that," Drizzt replied, throwing a wink at his wife.

Zaknafein looked at her curiously.

"The Harpells of the Ivy Mansion on the hill and I are doing promising research into dweomers that could safely extend Guenhwyvar's time on this plane of existence each week—each day, even," the woman explained.

"And to show you, perhaps," Drizzt then admitted. "I am well, Father. My life has been one worth living, in ways I never imagined."

"Like taking a human for a wife?"

"That is no longer up for discussion," Drizzt said coldly. "She is my world. Here and now and forever. As will be our child. *Our* child."

Zaknafein noted no room for debate in Drizzt's voice, so he bit back a stinging retort and heaved a great sigh. "I have much to learn," he conceded. "I hope that I can."

He knew there wasn't much optimism in his voice, but he saw no way to remedy that.

Catti-brie, who was also not smiling, started to respond, but Drizzt put his hand on her shoulder, silently bidding her to let him take the lead here.

"I have walked a wondrous road, Father," he said quietly. "I have seen things I could never have imagined, learned so much beyond the sphere of the Spider Queen and her matrons, and found love— true love." He paused to share a look with Catti-brie. "A partner to walk with me throughout this amazing journey."

Zaknafein was trying to find a way to respond when Guenhwyvar issued a long, low roar from out in the forest.

"Werewolf?" Zaknafein asked hopefully, thinking this might be just the thing to get him away from this unbearable tension and unanswerable dilemma.

"So it would seem," Drizzt replied. He glanced at his wife, who nodded, then gave her a quick kiss and took his leave.

Zaknafein, suddenly alone with his daughter-in-law, then realized that perhaps the cat's interruption wouldn't be the reprieve he desired.

Catti-brie walked past him and closed the door behind her husband. She moved to the table and cast some spells, conjuring a feast to fill the bowls and wine to fill the goblets.

"Sit," she bade Zaknafein. "Drizzt will not be long."

He looked at her, trying not to be suspicious.

"Sit," she said again, more commandingly. "It is past time that you and I had a talk."

"A blunt one?" he said with a snort.

"An honest one," she answered dryly.

Zaknafein walked over and took a seat, then said, not hiding his condescension, "I feel as if I am about to be scolded."

"You are about to be informed, if you'll listen, not scolded."

"They are often one and the same. Perhaps human women are not so different from the drow matrons after all." He said it with a grin, but Catti-brie was clearly not buying into such a comment as a good-natured jab.

"I expect that you are about to learn the choices before you," Catti-brie answered. "What you do with those choices will be up to you. Not me, and not Drizzt."

"The choices from *your* perspective."

"No, the story of who Drizzt has become, from the day I first met him on the slopes of a mountain called Kelvin's Cairn to now. His has been an incredible journey since his arrival on the surface of Toril, and I have been beside him for most of it. So I will tell you, and, I'm sure, Drizzt will tell you when he returns. With that knowledge, your choices, whatever they might be, will be more informed."

"My choices about what?" Zaknafein asked, sitting back and studying the surprising woman more carefully.

"About . . . everything. Everything to do with your son, at least."

"You fear my opinion."

She snorted, and Zaknafein was surprised at the sincerity of her retort. This one was confident in her position here. That gave him pause.

She began her tale. Zaknafein ate and drank, but he listened, and quite intently.

ANOTHER MEETING OF THREE WAS TAKING PLACE TO THE west of Longsaddle, in the grand chambers—physical and extradimensional—of Gromph Baenre in Luskan.

Two female drow circled about the wizard, staring at him unblinkingly, measuring him, trying to get into his thoughts and seeking any clue at all. No drow other than the matron mother herself would ever attempt such a stare at Gromph, but these two were not actually dark elves. They only made themselves look that way to strong effect, for their actual appearance, the half-melted-candle-of-mud form of a yochlol, would keep any drow with whom they spoke far more on his guard.

Not that Gromph had any illusions about the nature of his guests.

"What have you learned of Zaknafein's return?" Yiccardaria asked, her voice husky and suggestive—magically so.

Gromph snorted at that effect, as if such a minor dweomer could entrap him, even if issued by one who often stood beside the Spider Queen.

"Nothing," the wizard replied. "Zaknafein has been reunited with his son, though I don't know the outcome of that circumstance."

"They accept the return of Zaknafein?" asked Eskavidne.

"What is to accept? He is here."

"And they are not curious as to why or how?" the handmaiden pressed.

"Of course they are. Jarlaxle—"

"Yvonnel?" Yiccardaria interjected.

"Yvonnel, too," said Gromph. "They inquire wherever they may. They asked me if I had learned anything upon my return from Menzoberranzan—"

"And you told them?" Yiccardaria asked, rather sharply.

Gromph shrugged as if it hardly mattered. "Told them what? That all believed it to be truly Zaknafein Do'Urden resurrected? Yes. But that is nothing they could not have easily discerned on their own."

"Perhaps they wished to learn of the news from Menzoberranzan to discern if suspicion of the resurrection was falling upon them," Yiccardaria reasoned, but Gromph just snorted in response.

"Zaknafein is here, however it happened," the former archmage said. "This is the new truth of the region, but it is only one."

"Tell us others," said Eskavidne.

"The dwarven gate between Gauntlgrym and this very tower and the one between Gauntlgrym and the Ivy Mansion are operational and working even better than I would have thought possible. King Bruenor will have a third portal in place within a tenday or three, connecting Gauntlgrym to Mithral Hall. When that is working, it will allow him to bring in material and soldiers from the Silver Marches at a moment's notice—putting Bruenor closer to becoming untouchable by the petty humans of the Sword Coast, unless they desire a war with the entire race of Delzoun dwarves. It is quite impressive."

"And the Hosttower?" asked Yiccardaria, apparently unconcerned by the goings-on of the dwarves. So be it.

"Look around you. Have you seen anything on the Material Plane to rival this magical creation, other than Ched Nasad's web city, perhaps?"

The handmaidens looked at each other, grim-faced but with clear intrigue.

"I share your interest," said Gromph. "This act of creation with the primordial—I have learned its name to be Maegera—holds wondrous promise for us all. I am your eyes and ears here."

Yiccardaria arched a delicate eyebrow at that, indicating that her trust level regarding Gromph Baenre was not as high as he was pretending with that statement. But indeed, what choice did she have?

"Should we fear to allow the dwarves this power?" Eskavidne asked, as clearly she didn't share Yiccardaria's indifference. "Will they send the armies of the north crashing against Jarlaxle in Luskan? Will King Bruenor bring in his kin from the Silver Marches to swarm the Underdark all the way to the City of Spiders?"

"Yvonnel holds within her the keen pain of King Bruenor's keener axe," Yiccardaria reminded, for it was this same Bruenor who had split the skull of Yvonnel the Eternal.

"Even if she didn't, I do not foresee such adventurousness in Bruenor, not for conquest, at least," Gromph answered.

"Has your time hiding among these *iblith* softened you?"

The former archmage cast an amused expression at Yiccardaria. He understood her added cynicism and anger here. The treachery of Yvonnel had defeated Yiccardaria and banished her to the lower planes—only the great weakening of the Faerzress and the intervention of Lolth herself had allowed this particular handmaiden to walk the lands of Faerun once more. And more than anything else, the proud demon yochlol's pride had been punched, as she had been punched, quite literally, by the human Grandmaster of Flowers.

"What other events will you report, servant of Lolth?" Eskavidne asked, ignoring her fellow handmaiden's question, as Gromph did.

He actually chuckled at that. "Intrigue with the lord protector of Neverwinter, as usual," he answered. "There are some strange stirrings, but nothing worthy of your time . . . at least, not yet."

"We would not have King Bruenor allied with him," Eskavidne made clear. "You must not allow it."

"Hardly a worry."

"Jarlaxle will monitor and we will know?"

"You can know already," Gromph assured her. "The dwarves of Gauntlgrym hate Dagult Neverember, and the feeling is quite deep and quite mutual."

The handmaidens again exchanged those interested glances.

"Do not think for a moment that enmity is an opening for any of Menzoberranzan with the open lord," Gromph insisted, making certain his tone conveyed the depth of his urgency. "Lord Neverember is a bothersome idiot and would be more trouble than gain, do not doubt."

"He is an open lord of Waterdeep, is he not? Surely he has allies," Yiccardaria said.

Gromph conceded the point with a shrug. "We are watching those allies."

"And they are?" the impatient handmaiden demanded.

"A Waterdhavian noble house, Margaster," Gromph admitted.

He was surprised at the twang of guilt that accompanied those words. Since when did it bother Gromph to think himself acting against the best interests of Jarlaxle and these strange companions with whom the self-serving fool had surrounded himself? Still, he was walking the fine line in giving away information that could be had elsewhere anyway, and that would not be too detrimental to his adventurous brother.

No matter, he thought, and he dismissed the whole notion out of hand. These were emissaries of Lolth herself, and as in Menzoberranzan, Gromph would do what he needed to do to continue his work here and now—work that had become so precious to him once more with the inclusion of his training in psionics.

Primary among Gromph's priorities was self-preservation, something he thought more likely by staying on the good side of Lolth.

HOOFBEATS OUTSIDE THE COTTAGE ALERTED THEM OF AN approach, and Catti-brie, who had nearly finished her tales of Drizzt, moved over and peeked out the small window. "It is Drizzt returned," she told Zaknafein, and then added with a smile, "I warn you now, keep your swords sheathed, both of you."

"He drew first," Zaknafein replied, as lightheartedly as he could manage.

"I let you have your squabble last time, though I'll be a tenday of tendays replacing the broken things. But sometimes one must let children learn their own lessons, I suppose."

"Children?"

Catti-brie held up her hands and shrugged, letting the comment stand.

Zaknafein, however, couldn't ignore it. "Good lady, where I am from, children who battled as we did in the house proper would have been disciplined at the end of a living serpent on a priestess's scourge."

"Where you are from?" Catti-brie asked with an arch smile. "You mean where the superior race lives."

Zaknafein started to respond before he had fully digested that remark, but just surrendered and even chuckled.

The cottage door opened and Drizzt entered. He unstrapped his weapon belt and hung it on a hook beside the door, almost as if he had heard the previous conversation. As he did so, he looked curiously at his wife, then to the chuckling Zaknafein.

"Things are well?" he asked.

"Werewolves?" Zaknafein asked, still not quite sure how to answer that seemingly simple question.

Drizzt shook his head. "We thought we had the trail of one, but no."

Catti-brie motioned to a chair at the table, then took her own seat.

"I was telling your father of your life since our days running the foothills of Kelvin's Cairn," she explained. "From my perspective, .of course. I am sure he would like to hear it from you."

Zaknafein felt Drizzt's questioning stare fall upon him. "I would," he confirmed, and he wasn't lying. The human woman had, surprisingly, given him a lot to think about, and perhaps hearing the same stories from his son's perspective would help him better appreciate her words and feelings.

The three remained at the cottage long into the night, with Drizzt telling his story, from Kelvin's Cairn to Mithral Hall, of all the places in between and all the places beyond. He paid particular attention to one tale that Zaknafein couldn't help but appreciate.

"I returned to Menzoberranzan," Drizzt explained. "Openly, and in surrender."

"I gave my life so that you would not have to do such a thing," Zaknafein interjected, and he didn't try to hide his anger about such a ridiculous choice.

"I had to," Drizzt explained.

"You *thought* you had to," Catti-brie interjected, to which Drizzt nodded.

"They hunted me, imperiling those I came to love," Drizzt said. "I could not allow that."

"Those who loved you would rather die beside you than have you give yourself to House Baenre," Catti-brie insisted.

That raised Zaknafein's eyebrow. "Do tell," he said to Drizzt. "All of it. This is a tale your wife seems to have forgotten."

Drizzt laughed at that, which surprised his father. "She alone came for me," he said. "She was no great priestess at that time, nor even a wizard, though now she is proficient in both the arcane and the divine. She was a fighter, and not yet one of great experience even." He cast a glance at his wife, one full of love. "But she came, alone. She walked the ways of the Underdark all the way to Menzoberranzan, and there, with the help of another human, a man you will soon meet if you have not already, she got me out of the dungeons of House Baenre."

Zaknafein started to laugh, but he bit it back as he realized that his son was not joking. "From *Baenre?*" he asked incredulously, and Drizzt nodded.

"A good bit of luck," Catti-brie admitted.

"I doubt it not. When was this?" Zaknafein asked.

"Six score years ago, perhaps," said Drizzt. "Not so long after King Bruenor retook Mithral Hall."

Zaknafein nodded, but then realized a great inconsistency here when he regarded Catti-brie. "You cannot be more than forty years of age."

Catti-brie snorted at that. "I am not halfway through my twenties, but thank you for that . . . I think."

"But you just said . . ." the flabbergasted Zaknafein said, looking back to Drizzt.

"That is another story, one as remarkable as your own, Zaknafein," Catti-brie answered. "And one for another day. It is late. The moon has set. Let us return to the Ivy Mansion and warm beds."

She rose and began collecting her things, and Drizzt did likewise. Zaknafein, who was wearing everything he had brought out to the cottage, remained seated and finished his drink, watching the two moving about, and watching, most of all, the way they looked at each other.

He tried to minimize his occasional winces, and to keep the scowl from his face, but even with all he'd heard that night, he didn't think he was very successful at either.

"WELL, THAT WAS MUCH MORE PLEASANT," CATTI-BRIE SAID when she and Drizzt were alone in their rooms at the Ivy Mansion. "And we don't need to build a new table!"

Drizzt didn't share her mirth.

"He hates you," he said.

"He doesn't hate me."

"He hates that we are together. He hates, most of all, that we are having a child, a half-breed that he will not accept."

"Fear can lead to hate, but they are not the same," Catti-brie said. "Your father has no experience in a multitude of friendly races and cultures, and this world—a world and time where such a thing as our baby could occur—have been thrust upon him so jarringly."

"Zaknafein is no child," Drizzt replied. "Nor is he the man I—"

"You keep calling him Zaknafein," Catti-brie interrupted. "Not father, but Zaknafein. Why?"

Drizzt didn't answer, but he considered the valid point.

"Zaknafein's not the only one who's afraid," Catti-brie added.

She knew him so well, Drizzt thought. He was afraid, indeed terrified. Zaknafein had been a symbol to him more than a real person over the last century and more. He had idolized a memory, because he never had to worry about the reality of who Zaknafein, removed from Menzoberranzan, might be.

It was so much easier to just project his own feelings and beliefs onto the ghost of the man.

"People are complicated, and people change," Catti-brie said. "Look at Artemis Entreri."

Drizzt's audible gasp at that gave his fears away, he knew, when Catti-brie looked at him more intently.

"Have patience, my love," she said, moving near to him and massaging his shoulder.

Drizzt nodded. What choice did he have, after all?

CHAPTER 12

Weirdly Drunk

Regis struggled and writhed and almost broke free, pulling himself nearly out of the fountain. But the water weird caught him and shoved him down again, harder this time, and he cracked his head on the bottom of the basin. He flailed and tried to splash, but the world was going darker, darker, until his consciousness left him.

He woke up sometime later, still pressed to the floor of the watery basin.

Surprised to be alive, the halfling tried to make sense of it, and it took him many moments of near panic before he recalled once more his genasi heritage. He would have drowned long ago were it not for that fortunate bloodline.

He wasn't sure just how long he'd been down—or how much time he might have left, planetouched genasi or no.

He didn't thrash now—the weird had nearly split his skull the last time he had fought against it. Instead, he quietly eased his hand to his hip and slid forth his three-bladed dirk, the outer two shaped like curving serpents.

Then he moved quickly, twisting and stabbing at the thing—once, twice, thrice!

The water splashed. The monster pressed him down and slapped at the halfling's stabbing arm with its tendrils. Out of the corner of his eye, Regis could see the dagger scoring its hits, but could see, too, that those hits were doing little, if anything, to the malleable weird. A few droplets splashed aside, though whether those were just water or pieces of the monster he could not know.

What he *did* know was that he couldn't win this fight. Soon the tendril caught his arm. Worse, the weird now pressed down on his head with tremendous force, crushing him against the basin bottom. He flailed once more, screaming useless bubbles. When his dirk was slapped from his hand, he tried to punch, claw—anything. His other hand went to his belt pouch, grasping around blindly, and when his fingers finally grabbed something, he smashed it into the water.

Three silver coins floated down beside his bulging eyes.

Then came a potion flask, overturned and half floating, its cork bumping against his face.

He tried to blow it aside, but alas, he was finally out of breath.

He was drowning.

He tried to scream, tried to turn, tried to rise. He punched, grasped, slapped, clawed, and he did manage to catch the bottom of the bobbing flask.

As his vision started to blur, strange thoughts flitted through his mind. One crazy idea hit him with desperate strength:

Perhaps the flask was unused and full of air!

Had his head been on straight, he would have known it to be wishful thinking. But he bit at the cork anyway, twisted and gnashed, and when it pulled free, he tried to gulp at the stem.

But no, it was not empty, and instead of sweet air filling his lungs, a dark liquid poured forth, coloring the water, and now he couldn't even see!

Darkness closed in once more, not unconsciousness this time but the deeper sleep of death.

At least he had relayed the important information to Aiberdelle. He had not let his friends down. Not in this lifetime, as so often in the previous.

He tried to focus on that, certain he was doomed, but then, so suddenly, the basin shuddered and the water heaved as if a tsunami had struck. Before he could register what was happening, Regis was flying through the air and back into the room. He landed hard on the floor, sitting on his butt, gulping air for all his life and trying to back away from that watery monster, watching the basin closely with every movement.

The weird rose up menacingly, like a liquid club, higher and higher. Then it swirled left, then around to the right, swaying in a mesmerizing dance, very much like a serpent.

"Oh no," Regis cursed, expecting it to lash out at him, hoping he was far enough away and knowing he was almost certainly not.

But the weird dove back under the basin edge, water splashing all about. Then it rose up again suddenly, but just a bit, before flattening. And again, and a third time, almost as if bubbles within were compelling it.

Regis shook his head, confused. Was this some sort of spellcasting? It didn't seem so, but looked more like some internal distress . . . hiccups?

He looked to the potion flask, still in his hand: gut chaser.

The halfling's eyes popped open wide and he stared incredulously at the bubbling, hiccupping basin!

He crawled aside, putting more distance between himself and the monster, but circling to retrieve his valuable dirk. He found it sticking into the floor, the fine magical blade cutting easily and deeply into a seam in the wood. He struggled to tug it free, finally taking a chunk of the wooden flooring with it, and he turned quickly to be out of this cursed room.

The glint of gold stopped him short, though, and the halfling's eyes widened indeed when he looked at that chip in the floor, when he realized that the subflooring of this particular room was golden!

Regis dug at the wood with his dagger, tearing strips and throwing them aside. No hungry dog ever went for a bone more determinedly.

He lifted gold coins into his hand, and gold bars, and platinum. And gems and jewels. All sorts of expensive bits, now suddenly just lying here for him to take. He began to stuff his pouch, giggling, for he knew that he could probably empty this entire room into that magical extradimensional space, and his mood was suddenly improved as thoughts of near death vanished with the shining treasure before him.

He fell to work, practically humming, until he heard behind him, "Well now, a little packrat, is he?"

"YOU WOULD BE WISE TO SUMMON MATRON SHAKTI HUNZ-rin to your home," Eskavidne told Matron Zhindia Melarn back in Menzoberranzan.

Matron Zhindia looked curiously at the two yochlols. Shakti had been there only two days before, and was often a visitor to House Melarn, particularly now, when Zhindia was helping her with her newest and most valuable trade pieces: fine jewelry that was much more than it seemed.

"What do you know?" Zhindia asked suspiciously.

"It is quite likely that Matron Shakti can supply you with unexpected support in your hunt for this reborn Do'Urden creature," Eskavidne explained. "She has installed on the surface powerful allies."

Matron Zhindia shook her head and harrumphed. This scenario had already played out once on the surface, after all, and not at all to her advantage.

"You will see," Eskavidne promised. She glanced at her yochlol counterpart and nodded, and the two disappeared in a flash, leaping through the planes to the antechamber of Lady Lolth's throne room.

"It will be an enjoyable spectacle," Eskavidne promised upon their return.

Yiccardaria, who had been less convinced of their course, though she dearly wanted to pay back Yvonnel and the others for their treachery, added, "Hopefully it will prove at least informative, sister, for that alone will properly amuse the Spider Queen."

Eskavidne let out a giggle, which turned into a gurgle, which turned into popping bubbles of sludge as she reverted to her natural form.

TWO MEN STOOD BY THE DOOR, ONE HOLDING A MACE, THE other a sword. They looked like Margasters, that same pale skin and pitch-black hair, and both were large and strong, obviously made of that Uthgardt stock.

Regis made a quick assessment of the room, silently calculating steps in various directions.

The Margasters approached . . .

. . . and up hopped the halfling, tossing his magical torch into the weird fountain, where it was immediately swallowed by the strange monster, greatly diminishing the light in the room. Regis ran left, but just a stride, then cut back to the right, then left again as he charged at the duo.

He feinted left once more, then fast back to the right, only to cut between the two, running past them. Any excitement was tempered by the fact that they were right behind.

He could barely see, but he had to chance it, and upon reaching the door he leaped high, catching the pendulum just above the blade and riding it out into the hallway. There, he raised his legs to set his feet against the wall and shoved off, throwing the pendulum back behind him. He let go, fell to the floor, and rolled aside immediately, coming to his feet and drawing his weapons.

A torch flared to life inside the room as the pendulum came swinging back at him, then back into the room. As soon as it disappeared, out leaped the first of the Margasters, coming fast at the halfling.

He held his dirk at the ready but didn't intend to use it up close if he could help it. With a quick motion, one of the side blades came off in his hand, and with a flick of his wrist, he launched it at the charging man. That snake-shaped weapon catcher then became a real serpent, and it rushed up the man's chest to loop about his neck, a living garrote, choking him. At the same time, a leering specter appeared over his shoulder, a manifestation of the wicked weapon, and it tugged mightily, easily yanking the powerful man to his back on the floor.

Before he even landed, the halfling had the second missile away at the remaining opponent. That Margaster flew into the air as well, his torch sailing from his hand and bouncing off the returning pendulum when the heavy blade hit the poor fellow across the legs as he tumbled backward.

Regis winced, seeing the gash in the poor man's legs, and grimaced even more as he watched the strangling specters do their work. He hadn't come in here to kill anyone.

Then again, he hadn't come here to die, either.

He started back into the room—jarred by the impact, the pendulum wasn't swinging anymore—but stopped short. He glanced farther along the tunnel and decided no on that route as well. The problem was, he had to get out of there, but didn't want to face the prospect of the freezing canal again while being pursued. Other than that, however, he didn't have the slightest idea where to go.

He started past the first man, who was flailing helplessly, turning blue. Regis stopped and waited, watching closely.

The man's struggling decreased with each passing second. He issued a little gurgling sound, but Regis waited a bit longer. He had to make sure the man was down for a while, at least. Beyond the pendulum, the other Margaster lay very still, perhaps already dead.

"Damn, damn, damn," the halfling cursed, moving his rapier closer, almost stabbing the specter, but waiting. He had to wait.

Finally the man subsided, falling limp, and Regis poked the specter with his rapier, destroying it. He started to bend for the man, unsure if the fellow was dead or alive, but he shook his head in frustration, for he had not the time. He rushed past the pendulum, scooped up the Margaster's dropped torch, and poked the second specter, freeing the second man. He heard a cough behind him, which made him feel somewhat better as he raced back down the hallway.

He neared the entry cavern, hoping the poisoned chamberman

was still resting comfortably. He grinned as he neared, hearing snores, and so he went in feeling confident. That feeling quickly dissipated, though, because what awaited was the frozen canal. It probably wouldn't kill him, but it certainly wasn't warm.

He found the man where he had left him, snoring loudly. Wasting no time, Regis began to strip, stuffing his cloak, his boots, and his shirt into his magical pouch.

He had just pulled the hand crossbow from around his neck when he heard sounds from down the hallway, and sighed, thinking one of the guards had recovered from the choking and was stubbornly pursuing. "Alas and ah well," he whispered, setting a bolt and cocking the hand crossbow.

The door opened and yet it was not one of the guards who walked in, but a woman, tall and raven-haired and quite pretty.

Inkeri Margaster, the one who had been standing beside Lord Neverember when the dwarves had come with the payment, walked in calmly.

"What mischief is this, little one?" she said.

Regis sighed, not wanting to shoot a lady.

But he did anyway.

The quarrel flew across the room to catch her right in the chest. She gave hardly a yip, then looked down at it curiously, then back up at Regis.

"Well now," she said, pulling out the bolt and tossing it aside.

Regis stared at her from across the way, looking for some sign that the poison was taking effect. But no. She rubbed her hands together and moved closer. As she did, a gemstone pendant hanging about her neck flickered with an inner light, and Inkeri began to expand.

At first Regis thought it a simple wizard's spell, but then her face reshaped suddenly, growing a snout, and two more arms sprouted up above the normal ones—and these ended not in hands, but in huge pincers. And even then his eyes were drawn away, to the tail now growing behind her.

He didn't think she looked so pretty anymore.

And, more certainly, she was nothing Regis wanted to battle. He

hadn't even fully finished his turn when he dove for the water, his bad
angle causing him to scrape painfully on the edge of the stone floor as
he went in. He ignored the pain, and didn't dare turn back to try to
swim against the current to the spot where he had first entered. No, he
just swam for all his life, deeper under the castle.

He heard the commotion behind him when the monster jumped
in, and so he swam faster, frantically. In complete darkness, fully sub-
merged, he paddled and kicked wildly. He tried to come up for air but
could not, instead banging his head hard on the ceiling of the tight
tunnel.

Again he resisted the urge to look back—he couldn't see anything
anyway—and just swam blindly as fast as he could, hoping against
hope that he'd find a way out . . . and that the monster chasing him
would not catch him.

On and on he went, and his lungs began to ache. He stopped and
called to his pouch, bringing a small ceramic ball to his hand. He
knew he'd be marking himself clearly, but he could only hope the fiend
wasn't nearby.

He broke the ball, freeing the stone inside, one coated with dayglow oil. He saw the floor, he saw the walls, he saw the ceiling. Up
he went carefully, clearing the water just enough to suck in another
breath. He dropped the light source then, and swam on for some distance, this time looking back to the lighted area.

Just as he was growing somewhat confident, a large form crossed
into the light. Regis couldn't make it out fully, but he really didn't need
to. There was only one thing it could be.

On he swam, back into complete darkness, sometimes crashing
into a wall, once scraping painfully on a shelf in the floor, more than
once banging his head as he went up to try to draw in a breath. And
while he was at least getting air into his lungs, his muscles were starting to ache from the exertion and cold.

Then he crashed into something—a pole, he thought. He tried to
go around it, but no, it was not a pole. It was a grate.

He fished another dayglow ball from his pouch and lit the area, to
find himself trapped at a portcullis. He looked all about, but no, there

were no levers to be found. He grabbed at the bars and tried to lift, to no avail.

Panic began to set in—he was trapped.

After a moment of futile tugging and searching and even trying to squeeze through the bars, the halfling turned back. Dare he hope the fiend had broken off pursuit and he might slip by?

The thought lasted only a moment, because a dark form appeared at the edge of his light. He went for his rapier but knew that he had no chance fighting such a monster. Still, he reached for his dirk, too, single-bladed now. He paused, his mind whirling, seeking some answer. None came, other than the surety that he was about to die.

He had his hand by his magical pouch, though he didn't know why. Perhaps to grab more light sources to try to drive the monster away? To grab a gut chaser or two to numb himself from the pain and the horror of certain death?

He saw the monster clearly now, eyes drawn to its pincers, either of which could easily snip him in half; they were already eagerly snapping in the water. He saw the doglike face, leering, seeming like it was smiling.

Regis wanted to cry. He didn't want to die like this, half-naked in the cold water, in a place where his friends, where his beloved Donnola, would likely never find him. He resolved to fight ferociously, and nearly laughed at himself for the absurd thought. Even if he could defeat this thing, surely he would do so only to drown before he could find air.

And only then, in that moment of complete resignation and hopelessness, did the halfling remember. And in doing so, he cursed his own foolishness.

For Regis had not come down here expecting to swim back out. He would find his way to the back stair, or . . .

He pulled a small vial from his pouch, his most expensive and impressive potion.

A pincer came out at him as he quaffed it, and he felt the sharp edges cutting against his sides. His mouth opened as he started to scream.

But then his mouth was gone, and then his body was gone, insubstantial, a gaseous form, and the pincer closed harmlessly *through* where he should have been.

Regis, no more substantial than a cloud, slipped through the portcullis and drifted along, no longer feeling the cold, no longer feeling any compulsion to draw breath. He did note the fiend tearing at the portcullis, bending the bars, and so he willed himself to go as fast as he could, which really wasn't very fast.

He couldn't swim, after all, having nothing with which to push against the water. He was moving, though, and faster than the current, at least. Still, it seemed like forever before he at last crossed out from under the castle, from under the main boulevard of Neverwinter, from under another cluster of houses, and from under Neverwinter's city wall.

He came up out of the water, scrambling to the muddy land, and barely had he emerged when his potion wore off and he became a sputtering, freezing, half-naked halfling, sitting beside an icy canal in a snow-filled forest. He went for his pouch immediately and brought forth his cloak, scrambling all the while, trying to put some distance between himself and the water.

He ran, stumbling repeatedly but stubbornly pulling himself back up every time, ever onward. Ever *away*.

He didn't know how far he had gone when he heard a shriek from far behind. An otherworldly, hideous, bone-chilling shriek. And Regis knew that he had not evaded the pursuit.

So he somehow got his boots out, finally, and put them on, and he ran even harder, because what else could he do?

The night was not dark, and with the reflections off the snow, clinging stubbornly to the shadier areas in the forest, the halfling could make out his way fairly easily. He also saw the shadows, though, moving shadows, flitting from tree to tree in the distance to his right. Then more to the left.

Regis put his head down and ran faster, ran for all his life—which he was pretty sure was no exaggeration—fearing that he was being flanked on both sides by some hellish demons. Behind him, he heard a shriek and a guttural roar—not nearly far enough away for his liking. Somehow he knew these monsters wouldn't tire, and he would never make it out the other side of Neverwinter Wood. He needed another plan.

He needed a place to hide.

Before he had even truly considered it, he skidded to a stop and crouched, letting the shadows pass him by, then ran behind them to the east, toward, he believed, Aiberdelle's stable. Only a short while later, he broke out of the underbrush and onto the muddy road. Right—back toward Neverwinter—would take him to the stable, and so he started to turn that way.

But no, he realized. How could he bring such a horde of fiends upon the poor elven woman?

He sprinted to the left, north. He shook his head with almost every step, however, knowing that he'd never get ahead of the pursuit.

His lungs burned; his legs ached. He was cold, and the scrape from diving into the waterway was bothering him more than he wanted to admit. Down one straightaway, he happened to glance back, in time to see a hulking four-armed fiend crash out onto the road. Along the sides, hidden in the brush and tangle, he heard hissing now, and the occasional grunt, and cracking branches and twigs. He focused forward, even though there was no point.

It would be over soon.

He felt as if he were rushing toward his end, a thought amplified when he heard footsteps ahead on the road. He was out of places to run. He had to go left or right, and quickly, so he tried to discern which side likely had the fewest monsters.

Left, he decided, and he turned, only for the footsteps on the road to become louder. . . .

No . . .

He skidded to a stop. It wasn't footsteps he'd been hearing, but hoofbeats.

A rider!

Away he ran again, toward the sound, thinking it his only chance. He slipped on some ice and crashed down hard, but came up immediately, scrambling, trying to get his feet under him, and he let out a yell when just around the bend before him came a large dark form. He dove back to the ground and covered up, cowering.

He felt the splash of mud over him, and heard the screech of scraping iron shoes over cobblestones.

"Spider!"

The surprised halfling looked up to see Aiberdelle staring down at him.

He leaped to his feet and leaped again at her, to her reaching hand, and as soon as he caught it, he cried out, "Ride! Ride! Ride! For all our lives, ride!"

The horse whinnied and reared and Regis nearly fell from her grasp, desperately trying to set himself as the skilled elf horsewoman turned her mount about, then kicked the steed away furiously, never once asking a question. It wasn't until Regis got into his seat behind her and glanced back that he understood her quick actions—it was less to do with his urgent words and more to do with the four-armed, dog-faced demon running behind them, almost keeping stride. From the bushes on the side, the shadowed monsters found form and leaped as well—all manner of misshapen fiend, some no more than zombielike humans, others black-skinned and froglike but running upright, with clawed hands and rows of formidable teeth.

Through the grotesque menagerie went the galloping horse, demons leaping and clawing the air, biting hard with click-clicking sounds all about the fleeing duo. Regis tried to block his ears and scream it all away. But it mattered little.

The cacophony of hellish hunger did fade, though, as the strong horse outran them, its nostrils flaring, puffing steam into the night with every long stride. It was going hard and needed to rest, but Aiberdelle didn't dare let up. Not that she needed to encourage their mount all that much.

The road bent to the right for a long way, then straightened back to the north, but just as Aiberdelle eased the mount to the left, a creature leaped out of the brush to block the path, and the elf pulled up hard on the reins, skidding the horse to a stop.

Apparently the four-armed demon, Inkeri Margaster or another fiend just like her, had taken a shortcut straight through the brush, clearing it away with great pincers, hardly slowing at all to cross out ahead of them on the circuitous road.

Just as apparently, the elf and halfling were in a great deal of trouble.

"We fight it," Aiberdelle said, for what else was there to do?

Regis, gasping and huffing too much to verbally respond, nodded and grabbed for his rapier, thinking to slide off the horse. "I'll take it aside," he said when he at last found his breath, his boots splashing down in the mud. "Get to Bleeding Vines and tell them!"

"No," she started to argue, but she stopped short and so did Regis in his demand, for a flash of fire erupted in the road right in front of the fiend.

More chaos on an already chaotic night.

With the fire another form dropped down from on high, falling right behind the monster, swords in hand and slashing at the fiend's back before it could even register what was happening.

"Ride, you fools!" the newcomer called, diving aside as the fiend spun about, batting with all four arms.

Regis thought he recognized the voice and the lithe form, not to mention the graceful movements as the newcomer rolled aside, came back to his feet, and drove in at the fiend, his blades spinning in a deadly dance.

Even as the halfling tried to speak out his name, though, he felt a hand grab his cloak at the scruff of his neck, and he was jerked from his feet so forcefully that he nearly lost a boot. Right by the battle went Aiberdelle's mount, and Regis got a look at their rescuer, and realized it to be a drow he certainly knew.

CHAPTER 13

Tendrils of Lolthian Chaos

The halfling Wigglefingers found the man in an alley beside a tavern, one of five predetermined meeting spots for this most particular spy.

"My payment, wizard," the man said upon his approach. He was not tall for a human, but towered over the halfling spellcaster.

Wigglefingers sighed and tried to hide his disgust. "Do you not even care about the consequences of this most urgent information?"

The man, Artemis Entreri, seemed genuinely amused by that.

"I thought you cared for Jarlaxle, for Drizzt Do'Urden, even!" the exasperated halfling added. How he wanted to create some great magical cataclysm and wash this fool away.

The man shrugged and gave a little nod.

"Yet you ask for payment straightaway!"

"Of course," said Entreri. "Dahlia and I have decided that we should find a better housing arrangement. For that, I need the payment."

"And if I didn't have it?"

"You wouldn't be here."

"No, no, no, put that aside," said Wigglefingers. "Suppose I found you here this day, desperate for the news but unprepared to pay you. Would you tell me the information, that I could relay it to Jarlaxle and Lady Donnola? Or would you sit quiet and let others suffer?"

"Perhaps someday you will find out."

"I grow tired of your games."

"Then take a nap. In the meantime, remember this isn't a game—I do a job, I get paid."

The halfling could only sigh and even chuckle a bit. He didn't believe that this one was as irascible as he pretended, and he had fully soured on the man's dangerous reputation. There were plenty of capable halfling scouts working Waterdeep's streets, and yet Lady Donnola had specifically instructed the wizard to visit this human.

Which bothered him even more, because Entreri was Jarlaxle's man and not Donnola's. That knowledge didn't help Wigglefingers's mood very much, either. Anything that he garnered from this rogue would almost certainly be given to Jarlaxle long before Donnola heard it—and cleared by Jarlaxle, the halfling wizard assumed. He couldn't deny Entreri's reputation as a spy, as Jarlaxle considered the man one of his very top lieutenants, and surely the human knew his way with sword and dagger. But this was the northern Sword Coast of Faerun, a region called the Savage Frontier, and swordsmen were a crowd a copper.

The notion that this one above all the others could get the job done deeply insulted the fiercely proud halfling, who had, after all, personally trained most of Donnola's younger scouts.

Yet here he stood, disgusted by how much he needed what Entreri had for him. Wigglefingers reminded himself that it was not his place to question. Not then. He produced a small pouch of gems and handed them over. Surprisingly, Entreri didn't even look inside. Only then did it dawn on Wigglefingers: *The man figures he doesn't have to because he assumes no one would dare short him on such a payment.*

Such hubris was almost enough to make the wizard laugh.

Or cry in frustration, especially when Entreri said nothing.

"The Stoneshaft Clan bought Thornhold from Lord Neverember,"

Wigglefingers prompted. "And Lord Neverember had previously pur-chased the castle from House Margaster, we believe . . ."

"Just last year," Entreri confirmed. "For forty thousand pieces of gold."

"Forty thousand? That is a paltry sum—it makes no sense!"

Entreri shrugged.

"And only last year?"

"Last summer," Entreri answered.

"But why?" the wizard muttered, more to himself than to Entreri, cupping his chin in his hand and staring at the floor. He looked back up at Entreri a moment later. "We need you to look more deeply. How long did the Margasters own Thornhold before the transaction with Lord Neverember? And why would they sell to him at so low a price? Did they not know of the dwarves' interest?"

"Should I deliver the lord of House Margaster to Lady Donnola in chains so that she can spend a decade interrogating him?" came the predictably sarcastic response.

"Just those three simple questions," Wigglefingers replied. "Oh, and a fourth: Are the Margasters not angered at Lord Neverember's apparent windfall? Forty thousand gold, you say? We believe that Neverember garnered twenty-five times that value."

Entreri didn't even blink. "And you ask me to care about these games as if the lives of my friends depend upon them?" he said after a long pause. "For Neverember and all the others, this is more about stature than value. A million gold? What will Neverember do with that sum that he could not already do? Bury it under a castle while people around him starve or freeze in the dark of winter? And you ask me to care?"

"But you care about your payment," the halfling pointed out.

"I like to eat, and prefer to respectably buy my food instead of hurt-ing people to get it."

That silenced the halfling.

"Four questions," Entreri agreed. "But it may take some time. A lot of good men could die giving this information."

Wigglefingers nodded, but then scrunched up his face as he con-sidered the odd phrasing. "You mean 'getting.'"

And then Wigglefingers saw it, that particularly cold look, and so the assassin's eyes told the wizard that he had not misspoken. In that terrible moment, Wigglefingers feared that he might someday be one of the necessary victims to whom Artemis Entreri had just referred.

The halfling left the meeting almost immediately, taking with him valuable information about the Margasters and Lord Neverember for Donnola, and perhaps even more information for himself about the true danger of this strange human.

Indeed, the assassin's stare would linger with the wizard for a long time after he discharged his newly bought intelligence.

A SINGLE CANDLE BURNED ON THE TABLE BETWEEN DON-nola Topolino, Wigglefingers, and Jarlaxle, a fittingly quiet light for a discussion that had to be whispered.

"Regis thinks the price near to a million pieces of gold," Donnola confirmed.

"A treasure King Bruenor would be hard-pressed to muster," said a curious Jarlaxle. "Yet this Stoneshaft clan, hardly known . . ."

"I told you it was intriguing," Donnola replied with a soft laugh.

"You said a *bit* intriguing, if I recall. It is more than that, it would seem."

"More still," said Donnola. She looked to Wigglefingers.

"Your agent in Waterdeep told me that Lord Neverember pur-chased the stronghold only a short while before from House Margaster for a fraction of the price to the dwarves. But of course, I expect you already know this."

If Jarlaxle took umbrage at Wigglefingers's accusation, he didn't show it. Instead, he just sat back in his chair, tap-tapping his long slender fingers together, digesting it all, assembling the pieces of the puzzle.

The wizard continued. "Many of Margaster's nobles were there in Neverwinter, in Neverember's own court, when the dwarves arrived with their payment, and we've reason to believe that another of the Margasters may well have ridden north to meet the dwarven caravan on their way to Neverwinter."

"Their roundabout way," Jarlaxle said, and the other two perked up, for Jarlaxle typically accepted more information than he ever offered.

"The dwarves sailed around Neverwinter to the north, to Port Llast, as you suspected," the drow mercenary confirmed. "There they disembarked and the ships sailed away in the night, and the dwarves marched south, straight from the docks, with no announcement and little fanfare."

"It could not have been easy to arrange that," Wigglefingers reasoned.

"Even less than you would believe," said Jarlaxle. "The folk of Port Llast are often besieged. To bring a heavily armed dwarven force of that magnitude through the city in the dark of night surely meant more than a few bags of gold sliding into the right pockets."

"We know they had the gold," Donnola said dryly.

"It would take more than just gold, though, wouldn't it?" asked the halfling wizard.

Jarlaxle offered a slight nod but no words as he sat back in contemplation, tapping his fingertips. Why weren't the Margasters upset about Neverember's apparently huge windfall on a property they had only recently sold to him? They were there, in the court. Regis had seen them. And there in great numbers in the inn, according to Donnola. This was no happy face they were painting on for optics, Jarlaxle believed.

They were truly glad for the sale.

The term "money washing" ran through his mind, just as it surely did through the minds of his rather worldly associates at this table. Certainly Donnola and the wizard had seen their share of this back in Aglarond—it was a favored game to secretly tip the scales of power until unwitting rivals could do nothing to preserve the current order.

Lord Neverember had bought low from the Margasters, who probably didn't even actually hold the deed to the place. House Margaster then funneled a vast treasure to the little known, little cared about Clan Stoneshaft, who delivered it to Lord Neverember under the guise of repatriating themselves to a fortress they once considered their home, to great fanfare and celebration. As sure as an annoying elf

202 R. A. SALVATORE

launching into inane song, everyone knew that dwarves would always go to great lengths to regain lost homelands.

And, of course, Clan Stoneshaft had likely been in possession of, probably even living under, this place called Thornhold the whole time. The entire purpose of the transaction, then, was simply to wash ill-gotten gold and get it out of Waterdeep.

"And now the newest twist," Donnola said after all three had mulled in silence for a long while. "House Margaster is, perhaps, much more than it appears. Much more sinister."

The door cracked open and a halfling attendant poked his head in. "Milady," he said, "your husband."

The attendant pulled the door wide and a shaky Regis entered.

"You should be in bed," Donnola said, standing and starting for him, but Regis held her back with an outstretched arm.

"We'll all rest when this is done," he said, taking a seat at the table. He gave a great exhale as he sat, clearly exhausted and over-whelmed. "Trust me that I am glad I am alive to sit here and join this meeting. All because of good fortune and good friends," he added, looking to Jarlaxle.

"You dismiss your own cleverness in getting out of those tunnels?" Donnola asked.

"I already said—good fortune," said Regis. "I am luckily more at home in the water—nay, under the water—than a halfling ought to be."

"Whatever the reason," said Jarlaxle, lifting a goblet of wine, "we are glad of the outcome."

"And doubting my story, I expect," said Regis. "As am I!"

"Aiberdelle's was identical, though," said Wigglefingers.

Regis gave the wizard an appreciative nod, and was glad that the information had come from him, whom Regis thought the least supportive of the three.

"Now we must discern what lives under Lord Neverember's castle, and in Neverwinter Wood, it would seem," Donnola said.

"That forest is no stranger to creatures of the lower planes," Jarlaxle told them.

"The Ashmadai?" Donnola asked. "I thought they were gone."

"Such cults are rarely ever gone," the drow replied. "Dark dandelions, one and all, and my sources whisper that Asmodeus has gained a fair number of followers in Waterdeep."

"Asmodeus is an archdevil," Regis interrupted. "These were demons, not devils."

"How can you know?" Jarlaxle asked.

"We just stepped this dance in the Bloodstone Lands," Regis reminded. "Trust me—I watched the lady Inkeri transform before my eyes into a glabrezu, a demon I have known before."

"I do not doubt you, my friend," Jarlaxle said as the same attendant to Donnola poked his head into the room again, "but a devil could do the same, and many resemble—"

"No devil," said another drow, pushing into the room, walking with a limp, his left arm held tight to his side. "Glabrezu."

Jarlaxle leaped from his seat and rushed to help his wounded soldier. Donnola called to the attendant to fetch a proper priest.

"I will survive," Braelin Janquay assured them, nevertheless taking Jarlaxle's offered seat.

"Glabrezu?" Jarlaxle asked him.

Braelin nodded. "And chasmes, and others. Demons all. A remarkable collection, thick about Neverwinter Wood, but coming from the city itself in pursuit of Regis, I would guess." He turned and winked at Regis. "This is twice now that you owe me your life, halfling. Perhaps Jarlaxle would be wise in extracting my pay from your pocket."

"Twice?"

"The woman with the bow on the lake bank in Icewind Dale," Braelin explained. "Did you think your own shot so lucky?"

Regis's lips moved too fast for any actual words to spill out for a short while, before finally managing to blurt, "That was you?"

Braelin managed a little laugh, followed by a blood-filled cough.

"Is there anything in the north that Jarlaxle does not watch?" Regis asked, his voice heavy with sarcasm.

"Not if I can help it," Jarlaxle replied, rubbing Braelin's back and trying to ease the wounded soldier's obvious discomfort. Fortunately, a pair of clerics, halfling and dwarf, bumbled into the room then, holy symbols in hand.

Jarlaxle stepped back as they went to work on Braelin. Confident that the drow's wounds were not mortal, he let his mind go to the matters at hand. He didn't doubt the veracity of the reports from Regis and Braelin; the rise of supporters for Asmodeus in Waterdeep, after all, had come about because so many more demons had been showing up all across Faerun of late. Some foolish humans, desperate and afraid, had come to believe that allying with the lawful devils was somehow better than risking the dangers of the unpredictable demons.

There was some truth to that, Jarlaxle had to admit, but only in certain circumstances. Devils were more predictable than demons, which generally were little more than vile killing machines with less subtlety than a trebuchet throwing baskets of fire into a village. The catch was that getting a devil out of your midst, especially one to which you owed a favor, was never an easy or inexpensive task.

But Waterdeep was a worry for another day. The more immediate challenge involved the lord protector of Neverwinter and his strange partners in crime.

"Demons," he whispered under his breath to focus his thinking, and he suspected then that the source of these unwelcome visitors along the Sword Coast might well be the same as the ones who brought Malcanthet, the Queen of the Succubi, to the Bloodstone Lands not so long ago.

He needed some information, and fast—and he had an idea of who might be best able to get it for him.

"SO GOOD TO BE BACK IN LANDS I'VE NE'ER SEEN," AMBER Gristle O'Maul remarked, skipping down the road, her huge two-handed mace, Skullcrusher, resting on her shoulder.

"If ye ain't been in 'em ne'er, then how're ye back in 'em, eh?" teased her companion—her lover, her best friend—Athrogate. The thick-limbed fellow had found some fresh cow pies that morning to better braid and tip his huge black beard, and Amber found the aroma intoxicating.

"I know someplace ye're not soon gettin' back into, me clever hubby."

Athrogate gave a great harrumph at that, though he was hardly unaccustomed to that line from Amber, and knew that his amorous companion never meant it—or couldn't hold to it if she did.

"Yer legs gettin' tired yet?" Athrogate asked. "I can bring out me pig." He grabbed at his belt pouch, in which sat the figurine he used to summon a magical hell boar.

"I can always bring out the pig in ye," Amber remarked, unable to resist. "But no, me love, let's walk and skip and dance in the day. Oh, but a beautiful one she is!"

Amber looked all about at the sky, bright blue and dotted with puffy white clouds, but Athrogate just stared admiringly at her as he replied, "Ah, but suren she is."

They walked for the rest of the morning, talking lightly, enjoying the day, anticipating that they'd be back in Bleeding Vines soon enough, though they had left the place far behind. The day was warm for the season, but winter held and so the caravans had not yet begun their spring travels, giving the dwarven pair the road to themselves. Better still, they were moving back near the coastline now, as they had nearly circumvented the Mere of Dead Men, and so the smell of bog was being quickly replaced by the refreshing aroma of salt and brine.

When looking for a place to break for some lunch, they happened upon a road turning west off the Trade Way, and following it to the next rise, they soon came in sight of the ocean . . . and more importantly, a plain gray fortress with a squat central keep, flanked by two towers.

Amber took out the rough drawing Jarlaxle had made for her and nodded to Athrogate. "Thornhold," she said.

"A million pieces o' gold ain't buying what it used to," Athrogate lamented, for indeed, the fort was not overly impressive, nor strategically located. "Well, good enough for them Stoneshafts, then. Let's go see what we can see. I'm thinking they got the money for a proper feast!"

They clambered down over the broken rocks to what seemed to be an entry road, though one long reduced to tangled vines and rubble. Before them loomed the fortress's main gate, a pair of gigantic iron-banded wooden doors that looked as if they could once have held back a horde of giants. Once, but not now, for they hung a'kilter, one missing its top hinges, which left it angled, creating an opening wide enough for a dwarf to walk through without bending, as was proven even as Athrogate noted it when a yellow-haired dwarf walked out and stepped to the side. He crossed his burly arms over his chest, shield presented in the top one, mace held high in the other.

Up above, more dwarves peered over the wall.

"Clan Stoneshaft, I'm guessin'," Athrogate told his love.

"Aye, and an ugly-lookin' bunch, what," Ambergris replied.

A second dwarf came out, then a third and fourth, forming a line and stepping forward toward the oncoming pair as more filtered out behind them.

"Well met!" Athrogate called to them, waving and scrambling over the last rock before the entry path, which leveled out somewhat. He reached back to help Amber over the stone, but she just hopped it and rolled, planting her huge two-handed mace as she went to prop her right to her feet.

"Aye, well met, and we're lookin' for some food," she called, moving right past Athrogate. "And glad to see dwarfs here in this unknown place, aye!"

"Well, who'd ye expect then?" asked one from behind the line of four dwarves, stepping up between them. He was a strong one, certainly, with yellow hair tightened into cornrows and a great beard that rivaled Athrogate's own. From the description Jarlaxle had offered, Athrogate figured this one to be Bronkyn, the commander of the force that had gone to Lord Neverember's castle.

"Weren't knowin'," Athrogate said before Amber could respond. "Been walking a long way and not knowin' what to expect. Too far south for that new Delzoun home, aye, and not north enough yet for Icewind Dale."

"New Delzoun home?" the yellow-haired dwarf asked, coming forward along with a dozen of his compatriots, all moving out and around to fully flank the incoming couple. "Ye're meaning Gauntlgrym, then? Or this home ye're now seeing?"

"Gauntlgrym, aye," Athrogate answered. "Not knowin' this one ye're speaking o', but eh, are ye Delzoun dwarf now or ain't ye?"

"And if not?"

"Thought all dwarfs in the north were o' that blood, is all," said Athrogate.

"Might we are, might we ain't."

Athrogate shrugged as if it didn't matter, though the line of answers surely seemed inappropriate and surprising to him. The Delzoun heritage had represented the great Northkingdom of the dwarves for centuries, and almost all dwarves in the north of Faerun now identified with the name, or at least showed some measure of reverence for it.

"Might ye are, might ye ain't, then," said Amber. "But suren that we're glad to see ye, whate'er, for I've a mighty thirst and a grumblin' tummy, and a dwarf's a dwarf if he's not a gray one, eh?"

"Eh," answered the Stoneshaft leader, though he didn't sound convinced.

"So what're we eatin' then?" Amber pressed.

"Nothing's on the spit." The flatness of his tone spoke of a threat.

"So put something on," Athrogate said. "Ye're not turnin' kin aside, are ye?"

"What kin?" another Stoneshaft said.

"Kin o' Bruenor, not for doubtin'," added a third, and she spat on the ground.

"Ye got a problem with King Bruenor, do ye?" Amber asked. "And what might that be, then? He's got Gauntlgrym back from the ruins and running strong."

"Aye, if there's a problem with that, then might that ye'll be telling us, eh?" Athrogate added. "We be lookin' for him and the place, and hopin' it's worth the journey. What ain't we knowin'?"

"Bruenor got no friends here," the one Athrogate believed to be Bronkyn flatly stated. "Friends o' Bruenor got no friends here."

"Who ye be, then?" asked Amber. "And what's this place? A better stop for weary dwarfs?"

"Ain't that," one of the Stoneshafts muttered.

Both Amber and Athrogate looked in the direction of the mutterer, then back at the leader, who merely shrugged, not disagreeing with the assessment.

"Ye're telling us to be leavin', then," Athrogate said.

"Said no such thing," answered the leader.

"He'll be running right to Bruenor," said another.

"Who'd be back with an army, as all must kneel or die," said yet another.

"Aye, but he's the king o' all, don't ye know?" said another. And while they were talking, they fanned out even more, nearly closing the circle around the couple.

"Ye're not showin' much kinship, mate," Amber told the leader. "Ye didn't even ask our names or offer yer own."

"Her name's Amber, and his's Athrogate," a dwarf on the wall called. "Bruenor's spies."

"Worse," said a dwarf to the side of the couple, pulling a battleaxe from his back and resting it on one shoulder. "These two're spies for the durned drow elfs."

Athrogate tried hard to keep his jaw from dropping open. How could they know any of that? How could they know more about Jarlaxle than Jarlaxle knew of them? It never worked that way!

But now he and Amber had no choice, and while she brought Skullcrusher out before her, Athrogate pulled his flails from over his shoulders, setting the balls to spinning immediately.

"We didn't come looking for trouble," he told the leader.

"Funny what ye find."

"Just wonderin' o' the new unannounced neighbors," Amber added. "Any dwarf'd understand that."

The ring began to close around them, Stoneshaft weapons at the ready.

"Ye're making a mistake, boys," Athrogate warned.

Even as he finished, a dwarf wielding a shield and mace leaped at him, bulling in—or trying to, for Athrogate called to his flail Whacker, summoning a coating of special oil that exploded when he brought the ball swinging against that shield, splintering the buckler into a dozen flying shards and launching the dwarf back a dozen strides. He feared he had killed the poor fellow, but what else could he do?

The other Stoneshafts came in a fast couple of strides, but fell back in unison short of the swipe of Amber's murderous two-handed mace.

"Yerself and meself!" Athrogate challenged the leader. "Or be Bronkyn Stoneshaft a coward?"

The others laughed at that, but those laughs sounded strange somehow.

Bronkyn just smiled and nodded. "I'll be liking that."

But he didn't come on. He nodded left and right and the ten remaining Stoneshafts on the perimeter all threw their weapons to the ground. At first it seemed as if they were giving up, but then they leaped as one high into the air toward the couple. Not leaping, actually, but diving, as if into a pool of water.

And they hit the ground and sank into it, disappearing, like otters into a lake.

"The Nine Hells?" Athrogate stammered, and the ground all about him and Amber began to bubble and ooze with some black tar-like liquid. From that liquid, the Stoneshaft dwarves returned, but not as dwarves. Ten black tendrils rose up around Athrogate and Ambergris, their tips ending in claws, their sides lined with suckers, like the arms of an octopus.

Athrogate went into a wild spin, batting at the nearby tendrils. Ambergris, too, tried to fight them off, though less successfully with her single heavy weapon. She did bat one, sending it rolling out the other way, but a second whipped her from behind, cracking her along the back and sending her sprawling—or she would have been sprawling, except that the hook and top suckers caught her and brought her right back to her feet, then up into the air, swirling her all about before bringing her down again with tremendous force.

Athrogate heard her heavy grunt amid the slaps of his spinning flails as she kissed the stone. Furiously, he pressed toward her, whacking with abandon.

Up went Amber again, her face all bloody, but this time, she spun around and grabbed at the tendril with her arms and with her teeth—and to great effect, it seemed, from the way the arm began thrashing about.

Athrogate rolled under the crack of a snapping claw and came to his feet to see the leader laughing and pointing. He glanced at his love and knew he had to trust in her. Out he charged, smacking aside the grabbing arms. One caught him, wrapping around his waist, but the tough dwarf turned with it, rolling to loop the thing tighter, like a rabbit rolling into the python!

Except that this rabbit possessed the strength of a storm giant, and he clamped his arms about the tendril, rolled in even more, then tugged with all his strength.

A piercing shriek erupted from . . . somewhere, as the tendril began to tear from the ground. Other tendrils snapped at the dwarf, but he roared and ignored them and drove on, ripping out the grasping arm.

The tendril went limp, its coils falling off him, and as soon as it hit the ground, twitching in death throes, it reverted and became again a dwarf, albeit a broken and dying one, spitting black blood.

Athrogate's eyes widened in horror. What was this madness?

He spied the dwarf leader, staring back at him hatefully now. He was no longer laughing. Bronkyn motioned to a dwarf beside him, who tapped a pendant hanging around his neck. It flared with an inner black glow, and the dwarf flared, too, growing suddenly, sprouting extra arms, his hair becoming fur, his dwarven face becoming that of a dog demon.

"Mystery solved!" Athrogate roared, and he charged at the glabrezu, shouldering aside another writhing tentacle, whacking yet another. "Come on, Ambergris, me girl!"

Athrogate almost got to the waiting four-armed demon, but with surprising coordination, and apparently at a command from the watching Bronkyn, two tentacles reached out at him, coming in low, wrapping his ankles and dropping him hard to his face. The dwarf's first instinct was to grab at a stone, but his rage got the better of him and he turned at the tentacles instead, thinking to splatter them, for Whacker had another coating of oil of impact ready.

Before he could begin his swing, though, Athrogate rose up suddenly into the air, circling right over as the tentacles moved in unison, to bring him crashing down into the black goo and hard stones beneath.

He bounced once, felt his flails go flying, and then *he* was flying, hoisted straight back up . . . only this time, the tentacles let him go.

High into the air Athrogate soared, spinning willy-nilly. He called for his love, then saw her, suspended in the air, spread-armed and spread-legged, held at each wrist and ankle by a tugging tendril. And there beside her stood the glabrezu, looking back at Athrogate and smiling wickedly, so wickedly, its pincer clamped about poor, helpless Amber's waist.

Cutting . . .

So slowly . . .

He had to get to her . . .

That was his only thought, his last thought, as he slammed into the ground once again and knew no more.

ZAKNAFEIN WAS GLAD FOR THE WORK, GLAD TO BE BACK ON the road of adventure once more—especially an adventure that might offer him the chance to kill a drow priestess, which had always been a pleasure for him—and glad, most of all, to be away from a situation he could not comprehend or properly digest. He had listened to the tales of the human woman and his son, and he could not deny that within them he had found some comfort and hope. But he could not bring himself to accept a human as his daughter-in-law, and her child, a half-breed . . .

He shook the notion away and focused on his mission.

He was grateful to Jarlaxle for trusting him with this. He looked back at the two dark elves trailing him, Braelin Janquay and Jeyrelle

Fey, one of the few women in Bregan D'aerthe and a priestess of some goddess who was, remarkably, not Lolth. Zaknafein had asked the beautiful amber-eyed drow for some details regarding her deity, but she had just scowled at him and told him to take the point position as Jarlaxle had instructed.

That had only made Zaknafein more attracted to her, but that wasn't really all that surprising, as a drow woman with the courage to take her clerical skills to a goddess other than the Spider Queen was about as attractive as anything to Zaknafein.

He was at the point now, twenty strides ahead of his companions, walking the tunnels of the upper Underdark, and so he reminded himself that he should be concentrating on the winding passage before him and not the companions behind.

"Question: how does one find a drow?" he asked under his breath, and he smiled at the long-ago conversation he had exchanged with Jarlaxle in tunnels much deeper than these.

Zaknafein considered the answer; he had found those centuries before in Menzoberranzan, but he didn't have any halfling captives with him this time, and was glad of that. Jarlaxle had assured him that things would be taken care of.

"How, indeed?" he whispered, and on he went.

PART 3

Lessons
of the Past

Age breeds wisdom because age brings experience. Thus we learn, and if we are not frozen in our ways or wedded to a manner of looking at the world that defies experiential evidence, we learn.

The rhyme of history is, in the end, the greatest teacher.

The question, however, is whether the students are sufficient. Yes, Menzoberranzan would look very different to me now, with my wealth of experience accompanying me back to that dark place, and yes, an individual may learn, should learn, must learn, through his or her journey. But that doesn't happen to all individuals, I have seen. And is it true at all on a societal level? Or a generational level?

I would expect the elves, including the drow, to be the learned guides of this turning cycle. Having seen the birth and death of centuries, the memories of the long-living races should cry as warnings to another fool king or queen or council of lords to change course when they are walking the road to catastrophe. For we have witnessed this marionette show before, and the puppets all died, and the principals who lived did so with great regret and even horror at their own actions. A dark path is walked in tiny steps.

So the elves should be the clarion call of warning, but, sadly, it is the shorter life span of the humans that seems to most dictate the cycles of destruction, as if the passing of a generation that knew great strife or war or insurgence erases, too, the societal memory of a road's tragic destination.

In the Monastery of the Yellow Rose, they have a great library, and in that historical repository is a timeline of devastating, world-shattering events.

The occurrences appear with alarming regularity. Every seventy to one hundred years, there comes a time of great strife. Oh, there are other events, often tragic, from time to time, but these are often anomalies, it seems, the rogue acts of foolish kings.

The events of which I speak appear more to be a maturation of devastation, a perilous journey of thousands of tiny steps that culminates when the last of those humans who remember have died away.

Then, again, darkness falls.

It is more than coincidence, I think, this backstep, this backward downslope of the rolling wheel of the centuries, and so I have come to believe that enlightenment may occur in a straight line for individuals, but only within that slowly turning wheel for the world at large.

There have been Lord Neverembers before, with different names but similar shortsightedness.

Hereafter, perhaps I shall refer to the lord protector of Neverwinter, Lord Never-remember.

His attitude toward King Bruenor raises great alarms. His clamor for supremacy knows no common sense. His selfishness leads to hoarding that is greatly detrimental, even fatal, to those he calls his subjects.

Everything is faster for the humans. Their compressed lives lead to compressed kingdoms, and to repeated wars. Perhaps it is the urgency of trying to achieve too-high pedestals too quickly, before the unbeatable death closes in. Or perhaps, because they are shorter-lived, it is simply that they have less to lose. A king who has passed his fiftieth year might lose twenty years of life if he dies in battle or the guillotine finds his neck after a failed grab for even more power, while an elven king could lose centuries, or a dwarven king might lose many decades.

As old age sets in and the joys of life are compromised, perhaps this human king must grab for something glorious to replace the excitement of his rise to power, or the distant pleasures of the flesh, or the simple absence of pain when he crawled out of bed each morning.

For all this potential tragedy and darkness, though, I must remind myself that the wheel does inevitably move forward. The world was a darker, harsher, crueler place a hundred years ago, and much more so a thousand years ago.

And this gives me hope for my own people. Is our wheel similarly turning, though at a vastly slower pace?

Is Menzoberranzan truly evolving toward a lighter and more generous existence with the passing of each drow generation?

That is my hope, but it is tempered with very real fears that the wheel turns so slowly that its momentum may not be enough, that events and unscrupulous matrons could not just stop it but push it in the other direction.

And that's to say nothing of the vile demon goddess who holds those matrons in thrall.

Drow heroes are needed.

Fortunately, Menzoberranzan has produced a surprising number of those, usually hidden in the shadows, of which there are many.

It is my desperate hope that one of them, one I dearly loved, has returned to the world.

—Drizzt Do'Urden

CHAPTER 14

City of Shimmering Webs

For five tendays, a dozen small wagons and carts bounced along the lightless tunnels of the Underdark, pulled by large lizards. In the middle of the line, goblin drivers managed a group of the common cattle, rothé, while the cows stood and lowed on a floating floor, hemmed in by fences of lightning energy. The magical designs of that cattle cart were quite interesting and powerful, and surely such an item would have been coveted by many in the Underdark, including the mining dwarves and even the mushroom myconids for their great stalk harvests.

Few, though, would dare to try to take it, for veteran drow scouts flanked the caravan and trailed it, outfitted with fabulous armor and weapons. Word went out before the caravan that it had been sanctioned by a great house of Menzoberranzan, with the full protection of the city's Ruling Council. To attack this train was to go to war with Menzoberranzan.

The three dark elves in the party who were most capable of such scouting and guarding, the three who would be avoided by anyone thinking them enemies, did not participate in the mundane duties of the caravan, however. Instead, Jarlaxle, Zaknafein Do'Urden, and Arathis Hune kept to themselves, usually in the covered cargo hold of the one cart driven and guarded by Bregan D'aerthe operatives, the last cart in the caravan line.

"Matron Sheeva Zauvirr," Jarlaxle revealed at one quiet meeting of the three. He produced a drawing of the woman, a strong and sturdy priestess with her wavy hair dyed blue, except for a tight bun on one side of her head that was left the more natural white. Her red eyes shone all the more because of the glowing ruby she had pierced into the side of her nose.

"Quite attractive," Arathis remarked, clearly impressed.

"And easy to find," Zaknafein added in very different tones, ones that did not hint at carnal desire. For Zaknafein, Jarlaxle knew, felt that drow Lolthian priestesses were most visually pleasing when they were dead.

"Wait," Arathis added, seeming suddenly perplexed. "Zauvirr? The trading family?"

"Black Claw Mercantile," Jarlaxle confirmed.

"They are friends of House Baenre," Arathis Hune replied, seeming alarmed, or at least surprised.

"They will be again," Jarlaxle assured him. "When the error is corrected."

"And that error is this Matron Sheeva creature?" Zaknafein asked.

"She bent to ambition and overplayed her position," the mercenary band's leader replied. "She spoke ill of Matron Mother Baenre to a handmaiden of Lolth, a dutiful creature who, of course, was quick to report the transgression back to Matron Mother Baenre. Matron Sheeva is trying to find a bit of independence, perhaps. Her reasons do not matter and are not our concern. All we need know is the task before us, put to us by the matron mother of Menzoberranzan. She is the head. We are just her hands, albeit ones holding weapons.

"It is just business."

"None here believe that such a dispassionate and logical view of murder infects all three of us," Arathis Hune remarked dryly.

Jarlaxle smirked and looked to Zaknafein.

"Allow me my delusions," Zaknafein scolded Arathis Hune.

The rogue laughed at the new Bregan D'aerthe warrior. "You would choose to believe that this is an edict for murder from Lady Lolth herself? I have never known of you to be so devout, warrior."

"Sacrosanct?" Jarlaxle asked with a snicker. "Do tell us your delusion, good Zaknafein."

The Do'Urden weapon master shrugged. "That I may find peaceful reverie, I convince myself that there are a finite number of them, and that another one killed brings me closer."

"'Them'?" Arathis asked.

"Matrons and priestesses," Jarlaxle answered before Zaknafein could.

"And when he says closer?"

"The ultimate Zaknafein fantasy," Jarlaxle replied. "That he would kill them all, right to—and right *through*—Matron Mother Baenre."

Arathis Hune chortled and turned to Zaknafein.

"Everyone needs a hobby," the weapon master said with a shrug.

The cart hit a bump in the rocky corridor as he spoke, and all three heads involuntarily bobbed, as if in agreement.

BACKED BY THE REPUTATION OF THE DARK ELVES AND THE obvious power guarding the caravan, they encountered little trouble even in the open Underdark. One scout did get injured by an umber hulk, but the monster was quickly dispatched, and displacer beasts were run off on two separate occasions.

By Underdark standards, all of that counted as uneventful.

So as they neared the middle of the seventh tenday out from Menzoberranzan, the caravan came to smoother tunnels, well worked and swept of loose stones, with several intersections clearly marked by faerie fire signposts, pointing the way for those who knew how to read the drow codes and separate the truth from the diversions.

"You have never been out of Menzoberranzan, then?" Jarlaxle asked Zaknafein, the two sitting up beside the cart driver.

"Many times."

"Truly?"

"Not far," Zaknafein explained. "The adjoining tunnels only. House Simfray was ambitious and wanted to explore the possibilities of becoming an extra-Menzoberranzan trading party."

"That is always the way, isn't it?" Jarlaxle mused with a chuckle. "When the path to any real ascension is blocked, the ambitious look beyond the immediate walls."

"Like Jarlaxle?"

The mercenary leader brought two fingers to his forehead in salute at the observation. "Someday I will look outside the City of Spiders, even more than this, likely," Jarlaxle confirmed. "For now, however, there is plenty of room for Bregan D'aerthe to grow within the cavern of Menzoberranzan. I see great strife among the noble families in the near future, with many lesser houses trying to capitalize on the confusion."

"And from great strife, Jarlaxle finds gain."

"As do we all."

"But someday, perhaps, you will move beyond the cavern, beyond the immediate reach of the matron mother and her Ruling Council," Zaknafein reasoned.

"Perhaps, but it is nothing I care to even discuss," Jarlaxle replied. "I am quite content right now, my friend, and I see a path of tremendous luxury. We are safe in our caverns beneath the Clawrift, and protected by the most powerful house in the city—one more powerful than any other two houses, perhaps even any other three houses, combined. So I am more than glad to serve Matron Mother Baenre."

"But not Lolth?"

Jarlaxle's fingers flashed his response, trying to silence his brash companion. Matron Mother Baenre surely knew the truth of Jarlaxle—that he was not a loyal follower of the Spider Queen, or of anyone, for that matter. But to have such information out in the open would not serve him well in his dealings with the merciless Yvonnel Baenre!

"Let me prepare you for Ched Nasad," Jarlaxle said aloud, changing the subject. "It is quite unlike Menzoberranzan, and spectacularly so."

Zaknafein stared at him hard.

Not here, Jarlaxle's hands signed to the weapon master.

"I have heard that the design and construction of the City of Webs are truly inspired," Zaknafein said, rather loudly (perhaps too loudly, Jarlaxle thought, as was typical of people not used to weaving such deflections or lies).

"Words can do it no justice." Jarlaxle pointed far up ahead, to a shimmering wave of faerie fire set on the corridor wall, indicating a sharp turn. "You will see in a moment."

The caravan paused when the first cart rounded that bend, then paused again with each subsequent cart, the drivers and riders taking a moment to soak in the grand scope of the city before them. Zaknafein watched it curiously, quickly coming to realize from the expressions of those turning the bend that Jarlaxle had not been exaggerating. For all of that, though, the House Do'Urden weapon master was still not prepared for the vision when at last his cart turned the corner to show Ched Nasad spread before him.

It was built in a grotto, a vast V-shaped cavern with steep walls climbing thousands of feet. Called the City of Webs—or more formally and regally, the City of Shimmering Webs—Ched Nasad certainly lived up to that moniker. In Menzoberranzan, most of the drow houses were built within gigantic stalagmites and stalactites, with a few, like House Do'Urden, set into caves in the wall, but in this city, almost all of the houses were a combination of cave and petrified webbing. Some of the chambers were formed of multichanneled giant web cocoons.

Those webs, endless webs, lined the whole of the place, climbing the walls, with web bridges spanning the various cavern levels. And not just thick gray webs, but webs glowing in faerie fire, purple and blue, amber and green, even yellow, and ever changing, ever shifting, climbing and descending, a cascade of colors that seemed almost alive.

The sound of rushing water created a background hum that only added to the strangeness of the place, and so attuned were the magical lighting and strange construction that it took Zaknafein a long while to even notice the sound at all.

"We'll be climbing quite high," Jarlaxle explained. "Ched Nasad's Qu'ellarz'orl is up away from the stink of the refuse and the goblin slaves who tend the rothé herd and farm the fungi and lichen on the cavern floor."

"The noble houses?"

Jarlaxle nodded.

Our mark is a noble matron? Zaknafein's fingers asked, and Jarlaxle couldn't tell if his companion was hoping for that or not.

"No," he said, and Zaknafein's crestfallen look became obvious. "But not far removed. Matron Mother Baenre demanded that I inform one ally of our coming. Just one."

"You keep calling her by her title, and with apparent reverence. I am not used to that from you."

Zaknafein felt the flick of a finger against his back, and he turned halfway around in his seat.

You are surrounded by House Baenre agents, Arathis Hune's fingers flashed from behind Jarlaxle, in the back of the cart and down low.

Zaknafein's expression soured at that, but he nodded his understanding.

"Secure our lodging," Jarlaxle told Arathis Hune.

"Under what name?"

"House Hunzrin, of course," Jarlaxle explained. "We have brought a handful of bull rothés to improve the health of the Ched Nasad herd, and will take some of their bulls back to Menzoberranzan so that our herd becomes less an orgy of brothers and sisters."

"I wondered why we brought the smelly things along," Arathis Hune said with a chuckle. "I had hoped we might slaughter them for steaks along the way."

"That would not have been wise."

"Still, I cannot believe that the Hunzrins let their most valuable floating barge depart Menzoberranzan for half a year!"

"I could say the same for Matron Do'Urden and her preferred bull," Jarlaxle teased. "But as with Matron Malice, the Hunzrins were not given much of a choice in the matter."

"Matron Mother Baenre really wants this particular creature dead," Arathis Hune said.

"The matron mother does not take insult lightly, and really, arranging for such things gives her something to do to pass the hours, and at no great cost by Baenre measures."

The caravan rolled up to a huge side cavern that served as a grand stable for the city, and while the drivers and scouts went about the task of securing their wares, Jarlaxle and his companions moved out for their respective tasks. As beautiful as the shimmering webs were, Zaknafein found them even more amazing when he and Jarlaxle began their climb, for the web ramps grabbed at his feet, securing his every step even up nearly vertical walls, but magically let go their grasp at just the right moment as he lifted his foot, affording amazing traction without any hindrance whatsoever.

"I feel like a spider," Zaknafein remarked to Jarlaxle as they scurried up higher on the side wall of the cavern.

"You please Lolth with such words."

"Say that again and I'll please her by throwing you from this perch."

Jarlaxle looked back at him and grinned. "And you believe that I do not have a contingency plan for such an unexpected flight?"

Zaknafein could only sigh, return the grin, and shake his head. This was the fellow, after all, who kept a portable hole in his pouch. There was nothing "unexpected" in Jarlaxle's life, as far as Zaknafein had seen. He didn't know this strangest of dark elves very well, but the mere fact that Jarlaxle was surviving, and apparently thriving, in the brutally matriarchal drow city told him all he needed to know about the mercenary's preparedness and cleverness.

They walked and climbed for a long while, moving near to the noble city houses that were scattered along the highest web balconies of the city. The open routes before them quickly became very limited, and scowling guards eyed them from every cocoon-like structure and from the cave openings at the back of the terraces.

Why are we up here? Zaknafein's fingers flashed. *Didn't you say that Zauvirr was not a ruling house?*

It's not, Jarlaxle signed back. He held up a small parchment, glanced at it, then looked all around, getting his bearings. He motioned toward a wide crack in the wall farther along and across the way, then led Zaknafein to the nearest web bridge that they could cross.

"House Nasadra," Jarlaxle explained as they approached the house that flanked the natural-looking tunnel in the cavern wall. They went behind some web walls, then through a maze of the opaque things, finally coming to an exit inside the wall crack they had seen from across the way. Quite a far way in, too, for the lights of the city were distant and cast little illumination into this natural alley.

Taking great care with every step, the duo moved along the uneven and descending narrow gorge, down and around several boulders and into a deeper gloom. Even with their exceptional drow darkvision, they had to feel their way as much as see it, carefully placing one foot in front of the other as they crept along.

They came to a fork in the narrow trail and were greeted by some light as they neared, from glowworms crawling across the ceiling, casting a bluish glow.

Jarlaxle pointed to the left fork, then motioned for Zaknafein to lead.

The glow intensified after a short distance, and the tunnel became an open room. Before they even saw the two dark silhouettes ahead of them, Jarlaxle and Zaknafein realized they were not alone.

"That is far enough," came the voice of a woman.

"Matron Nasadra?" Jarlaxle asked when the woman, along with another, came somewhat into view along the far wall, which was natural and uneven.

The woman laughed. "You think yourself important enough to warrant an audience with the great Nasadra?" she replied. "This is not Menzoberranzan, mercenary."

"I was told to announce my arrival to Matron Nasadra."

"And you have come to the appointed place," the woman answered.

"And found the emissary of Matron Nasadra. I am a priestess of House Nasadra, perhaps out of favor with my matron for some reason of which I am not aware, for she sent me here, to meet . . . you."

"Perhaps with some—" Jarlaxle started to say, and Zaknafein was caught off guard by the shakiness in the rogue's voice.

"Your arrival is announced," the woman harshly interrupted. "Be on your way."

"Matron Nasadra is in agreement with my—"

"Be on your way," the woman repeated, and she turned and melted into the shadows, her companion, another priestess, moving behind her.

They were quickly out of sight, but Jarlaxle offered a parting bow anyway before turning and going back the way he had come. He said not a word nor signed to Zaknafein until they were out of the side tunnel and far down the cavern's walls once more.

"That was the first priestess of Nasadra, I am fairly certain," he explained to Zaknafein. "Aunrae. Quite a beautiful thing, and a dance worth taking."

Zaknafein looked at him skeptically. "She didn't seem much taken with Jarlaxle."

"Of course not. If I am correct, the woman beside her was Ssipriina Zauvirr, youngest daughter of the woman we were sent to . . . teach." He glanced around to make sure no others were nearby or paying them much heed.

"House Zauvirr knows we are here?"

"Just the little one—I hope."

Zaknafein stopped abruptly at that revelation and let Jarlaxle walk ahead. He stared at the mercenary curiously, feeling suddenly vulnerable and out of sorts. "The shake in your voice . . ." he said.

"Intentional," Jarlaxle replied without looking back. "House Nasadra is grooming Ssipriina to eventually ascend. It is good for her to have some hope that her mother may overcome the likes of us, particularly if she, Ssipriina, does not understand the truth of the darkness that has come for Matron Sheeva. Perhaps Ssipriina believes, even dares hope, that Matron Sheeva will win out. When she does not, Ssipriina will think less of her older siblings, who could not prevent disaster from the likes of two shaky-voiced males."

He kept walking until he realized that Zaknafein wasn't following anymore. Then he turned on his heel to see his companion's confused expression.

"I suppose you believe that Aunrae Nasadra was truly scowling at me, at us." Jarlaxle flashed that grin and shook his head. "My dear Zaknafein, you are going to have to better learn to see through such obvious ruses if you are ever to be of substantial value to me."

Zaknafein continued to stare for a while, obviously replaying the events that had just occurred. "Is nothing what it seems in the world of Jarlaxle?"

"If I am doing it right," the mercenary answered, and started away.

"Even our friendship?" The most unexpected question came from behind, and Jarlaxle spun about again.

"I do not deceive Arathis Hune," Jarlaxle said. "I do not deceive those I pull closest to my side in Bregan D'aerthe."

"And what does that mean for me?"

"You will learn soon enough, I expect."

Zaknafein didn't blink, but his hands went to his weapon hilts reflexively.

Jarlaxle just smirked and turned away once more, leading Zaknafein across the middle levels of Ched Nasad to the inn where Arathis Hune waited.

"I'M NOT FOND OF YOUR CHOICE," ARATHIS HUNE SAID when Jarlaxle and Zaknafein joined him in the suite he had rented under the name of House Hunzrin. The room was well furnished, with three comfortable beds, but the webbed ceiling hung very low, barely above the head of Jarlaxle, who was the tallest of the three.

"It was the best choice," Jarlaxle replied. "The innkeeper is a friend."

"You mean the dead guy out at the desk?" whispered Zaknafein, who was standing at the door, holding it slightly ajar and looking out at the main area of the establishment.

"Priveer Bar'cl—" Jarlaxle started to reply until the weight of Zaknafein's words hit him.

The weapon master swung wide the door and leaped out, dodging a flare of fire as he did. "Down!" Zaknafein yelled to his companions still in the room, and he dove, too, flying to the side of the open door even as a magical fireball exploded within the apartment.

Zaknafein rolled right back to his feet, weapons in hands, as the drow wizard, his invisibility spell ended by the attack, came into view. Zaknafein was no veteran of battling wizards, but he had certainly killed more than a few priestesses in his years, and so he figured the tactics were much the same: get in close.

That would not prove easy, though, as a pair of swordsmen leaped from concealment, one from behind the desk, the other from behind a web screen over by the room's far corner, both rushing to block his way to the spellcaster.

Which meant he wasn't going to get to the wizard in time, and the drow was already casting another spell.

Zaknafein cut left to intercept the man from the corner, but stopped short and snapped his right arm around, throwing his sword like a spear at the warrior coming the other way. That drow got his swords up together to deflect the missile, but it still clipped his shoulder, drawing a painful gash and putting him back on his heels.

The other warrior came in hard, both swords stabbing, but with his left hand alone, the skilled weapon master blocked and parried, even riposted with a sharp and true counter to defeat the attacker's forward push and even drive him back a step.

Zaknafein used the moment to tug the whip from his belt. He brought it spinning up above his head, dropping back on his right foot to turn to face the newcomer. The mere action of the whip had that drow slowing, which was exactly what Zaknafein had counted on as he half turned back and snapped the whip into the face of the spellcaster instead.

The wizard's magical wards stopped the weapon from connecting, but the snap so near his eyes distracted him and interrupted his spell.

And all the while, Zaknafein worked his left-hand blade, keeping the warrior drow at bay. The other was coming back again, though, and Zaknafein knew he had to retreat. He started back a step, but heard a heavy grunt and watched the incoming warrior lurch and stagger to the side.

Most dark elves carried small hand crossbows. Arathis Hune, though, kept a sizable one on his back, one that threw bolts that needed no poison to drop a foe. And he knew how to use it.

The wounded drow staggered, a quarrel deep in his thigh. He grimaced and tried to straighten, but then began howling.

Because the large bolt was poisoned anyway, Zaknafein realized. Why not?

He cracked the whip again at the wizard, though that one had already fallen back out of range. Unfazed, Zaknafein came around, still working the whip, and short-snapped it to the side of his closer opponent's swords, once and then again.

"Get the wizard!" he yelled to Arathis Hune, but even as he cried out, a line of fire raced behind him, not from the wizard, but *at* the wizard.

A lightning bolt followed, then a flying blob of viscous goo that slammed the surprised wizard and drove him up against the wall, sticking him there.

And another lightning bolt roared into the poor fellow, and Zaknafein understood then that Jarlaxle was outraged—he had never seen such a barrage from the mercenary. He figured that the innkeeper must have been a good friend, perhaps even a Bregan D'aerthe agent, but when he glanced at Jarlaxle, he saw another possible reason.

The mercenary's hair, what was left of it, was still smoking.

Back beyond Jarlaxle, Arathis Hune had reloaded and was aiming, but toward the inn's door, where more assassins were coming on fast.

No time now for games or subtlety. Zaknafein snapped the whip in the air above his foe's head, but only for effect and to put it in line for his real attack. With great skill and dexterity, Zaknafein reached far forward with his right hand and swept the whip out to the left, deftly shortening the stroke to send it swinging over the twin swords he continued to parry.

His opponent saw the trick and tried to retract, but Zaknafein was quicker with his tug.

He couldn't keep the swords engaged, of course, nor did he pull either from the drow warrior's grasp, but he tangled them just enough to pull them to his right while he slid past to the left.

He could have killed that drow—were it a priestess of Lolth, he surely would have—but instead he punched out with a sweeping left hook, slamming the fellow across the jaw with the ball pommel of his sword. The warrior staggered and went to one knee, and Zaknafein kept spinning and leaping, easily clearing the last cut of his opponent's freed blades.

Down came Zaknafein from on high, the momentum of his drop and his spin adding power as he brought his hard boot into the warrior's face, laying him flat out on the floor. He kicked one of the swords away and stomped down hard on the drow's other wrist, then threw aside his cut whip, damaged by the blades it had entangled, and scooped up the freed weapon as his own.

He saw the other warrior as he came around, the man leaning heavily against the wall, screaming in agony, clutching at his leg and, Zaknafein could tell, at his very consciousness.

Behind the warrior, the wizard hung on the wall, looking more like a hunting trophy than a threat.

The battle was far from won, though, for over at the entryway of the tavern, another pair of drow warriors appeared, and as soon as Zaknafein—and Arathis Hune, coming from the opposite wall—started for them, they parted and sent a line of powerful bugbears streaming into the fight.

"Left flank!" Zaknafein called to Jarlaxle. Zaknafein and Arathis Hune met the bugbear charge side by side, holding a line, but not near enough to the door, and so more of the brutes were pouring in, sweeping about to Zaknafein's left, threatening to flank the pair.

And where was Jarlaxle?

Something flittered past Zaknafein as he was forced to drop his left foot back to intercept a bugbear trying to rush past. He had no idea what Jarlaxle might be up to, if it was even Jarlaxle who had sent the strange missile. Whoever it was, it made no sense to him, because it wasn't some caltrop or magical burst.

No, it was a feather. A huge, strange feather.

Until it touched the ground, and then, so suddenly, it became a gigantic, flightless, thick-bodied, thick-legged, huge-clawed monstrosity.

Zaknafein shied reflexively, as did the bugbear—or at least, the bugbear tried. But the giant bird was quicker and it pecked the goblinoid atop the head with its massive beak, a punishing blow that sent the bugbear straight to the floor, its eyes rolling, its skull shattered.

The left flank secured, the giant bird leaped ahead fearlessly, hopping, raking with its murderous claws, batting its short thick wings, and driving back the press of bugbears.

A twist, a feint, a step back as if in retreat, and a sudden reversal led by a thrust dispatched the bugbear standing before Zaknafein, and a second, surprising stab with his right-hand blade went immediately over the falling monster and straight into the face of the one thinking to take its place.

Beside Zaknafein, Arathis Hune dispatched his immediate opponent but found himself facing a pair of replacements.

"Jarlaxle!" Zaknafein called again, for he was suddenly too engaged to help his flanked companion.

Even as he called for the help, though, it seemed a moot point, for another pea of flame soared in through the door.

"Break and flee!" Jarlaxle shouted from somewhere behind, and with a fireball about to explode, neither Zaknafein or Arathis Hune was about to argue. As one, they turned to retreat . . .

Only to wonder where they could retreat to.

The answer became apparent when they spied the magical hole thrown against the back wall by their companion, who was already diving out of the establishment.

So went Arathis Hune, and so went Zaknafein, and so went a

pursuing bugbear, but that one came through aflame as the fireball exploded within the inn, filling the common room with fire and the cries of bugbears and the shrieks of a flaming giant bird. A burst of flames came roaring out, as well, but it was abruptly extinguished as Jarlaxle tugged his portable hole away from the wall, returning it to normal—and an instant later, there came a heavy thud as another bugbear tried to charge out of the conflagration through the hole that was no longer there.

"Do not let them escape," Jarlaxle said with a hiss, and that sound was telling to Zaknafein, who was already up and running around the side of the inn. He had never heard the mercenary leader so obviously upset.

No time to consider that now, though, for on the other side of the small inn stood a drow wizard and her two guards, at ease and staring at the burning inn, clearly believing that their targets remained inside the killing flames.

The looks on their faces when Zaknafein leaped around the edge of the structure into their midst brought a smile to the deadly weapon master's lips. The looks on their faces as his strike gracefully took the throat from the wizard and his second sword swept past the nearest warrior to cut him across both wrists as he turned to react were even more delightful.

Zaknafein turned, too, facing him, and his left hook took the man in the cheek while he flipped his right-hand sword over and stabbed it straight behind him, catching the other leaping warrior by surprise— right in the chest.

Jarlaxle and Arathis Hune came running around the building at just that moment, to find all three of the remaining drow defeated: the wizard rolling on the ground grabbing tightly at her bleeding neck, the impaled warrior lying quite still, and the other holding his cut wrists as he knelt there unsteadily on one knee, his nose dripping blood.

"Go get my feather," Jarlaxle told Zaknafein, moving past toward the fallen sorceress. At that same moment, Arathis Hune's sword tip settled against the back of the wounded warrior's neck.

Zaknafein stepped back and stood up straight. With a glance

around, he sheathed his swords and turned back for the burning structure, though it was more smolder than conflagration at that point, since much of the inn was constructed with thick but easily melted webbing. He moved to the door and kicked it, expecting it to fall in. But it caught on some strands of gooey webbing and toppled back outside instead, hitting the ground with a whoosh of sparks.

In the main room, Zaknafein found some bugbears writhing but posing no threat. A quick scan and he saw the smoldering carcass of the giant bird Jarlaxle had summoned.

The only unburned feather that he found seemed hardly worth retrieving, looking more like a twig than a bird's plumage. He shrugged and picked it up, pocketing it, then moving to the wizard hanging on the wall.

That drow was alive, most of the goo burned away, though enough remained to keep him aloft and his feet were still off the floor. The warrior shot by Arathis Hune had expired, though whether from the fireball or the poison, Zaknafein couldn't tell, and didn't care, but the drow he had knocked out was still alive, and just starting to stir.

Jarlaxle walked into the room. "I count two dead drow, seven dead bugbears, and four prisoners, including a wizard," he said.

"And we are unscathed," Zaknafein replied.

"An easy remark for you to make," Jarlaxle said and patted his once-again singed head, where most of his hair had burned away and much of his skin looked as though it had been caramelized. His subsequent growl made it clear that he was not amused.

With a shrug, Zaknafein handed him the feather. "Your bird—was that a bird?—too," he explained. "Might be good eating, though."

Jarlaxle took the feather stub and put on his wry grin once more. "It will grow back," he said.

Zaknafein looked at the mercenary leader's pate and tried to appear encouraging.

"Not the hair," Jarlaxle explained. "Though I will see to that with a priestess when we return to Menzoberranzan."

"Perhaps the gods are trying to tell you something," Zaknafein quipped. "Every time I see you, your head is on fire."

"Not the hair,"' Jarlaxle said again, in even and grim tones. "The feather, the bird. The feather will grow back, and so return to me my useful pet when I need it."

Somehow, Zaknafein wasn't surprised. The man carried holes, grew giant birds from feathers, and acted as if the matron mothers worked for him.

And perhaps, in Jarlaxle's mind, they did.

It occurred to Zaknafein Do'Urden then that it probably wasn't a good life decision to remain near this dangerous character, but he shook the notion away, more than willing to take the risks.

Because it was so much fun.

CHAPTER 15

Self-Starter

W here are they?" Zaknafein said from the scorched door, which he had propped back up against the shell of the inn. Behind him, Jarlaxle and Arathis Hune sat with the four drow prisoners, all bound with the magical cord that was Jarlaxle's belt. They were gagged, too, except for one, the man Zaknafein had laid low with the butt of his sword.

"That fireball had to have been seen by everyone in the region, this level and those above and below," Zaknafein pressed.

"Sure," said Arathis Hune.

"So where are they?"

"Who?"

"Onlookers."

"Hiding, and wisely so."

"Then the city guard?"

"Oh, they are coming," Arathis Hune assured him. "From above, no doubt, and shortly, and in overwhelming numbers. Nothing like a fireball to rouse the defenders of a city built with webbing."

"And we are leaving," Jarlaxle said, standing up. He looked to that one drow who seemed conscious enough to comprehend. "We're not going to kill you," he said, eliciting a surprised and doubting expression from the man. "Though I'm not certain that two of your friends will survive anyway."

From the door, Zaknafein looked on curiously. Jarlaxle was leaving witnesses. True, these drow had initiated the fight, but that was certainly not the story they would tell to Ched Nasad's matron mother and Ruling Council.

"I wish you well," Jarlaxle went on. "And if House Zauvirr falls and you become houseless rogues, as seems likely, remember the name of Bregan D'aerthe."

"And if my house survives, should I remember that name, rogue?" the prisoner asked rather impudently.

"Oh, do," said Jarlaxle. "And remember that three of us defeated six of you and a host of bugbears besides—and that on an occasion when you attacked us unprovoked and with the favor of surprise. So do, please, forever remember how badly you were beaten by less than half of your number. And remember, too, that Bregan D'aerthe outnumbers House Zauvirr, as surely as Menzoberranzan outnumbers Ched Nasad."

With that, and with Arathis Hune in tow, the mercenary leader moved to the door, pushing it down and walking out of the burned-out inn.

If they survive, that will be more for us to fight in House Zauvirr, Zaknafein signaled to the pair.

We will be long gone from this city before they are returned to their house, Jarlaxle replied.

"Where now?" Arathis Hune asked.

House Zauvirr, of course, before the city guard descends upon the place, and before Matron Sheeva realizes that we did not simply flee, and were not wounded or killed in the assault.

He pointed down three levels and across the chasm. To the right of a small waterfall.

"Are you ready for another fight?" he asked quietly.

"We had better be!" Arathis Hune answered suddenly. Following his gaze, the other two saw why, as armored drow soldiers, some carrying the snake-headed whips of Lolthian priestesses, swarmed down at them, riding magical war spiders. The arachnids scrambled across a higher level, producing draglines from their spinnerets to lower down to the next level.

"No fight," Jarlaxle assured them, and leading by example, he ran away, his two companions in close pursuit.

They encountered few other drow, and it seemed clear that Arathis Hune had been correct, and those nearby were in hiding. The trio crossed a marketplace situated at a wider alcove in the chasm wall, but it, too, was nearly deserted, with one or two merchants peering out nervously from behind their carts.

"We need to split up," Jarlaxle said.

"There's only one way," Arathis Hune protested. "And only one ramp near to the next level, and one going up from here. Where would you like us to go?"

Zaknafein, though, moved to the lip of the ledge, as if he meant to leap away. He ran along it instead, dragging his sword heavily just a finger's breadth in from the drop, as if cutting into the webbing. Slowed by the drag, he was outdistanced by the other two, who turned back curiously.

"Go!" he called to them, and pulling up abruptly, he brought his blade up high only to slam it down hard against the edge of the web ramp.

"What is he doing?" Arathis Hune asked, but before Jarlaxle could answer, Zaknafein reached down and grabbed the webbing he had cut with his sword, then leaped over, holding fast his makeshift cord.

That line he had cut into the webbing tore under his weight, like a piece of cloth ripping, carrying him from sight.

"What?" a shocked Arathis Hune stuttered. "He . . ."

"I told you as much about that one," a proud Jarlaxle replied, and on they ran.

ZAKNAFEIN HAD ESTIMATED HIS CUT VERY WELL, AND HE was quite relieved that his guess about the strength and integrity level of the webbing had proved accurate.

He swung down from the ledge in a controlled manner, the webbing tearing evenly as he moved lower, going right past the level below and, he hoped, to the floor of the one below that. He came up a bit short, and so twisted to angle his drop to the roof of a building made of mushroom stalks and web cocoon, a large establishment that seemed to be another tavern or common room of some sort.

Many eyes were upon him down here, though, drow looking up curiously.

As he let go of the web and fell free, he summoned a globe of darkness ahead of him, at his estimated landing place. He entered the darkness and hit the roof hard, fighting to maintain his balance. He had no room for error here and held tight to the image of the landing area, and so moved within the darkness globe to the back edge of the roof, then flipped right over it, dropping between the structure and the chasm wall. There he found some good luck in the form of a back door, and he went in without hesitation, correctly guessing that those inside were quickly exiting to see what the fuss was about.

Calmly moving through the small rooms and narrow corridors, Zaknafein exited right behind many other dark elves, seeming to all who took notice to be just as surprised by the unexpected crash on the roof as the rest of the patrons.

He melted away quickly among the crowd of drow milling about, then slipped through the marketplaces and around the buildings, moving fast to the nearest bridge that would bring him across the chasm.

He looked back several times, hoping to catch sight of Jarlaxle, but saw nothing.

He remembered the mercenary's words, though, and so he knew

where to go. House Zauvirr would never be more vulnerable than it was at that very moment.

"GO DOWN A LEVEL AND I'LL GET ACROSS THE CHASM," JARL-axle called to Arathis Hune as the pair approached a ramp.

The rogue nodded, or tried to, for at that same moment, four stone sheets appeared in the air above him, hanging horizontally and moving with him for just a moment before swinging down as if on an invisible hinge, thumping together around the surprised drow, forming a sarcophagus around him, magically closing the top and bottom. It stood only briefly, then fell over with a dull thud and the muted groan of the surprised and suddenly battered rogue caught inside.

Jarlaxle knew the spell—only a very skilled high priestess could create such a prison in the air.

They were in trouble.

He saw soldiers coming up the ramp before him and knew he was out of options. He ran to the ledge and leaped away, planning to fall almost to the floor before breaking the plummet with a dweomer of levitation.

But he hadn't even passed the ledge when he knew he was caught, for there sat riders upon spiders—spiders turned away to face the chasm wall at the back of the ledge.

Spiders spitting web lines all around Jarlaxle.

The mercenary grasped a wand reflexively to dispel the magical webs. He considered his portable hole, wondering how he might climb in and disappear. So many different options whirled in his thoughts about how he might find a new avenue of retreat. But in the end, he didn't bother.

He was caught, just as Arathis Hune was.

He could only hope Zaknafein was still free.

MANY EYES TURNED ACROSS THE CHASM TO THE SMOLDER-ing ruins and the activity along the upper ledges. Zaknafein was glad of that—better to have wary drow looking there than noticing him as he hustled across the level, moving determinedly toward the house Jarlaxle had pointed out as Zauvirr.

Using the waterfall as a guide, he ran true, coming before House Zauvirr in short order.

He feared it wasn't short enough, though, because when he came in sight of the place, he found house guards arguing with a contingent of armored soldiers, wizards, and many priestesses who had assembled out front.

Zaknafein heard one invoke the Ruling Council a couple of times, and recognized that this gathering had come about in response to the assassination attempt. As in Menzoberranzan, it was acceptable to murder someone in Ched Nasad, but it was not okay to be *caught* trying to murder someone.

Zaknafein slipped down an alley at the side of the house. The confrontation in front was right in the open, a negotiation more than a fight—as it would have to be, since the force assembled to confront the relatively weak House Zauvirr appeared to be a massive alliance of the city's greatest houses.

Confronted with such a challenge, the Zauvirr guards weren't watching for quiet infiltrations at that time. So over the wall went the weapon master, confident that he had correctly identified the guard posts in that area and had found a suitable spot equidistant to both.

He slipped between hanging webs, around walls, and through shadows, finding a surprisingly easy route to a side wall of the house within the gate. In he went, moving silently along a tunnel going into the stone of the chasm wall. When he came to the end, to a door opening to his right into the house proper, he drew his weapons, expecting a fight.

He tried to lay out a logical floor plan in his thoughts—how he wished that Jarlaxle had supplied one earlier—hoping that the houses in Ched Nasad were of similar interior design to those in Menzoberranzan. He considered his steps to try to approximate his depth within the wall, then decided that the matron's throne room would likely be deeper still.

Through the door he went, into a large empty sitting room. Not pausing to consider his good fortune, he was away immediately, moving deeper along the passageways.

He passed a couple of occupied rooms, but again didn't pause, as he heard conversations within that did not seem like the chatter of a matron.

Around one bend and down a low, tight side tunnel, he found a wider area, one that ended with ornate double doors sculpted with images of the Spider Queen, and knew at once that he had found the throne room.

The door was likely warded, and heavily so. He had no way to defeat any such protections, so he chose speed as his ally.

He burst through, diving into a roll, once and then again, as if flames and lightning were chasing him. He came to his feet unscathed, noting surprised guards at either side of the room and a pair of young women, barely more than girls despite their priestly garb, gasping and falling back to either side of the raised dais in the center.

Kneeling before an altar there was an adult priestess, her head bowed, her silver hair shining in the shimmering magical lights that danced in the webbing flanking the altar.

He noted a pair of magical guardians, too, in the form of small jade spiders, and it surprised him that they had not animated against the threat, with the matron so readily exposed and so soon to be dispatched.

"She is not here," the woman kneeling at the altar said without turning.

Was she talking to him?

The guards hadn't moved; the spiders hadn't rushed at him. The whole thing seemed somehow out of place.

He stalked slowly to the kneeling woman, weapons drawn, and, amazingly, she waved aside the younger girls and made no move to stop him.

"Matron Zauvirr is gone," she said when Zaknafein's sword settled on the back of her neck. "She'll not be back."

"And who are you, then?" he asked. "Where is she?"

"Be gone!" the priestess snapped, but not to him, and the younger women and the guards hustled out of the room.

Slowly, the woman stood and turned to face the assassin.

"I know why you are here, and do not disagree with your intended course," she said.

"Even if that course is to kill you?"

"You have no reason," she said with confidence. "I will ascend here in the absence of Matron Sheeva, and on terms friendly to your employer. It has all been arranged, and I do not think your Matron Mother Baenre will be pleased if you put that blade to use."

"I am to trust the word of a high priestess?"

"I am Ssipriina, daughter of Sheeva, who will be Matron Zauvirr soon enough, assassin."

"I know who you are," Zaknafein replied, recognizing her from the meeting with Aunrae Nasadra. "You will be matron? For that alone I should kill you."

"Should you? The cost will be enormous to your mercenary companions, I assure you. And perhaps, as well, you should consider that such an act will not be as easy as you seem to believe."

He had, of course, considered the second part. No powerful priestess would be such an easy kill as this now appeared. In fact, it was that very apparent vulnerability that had given Zaknafein pause in the first place.

Yes, he believed, this was the priestess who had squealed on Matron Sheeva's mealymouthing about Baenre to a yochlol handmaiden. The conniving witch had condemned her own mother in her lust for power—hardly a new story among the drow, but still reprehensible in his mind. How Zaknafein hated her, hated them all, and he certainly still wanted to kill this one—he wanted to kill any priestess serving Lolth.

But he understood his responsibility to Jarlaxle and so he sheathed his weapons.

"A wise choice," she said.

ARATHIS HUNE LEANED AGAINST THE WALL OF THE NATU-ral cave, his arms up above his head, shackled to the stone. Shackled magically, with no locks to pick and no way to get out short of cutting off his own hands.

Oh, and no knife to be found.

Even if he somehow managed to wriggle free, where was he to go? In the stone sarcophagus that had captured him, he had been carried to this dark place—somewhere within the chasm walls surrounding Ched Nasad, he supposed, but could not know—and then unceremoniously dumped into a pit. There he had been tormented with stinging needles shot from hand crossbows until he had stripped naked and handed all his gear up to his captors.

They had dragged him to this place and left him here, enchained and with just enough magical light to keep him looking at the many dancing shadows, to keep him on edge. *Better to have complete darkness than this,* he thought.

Still, it could have been much worse. He had not felt the burning bite of any snake-headed whips, nor had any priestesses left magical symbols of pain or despair hanging in the air to devastate him in his solitude. He didn't dare hope that the matrons of Ched Nasad were less skilled in torture than those of Menzoberranzan, though, and he had heard the word "drider" uttered more than a few times as his captors had departed.

Was that his fate? To become an eight-legged abomination, half drow, half spider, and forever tormented?

Arathis Hune had to hope that time was on his side. Yet even as he considered that, he shook his head. If word got back to Menzoberranzan and Matron Mother Baenre, would she protect him?

The rogue sighed at the thought, for he doubted that the mighty Baenre would spend an ounce of treasure or political capital on the likes of him. Jarlaxle, maybe—he would probably walk free, of course, coming out of this somehow in a better situation than he had entered it—but not Arathis Hune.

The rogue tried to swallow his bitterness. Jarlaxle had saved him, he reminded himself many times. His minor house had been all but obliterated decades before, with only Arathis and a few others managing to escape. But surviving was not thriving, and the few remaining

Hunes had then faced a miserable existence of bare sustenance along the ever-dangerous Stenchstreets, where disease would find one if murder did not. A reprieve seemed at hand when the remnants of House Hune had joined with another minor house, Ozzl, but there was no place in House Ozzl'Hune for Arathis, who had assassinated one of House Ozzl's nobles years ago.

Which left him on the Stenchstreets, and that's where Jarlaxle had found him two decades earlier. Found him, and befriended him, and brought him and three others from his fallen house into this band of brothers he was somehow creating, remarkably, with the quiet blessing of the great Matron Mother Baenre. Their friendship had survived the decades—that in itself was a remarkable thing in Menzoberranzan, Arathis Hune knew—and the trust between the two had grown to the point that they had become like brothers, and not in the typical drow meaning of the relationship, with competition and jealousy and gain found at the end of a bloody dagger.

But now the inevitable politics of Spider Queen treachery had wedged between them, and in this dark place, shackled helplessly to a wall, Arathis Hune had to work very hard to hold hope that Jarlaxle's loyalty to him would climb some very tall barriers.

If Jarlaxle was even still alive, let alone in any manner of control of this situation.

The rogue sighed again, then rolled up acrobatically, turning his shoulders and bringing his feet right up over to plant against the wall. There he stood straight out, as far as the shackles would allow, then pressed off the wall with all his might.

But to no avail. His wrists ached, the bottoms of his bare feet bled, but there was no yield in the magical bonds that held him.

He rolled back down and rested, falling within himself, trying to find a place of emptiness where his fears and bitterness would not consume him.

He became unaware of his surroundings, of the physical world around him, and so he didn't know how much time had passed—was it one day or three?—when some stirring off in the darkness brought him from his forced reverie.

He strained his eyes, catching movement, hoping for Jarlaxle, then recoiled physically and emotionally when he noted the approach of a trio of drow, two male guards and a priestess of some rank, judging from the ostentatious collar of the ornate robe climbing up behind her head.

She walked right up to him and stared hard, then lifted her hand and waggled her fingers, chanting softly, while one of the guards moved up beside her and dropped a wrapped pack to the ground before him.

Arathis Hune braced himself, expecting some horrid magical pain to strike him, but instead, suddenly, his arms fell free, the magical shackles simply letting go.

The priestess motioned to the bundle on the ground before him.

Arathis Hune eyed her suspiciously, glancing down at the pack and back to meet her gaze.

"We are leaving," she stated sternly, motioning her chin toward the pack as she did and making it clear from her tone that when she said "we," she was including Arathis Hune.

Figuring he had nothing to lose, the rogue bent and pulled back the blankets wrapped about the items, his eyes widening as he realized that this was his gear—*all* of it, including his weapons.

Including his vials of poison, even.

"By order of House Nasadra, you are no prisoner of Ched Nasad," the priestess explained. "Dress quickly and come along."

"Jarlaxle," Arathis Hune muttered appreciatively, pulling on his clothes.

They left the tunnels soon after, coming out onto one of the middle levels of Ched Nasad. They didn't ascend, though, to where Arathis Hune knew the great House Nasadra to be, but rather went down, level by level, until they were on the floor of the chasm, near the exit from the city.

Were they going to set him free out into the open Underdark?

But no, they led him instead to the wall just beyond the V-shaped chasm, and there one of the guards opened a secret door, cleverly designed to look like part of the natural stone. Through the narrow door and down an equally narrow tunnel, the priestess led Arathis Hune while the two male guards remained outside.

Guided by glowing purple orbs, they reached a chamber, comfortably appointed with large pillows thrown all about the floor and a rack holding many fancy bottles above a shelf of crystal goblets on one wall.

Arathis Hune was taking it all in when the priestess grabbed him by the wrist and pulled his arm out wide. He watched her in disbelief as she cast a spell of healing, flooding him with warmth and removing all the pain inflicted by his shackling.

"I accept your apology," he said slyly.

The priestess chortled, a mixture of disgust and amusement, and walked away to pour herself a drink.

"Are we to make this our home?" Arathis Hune teased. "The pillows seem quite soft."

"I will take you at my pleasure or I will not, as I choose," said the priestess. "You have no say here, foolish outsider, and no power. Do not mistake my actions for anything more than my obedience to Matron Mother Nasadra."

"And to Lady Lolth, of course," Arathis Hune said with a bow. Before he came up from that bow, he heard the scraping of stone on stone at the back of the chamber and looked over to see a portion of the wall sliding aside.

In walked another priestess, magnificently adorned and of regal bearing. Arathis Hune glanced over at his rescuer to see her bowing her head, eyes lowered deferentially, and he followed her lead.

From that bowed position, he did dare to peek over at the new priestess to notice a second and more familiar person entering the room.

Arathis Hune stood up straight to greet Jarlaxle, but was caught off guard by the sight of the man. The little hair he had left had been greased and straightened upright, like a trio of small spikes protruding from the top of his head. Arathis had seen a similar, fuller set of hair spikes on Uthegentel Armgo, he recalled, and while Jarlaxle's were framed by skin reddened by fire, it was still a quite striking—and quite handsome—look for the mercenary.

Always did Jarlaxle come out better off, even regarding his hair.

"I give you First Priestess Aunrae Nasadra," Jarlaxle said. "Named for the matron mother. Aunrae the Second, I believe."

"Third," she corrected.

"Even more impressive," Jarlaxle said with a bow.

"I knew you'd come for me," Aratahis remarked.

"I would take the credit if I could, of course," Jarlaxle replied. "But alas, I expect that I was quite recently in the same situation as you."

"House Nasadra was not aware of your arrests," Aunrae explained. "You and the House Zauvirr assailants who attacked you were taken by the Red Guard, who answer only to the Ruling Council—and that's only when they deem it necessary."

"We would have been executed, I am told," said Jarlaxle. "Killed in dark holes and left for the rats."

"I'm glad that you discovered us, then," Arathis Hune said to Aunrae.

"Not by accident," Jarlaxle remarked, drawing a curious look from his associate. "Zaknafein," the mercenary leader explained. "He went straight to House Zauvirr to finish our task. But he could not, because Matron Sheeva had fled the house and the city."

"Sheeva is no longer to be titled as a matron," Aunrae corrected. "She is afflicted and beyond redemption."

"Afflicted?" Arathis Hune echoed.

"*Payz izi covfefe narz iz cyzt,*" said the priestess who had brought Arathis Hune to this place.

"The affliction of mirrors," Jarlaxle agreed with a nod, but Arathis Hune wore a confused look.

"She fell in love with the image in the mirror," Jarlaxle explained. "All the world came to her through that narrow prism."

"That is why she thought she could challenge Baenre," Arathis Hune reasoned.

"Matron Mother Baenre," the priestess beside him corrected with a backhanded slap for his insolence.

Jarlaxle just shrugged and nodded, then, almost as an afterthought, added, "The affliction of mirrors is key to the power of Matron Mother Baenre, a great advantage."

"You think her afflicted?" Arathis Hune asked, stuttering through the words and wisely ducking aside when he realized that he had spoken them aloud.

"Quite the opposite," Jarlaxle replied. "Never is this insanity found in the first matron in the founding of a house, which Yvonnel the Eternal is, and rarely in the second generation of matrons, for, you see, it is not usually an affliction that attacks those who have earned their power, only those who have such power given to them. And even then, it is somewhat rare, and is quickly corrected."

"Corrected?"

"The mirrors will shatter," said Jarlaxle. "Pride will take the afflicted too high, and so to a great fall."

"*You're* quite fond of your reflection," Arathis Hune pointed out.

"Who could blame me?"

"And now Sheeva has climbed too high," Aunrae said, "to peaks where she can only fall. But for the work of your companion, she might have survived longer, but now . . . now she will be removed."

"Zaknafein," Jarlaxle said.

"Impressive for a new recruit," Arathis Hune admitted.

"Not unexpected," Jarlaxle replied with a grin. "But please, do not tell him that when he joins us. I would not have him thinking too highly of himself when we have such a dangerous hunt ahead of us."

"Sheeva?"

"You have unfinished business," Aunrae confirmed.

"But first, I think we have earned a bit of respite and a celebration," Jarlaxle said, rubbing his hands together briskly and motioning at the bottles of fine liquor across the room.

"I've earned it, at least, for saving your pitiful self," Aunrae agreed.

"Then we will celebrate together, and I will try to serve you well, my lady," Jarlaxle promised, and bowed.

HOURS LATER, JARLAXLE AND ARATHIS HUNE WERE RELAX-
ing in the secret chamber when the door to the chasm floor opened and Zaknafein Do'Urden walked in, looking quite refreshed and relaxed.

"You kept us waiting long enough," Jarlaxle greeted him sarcastically.

"I was considering retiring to House Zauvirr," the weapon master replied. "The new matron is quite endearing."

"She is still a priestess of Lolth," Jarlaxle reminded him.

"I didn't say I wouldn't kill her eventually."

Jarlaxle started to reply but held his tongue—amazingly—and just nodded.

"A new look?" Zaknafein asked, staring at Jarlaxle's spiked hair.

"Dashing, don't you think? I am rather fond of it."

"By your own edicts, is it not in the best interest of an underground band to be inconspicuous and not stand out?"

"It is better for me that Bregan D'aerthe's soldiers do not stand out, indeed," Jarlaxle replied. "But I have come now to learn something about my reputation preceding me—a reputation that will only grow when we bring back the head of Matron—excuse me, of the *former* matron Zauvirr. It is better for you, I expect, that I am recognized, that our targets take note and so lose heart."

Zaknafein and Arathis Hune exchanged doubting looks at that proclamation. But they just shrugged, neither really surprised by anything Jarlaxle might say or do.

"East and south, beyond the giant mushroom grove, is where we should begin our search, I am told," Zaknafein said.

"You have narrowed it down to half a world," Arathis Hune remarked.

Zaknafein shrugged. "She is out of the city, into the open Underdark, by all accounts. Is there a better plan to be executed?"

Jarlaxle moved over and handed Zaknafein a glass of brandy. "Question," he said. "How do you find a drow?"

Taking the glass and a long swallow, Zaknafein considered the puzzle for just a moment. "Answer," he replied, "you don't. You let the drow find you."

CHAPTER 16

The Temptation of Revival

W hat are they?" Zaknafein asked, for he had never seen such creatures. They looked rather human but stood barely half the height of a surface human, and appeared soft and a bit round, even after being held in near starvation as prisoners in a drow city.

"Halflings," Arathis Hune explained.

"Beardless dwarves?"

"Nothing like the dwarves except in stature," Jarlaxle's lieutenant answered. "These little ones prefer the sunlight and the soft luxuries of the surface world, not the caves of the upper Underdark or the tunnels of the lower."

"How are they here, then?"

"We told Aunrae Nasadra that we needed bait. She gave us bait."

Zaknafein stared at the living lures, five pathetic-looking creatures shackled together and milling about nervously. They looked like children to him, except that he noted facial hair on two of the group, and the fifth clearly had the figure of a woman grown—just not the height.

The weapon master winced, not quite liking this arrangement. He held no affinity for halflings, of course, seeing how he had just learned of their existence, but it was clear that this was no band of rogues or warriors imprisoned for transgressions. Just unfortunate victims. This group of poor folks would be put out in the open, prey for Sheeva and her entourage. He looked at their faces, at their eyes, and saw the fear, the helplessness, and for a moment, he shared a piece of it with them.

He wanted to say something, but Jarlaxle walked over then, carrying something underneath a plain white sheet, a magical disk floating behind him.

"Sheeva has not abandoned her desire to hold on to her house," the mercenary leader explained. "She seeks some way to regain the favor of Ched Nasad, to be protected from Baenre and from those in the City of Shimmering Webs who now see her as a danger to the integrity of their order." He reached over and pulled back the sheet, revealing a magnificent, gem-studded spider statue.

"It is a mock of the one that graces the table of the Ched Nasad Ruling Council," he explained. "Whispers have slipped from the city that a band of diminutive thieves from the surface world stole away with it."

"You think this will lure Sheeva?" Zaknafein asked, his tone revealing his skepticism.

"The temptation of revival," Jarlaxle replied. "There is nothing a former matron desires more than to return to her throne after she is deposed. Rescuing this from these fearsome halfling highwaymen will be Sheeva's invitation back to the Ruling Council. Except, of course, it will not."

"It seems a lot of trouble. Can't we simply hunt her down and be done with it?"

"How do you find a drow?" Jarlaxle reminded him.

Zaknafein had no response. He looked at the prisoners and heaved a sigh, already trying to envision how he might properly protect them if Sheeva came hunting.

"Highwayhalflings," he muttered with a helpless chuckle.

◆ ◆ ◆

AT THE BACK OF A GIANT MUSHROOM GROVE, IN A SMALL alcove sheltered from the light of the glowworms on the main cavern's ceiling, the five halflings sat around a small, low-burning, recessed fire eating a meal Jarlaxle had provided—quite a fine meal, indeed, and one that the famished prisoners did not try to refuse. Behind them in the shallow, the spider statue rested on a natural shelf, in clear view to anyone who happened upon the band.

To the side of that alcove, a dark crack in the wall revealed the almost-closed mouth of the extradimensional chamber Jarlaxle had created with his portable hole. From inside, the three drow took turns watching their bait—Arathis Hune, who had once fished the waters of Lake Donigarten in Menzoberranzan, had nicknamed the leader of the halfling troupe Bobber, and had teased all the prisoners about how they'd soon be gobbled up.

Aside from the cruelty of the assassin's taunts, which bothered him more than a little, Zaknafein didn't think the strategy effective.

"You taunt them with certain death, so what have they to lose?" he had asked when they had entered the extradimensional chamber this day, their tenth out of Ched Nasad.

"I don't give much thought to their loss. But it is a way to pass the time," Arathis replied.

"They are more likely to attempt to flee, or to fight, if you keep provoking them," Zaknafein argued, thinking practicality would have a better chance here than simple decency.

But Arathis Hune just shrugged as if neither thought bothered him and crawled into the hole.

Zaknafein looked to Jarlaxle for support, but the mercenary leader was having no part of their growing argument. They had one mission here, one alone, and they would be wise to complete it successfully, Jarlaxle had reminded him.

Like Arathis Hune, he didn't seem to care about anything else.

But Zaknafein did.

He thought about that as he took his turn at the exit, peering through to see the gathered halflings in their makeshift camp. House

Simfray had been but a minor house, with few in bondage other than a handful of goblins, and so Zaknafein had not been exposed to many slaves, and certainly none like these. Goblins were thoroughly wretched creatures, with no redeeming value that Zaknafein had ever noted. Their entire existence had seemed to be one of plotting misery and destruction, even to each other.

Still, seeing them as slaves had never sat well with the weapon master. And this . . . Zaknafein knew in watching the halflings, with their frightened glances—but also their occasional laughs and many seemingly comforting exchanges with one another—that these creatures were not like goblins, not at all.

Yet here they were, bait dangled before terrible enemies with terrible designs, who would quite possibly murder them before the three onlookers could stop it.

And his two companions didn't give a damn.

One of the halflings rose and walked about, stretching his arms as he went. He yawned and sat back down, but off to the side and against the alcove wall.

Zaknafein looked back the other way to see the halfling woman also stretching out upon the ground, apparently already asleep, and when he looked back to the wanderer, that one, too, was quietly curled in slumber.

Jarlaxle had told him that this race was very good at two things, eating and sleeping, and it was a hard observation to dispute in that moment. In a matter of just a few heartbeats, two were seemingly deep in sleep, and the other three just sat there, apparently absorbed in their food.

The thing was, they were sitting *too* still, but Zaknafein didn't immediately realize that, not until it occurred to him that he couldn't hear the crackle of the small fire any longer. The fire was still there, he just couldn't hear it.

The weapon master sucked in his breath and turned back to wave to his companions, his fingers signaling, *They have come!*

Zaknafein rolled his fingers, eager to leap out, but Jarlaxle grabbed him by the shoulder and signed, *Patience!*

"Patience?" Zaknafein returned, almost loud in his disgust. Their patience would likely result in five slit throats.

Seven, Jarlaxle's fingers reminded him, for as far as they could tell from the witnesses at House Zauvirr, Sheeva had fled the city with a half dozen loyal followers.

Onto the scene before them came a pair of drow warriors, the two men with swords drawn, moving cautiously into the firelight.

The sitting halflings didn't move. The sleeping halflings didn't wake.

The first drow moving among them punched a halfling in the side of the head. His fellow went further, stabbing a seated halfling in the shoulder—not deeply, but enough so that the fellow couldn't fake his immobility, certainly.

Zaknafein knew this insidious priestess spell. The halflings were very much aware of their surroundings, and very much aware of the pain being inflicted, but unable to even call out in protest or agony.

It was all he could do not to rush through the portal and take his chances.

Another drow pair came into view, a man and a woman, both finely dressed. Sheeva Zauvirr had fled with a daughter and son, they had been told, and Zaknafein figured these two to be that noble's progeny. The woman was signing in the silent hand code, but from this distance, Zaknafein couldn't make out every word.

He glanced at Jarlaxle, though, and saw that the mercenary leader had taken out a curious item, an eyepiece. He was looking through it at the scene before them and basically repeating the signs from the priestess.

How could they have escaped, and with this? the daughter of House Zauvirr was saying, adding that her troop should take all precautions.

All precautions will not include the possibility of us, Zaknafein quickly signed to his companions, eager to be on with this fight.

Of course you are eager, Jarlaxle signed.

Zaknafein could only grin at his friend's sarcasm. There was a priestess of Lolth out there, and Jarlaxle knew well that having her in

Zaknafein's sight was like putting a wounded rothé calf in the path of a displacer beast.

Jarlaxle shifted away from the crease, put away his eyepiece, and signaled one word to his team: *Furiously!*

Zaknafein crashed out of the extradimensional pocket, predictably running right for the priestess. The warrior they thought the noble son of Sheeva intercepted, stabbing a sword at the charging weapon master, but Zaknafein sidestepped outside the thrust, right sword down-facing and backhanding the enemy's sword away.

The drow noble tried to counter by cleverly bringing his left-hand blade under and stabbing out, but Zaknafein had seen this rather mundane routine many times before and was ready for it, executing an upward parry with his own left-hand sword, lifting his opponent's sword up even before it had cleared the extended arm.

Yelping at the cut of his own sword, the Zauvirr warrior tried to dodge aside, but Zaknafein went with him, stabbing once and then again into the drow's thigh.

Down the son of Sheeva went, summoning a globe of darkness in a desperate move to prevent the kill.

Zaknafein was done with him anyway, though, already moving on to the daughter of Sheeva, a priestess of the vile Spider Queen.

His coveted prey.

ARATHIS HUNE, OUT RIGHT BEHIND ZAKNAFEIN, VEERED for the halflings and the drow pair milling about the frozen creatures. The assassin came in with two swords spinning, and three blades and a hand crossbow rose against him.

He threw one sword straight up into the air, accepted the sting of the crossbow bolt (having long ago trained his body to resist drow sleeping poison), and drew forth his own crossbow, one considerably larger than the diminutive weapon that shot at him.

There was no poison on Arathis Hune's set quarrel this time.

There didn't need to be.

Now there was one blade, and one empty hand crossbow, facing

Arathis Hune as he caught his falling sword. He went in with a flour-
ish, furiously, as Jarlaxle had ordered, his blades cutting all about the
warrior, overwhelming him, keeping him on his heels, the Zauvirr
drow moving and turning so crazily to avoid sudden death he had no
time to even think of drawing his second sword.

It seemed a fitting irony when that warrior stumbled over a felled
halfling, tumbling down. He executed a backward roll and even managed to draw out that second blade as he went, but Arathis Hune was
faster, waiting at a spot the warrior couldn't begin to defend as the
drow started to stand.

So the Zauvirr warrior had to roll again, and again after that, and
on and on, Arathis Hune determined to wear him out without ever
landing a blow.

DESPITE HIS INSTRUCTION TO HIS FELLOWS, JARLAXLE
didn't come out of the extradimensional pocket with flair and energy.
He slipped out instead, quietly taking down the hole behind him, and
slithered off through the shadows for the greater and more dangerous
prey he knew to be near.

He called upon his magical boots, willing them to absolute silence,
and also called from them the essence of the spider, granting him the
ability to walk along the wall as easily as an arachnid.

The shadows were better there, he thought.

He saw another trio of drow warriors charging in, heading straight
for Zaknafein, who was engaged then with the daughter of Matron
Sheeva. "More than seven," he whispered under his breath, and he feared
then that a horde of drow might soon overwhelm his companions.

He had to trust in his weapon master friend, he reminded himself, and so he backtracked the way those soldiers had come, creeping
around a bend in the high corridor nearer the ceiling than the floor.

And there she was, Sheeva Zauvirr, holding a snake-headed whip
and tapping a wand against her leg, no doubt ready to launch a catastrophe.

Surprised at finding her there alone, Jarlaxle became even more cautious. He used his monocle again, turning its outer, sliding rim ever so slightly to see into a different spectrum, that of magic. Sure enough, the floor and walls all around Sheeva glowed with runes and glyphs. As did the woman herself.

Simply because she was out of favor with the other matrons of the cities didn't mean that she was out of favor with the Spider Queen—in fact, given Lolth's desire for chaos, it was probably quite the opposite. She was still a high priestess, Jarlaxle reminded himself, and he had dealt with the wards and protections of powerful matrons before.

He had little desire to try to deal with them again.

He crept up higher on the wall, finding a shallow alcove, allowing Sheeva to come to him.

She did move eventually, pausing with every step to listen to the sounds, smiling particularly when one group of her minions—the last three into the fight, Jarlaxle presumed—began claiming that their opponent was surrounded and so should surrender.

Trust him, Jarlaxle silently told himself once more, reminding himself of Zaknafein's prowess and trying to keep his focus here. Sheeva was a former matron, but that was a political distinction and had little to do with the power she could wield. His plan could wash away on the strength of a single spell.

Sheeva kept moving cautiously, reaching the bend and peeking around.

Jarlaxle took some pleasure in her angry hiss.

She immediately started chanting in a low and gravelly voice, one filled with mounting rage.

Jarlaxle had to move quickly, but he still wasn't sure how he might intervene. She was fully warded, and no weapon or spell he could throw would get through her magical defenses quickly enough.

The mercenary shrugged and thought maybe he should be the thing moving quickly . . . and as far away as possible.

SHE HAD A WHIP. NOT A SNAKE-HEADED MONSTROSITY LIKE those carried by most high priestesses, but a bullwhip, black and braided, swaying, swerving, and dancing like a serpent anyway in the priestess's obviously expert grasp. Zaknafein admired her clear proficiency with the weapon and wished he could respond in kind, but alas, his own whip had been ruined at the inn. Still, he was quite glad of his understanding of that unusual weapon now, for he knew the many possible angles and tactics his opponent could employ.

He measured the cant of her arm when she moved to strike at him, and instantly knew the range. So he skidded to a stop and fell backward, bending at the knees, allowing the whip to crack above him as he lay out faceup. He meant to touch down lightly with his shoulder blades, then lift right back up to close the gap before the priestess could bring the whip to bear again, but this was no ordinary whip. It cracked in the air as expected, the lash drawing a sudden and sharp line right above him as he descended. But the snapping tip did more than that, and cut a line *into* the air itself, as if tearing the very fabric of the Prime Material Plane. To Zaknafein, it seemed as if the weapon had struck not the time-space around him, but a painting of the area, with him in the painting, and had gashed that painting to reveal an inferno beyond.

For now there was a line of flames right above him, so hot that it burned his eyes and eyebrows even, and dripping molten fire down at him, as if it was bleeding lava.

Zaknafein threw his arms across his face and rolled out of the way of that descending hell. Trying to settle his sensibilities after the shock, trying to make sure he was not on fire, he moved to regain his footing fast—and faster still when he heard the priestess ordering new arrivals to slay him.

Up leaped the weapon master, his back to the priestess and the newcomers, and on instinct he sent his swords spinning up and back over his shoulders, one angled down, the other with the blade toward the high ceiling.

He spun to his right, pivoting about, leaving that right-hand blade behind to pick off yet another cut of a drow sword.

He saw three enemies, one flanking on each side, one coming right in at him in fierce pursuit. Zaknafein didn't hesitate—not even an eyeblink to find a solution to the encirclement.

There was no solution, the weapon master knew, other than to grab the initiative and hold it.

So he did just that. Instead of backpedaling to prevent the full flanking, he welcomed it and moved the opposite way, boldly at the drow before him. His blades worked left and right, spinning down and leaping up, the sheer suddenness of a dozen attacks driving his opponent backward.

He put his immediate opponent even more off balance with another surprise, stabbing straight out with his right hand, then retracting fast, then throwing the sword, spearlike.

The drow dodged easily, renewed confidence displayed upon his face, thinking himself the target, thinking he had dodged the anticipated killing blow.

His smirk disappeared when he heard the priestess behind him yelp in surprise, and in that moment of surprise, Zaknafein leaped forward—just ahead of the swords coming in at him from behind.

Zaknafein's left-hand sword swept a wide, horizontal backhand arc, parrying both of his opponent's blades. He cut that sweep short, though, and reversed the sword down and to the right, under his opponent's left blade, immediately lifting it and stepping forward under the rising arm.

In that same movement, in an incredible act of inspiration, Zaknafein's free right hand cupped the fingers of his opponent's left hand and bent the drow's wrist sharply, breaking his hold on the sword—which Zaknafein caught and carried as he backed up right beside that poor fellow's shoulder. Both his arms did not remain extended, though. Zaknafein jerked back his right hand, driving the pommel of his opponent's own sword into the drow's face while he turned in and brought his left sword snapping across to defeat the meager counter the now-falling drow was attempting.

Zaknafein broke free of the falling warrior, his blades immediately working opposing sweeps before him, always in balance, always in line, yet always ready to veer. Metal screeched then, as two swords parried four, over and over. With seemingly minimal effort, Zaknafein kept the barrage at bay and sought a path for gaining advantage.

The idea of an advantage quickly faded when he heard an ominous sound behind him.

Apparently, he hadn't quite finished the priestess with his thrown sword.

HE WONDERED WHY HE HADN'T MOVED. A HIGH PRIESTESS, a former matron of a drow house, was about to call down some eldritch destruction, and yet he hadn't moved.

It was a strange feeling that came over Jarlaxle then, one with which he was not overly familiar.

He wasn't fleeing to save his own skin.

If you can't hit your target, hit her associates, Jarlaxle silently mouthed, recalling the first rule of ambush. The problem with that rule, though, was that he couldn't see any of the other House Zauvirr traitors.

So that wouldn't work.

"If you can't hit her associates, attack the battlefield," he said quietly, and this time, he *could* follow the rules. He cast a globe of darkness at Sheeva—not to fully encompass her, but specifically to clip her from behind, just enough to prod her forward.

For at the same time he summoned the darkness, Jarlaxle threw out his portable hole, spinning it so that it widened with every rotation down to the floor right before the priestess, who hopefully wouldn't notice it until it was too late.

The darkness nudged her, and giving an irritated look behind, she didn't look where she was going as she unconsciously stepped forward . . . into the hole!

Jarlaxle leaped down from the wall and ran across the hallway, scooping up his toy and securing it. His ten-foot-deep pit was once again an extradimensional pocket, this time with a drow he might consider even more dangerous than Zaknafein had been all those months ago.

With the weapon master in mind, he hurried around the bend to see Zaknafein in the middle of a wild brawl with three Zauvirr foot soldiers, and to see, more ominously, a priestess turning, with a mace hanging from the side of her robe but a bullwhip in hand and rolling above her shoulder.

Cracking right for him!

He ducked the blow, but learned of that whip's plane-cutting properties the hard way, for unlike Zaknafein, Jarlaxle didn't see the lava.

He felt it.

On his head.

With a howl, the mercenary leader rushed back around the bend, slapping at the fiery sting upon his scalp.

ZAKNAFEIN WINCED WHEN HE HEARD THE CRACK OF THE whip, and more so when he heard the yelp from Jarlaxle. He stayed focused, though, too engaged to go to his friend.

This time, his familiarity with the priestess's weapon saved Zaknafein, not just because he recognized the sound behind him as the telltale whoosh of the whip rising and rolling, but because he knew what it was fully capable of.

With his back to the priestess and two warriors before him, he had a decision to make . . . and fast.

He didn't hesitate, had no time to even consider consciously that which his exhaustive training had ingrained in his muscles. He leaped backward, spinning and landing in a run. He didn't try to deflect the whip as it rolled out in his direction, this time from the side and not above. Instead, he rushed inside its reach as he had intended to do the first time, before he'd been surprised by the weapon's "talents."

And as he did, the two warriors pursuing him ran right into the whip's strike zone.

The priestess's tear into the Plane of Fire caught right in the faces of her minions, and both fell aside, howling.

Giving Zaknafein the time he needed.

He dove and rolled, coming up with his two swords and working furiously.

Stabbing the priestess's gut . . .

Slashing at the side of one leg . . .

At the other hip . . .

Slicing up under her chin . . .

Each strike brought forth a burst of magical light, a repelling spark, as her wards held up. But each burst was a bit dimmer than the previous, for clearly she wasn't powerful enough to keep up perpetual wards.

He hit her five times, ten times. Too close for her whip to be of use, his assault too furious for her to even attempt a spell, the priestess brought up one of her other weapons, trying to slow Zaknafein's momentum with a powerfully magicked mace.

She was very skilled with it, and could likely defeat most drow males in simple combat.

But Zaknafein wasn't most *drow*, let alone most males.

To her credit, she *almost* blocked one of Zaknafein's next dozen or so attacks. Her wards were gone halfway through that barrage, and so she was too wounded, too shocked and pained, too gashed to even attempt to block his subsequent flurry.

Zaknafein worked his way around her as he cut her to pieces, concerned only with the act of destruction he was performing on the priestess. He had no reason to worry, anyway, for the warrior he had slugged with the sword pommel was still on the ground, writhing. A second of the trio was down, too, on his face with wisps of smoke rising from his clothing, trembling fingers trying to reach behind his back at a crossbow quarrel stuck there. The third had turned about, weapons dropped, hands held high in surrender to Arathis Hune's leveled crossbow.

Those three mattered little to the weapon master. The only thing that held his attention was the vile servant of Lolth before him. The priestess finally crumpled to the ground, gasping in the last breaths of her life, her eyes opening wide at the reality that she was passing into the nether realm.

Zaknafein could have stabbed her and ended her horror.

Instead, he spat upon her, then wiped his blades on her robes.

"Enjoy the embrace of your goddess."

CHAPTER 17

The Power of Conscience

B y the time Jarlaxle came walking around the corridor's bend, the fight was over, with his associates the only ones left upright—at least, upright and still moving, for a couple of the halflings remained as they had been, perfectly still in the continuing thrall of the priestess's debilitating spell.

With a thought, Jarlaxle willed his magical boots to click against the floor, and he sauntered over casually.

"Nice of you to join us," Zaknafein greeted him, though he didn't turn to regard his friend carefully. He stood flexing the fingers of his hand, which he had bruised against the face of an enemy.

"Well, there was a matron to be dealt with," the mercenary replied.

"And where is—?" Zaknafein asked, but bit the question short, seeing the wide-eyed expression of Arathis Hune as the rogue looked past him toward the mercenary leader.

"Far away in another dimension, yet very near," Jarlaxle said, and held forth a small circle of black cloth.

Zaknafein turned and sputtered, snorting even. "Your hair *again?*"

And despite the carnage about him, despite his uneasiness with the halfling slaves, despite the blood on his hands and blades, he had to work hard to bite back a laugh. For indeed, Jarlaxle looked ridiculous, with the little spikes of hair now blackened (no doubt from the grease he had used for the sake of vanity) and wafting lines of smoke. It might have been steam from his ears for all the joy Jarlaxle was displaying, though. It was clear that the burns on his head were more than a bit uncomfortable.

"Shut up," he said.

"Perhaps the gods are telling you that they don't like your hair," Zaknafein said anyway.

"*Shut up.*"

"I think you look rather dashing—or at least useful. Like a wind-blown torch waiting to be relit."

Jarlaxle scowled and Zaknafein laughed all the harder.

Behind him, though, Arathis Hune was not amused. "Your silly toy won't hold her," he warned. "She will dispel the magic long enough to make her escape."

Jarlaxle looked at him, then at the cloth, then back at Hune. With a shrug, he sent the cloth spinning high into the air behind him, up and up, until it slapped against the ceiling and there stuck, opened.

Matron Sheeva came tumbling out, headfirst. She flailed and, predictably, went for her house emblem to activate a levitation spell.

But Jarlaxle had already acted, drawing a wand and spitting forth a glob of goo, perfectly aimed, that caught the priestess's torso, locking her hands in place.

And she fell, head down, nearly thirty feet, to smash against the stone floor.

She had protected herself against evocation magic, against fire and cold and lightning, against arrows and bolts, against weapons edged and blunt.

But not against falling.

Yes, her protection spells absorbed the initial impact, and so her skull didn't shatter, but they were of little use as her neck was bent too quickly to the side, the bone protesting with a sharp, echoing retort.

Jarlaxle, Arathis Hune, and the Zauvirr warrior who was not writhing on the floor all winced at the sickening sound of Sheeva's neck snapping.

Not Zaknafein, though, for this was a high priestess of the Spider Queen. Killing her daughter had been satisfying, but this felt even better. He casually walked over to cut Sheeva's throat for good measure, though his blade did not sink in. Priestesses and their wards!

"Collect the trophy," Jarlaxle told Zaknafein as he walked past to look at the wounded and captured Zauvirr warriors.

With a shrug, Zaknafein moved over the fallen matron and sent his blade into a circular motion, winding up for the next blow. He stopped, however, and kicked her first to see if she would stir. She did, though with only a gurgle.

Good, he thought. He wanted her to know.

Around came his blade again, slashing down hard at the dying Sheeva, and again her magical defenses flashed and deflected it harmlessly.

"How many do you have, foul priestess?" Zaknafein muttered, his sword coming around again and again, drawing forth and expending more of the wards. With the fourth swing he drew blood across her throat, and so he pressed faster, each revolution cutting a bit deeper.

Sheeva gurgled again, more than once, and Zaknafein knew that she was feeling the pain and was realizing the horror that her life was at its end.

That made him happy. Some thought Zaknafein to be a drow of conscience and generosity, and indeed, for most, he was. But not to, *never* to, matrons of the Spider Queen.

"Put down your hands," he heard Arathis Hune say, and when his next cut took Sheeva's head from her neck, he turned about to regard his Bregan D'aerthe companion.

One of the warriors on the floor had stopped squirming but seemed to be alive. The other, the one Zaknafein had punched in the face, had rolled to his belly and set his hands as if trying to get up.

The third, the one to whom Arathis Hune was speaking, was on his knees, hands presented in the air.

"We're not going to kill you," Arathis Hune went on. "Not now, at least. In fact, there may be an opportunity for you here. You are a houseless rogue now, and a fugitive from Ched Nasad and from the new hierarchy of your own house. It would seem like you two—or three, if that one lives—have few options. However, I tell you now that Jarlaxle is one of a generous nature."

"To join with him?" the Zauvirr drow asked skeptically. "He would trust us?"

"To not trust you would imply that he fears you might do him harm," Zaknafein interceded, more than a little mockingly. "You cannot."

"Go and tend to your companions," Arathis Hune told the Zauvirr soldier. The rogue spun about and sheathed one of his blades, but kept the other in hand as he turned to the halflings, several of whom were now beginning to stir as the spells wore off.

They saw the murderous rogue coming for them. They had nowhere to run, so they cowered, expecting to die.

They cowered tighter when Zaknafein came sprinting toward them, but he turned short of the group, spinning back on Arathis Hune.

"What are you about?" he demanded.

"What do you mean?" the rogue answered.

Zaknafein drew his blades.

"Seriously, what are you about? Tell me your plan."

"My plan?" an incredulous Arathis Hune echoed. "I'll tell you what isn't my plan. I do not plan to go back to Ched Nasad. The trophy is for Matron Mother Baenre, and it is her place, not ours, to inform the Ched Nasad Ruling Council of Sheeva's fate."

"I agree."

"And I do not plan to spend seven tendays wandering the corridors of the Underdark with these wretches along."

"So let them go," Zaknafein posited.

"To kill us while we sleep?"

"You do not believe that."

Arathis Hune snorted derisively. "And you can't believe that letting them walk from this place into the open Underdark would be merciful," he said with a laugh. "I will make their deaths easy, at least." He drew his second blade and came forward.

"No," Zaknafein demanded, stepping between Arathis Hune and the cowering halflings.

"Don't be a fool," the assassin chided. "If you allow them to walk from this place, they will wander the dark tunnels helplessly until an almost certainly more horrible death befalls them. You think that preferable?"

"You are not murdering them," said Zaknafein.

"Who's talking about murder? They are *iblith*, nothing more!"

Zaknafein just shook his head and held his ground.

"Get out of my way, Zaknafein Do'Urden."

Zaknafein shook his head.

"You serve Bregan D'aerthe," Arathis Hune demanded.

"I hunt with Jarlaxle," Zaknafein corrected. "You are not killing these halflings—"

"Unless I kill you first," Arathis Hune finished the thought.

"That is usually how this plays out, yes."

"Then I shall," Arathis Hune promised and dipped a bow of challenge—and as he lowered, Zaknafein realized that Hune had rearranged his crossbow on his back, and had reloaded it, and now cleverly sprang his trap, pulling a secret cord attached to the trigger of the secured weapon to let fly.

As if he'd practiced this very movement a million times before, Zaknafein dropped to his knees and lifted his sword, held horizontally before him, straight up. The quarrel clipped the blade and flew harmlessly high.

"You can try," Zaknafein said, leaping immediately back to his feet, and just in time, for Arathis Hune had come out of his phony bow with a charge, as if in anticipation that his crossbow trick wouldn't finish off this skilled weapon master.

Zaknafein knew from the drow's expression as they engaged, though, that Arathis Hune had expected some level of wound, or at least to have caught Zaknafein off balance.

But no such luck for the assassin. Zaknafein was up to meet the charge, if a bit on his heels, his swords out before him in complete balance, turning one strike after another.

With a blinding roll and thrust of his blades, Zaknafein worked himself forward to the balls of his feet, stealing Arathis Hune's momentum, driving the rogue back to even ground.

Arathis Hune had never held the title of weapon master, but he could fight like one, surely, and he quickly accepted and countered Zaknafein's turning of the tables with equal ferocity and speed, their swords becoming a blur of ringing metal between them.

The rogue began working his right-hand blade in short circles, parrying inward.

He favored his left hand, Zaknafein realized immediately, and he let the first few parries succeed, moving his own left blade across his body slightly. Zaknafein knew the break point here, knew when his opponent would get both of his swords over to that side far enough to execute a double-thrust, or a left thrust–right slash, or whatever other combination Arathis Hune had perfected.

As the clanging swords neared that point, Zaknafein thought to parry the parry, to throw all his weight behind a counterstrike to drive his opponent all the way back to the right.

Something stopped him. Some subtle shift in Arathis Hune's feet, perhaps, or the look on the rogue's face, or the way his knuckles shifted on his circling sword.

Instead of going left, now thinking that to be exactly what Arathis Hune wanted, Zaknafein stepped back and spun down to his knees, coming fully around with his left blade diving low across to the right, his right blade lifting fast.

And just in time, and correctly angled, he knew with relief, when that lifting sword caught not the left-hand blade of Arathis Hune, but his right sword, coming across suddenly, clearly in anticipation of Zaknafein's turn, and now, because of the reversal, duck, and spin, hitting nothing but air, then being hit and carried high by the weapon master's upward block.

Arathis Hune had another counter, a clever reangling of his

circling left-hand blade that had it diving under his other extended weapon, and also under Zaknafein's block.

But that was foreseen by Zaknafein as well, and while his opponent executed it precisely and with blinding speed—and while it certainly would have finished a lesser fighter—it got nowhere near to hitting Zaknafein. Indeed, instead, the speeding weapon got hit, and forcefully, by Zaknafein's rising left-hand blade. The block caught the down-angled and thrusting sword, slapping it up against the underside of Zaknafein's blocking right-hand blade.

As if that beautiful block weren't enough, Zaknafein went a bit further. With stunning balance and practiced strength, the weapon master locked the top blade firmly in place while he jumped from knees to feet, driving upward with everything but his locked right arm.

The suddenness and ferocity of the movement turned the angle of that thrusting sword sharply, and too swiftly for Arathis Hune to adjust, and so Zaknafein's powerful move took the sword right from the rogue's hand.

He could have released it, sent it flying and spinning into the air, and such a movement would have freed that rising lower blade for a sudden outward spin and slash at Arathis Hune's vulnerable right side.

The rogue saw it and had already begun a half turn to defend.

But Zaknafein didn't release that blade, and instead slid his sword up to the hilt, caught it, and brought it rolling down and out with his own blade to become a guided spear, flying fast for the rogue's face.

Up and across came Arathis Hune's remaining sword, knocking it aside, but in behind it came the fury of Zaknafein, two swords charging ahead.

Arathis Hune parried once, twice, thrice, backpedaling with each deflection, and seemingly on the edge of disaster.

Too easy, Zaknafein silently mouthed, warning himself, and instead of taking the obvious route forward, the weapon master instinctively leaped off to the side. When he landed and turned, he nearly laughed aloud, seeing that the clever rogue had dropped caltrops in his expected path!

Undaunted, Arathis Hune went for his fallen blade, retrieving it just as Zaknafein arrived.

"How many more tricks have you to play?" Zaknafein asked, his swords working a brilliant routine of stabs from multiple angles, putting Arathis Hune on the defensive yet again. His question sounded clearly as a taunt, for by now it was obvious to both that Arathis Hune could not match Zaknafein sword against sword.

"I fight with the tools provided," Arathis Hune answered, falling into a rhythm of parries to keep Zaknafein's stings aside.

"You disappoint—" the assassin started to add, but stopped, gulping and leaping desperately as Zaknafein suddenly fell to one knee, lowering his slashing right-hand weapon. Arathis Hune tucked his legs and cleared the cut, and got his own right-hand sword down in time to intercept the backhand return slash, then up and across to turn aside Zaknafein's second sword, stabbing for his chest.

But now Zaknafein had Arathis Hune blocking twice with that one blade, and so, necessarily, dropping his left foot back a bit to keep that blade presented.

It was an advantage Zaknafein was determined not to relinquish, bearing in, working always to his opponent's right, forcing Arathis Hune to keep that one foot forward, to keep that one blade doing all the defensive work.

Knowing his off-hand was being pressed, the rogue responded with a drop turn like Zaknafein had earlier performed, summoning a globe of darkness over himself and Zaknafein as he went.

Zaknafein, seeing the first turn of the maneuver right before the light disappeared, didn't hesitate, diving high and forward, pitching a somersault right over the dropping rogue, twisting as he landed to come right in at the kneeling rogue's back.

Halfway through that turn, Zaknafein knew he had the kill. He had guessed right—Arathis Hune had dropped—and since the rogue had not gotten any blades up to hinder his dive, the drow was surely helpless.

However, just as he landed, the darkness unexpectedly went away.

He thought it Arathis Hune's doing, but it didn't matter, because darkness or no, there knelt the rogue, facing the wrong way, working his blades up and behind desperately.

Futilely.

But the rogue hadn't dispelled his darkness globe. Jarlaxle had, and Zaknafein spotted the mercenary leader back at the bend in the tunnel, two wands leveled.

Then the mere lack of magical darkness became magical light, brilliant and stinging.

Zaknafein growled and pressed on against the painful shine, determined to be done with this.

He did note a shimmer in the air ahead of him just before his stabbing sword hit a barrier, invisible but as solid as a stone wall, and he frowned. He looped his second sword out wider, thinking to come around the magical defense, but there, too, he hit the same barrier, a wall of nothingness.

Arathis Hune, his expression revealing that he believed Jarlaxle had come to his rescue, leaped up and spun about, stabbing hard for Zaknafein's face.

But his sword, too, hit the invisible wall Jarlaxle had placed between them.

"You are both stealing from me," Jarlaxle scolded. "That is something I'll not accept."

"Stealing?" Zaknafein and Arathis Hune answered together, then both looked at each other through the invisible wall and scowled.

"You are each trying to rob me of something valuable by killing the other," said Jarlaxle.

"You don't own—" Zaknafein started to protest.

"Out here, I do," Jarlaxle was quick to interrupt. "I grant you freedom from your wretched existence in exchange for your loyalty. It is a business arrangement, nothing more. Never. Forget. That!"

Zaknafein had never heard Jarlaxle speak to him quite like that before, and he didn't like it, not at all. He glared at the mercenary leader, measuring the distance to Jarlaxle and wondering if he could cover it before the too-clever drow played another of his many tricks.

"I see no priestess or wizard casting spells to control your minds, so would either of you have any explanation for why my two valued companions are trying hard to become my one valued companion?"

"I brook no murder," Zaknafein said.

"This one is less valuable than you believe," Arathis Hune said at the same time. "He is a fool of the highest order and will bring you— will bring *us* great trouble."

"It was Zaknafein who went to House Zauvirr when we two were caught," Jarlaxle reminded him.

"And Zaknafein who would let these slave halflings walk free," Arathis Hune protested. "To stab us in our sleep or to flee to gather allies!"

Jarlaxle stared hard at Arathis Hune for a few moments, digesting the words, then turned a suspicious stare upon Zaknafein.

"Is this true?"

"I brook no murder," Zaknafein said again.

"Murder?" Arathis Hune scoffed. "They are slaves! *Iblith!* Surface filth. They condemned themselves by coming to the Underdark. We do them a favor by killing them quickly."

"I brook no slavery," said Zaknafein.

"Menzoberranzan is full of slaves!" Arathis Hune protested, but Jarlaxle cut him short with an upraised hand.

"You would murder priestesses," Jarlaxle said, not quite a question.

"The Lolthian priestesses are damned by their choice and the consequences of that damnable choice," the weapon master growled.

"Yet you bed one every night," Arathis Hune quipped, and again Jarlaxle stopped him with an upraised hand, adding a stern gaze for good measure.

The slight didn't bring a wince to Zaknafein, of course. He wasn't sleeping with any Lolthian priestesses out of choice, after all.

"Did not these halflings determine their own fates when they came to the Underdark?" Jarlaxle asked.

"You do not know how they came to this place," said Zaknafein.

"What's more likely? They came to a place they almost certainly knew they couldn't survive, or that a slave trader captured them from their village above and dragged them here? They look like no adventuring band that could have traversed so far and so deep."

"Whatever the case, what would you have me do?" Jarlaxle asked Zaknafein, then he added, "And you," turning to face Arathis Hune.

"Free them," Zaknafein said.

"Kill them," Arathis Hune said at the same time.

"Free them to do what?" Jarlaxle asked.

"Or at least take them to Menzoberranzan and sell them!" Arathis Hune insisted.

"They'll not survive these tunnels," Jarlaxle continued, talking to Zaknafein alone.

"Then we take them back to their surface world and there release them," said Zaknafein.

Jarlaxle snorted, and Arathis Hune choked . . . then laughed outright at the seemingly absurd suggestion.

"We have no time for such a detour," Jarlaxle said. "We have a trophy to deliver to Matron Mother Baenre."

"Who would not be pleased to learn that we freed valuable slaves," Arathis Hune added. "Slaves Jarlaxle could sell for a tidy profit."

"Then I will buy them," said Zaknafein.

This drew a smile from Jarlaxle.

"You are an idiot!" Arathis Hune shouted at him, but Zaknafein didn't even bother to look at the assassin. The drow was talking only because Jarlaxle had prevented Zaknafein from killing him, so his were the words of a ghost at this point.

"For my share of this adventure's profits," Zaknafein told Jarlaxle. "Give them to me and show me the way to the surface."

Arathis Hune started to say something, but Jarlaxle walked over—apparently his invisible magical barrier had dissipated—to stand right before Zaknafein.

"You know not even what your share might be," he said to the weapon master.

"Enough to pay for a few scrawny halflings," Zaknafein said. He settled and locked stares with his friend, then very quietly added, "I played my role and did as demanded."

"More than that, I would admit."

"Then give me this. My share for the halflings, and show me the way that I can properly set them free."

"And then?"

"Then I return to Menzoberranzan, as pleased with the results of this expedition as is Jarlaxle."

Jarlaxle looked from Zaknafein to Arathis Hune. "We split his share?"

The rogue laughed and nodded.

"I will have from you both, then, a promise that you will not try to steal from me again. You understand my meaning."

Neither did more than grunt, and certainly it was no solid commitment. But it was as good as could be expected in the Underdark, and thus enough for Jarlaxle.

Soon after, Jarlaxle, Arathis Hune, and three former Zauvirr warriors marched again for Menzoberranzan, the mercenary leader carrying the head of Matron Sheeva Zauvirr in a sack. Jarlaxle caught Arathis Hune staring at him more than once, and he recognized the swirl of emotions in his lieutenant's glare. Arathis Hune had, until this day, been the unquestioned second in command of the small Bregan D'aerthe band, but now he was afraid that Zaknafein might be threatening that position.

Jarlaxle smiled. Arathis Hune was right, he realized, and not only because of Zaknafein's prowess with the blade and his willingness to finish the mission even when it looked like Jarlaxle and Arathis Hune had been taken off the field.

Many in Bregan D'aerthe would perform similarly, though of course none was as good with the blade as Zaknafein.

But no, that was not why Jarlaxle now believed that Zaknafein would rise to his side.

It was because Zaknafein wouldn't kill the halflings.

It was because Zaknafein was possessed of mercy.

Would Jarlaxle himself have been brave enough to champion the cause of the helpless little folk?

Inwardly, he smiled all the wider.

He smiled wider still when Zaknafein walked into the Oozing Myconid less than a tenday after Jarlaxle had delivered the head to Matron Mother Baenre and shown the three new Bregan D'aerthe soldiers to their quarters. The mercenary leader had been in the tavern every day since his return, waiting and watching.

He didn't even try to contain his smile when Zaknafein walked over to join him.

Zaknafein grabbed the back of a chair to pull it out from the table but paused, staring.

It took Jarlaxle a few moments to understand the man's confusion, but then he ran his hand over his completely healed, and completely bald, pate. Not a scar showed, and not a bump, as if the perfectly shaped head had been sculpted by the finest of Menzoberranzan's artists.

"It is becoming, is it not?" Jarlaxle asked.

Zaknafein snorted, sighed, and shook his head helplessly, but conceded, "Better than that stupid hair," as he took his seat. "I can join you?" he added as an afterthought, for he was already sitting.

"I saved that very chair for you," Jarlaxle replied with great enthusiasm and his dashing smile.

Zaknafein sighed again.

"Though I was not sure you would ever return," Jarlaxle went on. "You delivered the halflings?"

"Into an upper tunnel that led to sunlight, yes."

Jarlaxle looked at him curiously, a wry grin spreading. "Why did you come back?"

The question clearly caught Zaknafein off guard, and he sputtered a bit before replying, "Where else might I go?"

Jarlaxle just nodded and let it go at that. He was glad the weapon master had returned.

He was also a bit disappointed.

JARLAXLE'S QUESTION STAYED WITH ZAKNAFEIN ALL THE way back to House Do'Urden, and indeed, for many days afterward.

He had seen the sunlight of the surface, and though it was unpleasant to his eyes, which knew only the dim glows of the Underdark, he could not deny the allure.

He had thought of going forward into the open surface world, of leaving Menzoberranzan far and forever behind.

But how might he be received up there, where the elves were plentiful and no race held affinity to the drow?

And Malice would come for him, he knew, likely with the support of the Ruling Council, for such heresy could not stand.

Zaknafein had come back to Menzoberranzan unsure of his choice, particularly since he suspected that one excursion to be the best chance of escaping drow society he would ever know.

He feared he would regret his decision for the rest of his life.

It would prove a valid fear.

PART 4

Selflessness?

Where does the self end and the other, the community, begin?

It seems a simple, even self-evident, question, but I have come to believe that it is perhaps the most complicated investigation of all. And the most pressing one, if I am to find any true meaning in my life. Even more, on a wider level, this is the question that will determine the heart of a society, and possibly even its very life span—one way or the other.

If I were walking down the road and saw a person drowning in a pond, and I had a rope that would reach, of course I would throw it to the troubled fellow and pull him to safety.

But that is not a selfless act.

I might be called a hero for saving the person.

But that is not a heroic act.

No, that is merely the expected behavior of one worthy to live in a civilized society, and any who would not stop to help the drowning person in such a situation deserve to be shunned, at the very least.

If I were walking down a road and saw a person drowning in a pond, but I had no rope, I would dive in and swim out to try to pull the person to safety.

This is more selfless, and involves a small measure of danger.

Would I be a hero then?

Some would call me that, but the word would ring hollow in my ears. For I would have done only what I would have expected from my neighbor were I that drowning man.

This is what makes the community greater than the individual.

Suppose the drowning man was in a lake known to be inhabited by a killer gar. Suppose he was even then being attacked by such a creature. Suppose the lake was full of them, swarming, hungry.

At what point would my act of attempting to rescue him become heroic? At what point would my actions rightly earn the title of hero?

At what point would I not want my neighbors to jump into that gar-filled death trap to try to save me?

And there is a point, surely. There is a place where responsibility to self outweighs, must outweigh, responsibility to the community.

But where?

Likely, few have considered the above dilemma specifically, but the question posed is one that every person faces in his or her life, all the time. Where does one's responsibility to oneself end, and a wider responsibility to the community begin?

If I am a successful hunter and fill my winter stores, is it right and just for me to let my neighbor go hungry? If feeding my neighbor would mean rationing for me, a winter of privation but not death, is it still my duty to save the unsuccessful hunter?

I am surprised by how many people I have met who would say that it is not, that their growling belly is not worth a neighbor's life, and who justify their claim by blaming their neighbor for being less successful in the hunt.

Again, the example is extreme, but moving now toward the commonplace, toward the daily choices we all face in our lives, the choices are no less crucial. What is your responsibility beyond the self? To your partner, your children, your brothers, your parents, your cousins, your neighbors, a stranger?

These are the questions that will define you as a person, I think, more than anything else you might do.

The laws of a kingdom try to define these lines of responsibility in the daily lives of citizens. In the village of Lonelywood in Ten Towns, for example, a successful hunter is bound to share all bounty beyond one full meal a day, with any excess to be divided equally among all Lonelywood residents. But in Dougan's Hole, another of the Ten Towns of Icewind Dale, those who cannot hunt their winter food will very possibly starve, and successful hunters can defend their bounty to the death, even if that bounty is so great that much will rot when the spring melt falls across the tundra.

No one in Dougan's Hole tries to change these laws, or the common behavior that gives them credence. Certainly, though, there are folks in Bryn Shander, the hub of Ten Towns, who would like to see such changes, since the starving people of the Redwaters' towns inevitably try to make it to Bryn Shander's gates.

I prefer Lonelywood, as would my companions, for I have come to see philanthropy as ultimately self-satisfying, if not selfish!

There is in Bryn Shander an old woman who takes in the stray cats and dogs of the place. She works tirelessly feeding, grooming, hugging, and training the animals, and tries ceaselessly to find for them homes among the citizens of the town.

So dedicated is she that she eats little and sleeps less. I once asked her about it, about why she would give up that extra hour of sleep to hunt down a reported stray.

"Every hour I'm not at me work, a precious little one might die," she told me.

The people of Bryn Shander think her quite mad, and to be honest, I questioned her grasp on reality and priority myself. Until I spoke with her, and then I found in her one of the most sane and satisfied humans I have ever had the pleasure of meeting. The warmth of her heart touched me and made me know the sincerity in her smile. This was, to her, a calling, a way that she, a feeble old woman of little means, could make the world a better place.

I have met few nobles whose smiles can rival hers in sincerity.

For I see myself somewhat akin to this old woman, and more so now after my training in the monastery. The greatest lesson in that place of profound teaching was the constant reminder of how little I truly need and the mind-set to avoid the traps of acquisition.

The rich man is often owned by that which he thinks he owns.

The rich woman might elicit jealousy, and while satisfying to her, her provocation will harden the visages of those around her long before she has died.

Some people measure wealth in gold.

Others measure it in tears of those who mourn them when they have passed on.

I recognize and admit with contempt that my own preferences are not universal—not nearly—among the people I have met. Dougan's Hole is in no need of new residents, and any houses emptied by the harsh terms of that community will soon enough be full again, mostly with people grumbling about tithing or taxation, and ready to go to war with any who would demand one copper piece from them.

"If ye canno' catch yer food, ye've no right to live" is a common credo, spoken sternly about that town, and indeed, recited about all the reaches of the lake called Redwaters.

This is the ethical spectrum of reasoning beings, moving that slide between self and community.

My friend Bruenor is one of the richest kings in the region. The linked dwarven communities, from Icewind Dale to the Silver Marches to Gauntlgrym in the Crags, have come out of their wars brimming with wealth and power, and Bruenor himself already possesses a treasury that would make most Waterdhavian lords envious.

Is Bruenor bound, then, to open his gates wide to all who would come begging? How far ranges the responsibility of one who has gained so much? Farther than that of the farmer or the cobbler? If a farmer has saved a dozen silver coins and gives one to a poor man he meets at the market, should Bruenor, who has a thousand thousand times that wealth, dole out a silver to a thousand thousand needy others?

Or should he dole out even more than that, because his coins become less important to his own security and health once he has surpassed a certain point of wealth? Like dragons, the great lords of the north possess hoards of treasure beyond anything they might hope to spend in their lifetimes, or that their children could spend, or even the familial generation beyond that. Taking a silver piece from a man who has ten silvers hurts him and his family less than taking a copper piece from a family that has only ten coppers. And taking a gold piece from a woman who has ten gold means less to her family's well-being than the tithe imposed upon the man with the ten silvers.

And the rule holds true so on up the line of wealth. The more you have, the less you need, and once all the basic needs are met, the luxuries become redundant and indeed flatten the joy of purchase.

Menzoberranzan is not unlike Dougan's Hole. There is never enough gold and gems and jewels to satisfy the insatiable greed of the matrons. In Menzoberranzan, wealth is power, and power is all. And wealth is station, which implies more than power. For station breeds envy, and to the drow of my homeland, the envy of others is among life's greatest joys.

This philosophy of life seems foolhardy to me.

A beggar at the gates of House Baenre will be killed or enslaved.

A beggar at the gates of Gauntlgrym will find a hot meal and a bed.

This is why King Bruenor is my friend.

—Drizzt Do'Urden

CHAPTER 18

THE YEAR OF DWARVENKIND REBORN
DALERECKONING 1488

The Reality of Perception

Are you mad?" Kimmuriel replied to Jarlaxle after the mercenary leader's latest seemingly preposterous request.

Jarlaxle moved as if to respond, but Kimmuriel held up his hand and shook his head. "Bother not with the words," the psionicist said. "I already know that answer."

"Truly you wound me, my friend."

"I wound you, but you're to get me killed, beyond doubt," said Kimmuriel.

"Gromph is not going to kill you," Jarlaxle assured him. "After feeling the power of the illithid hive flowing through him to destroy Demogorgon, he is more likely to cast enchantments of love upon you than to lob fireballs your way."

"Thrilling," Kimmuriel dryly replied.

"He would give you a room at the Hosttower."

"To be surrounded by insipid wizards and their limitations?"

Jarlaxle sighed in surrender.

"My comment is not about Gromph, in any case," said Kimmuriel.

"This game you ask me to play now, I fear, is with a creature more dangerous than the former archmage, and one with less to gain by keeping me alive."

"Perhaps, but it is critical, or I would not ask. Yvonnel is much more than she appears, and her hand in all of this is larger than we understand. My instincts scream this to me, and I have learned to listen to them."

"You think her a handmaiden in disguise?" Kimmuriel asked.

Jarlaxle arched his eyebrows. "More."

It took a moment for that to sink in to the psionicist. "Lolth?" he cried. "You think Yvonnel a manifestation of Lady Lolth herself? You would have me *spy* upon Lolth?

"Are you *mad*?"

"To answer your last question, I will be honest: possibly. As for the first, I simply do not know," Jarlaxle admitted. "But, as pertains to the second, I think we must try to know, don't you?"

Kimmuriel replied, "I think we should move to the far ends of Faerun."

"BUT IT IS JUST AN ILLUSION," DRIZZT SAID.

Yvonnel smiled coyly. "I thought you would enjoy them." To accentuate, she batted "them," her eyes, which were now violet in hue, much like Drizzt's own, an aberration incredibly rare among the drow.

"They are beautiful," Drizzt admitted. "Everything about you is beautiful to anyone who looks upon you. That is your game, is it not? You maintain a magical illusion to let the viewer see what most pleases him or her when looking upon you."

"No," she said. "No more. At one time I played that game, as I willingly admitted to you. It was indeed a conscious manipulation. Those looking upon me couldn't help but treat me a bit better than they would another more mundane and, to them, less attractive person. I played on perception for advantage."

"That is dishonest."

"Is it? Do you not play upon your reputation for advantage? Does it not aid you when your opponents know that they are in battle with a legendary swordsman? Or even just being a drow. Certainly, it holds great disadvantages in some areas, but do you not think that many of Jarlaxle's business partners take greater care because of his skin and because of their fear of what retribution might mean?"

Drizzt fumbled for a response, then blurted, "This is different."

"No, it's not," Yvonnel insisted. "Are there not nights when Catti-brie puts on special clothes, or wears her hair just so? Do you not do the same? This is simply how I choose to appear. And to appear to all; no more is there a malleable illusion from viewer to viewer."

"But is it your natural appearance?"

"Does that matter?"

Drizzt started to answer, but he knew he was caught here and so he just shrugged.

"People sculpt their bodies, style their hair, choose their clothes, paint their faces—everything!—to shape their appearance. I have done nothing different." She flashed that coy smile again. "I just have better tools."

Drizzt laughed despite himself. He wanted to find some pedestal upon which to make a stand, but there was none. He thought of his own vanity, of how he worked his muscles so tirelessly each and every morning. Yes, most of that was practical and came from a drive to be the perfect swordsman so that he could use his skills to the greater good. All of that was true.

Yet so was his personal pleasure in sculpting those lean muscles. How many times had he caught Catti-brie spying on him during his morning routines, and how hard had it been to keep the grin off his face when he knew that she was there watching from behind a shrub?

"I struggled with this greatly in the recent past," Drizzt reminded her, referring to the affliction he had suffered that had blurred the line between reality and illusion, an illness of the mind wrought by the thinning of the Faerzress in the Underdark.

"This was your madness," Yvonnel agreed. "Where did perception end and reality begin? You could not tell, and so you could not trust that anything around you, even those you loved, was real."

"And yet, even if they were not real, the illusion, the perception that I had that these were indeed my friends, made them real to me. I lay with Catti-brie, in my mind, in my heart."

"Perception is reality, Drizzt Do'Urden," Yvonnel stated.

"There is no objective truth?"

"Of course there is! But until a falsehood is uncovered, the reality is what you perceive it to be. You cannot separate the two without a reveal. That you tried to do so was your madness."

Drizzt considered that for a few heartbeats, then laughed. "Are you warning me, lady?"

"No," Yvonnel said, and Drizzt could detect no insincerity there. "And now I tell you that Zaknafein is real. He is the same man who sacrificed himself so that you could walk from Menzoberranzan, then again when he was sent as an undead monster to kill you. The conscious being inhabiting that drow coil is Zaknafein, your father."

Drizzt nodded for a long while, replaying all of Yvonnel's contributions to this unexpected conversation in Bleeding Vines. He stopped, finally, and stared at the woman.

"I like your eyes," he admitted, and Yvonnel smiled.

"CAN YOU TELL?" KIMMURIEL ASKED JARLAXLE, WHO PEERED through his magical eyepatch to gain a true vision of the woman in the psionicist's scrying mirror. The two were in a private room in Twelve Hands, a tavern, inn, and stable in the halfling town of Bleeding Vines.

"No magic," he said, shaking his head and seeming quite confused by that. "This is how Yvonnel now appears. Her true image."

"But one altered by magic, as she admitted regarding her eyes," said Kimmuriel.

This elicited another shrug from his companion. "She chose her appearance and made it so, but at least the continual illusion, showing different things to different onlookers, is no more."

"You think that important?"

Jarlaxle paused, but then nodded. "I do not know why," he admitted. "But now she seems to me more true, more real, more . . ."

"More mortal?"

"Yes. Perhaps that is the best word for it. And it makes sense, given her decision to leave Menzoberranzan and come to this place. In Menzoberranzan, she could have become the matron mother. After she saved the city from Demogorgon, none, certainly not that pathetic Quenthel, would have dared stand against her. She could have lived as a goddess, yet here she stands, with us."

Kimmuriel didn't argue the point. He glanced back over his shoulder, then nodded his chin to draw Jarlaxle's attention to the image.

"She leaves him," the psionicist said.

Jarlaxle tipped his cap in appreciation of Kimmuriel's extraordinary powers.

"We would do well to learn the maneuvers of the drow houses regarding all of this," Jarlaxle stated.

"Isn't that why you sent Zaknafein?"

"To better learn of House Hunzrin's dealings in Waterdeep, yes. But I wonder now if this is more than coincidence that brings them to our particular region at this particular time."

"The great powers of Menzoberranzan would not come back at this time, not after the confrontation between Drizzt and the avatar of Lolth in the tunnels of the Bloodstone Lands, and surely not after the destruction of Demogorgon through the instrument of Drizzt in full view of the entire city. They just let Drizzt go. They're not going to come after him now, and if they were, wouldn't they just use this Yvonnel creature to get what they want?"

"It's more complicated than that."

"Isn't is always?" Kimmuriel asked dryly.

"Just the way Lolth likes it," Jarlaxle said. "And yes, you're correct that the city would not come forth at this time. But there are opportunistic matrons looking for advantage. Always. With all that has happened—with Drizzt, with Zaknafein, with our own growing alliances here—some might see a chance for advancement."

"Not Baenre," said Kimmuriel. "Not now, in the way you fear, at least. Yvonnel is Baenre, as is Gromph, and he visits—"

"You know of whom I speak," Jarlaxle interrupted. "And so you know your next task."

"Task? You address me as if I am in your thrall."

"Not thrall. But we can agree that you have a meeting, yes?"

"Ash'ala Melarn," Kimmuriel conceded. "She is to convene with Matron Zeerith Do'Urden soon, I am told, to determine if the former relationship between House Melarn and House Xorlarrin, which is now House Do'Urden, is beyond repair. I will find her in a quiet corridor after she sits with Matron Zeerith."

"In a space where she cannot be detected," Jarlaxle corrected. "In a dimension of your own making where no others can possibly hear. It is that important."

Kimmuriel nodded. "I will inquire of Ash'ala, in extreme privacy."

Jarlaxle tipped his cap again and rushed out of the tavern. He caught up to Yvonnel outside Drizzt's small house in the courtyard of Regis and Donnola's villa.

"How went your seduction?" he asked, approaching.

Yvonnel tilted her head and stared at him curiously.

"That is what all of this is about, is it not?" he pressed, falling into step beside the undeniably beautiful young drow woman.

"All of what?"

"Well, now, your appearance. Those eyes!"

"I'll not deny the symbolism of my choice."

"Or that they would please Drizzt?" Jarlaxle slyly remarked.

Yvonnel chuckled and offered a coy shrug.

"And the return of Zaknafein?" Jarlaxle asked, his voice suddenly low and serious.

"What of it?" Yvonnel replied, seeming genuinely surprised—but of course, she was very good at that kind of misdirection, so much like her namesake, Jarlaxle's mother.

"Did that not please Drizzt?"

"Don't dance, Uncle," said the daughter of Gromph, and Jarlaxle stiffened at the open acknowledgment of their familial connection.

"Very well, then. You brought him back to life."

Yvonnel scoffed.

"I know not how you did it, but you did, and this all seems a winding game to seduce Drizzt," he accused. "You heard Drizzt tell Lolth that if she was worth his worship, she would have returned Zaknafein without being asked." He stared at her hard, and reminded her, "You weren't asked."

"You think I want Drizzt to worship me?"

"To love you, then."

Yvonnel shrugged, but didn't shake her head to deny it. "A dark elf lives a long life. A human, not so long."

"Less long if she is killed by an enemy."

Yvonnel stopped and turned to face Jarlaxle directly, and when he turned to square up, she slapped him across the face.

"I am not Catti-brie's enemy and she is not mine," she said through gritted teeth. "I would not take the wife, the love, from Drizzt, even if she were."

"But you won't deny that he intrigues you."

"I won't."

It was so simply admitted, without the slightest hesitation or shame.

"And so Zaknafein's return," Jarlaxle reasoned.

"You keep saying that, but I know that you have no evidence, because none exists." She shrugged again. "Zaknafein has returned through divine intervention, it would seem, and I am no deity. Look to Mielikki, who returned to Drizzt his Companions of the Hall."

"That was planned by Mielikki from the beginning."

"Then look to Lolth," Yvonnel said. "Though Mielikki could still be the catalyst."

"Why?" Jarlaxle asked, truly at a loss. "Do you believe the nonsense that Drizzt will change her? That's what you told me when you announced the return of Zaknafein, yes? That Drizzt thinks he can change Lolth. Is that—"

"Perhaps the gods are gods because they can better see into the future to understand the ramifications of the actions of the present," Yvonnel interrupted. "And thus, they do not err for shortsightedness. I've thought much on this—I am uniquely equipped for this particular question, I believe—and it seems reasonable to me that Lolth under-stands the inevitability of our revolution, Jarlaxle, and understands that she cannot stop it."

"Inevitability?" Jarlaxle said with a snort. "I wish I shared your confidence."

"The changes in Menzoberranzan have begun. They will be there ever, whether they move forward now or not. Lolth knows this, and knows, too, that your role in it has been enormous."

"Please don't say that to anyone," Jarlaxle said, and he was only partially joking. The last thing he wanted was to see his own reflection in the spider eyes of Lady Lolth.

"Your city of Luskan is a grave threat to the old order," Yvonnel said. "The most powerful word in the drow language is *iblith*. Deni-gration of races who are different, of the other, is central to drow arrogance, and drow arrogance is rooted in the power and cruelty of the Spider Queen. But consider what you have accomplished in the City of Sails, Jarlaxle."

"I control it from the shadows, through a drow high captain who masquerades as a human," Jarlaxle protested. "That is no new trick for emissaries from Menzoberranzan."

Yvonnel laughed at him. "You are speaking of the past. In Luskan, the drow mingle openly with the surface dwellers—even powerful ones. In the new Hosttower of the Arcane, Gromph Baenre, the for-mer archmage of Menzoberranzan, studies beside Penelope Harpell, and Netherese lords, and wizards and sorcerers of great power from other races. The only one who thinks Beniago's disguise as High Cap-tain Kurth remains intact is you, apparently. All of King Bruenor's court and most of his city know the true power of Luskan. As do the halflings of this fine village."

"And so? What grave threat—"

"Because Lolth knows, as do you, that familiarity does not breed contempt among the reasoning races. Nay, it *erases* prejudice. Drizzt Do'Urden's greatest heresy was not that he walked out of Menzober-ranzan, but rather that he made himself welcome in Silverymoon and

Waterdeep. That is the threat to her. How does she keep her minions of the Underdark satisfied if there is a world accessible to them that isn't darkness and hatred and bloodshed?"

"She didn't kill Drizzt," Jarlaxle reminded. "An easy fix."

"Not so easy, no. Because she knew what that would bring. The symbol of Drizzt Do'Urden would become more powerful in martyr-dom. She didn't kill Drizzt because she feared the consequences."

"So she returned Zaknafein?"

Yvonnel shrugged again, wearing an expression of helpless bewil-derment, and Jarlaxle could only nod and try to sort it out. If indeed it was Lolth who had returned Zaknafein to Drizzt, was this the god-dess's way of admitting the inevitable? Of trying to hold on to her supporters—for what is a god without worshipers?—in a preemptive strike of kindness and contrition?

"It cannot be!" he blurted, his mind unable to make that leap.

"But it surely seems to be," said Yvonnel. "Especially to me, and I think I am a better judge of this particular situation than you are."

That set Jarlaxle back on his heels, for he prided himself on his abil-ity to evaluate and understand the rhythms of the world around him.

Yvonnel just shrugged yet again against that look of astonishment. "I have come to see time itself in a different manner," she explained, and she offered a self-deprecating chuckle. "My memories are older than my body, and my consciousness, by millennia! You cannot understand what that means, my uncle."

"I am not unversed in the past, and not so young," he replied. "Remember: I knew the person those memories came from—I share some of them."

"It is not the same. Not remotely. These are not simple tales told to me in the songs of a bard, even if those words all rang true. Nay, these are not just memories of a distant past, either. They are the experi-ences of a distant past that have become *new* memories to me, as if the events of a thousand years ago are only a few years removed from now.

"I can look back to Matron Mother Baenre's earliest fights and feel the wounds and smell the blood," she continued, and suddenly

Yvonnel seemed to be talking as much to herself as to Jarlaxle, as if her epiphany was finally playing out before her. "They're not merely memories! I can look back at Baenre's lovemaking and live it in my mind as vividly as if it had been me riding a partner and not my namesake. Vividly! I know, I experience, every feeling, even the great release, that Baenre found in those encounters. And not as if I am a voyeur to the scene, do you understand?"

"I'm not sure I want to."

"I know more than what she saw or what she felt," Yvonnel tried to explain. "I know, too, every conjured image, every exciting thought, in Baenre's mind when she drove herself to sexual ecstasy. I wish I did not, but . . ."

Jarlaxle was almost at a loss for words. "Did the illithid put more into your mind than just the memories of Matron Mother Baenre? Are you possessed, do you fear? Perhaps Kimmuriel—"

"No, it is not a possession, and not a haunting," Yvonnel calmly replied. "In the end, and despite the insult to certain sensibilities, it is a gift. With thousands of years of experiences to draw upon— experiences that seem so fresh to me—I feel that I will be granted from this a measure of foresight beyond . . . anyone. Older people are considered wiser because they have seen the outcomes in similar situations, and so the intimacy of Yvonnel the Eternal's imparted memories, feelings, revelations, and experience have given to me her wisdom."

"Is that why you can so patiently wait to see if Drizzt becomes available to you?"

Yvonnel laughed and Jarlaxle joined her. It seemed such a trite example of the horizons she might know.

Yet Jarlaxle joined her in that laughter because he recognized the sincerity behind it. He understood that Yvonnel was formidable in more than magic. In diplomacy and in deception, this was a dangerous woman, and yet this explanation, this line of reasoning, resonated as very convincing to Jarlaxle.

It all . . . fit. Somehow, it all seemed to click into Jarlaxle's wider understanding of the world. There was indeed a consistency in this incredibly unusual circumstance of Yvonnel.

He wasn't sure whether he believed her stated ignorance about Zaknafein's return—wasn't even certain that she had not facilitated that event.

But somehow, it didn't matter to him.

CHAPTER 19

Weapon Master

With Braelin and Jeyrelle Fey close behind, and another half dozen Bregan D'aerthe warriors following in the shadows, Zaknafein led his team through the tunnels of the upper Underdark, using every skill he had worked so hard to perfect. It had been nearly two centuries since he had done this, but by Zaknafein's internal clock, only a very short time had elapsed. These were not distant memories to him—he felt more as if he had been transported forward in time than that he had been absent from this place for decades.

He moved to one corner, three passages looming ahead, and closed his eyes, visualizing the model Jarlaxle had constructed back in Luskan before sending him forth. He reflexively put his hand on the folded map he now carried in his pocket . . . only to pull it away.

He had done his preparations and knew the way. He didn't need the map.

He signaled to his team to follow at length, then slipped across the entrances of the two nearest tunnels to the third, which would take him to the south along the coast, not far from the sewers of Waterdeep.

He sensed movement up ahead and fell into a crouch along the side of the natural tunnel, blending in seamlessly with the jags in the stone. Up ahead, he saw a lifted arm, just that, fingers waggling in the silent drow code.

Zaknafein stood up and brushed himself off, and the newcomer approached.

"Valas Hune, I presume," the weapon master stated. He lifted his hand to signal his band to remain back in the shadows.

"Well met, Zaknafein," the rogue replied. "Jarlaxle informed you that we would meet at this place?"

"Somewhere around here, though I am not familiar with these tunnels," Zaknafein replied, not wanting to tip his hand here, particularly given the last name of this drow.

"You are on the correct path, and before the day is through you will come to a region where the natural corridors intersect with worked stone," Valas Hune explained. "These are the Waterdeep sewers, and in this area you will find the Hunzrin merchants."

"One does not find a drow," Zaknafein said, remembering another place and another time, and an answer to a question posed. He spent a moment thinking of that adventure, then looked back to see Valas Hune eyeing him curiously. "It does not matter," Zaknafein said. "Just an old joke."

The rogue didn't blink.

"Do you have something for me?" Zaknafein asked.

Valas Hune nodded and slid a pack from his shoulder. From inside, he produced a small crystalline globe, one that fit neatly into the palm of his hand.

Zaknafein peered closer at the object, noting what looked like tiny stars floating and darting within the globe.

Valas Hune handed it to him.

"The command is 'Rumblebelly,' for some reason," the rogue explained as soon as he was no longer holding the item. "But do not invoke the magic until you are ready to fully use it. The item is charged, and each recharge is quite expensive."

"Is that not the nickname of my son's halfling friend?" Zaknafein asked.

"Is it? Well, then, perhaps the word is appropriate."

Recalling again that long-ago incident, Zaknafein smiled.

"I am told by Jarlaxle that you knew my grandfather," Valas Hune said.

Zaknafein stared at him hard. "I did."

"Then perhaps one day soon, we will share drinks in One-Eyed Jax and you can tell me all about him."

"Better to not have that conversation over potent drinks."

Now it was Valas Hune's turn to stare. "But you knew Arathis Hune?"

"I knew him better than he knew I knew him," Zaknafein replied evenly, his face and voice staid and serious. "And so he was surprised that I was not surprised when he crept up behind me with a bared dagger."

Valas Hune fell back a step, his hand reflexively going to his belt.

"He was of Bregan D'aerthe," the rogue said.

"So are you," Zaknafein said—a warning, since he was then staring at Valas Hune's sword hand.

"I would still have you tell me about him," Valas Hune said, relaxing.

"I didn't much like him."

"So I gather. Still. Perhaps your tales will allow me to walk better around Zaknafein."

"One that does not approach from behind is always preferred."

The two locked stares for a long and tense while, then Valas Hune took another step away and dropped a bow.

"Until we meet in Luskan, then," he said.

"You are not joining my adventure?" Zaknafein asked.

"I will be about."

"Ah. Jarlaxle has told you to hold back and watch, to report back to him in case I and my party are destroyed."

Valas Hune shrugged. "The Hunzrins are formidable and know the region very well. I doubt you'll even find them."

"I won't," Zaknafein replied. "After all, how does one find a drow?"

Once again the reference was lost on Valas Hune, and he just shrugged, took one last look at Zaknafein, and—in the blink of an eye—was gone.

Zaknafein measured the skill of the retreat, of how easily and completely, perhaps even magically, Valas Hune had disappeared from sight.

It seemed so very familiar to him. He had seen such skill before.

He hoped that this particular point of history wouldn't repeat.

"YOU ARE CERTAIN OF THIS?" ESKAVIDNE ASKED FOR THE third time. She was in the summoning chamber of House Melarn, alone with Matron Zhindia, and in her drow form.

"I have prayed," Matron Zhindia Melarn calmly replied.

"You ask for much. The price will be high."

"The reward will be the outcome," Matron Zhindia said. "More than worth the effort to you. The goddess will know of your contribution."

"You assume that such a reward is desired."

"I am devoted to Lady Lolth, and only to Lady Lolth. I have prayed."

"I have not told you the Spider Queen's desires," Eskavidne reminded her.

"Then you would not like a bit of the credit?" Matron Zhindia asked slyly.

"That is not for you to know," the handmaiden replied with equal aplomb. "Lady Lolth will know of my actions should I grant you that which you now beg. Of course she will. One cannot move such powerful toys about without notice."

"You will ask her permission?"

"I do not need her permission," Eskavidne said. "Nor do you, nor would it be denied or granted if you asked. The webs of chaos are not to be sorted for you by the Spider Queen. They are for you to decipher, rightly or wrongly, and take the blessing if rightly and the consequence if wrongly. It wouldn't be any fun otherwise, would it?"

Matron Zhindia closed her eyes and folded her arms comfortably over her chest, confident and at ease. "The webs of Drizzt Do'Urden," she said. "The War of the Silver Marches, the demons in the streets of Menzoberranzan, the destruction of Demogorgon at the gates of Menzoberranzan, the fall of Q'Xorlarrin to the dwarven friends of Drizzt . . . and with the help of Drizzt, of course. Always Drizzt! So many webs, and I have now found a strand to weave one of my own, and it is a good one, handmaiden. One that will, at last, finish the tale of the heretic."

"So you hope," Eskavidne said with a coy chuckle.

Matron Zhindia cast a stern look at the yochlol. "Hope implies doubt. I do not doubt. I have prayed. I have learned. I *believe*."

Eskavidne nodded. "And so you assume all the responsibility."

Matron Zhindia smiled.

"I will grant your request, Matron," the handmaiden said. "I will deliver the . . . diabolical toys to you, and forthwith. I hope that they will serve you well. And if they do not, if your web is not one of Lolth's desires, I will enjoy watching these gifts turn upon you, do not doubt."

"I have prayed," Matron Zhindia replied, smiling.

"YOU DON'T, VALAS HUNE. YOU DON'T FIND A DROW," ZAK-nafein whispered under his breath soon after he had parted ways with the rogue. He set the magical globe down on the floor. He feared it would roll away, for the natural stone surface was not level, but as he let go of it, the item didn't shift at all.

It took Zaknafein a long while to trust in that stability, but eventually he moved his hands back, knelt before the globe, and commanded it, "Rumblebelly."

The floating bits of light in the globe began to swirl and spin and coalesce, emanating an outward glow. Fearful of being revealed out in the open, Zaknafein moved away, scrambling over a couple of stones to exit the shallow alcove he had chosen for his trap.

When he looked back, his jaw slid open, for the magical globe was projecting images now. The item itself appeared to be gone, buried under a small cooking fire, and around that fire sat a handful of halflings, looking very much like the band Jarlaxle, Zaknafein, and Arathis Hune had used to lure Sheeva Zauvirr.

"You let the drow find you." Zaknafein motioned to his two nearest companions, Braelin Janquay and Egalavin Zauvirr, that latter of which had been on the other end of this trap those centuries before, and had since served well in the ranks of Bregan D'aerthe.

The three moved off into the shadows and waited, and Zaknafein wished that he also had Jarlaxle's portable hole along.

He had chosen this place carefully. Every tunnel, every possible approach, was now being watched by a pair of Bregan D'aerthe scouts, and the whole spiderweb of tunnels within those scouting positions was interconnected, thus word could be relayed to all of the party in short order.

Now they just had to wait.

Not always the easiest of tasks.

The day passed, and another, and a third after that. They had visitors—a mischief of giant rats, a cloud of bats, three different carrion crawlers, even a displacer beast—but none took interest in the scene of encamped halflings, and they were easily turned aside by the skilled drow.

Zaknafein had no idea how long the magic of the globe would last, but it hadn't dimmed, and thus they went into the fourth day, sitting and waiting and watching.

That day they were at last rewarded, as signals passed along the line that a drow troop, including at least three priestesses, was approaching from the south.

Zaknafein, nearest the illusion, crouched, with Braelin and Egalavin behind him, none with weapons in hand, though all had hands near those blades and crossbows and such. Zaknafein even gripped the handle of the whip on his right hip more than once, while his free left hand signaled a reminder to his two companions that this was a mission of parlay.

Still, one could never be too careful when dealing with priestesses, particularly high priestesses. No drow woman ever gained such a title because she was honest and kind.

With startling ferocity, the area before the three exploded in movement as a band of a half dozen net-carrying bugbears appeared as if out of nowhere and charged the halfling camp. So great was the illusion that the tall and hairy beasts didn't detect it as they came right upon the camp, throwing their nets wide and leaping at the halfling images with clubs in hand.

"Halt!" Zaknafein commanded, leaping from concealment, right hand pulling forth the whip, left grabbing the hilt of his sword, sheathed diagonally down his back from behind his left shoulder. He didn't draw the sword as he approached, though. Not yet.

The bugbears swung about, roaring in protest.

"Halt!" Zaknafein ordered again, aiming the command particularly at the closest one.

But the fool charged at him, hoisting a huge club up over its head in both hands, a weapon with such long reach that it could crush him before he was close enough for a sword strike.

Zaknafein, however, had a longer weapon still.

He cracked the whip with blinding speed and accuracy, bringing it above the seven-foot-tall creature's head to wrap about and entangle the lifted arms, with the tip coming back around to snap right in the bugbear's face. Zaknafein didn't call upon the plane-ripping power of the item, not against a mere bugbear, but it wasn't necessary anyway.

The creature stumbled and tugged, and stumbled off balance when the whip fell slack. One long stride let it set its feet firmly, though, and it brought its tangled arms down and pulled them wide, looking up only then to see if it could rip apart the ambusher.

But the ambusher wasn't there.

No, Zaknafein had moved simultaneously with that awkward bugbear stride, out of the creature's field of vision, and at the same instant the bugbear began to turn, feeling the whip tugging it from behind, Zaknafein's fine sword slid into its back, severing its spine with ease.

And Zaknafein, completely balanced, yanked the whip hard as

the bugbear started to fall forward, and with just the right angle and leverage to send the monster spinning, freeing his whip, which then went out immediately behind him, cracking once and again. It caught two other bugbears in the face with just the barest adjustment of his wrist, stopping them both in their tracks.

"What is the meaning of this?" a female voice yelled, and into the chamber came a host of Hunzrin drow: a high priestess flanked by two other clerics and a handful of drow men behind them.

But from every tunnel approach came more drow, Zaknafein's band, hand crossbows leveled, and behind Zaknafein came more: Braelin, Egalavin, and a third, Valas Hune, who appeared as if out of nowhere.

"Charri Hunzrin!" Valas Hune yelled over Zaknafein's attempted response.

The high priestess held back her charges and stared at the rogue, who stood with no weapons in hand, a disarming smile on his face.

"We are not here to do battle," Valas Hune assured her. "You know me, High Priestess, and know who I represent."

Zaknafein glanced back at the rogue only briefly, his expression conveying that he was less than amused. He knew he should have been glad for the intervention, but before him stood three priestesses. Couldn't he dispatch them and get the needed information from the remaining men?

"Yet battle was done, I see," Charri Hunzrin replied, motioning to the downed bugbear.

"Goblinkin," Zaknafein said, and spat on the corpse.

"Silence, houseless wretch," Charri Hunzrin scolded. Turning back to Valas Hune, she said, "Explain. And quickly, else I will punish this one severely instead of taking coin to pay for the dead slave."

"Coin?" Zaknafein echoed with a snort.

From her hip the high priestess produced a whip of her own, one with three living serpents, writhing and coiling, eager to strike.

"Don't kill him, I beg," said Valas Hune. "He is inexperienced and a bit of a fool, but he shows promise."

Zaknafein sighed and glanced back at the rogue once more.

"He could use a lesson, though, if you feel it necessary," Valas Hune then added, to the shock of everyone listening.

Charri Hunzrin howled and lifted her deadly scourge.

But Zaknafein had caught on to Valas Hune's plan. More important, he was quicker than the priestess, so much quicker than she could have ever anticipated, and his whip shot across suddenly, cracking right across the writhing serpents of Charri's scourge, and this time the weapon master did cut a line through the fabric of the multiverse to set loose the elemental Plane of Fire, a sizzling and angry white-hot rift that conflagrated the serpents immediately, giving Charri a writhing three-headed torch.

Everyone in the room gasped, except for Zaknafein and Valas Hune, and while Zaknafein used the distraction to leap forward into a roll, Valas Hune merely laughed.

The high priestess tried to respond with her scourge, but the serpents were quite dead already, just three flaking, smoking, limp cords that offered no bite at all.

Out of the roll, Zaknafein came up with his sword tip planted firmly against Charri Hunzrin's neck. He stared at her with eyes that promised murder.

"How many wards have you enacted, priestess?" he asked, and his red eyes sparkled. "Jarlaxle gave me this sword and promised me that no magical barriers would stop its bite. Would you like to learn the truth of his boast?" Zaknafein kept his expression quite steady here, with just a hint of eagerness evident to strengthen his bluff, for Jarlaxle had told him no such thing and while this sword was indeed quite fine, there was no such enchantment upon it.

"Enough! Enough!" Valas Hune demanded, coming forward and waving his arms at all of the potential combatants. "We have come only for information."

"And will pay for it," Charri Hunzrin dared to snap back at him.

"I can make a better deal with the women flanking you," Zaknafein warned.

"Call off your dog," Charri said to Valas Hune.

"You haven't figured it out yet?" the rogue replied.

The priestess eyed Valas Hune curiously for just a moment, then turned back, and the blood drained from Charri Hunzrin's face when she truly noted Zaknafein. When she looked at him as not just another male. When she, at last, came to understand the true identity of the murderer crouched before her.

She swallowed hard—Zaknafein felt his sword tip shift with the movement of her throat, and that brought him great satisfaction.

"I am no enemy to Jarlaxle and Bregan D'aerthe," she said.

It occurred to Zaknafein that this was the first time in his life that he had a drawn blade in range of a priestess of Lolth, other than Matron Simfray and Matron Malice Do'Urden, and had not struck. His grin reflected that as he withdrew the blade just a bit.

"What do you want?" High Priestess Charri Hunzrin asked, aiming her stare and words at Valas Hune.

"Information. That is all," the rogue answered.

"You will pay for it," Charri demanded again, apparently recovering her nerve. "And pay for my scourge."

Zaknafein lifted an eyebrow, and with that little gesture conveyed quite clearly that he would happily spring upon the impertinent witch and murder her most horribly just for continually bringing up payment when she had no leverage.

"Of course we will," said Valas Hune from behind him, and when the jingle of coins sounded, Zaknafein rolled his eyes at how quickly the other drow gave in.

Valas Hune came forward with a heavy sack. When he let it fall to the ground, some of the contents, gold coins, spilled out.

"Jarlaxle is always fair, High Priestess," Valas Hune said with a bow. "Ever has he valued the friendship of House Hunzrin above almost every other house." Then, tipping his hand regarding the information, he added, "I would have brought gems and jewels, but it seems that House Hunzrin is flush with those at this time."

"Not so much," Charri Hunzrin replied. She glared at Zaknafein. "Put that blade away!"

He did, but made a show of it, just so it was clear how close to death she was at his hands. As he stepped back, he couldn't help but feel quite unsatisfied.

But this was business, Jarlaxle's business, and Zaknafein knew his place.

"YOU ARE DISAPPOINTED BECAUSE YOU DID NOT GET TO murder a priestess," Jarlaxle observed when Zaknafein walked into his room at Twelve Hands.

The weapon master snorted but didn't otherwise answer, recognizing that this was Jarlaxle's roundabout way of letting him know that he had already heard some reports of the meeting, though his party had come straight back here with all speed.

"The Hunzrins know House Margaster," he explained to the mercenary leader. "They have bought many gemstones from High Priestess Charri and her agents. Dozens, including at least one major gemstone, perhaps more."

"Phylacteries, you mean, and major demons."

Zaknafein shrugged, conceding that Jarlaxle knew much more about this than he did.

"When Matron Mother Baenre invited demons into Menzoberranzan, when the Faerzress barrier between the Underdark and the lower planes had thinned, the streets of the city teemed with those foul denizens."

"Why would she do that?" Zaknafein asked.

"Quenthel believed that it harkened back to a glorious time of Menzoberranzan's past," Jarlaxle explained. "And also, it allowed her to strengthen her grip upon the city. The constant threat of uncontrolled demons brought several houses closer to her side. It was a brilliant plan to hold power tighter, even if many of our kin suffered for it."

"Nothing strengthens a queen more than an outside threat, even if she's the one who introduced it, I guess," Zaknafein said, shaking his head.

"Preservation of the tribe trumps all," Jarlaxle agreed. "There is also the not-so-little matter that many of the matrons and their high priestesses figured out that there was value in capturing those demons."

"To put them into phylacteries that the Hunzrins could sell on the surface world to unsuspecting *iblith*," Zaknafein reasoned. He shook his head at the diabolical planning. It was indeed so very . . . drow.

Zaknafein's face went very serious then, however, and he stared hard at Jarlaxle. "And Bregan D'aerthe?"

"What about us?"

"Have you . . . have we, engaged in such trade?"

"No," Jarlaxle answered without the slightest hesitation. "No, never. These phylacteries are poison. They will entrap the innocent and spread death, perhaps uncontrollably."

"But the profit," Zaknafein said teasingly.

Jarlaxle wouldn't take the bait, and shook his head resolutely. Zaknafein nodded, glad of that, because there were moral lines he would not cross, and acts that he knew his son simply would not tolerate, even from someone Drizzt called a friend.

He started to explain his relief, but didn't get the first word out of his mouth before he realized the look of horror on Jarlaxle's face.

"What is it?" Zaknafein asked.

"Dwarves," Jarlaxle replied, looking past Zaknafein, off into the distance, as if he was sorting through something.

"This Clan Stoneshaft?"

"No," said Jarlaxle. "In the Bloodstone Lands, the Hunzrins sold gems to dwarves, except they weren't dwarves at all, but strange creatures posing as dwarves when not in their usual giant form."

"Spriggans," Zaknafein said, and Jarlaxle nodded. "Do you think Clan Stoneshaft to be spriggans?"

Jarlaxle shook his head. "It doesn't matter. I was just reminded that Charri Hunzrin had dealt with dwarves before."

"She has been selling her wares to this House Margaster, so she admitted," Zaknafein replied. "She knows their nobles, and has dealt with them directly, if discreetly."

"But House Margaster is intimately tied to Clan Stoneshaft."

"How do you know?"

"Because they used those dwarves to wash their platinum and gold from the eyes of the other Waterdhavian noble families. It was Margaster gold that bought Thornhold from Lord Neverember. And those dwarves, Clan Stoneshaft, who appeared at Neverember's court with the ill-gotten coin, were well adorned with shiny baubles, according to Regis."

"Your agents," Zaknafein murmured, the mercenary's concern finally dawning on him.

"Athrogate and Ambergris," said Jarlaxle. "Into what hell did I send them?"

He rushed out the door, Zaknafein close behind, and didn't stop running until he arrived at the house of Donnola and Regis, where they found the governing couple enjoying their dinner.

"I've little time to explain," Jarlaxle replied to their questioning stares and Donnola's actual question. "The dwarves you saw in Neverwinter City," he said to Regis, who nodded. "Jewelry? Baubles?" Jarlaxle asked.

"An abundance," Regis confirmed. "Quite gaudy, I thought."

"Like the queen of Damara?"

Regis dropped a food-laden fork, something that never happened. Because he had been there. He had watched the whole thing. He had been lucky to get out of the Bloodstone Lands alive when Queen Concettina Delcasio Frostmantle had been possessed by the succubus.

"Gods . . ."

"What does this mean?" Donnola demanded.

"It means that for your sake, for my sake, for the sake of King Bruenor and everything we care about, you and your network now work for me."

Donnola's expression grew suspicious at that, but Regis stood up, looked to his wife, and nodded his agreement.

CHAPTER 20

To the Heart of the Matter

stride a nightmare summoned through an obsidian figurine, Jarlaxle pulled up on a high rocky bluff, looking down at the decrepit keep known as Thornhold. A few moments later, Zaknafein came bouncing up beside him, riding a summoned hell boar identical to the one that belonged to the very dwarf they were trying to find.

"You could not do better than this for an old friend?" an obviously rattled Zaknafein asked, trying to catch his breath after the bouncing journey.

"I probably could," Jarlaxle conceded. "But these items come at great expense, and time was a factor. If it makes you feel better, Gromph himself crafted the one you ride."

"You paid him to make this for *me*?"

"No, no, it was to be a gift to Ambergris, Athrogate's bride, upon their return."

Zaknafein nodded, then looked past his friend. "That is the place?"

Jarlaxle, staring down at the old keep, gave a little nod.

"A million pieces of gold for that?" Zaknafein scoffed. "I am not versed in the prices on the surface world, but I could find a better use for such a grand sum in Menzoberranzan, I expect."

"And that is the heart of the problem," Jarlaxle said. He dismounted and spoke a command word, reverting his pawing, fire-snorting steed to a tiny obsidian figurine once more.

Zaknafein was all too happy to hop off the uncomfortable hell boar, and Jarlaxle dismissed it, too.

"We'll wait for nightfall," Jarlaxle explained, and he led the way down into a small dell among the stones, out of sight of the keep but with a grand view of the rolling waters of the stormy Sword Coast.

"You seem especially dour this day," Jarlaxle mentioned as they shared an afternoon meal. "Although, I must admit, it is difficult to tell with you, since that does seem to be your humor."

"Or lack of," Zaknafein replied, but he growled at his own pun before Jarlaxle could possibly take that as a sign of any positive mood change.

"What is it? You have met your son once more. I would think such an event . . ."

Zaknafein didn't look up.

"And his bride, a most wonderful woman," Jarlaxle continued, measuring his words as carefully as he was studying Zaknafein. He caught a hint of a grimace there, and so pressed on, "His wife who is with the grandchild of Zaknafein."

Then Zaknafein did look up, unblinking.

"They were not happy to see you?" Jarlaxle asked.

Zaknafein shrugged. "Pleased enough, I expect."

"But you were not so happy to see . . . the changes," Jarlaxle reasoned.

"I didn't say any such thing."

"Your son married a human."

"You are ever a fount of information."

"Your grandson will be of half-human blood."

Zaknafein slammed his bowl down and glared at the mercenary.

"So?" said Jarlaxle.

"That's all you have to say about it? Any of it? Or am I to be blessed with a soliloquy of sorrow by Jarlaxle for my failing?"

"Failing?" Jarlaxle echoed.

"You float about these other creatures as if you were born to their mothers," said Zaknafein.

"I was not the one who escorted a band of bedraggled halflings out of the Underdark at great personal risk," Jarlaxle reminded him. "I was not the one who almost killed Drizzt when I thought he had murdered an elven child in a surface raid."

Zaknafein shook his head, muttered something unintelligible. He scooped up his fallen bowl and went back to his meal.

"You accuse me of judging you," Jarlaxle quipped. "Someone at this meal is certainly doing so."

"Just shut up, and do keep in mind that I'd rather be riding your nightmare than this stupid pig."

"I'm not trading."

"Then shut up."

Jarlaxle said no more and went back to his own meal. He understood Zaknafein's trepidation here, of course. It was one thing to free pathetic halflings and quite another to have his grandson be of mixed blood. He glanced up from his bowl to consider his old friend. He could see the pain there, the confusion, the anger, and knew that there was nothing he could say to make anything better. Zaknafein's feelings were Zaknafein's to own, and thus only one person could resolve them.

Or not.

The afternoon passed quietly, until the sun dipped low in the western sky, its last rays shining across the water, bright in drow eyes.

"How can you even look at it?" remarked Zaknafein, discomfort under the daytime glow etched across his squinting face.

"It was very difficult, at first, because it offended my drow senses," Jarlaxle replied. He paused a moment, and indeed, Zaknafein snapped a glare his way, catching the inference.

"But I grew used to it, and so it did not hurt for long," Jarlaxle went on. "Then, to my surprise, I grew quite fond of it, to the point where I actually prefer its warmth and shine to the cold darkness of the Under-dark. Though I suppose, as I ponder, that I quite like *both*, which gives me the best of both worlds to enjoy."

"You're not half as clever as you think you are," Zaknafein re-marked.

"Or twice as clever as I ought to be," Jarlaxle added with a grin. "I have been told that my wit will be my end."

"At least you'll die smiling, for no one finds Jarlaxle as amusing as Jarlaxle finds himself."

"Because no one is quite as smart as he is to truly understand him."

They let it go at that, for the westering sun began to sink below the watery horizon. As the shadows lengthened, they crept out of the dell and made their careful way toward the place called Thornhold.

Both studied the ground around them with every step, inching forward and looking for clues of . . . well, anything. The main entrance of the place was apparent, and there seemed only one logical approach, so if Athrogate and Ambergris had made it to Thornhold, Jarlaxle was confident that he was now retracing the exact last steps of their journey.

As they neared the gates, they came upon a scene of great inter-est. Even in the dimness of twilight, they could see dark stains on the broken stones, including some that looked almost like bubbled black goo.

Blood, Zaknafein signed, bending low to sniff one dark stain. *And not so old.*

I know this stain, Jarlaxle's hands responded, looking at a puddle of the black ooze.

Demon remains.

The Hunzrins had admitted to Zaknafein that they had been sell-ing gemstones in the region, and that House Margaster had become a favored client of Charri Hunzrin. The dots were all aligning here, and, given the absence of Athrogate and Amber, connecting to Jarlaxle's dismay.

The two drow stayed low and moved for the cover of a pair of tilted stones.

And not a heartbeat too soon, for even as they arrived, they heard a telltale clicking sound. Only their natural abilities coupled with their vast experience and warrior training sent both into diving rolls for the nearest cover as a crossbow quarrel sparked, skipping off the stone between them.

They looked to the wall and gates. A torch appeared above them, then a second, and a few moments later a fiery missile soared out, landing on the stone and there somehow still burning. More followed, landing in a strategic pattern to light up the entire area near where the two drow crouched.

"'Ere, ye skulkin' dogs!" came the call from the wall. "Show yerselfs! Show yer faces and be counted, or show yer arses and be shot runnin' away!"

Counted by dwarves or by demons? Zaknafein signed to Jarlaxle.

Yes, came the answer.

"We are emissaries from Luskan!" Jarlaxle called out. "Come to speak with the new owners of Thornhold, who were the old owners of Thornhold!"

"What business has the City of Sails so far down the coast?"

"Not so far for a ship," Jarlaxle replied.

"We ain't seein' yer sails!" a different dwarf from the wall yelled back.

"If you truly understand Luskan, when you see us, you will understand," Jarlaxle said cryptically. "There are the open powers of the city, and then . . ."

He let it hang and looked to Zaknafein, signing, *They've surely heard whispers of Jarlaxle.*

In Jarlaxle's mind, everyone speaks of him constantly, Zaknafein signed back.

That brought a wide smile to Jarlaxle's face, despite their precarious position here, for the relentless Zaknafein would not surrender his sarcastic wit even when speaking with his fingers. It occurred to Jarlaxle then that this irreverent, grousing drow was quite similar to another of his closest friends. He couldn't believe that he hadn't made that connection before, for the two spoke with the same voice, and they both so virulently hated the world in which they were trapped that it pleased them to stain their blades with the blood of those whom they believe oppressed them or did great wrongs to innocents.

Jarlaxle's other friend was human, which was probably why Jarlaxle hadn't seen them in similar light until now, because, superficially at least, it was hard to equate the world of men to that of drow.

Jarlaxle should have known better, though. Human kings or lords or landowners, or, well, just humans, were quite capable of being every bit as vicious as the worst of Lolth's priestesses.

Still, he was glad to have at least one of them by his side right now, for both the steadfast companionship and the ability to take care of the business at hand.

"Then show yerselfs!" the dwarf yelled, interrupting this revelation.

Jarlaxle motioned for Zaknafein to stay low, then brought forth his newest acquisition: a small circular wooden base with a group of feathers pinned flat atop it. Jarlaxle pulled them out and set them upright in four holes cut precisely for the feathers' shafts, equidistant around the circle's perimeter. He whispered, "Akadi," the name of the supreme aerial being of Toril, a goddess controlling air elementals. Immediately the feathers began to wave, then to spin, and the inner disk of the wooden base similarly spun.

The motion and the magic created a vortex above the wooden base, climbing up into the air.

Holding the item before him, Jarlaxle stood up from behind the stone.

"Myself, you mean," he called to the dwarf.

A crossbow clicked and a quarrel sped from the wall.

Jarlaxle didn't flinch. He couldn't see the quarrel, though he had heard the release. He did catch sight of it at the very last instant as it bore down upon him, nicking off the angled stone right before him and skipping up at his face.

The vortex caught it, though, as designed, and flung it harmlessly aside.

"Yer next lie'll get a better shot, elf!" the dwarf on the wall called. "We're knowing how to count to two!"

"You assail friends of House Hunzrin," Jarlaxle dared call out. "Would that please Lord Neverember, do you believe?"

A long silence slipped by with no response from the wall. Jarlaxle had taken a great risk here, he knew, and had tipped a big part of his hand. He didn't know where else to take this conversation, however, and figured that the chance of getting to Athrogate and Ambergris was worth the cost of a bit of his leverage.

"Yerself and yer friend come in," the dwarf called.

Jarlaxle looked to Zaknafein, who emphatically shook his head, echoing Jarlaxle's feelings on the matter.

"After that warm greeting, perhaps it would be best if you came out to us, initially, at least," he called back.

"Ye came to see us, so come in and see us," the dwarf bellowed.

"Better out here," Jarlaxle steadfastly replied.

"I'm fast to grow tired o' askin'!"

"Then don't weary yourself, good dwarf!" Jarlaxle called back. "Come out here that we might speak of glorious things to come."

Another long silence followed and all the torches along the wall went dark. Jarlaxle looked to Zaknafein and shrugged, and both watched the door.

"Here we come, elf!" came a shout a short while later, and so they did, but not through the door. With a great buzzing sound, a horde of man-sized insect-like creatures, resembling some grotesque cross between a housefly and a human, swarmed over the wall. The buzzing became a purposeful drone, and though they were elven, and so immune, both drow recognized the magical lullaby qualities of the wing-song.

Zaknafein, however, slumped down to the ground.

Jarlaxle glanced at him only once, not sure if he was afflicted or faking, but having no time to consider the implications, he gripped the wooden base of his item tighter and sent his will into it, demanding more from the magic.

He counted a dozen of the demons, and knew them as chasmes. Too many, he knew, for two warriors.

"Don't get stabbed!" he warned Zaknafein, who lay unmoving,

for Jarlaxle knew that a wound from a chasme's needlelike proboscis would keep bleeding for a long, long time.

Jarlaxle fell back. He wanted to reach for his nightmare, to bring it forth and ride away, but he discovered then that he couldn't let go of his new toy with either hand, for it was spinning furiously now, and any tilt or wobble would send it flying from his hands. Of course, he also had no idea what it was doing, or why it was spinning so furiously.

A globe of magical darkness fell over him, and not one of his or Zaknafein's doing. He wasn't surprised, though, and he didn't flee. Fully committed now, he just threw all his will into the magical item in his hands.

He couldn't see it, but he could definitely feel it and hear it, a great groaning whirlwind of power.

The buzzing grew much louder as a demon suddenly dove for him. Then another. He instinctively fell back and tried to angle his toy to intercept.

The buzzing became a thwapping sound, accompanied by human-like screeches, then groans as the pair caught in Jarlaxle's tornado began tumbling and spinning and crashing together.

Needing to see it, Jarlaxle backed out of the darkness fully, and there they were, two, then three demon creatures caught in the vortex.

And it was indeed a tornado, a mighty cyclone. But controlled, spinning tightly, battering the demons as it held them in its rotational grip.

The immediate threat to himself over, he looked at Zaknafein, only to see a pair of chasmes dive in for the kill.

With no way to get near his friend, Jarlaxle summoned a globe of darkness over Zaknafein and hoped for the best.

ZAKNAFEIN HAD NEVER BATTLED THIS TYPE OF DEMON BE-fore, but he had surely fought enough drow in his years to feel no surprise when magical darkness engulfed him. It might have even been Jarlaxle throwing the spell, he figured, in some attempt to shield him.

No matter. He heard the demons coming well enough, judging their distance from the sound of their buzzing insect wings, and trusted that they thought him an easy kill.

He pulled his whip from his hip as he rolled and snapped it up into the air, calling upon its powers to cut a line in the multiverse, a fiery tear now hidden in the magical darkness.

Rolling quickly, he went back over, gathered his feet under him, and dove away, taking some grim satisfaction when he heard a shrieking demon smash into the ground behind him.

A second turned with remarkable speed just above the darkness globe, however, and sped right for him. He didn't bother with the planar rift power this time, just snapped his whipcord tightly around the giant mosquitolike proboscis and yanked it down and to the left across his body. The chasme's head jerked down, giving Zaknafein a great view of its shocked insectoid eyes just as the weapon master's left cross brought his sword slicing across them.

Zaknafein slid aside while the chasme crashed down and tumbled over and over and over, bouncing and breaking.

"What in the Nine Hells," he muttered in disbelief, watching Jarlaxle rushing his way, bearing a . . .

Tornado?

Whatever it was, it was highly effective. The mercenary caught a fourth demon in the swirl, then a fifth. And the rest flew in every direction, some caught in the effects of the vortex, others clearly trying to swing wide of the powerful magic.

Howling from the wall caught the attention of the two drow, and the distant gate burst open and a pack of canines—hell hounds, of course—leaped forth.

"The mounts! The mounts!" Jarlaxle cried, but he needn't have, for Zaknafein already had his hell boar statuette on the ground, calling to it. And recognizing Jarlaxle's predicament, the weapon master grabbed the pouch from his companion's belt and dumped the other obsidian steed to the ground.

With a great roar, Jarlaxle swung his arms left, then jerked them back to the right, and the five spinning demons went flying from the cyclone, thrown like tumbleweeds. With their gossamer fly wings torn off in the cyclone, they couldn't recover and so they tumbled long and high, crashing down to smash against the stones.

Neither drow saw it, for they were well on their way, driving nightmare and hell boar with all speed, hooves clicking against the stone, lighting fires and trailing black smoke.

But they heard the sickening sound, and that was enough to make Jarlaxle shudder.

Long and hard they rode. Hell hounds wouldn't tire, but neither would the magical mounts, which were faster, and the pursuit eventually faded.

"GOOD TO BE HOME, ELF?" KING BRUENOR SAID TO DRIZZT when the drow ranger unexpectedly appeared at Bruenor's court in Gauntlgrym.

"My home is wherever I would find Catti-brie," Drizzt corrected. "Today I am visiting the house of my brother."

"Ha ha, good enough, then! And glad to have ye! So much afoot—I'm bettin' that stupid Neverember is up to little good and no good, and might not be in that order."

"Do tell," the drow prompted.

"Not much to tell yet," Bruenor replied. "Seems that Neverember sold a tower to some dwarfs—Stoneshaft Clan—down the coast. Rumblebelly seen it. Smelling like Neverember's burying ill-gotten gold, and I'd be happy as a gnome with a widget or a halfling with a pie to be the one catching him at it."

"I presume that relations between Gauntlgrym and Neverwinter City have not improved."

"Ha! The man's a fool."

Drizzt nodded and let it go. He had come here in the hopes of using Bruenor's newly activated teleportation gates to get to Mithral Hall in the Silver Marches. He wanted to buy something from Silverymoon for Catti-brie to commemorate the birth of their first child—he had a particular piece in mind, one that he had seen at Lady Alustriel's palace. The last thing he needed now was to get enmeshed in some nonsense between Lord Neverember and Bruenor, two of the most stubborn and headstrong people he had ever known!

At that moment, however, he happened to glance to the side, at Yvonnel, who was also at court that day, and her fingers fast-flashed him the message: *There is much more.*

"Do I still have my room, or did you sell it to some traveling merchant?" Drizzt asked, and Bruenor howled.

"Two, if ye're wantin' them! Nine Hells, ten! And more above in Bleeding Vines," Bruenor roared.

"Regis is in town?"

"Not for knowin'. He's been out and about many the tendays."

Drizzt bowed to take his leave.

"We're sharing mutton and ale tonight, eh?" Bruenor asked, and Drizzt readily agreed.

He left the court and meandered in the nearby halls for a bit until Yvonnel joined him, and the two went together to the entry cavern of Gauntlgrym, to the tram that would take them up to Bleeding Vines. They couldn't have a private conversation in Gauntlgrym, after all, where every ear was Bruenor's ear.

Drizzt had ridden this tram many times, and was never left less than amazed by the journey back to the surface. Coming down into the mountain was normal enough, a train of cars rolling down the tracks to the entry cavern of the dwarven complex, where a series of brakes and rises stopped the momentum and placed the train at the station on a high platform just before the underground pond and the gates of Gauntlgrym beyond.

The ride back to the surface, however, was a feat of engineering and magic as grand as anything Drizzt had ever known, including the web balconies of Ched Nasad. The tram rolled down from the platform and across the cavern, propelled again by simple gravity, but when it got to the steep incline, it rolled over with the tracks, upside down to the ceiling—except that wasn't upside down at that point, because Gromph Baenre and some other powerful wizards had reversed the gravity all the way back up the mountain.

The tram would then fall *up* the mountain, rolling back to the floor before exiting at the Bleeding Vines station.

Yvonnel was clearly not as entranced by such a feat, though, because barely off the tram, she took Drizzt by the arm and pulled him aside. And there, away from any eavesdroppers, she informed him that Regis had left town once more, moving back to infiltrate Neverember's court in Neverwinter City.

"He was the one who witnessed the sale to Clan Stoneshaft," she explained, "in that very chamber. And Regis was the one who made the connection to House Margaster of Waterdeep, though there are more connections he could not know."

Drizzt cocked an eyebrow at that.

"To House Hunzrin," Yvonnel explained. She told him then of the money washing, of Athrogate and Ambergris, who had gone off to Thornhold, and of Jarlaxle's fears that there might be even more nefarious characters afoot.

"I would expect this to come from Jarlaxle, not you," Drizzt admitted, making it clear that he still wasn't quite sure of this strange woman before him.

"He isn't here," Yvonnel answered. "He and Zaknafein went to find the missing dwarves."

"Missing?"

"They have been gone a long while," Yvonnel explained. "Perhaps they are drunk at the table of Clan Stoneshaft, celebrating a new dwarf kingdom in the region. But they went there to look for crimes, and they've not returned. With everything else we've been able to put together, it's hard not to think something untoward has befallen them."

"How long?"

"Two tendays."

"And Jarlaxle?"

"He left only a couple of days ago, but he is riding his . . ."

"Nightmare."

"And a hell boar for Zaknafein. I expect they are even now at Thornhold, or already on their way back."

Drizzt reflexively looked to the south and west.

"There's only one road," Yvonnel said, and it sounded very much like a suggestion.

Drizzt walked around the far side of the tram station, behind a mountain spur and out of sight of Bleeding Vines. He had meant to go to Silverymoon, as he had told Bruenor, but now that seemed ill-advised. He thought to go back to the tram, down to the dwarven portal, where he could be teleported back to the Ivy Mansion and Catti-brie. He would have liked to have her insight into these alarming developments. He could go, speak with her, and be back here in a matter of hours.

But then he looked to the south and scolded himself for his previous thoughts. They were just delays. He knew that in his heart. His road lay before him, a road where three of his friends had gone, likely into danger, along with a fourth, his father.

His *father.*

Drizzt wasn't sure what that meant, his confidence regarding Zaknafein's character thoroughly shaken by the man's prejudices. On a rational level, he told himself that he shouldn't be surprised—this was all so new and shocking to Zaknafein, after all, whose life had been lived wholly within the bounds of Menzoberranzan. Yet . . .

He looked back to the east, where, far beyond sight, lay the Ivy Mansion and his beloved, and the excuses he wanted to make for Zaknafein fell away. This was his wife, his partner in everything, and this was his child. Yet . . .

He reminded himself that this drow, Zaknafein, had willingly lain upon Matron Malice's sacrificial altar for the sake of Drizzt.

Drizzt nodded. He didn't need to go to Catti-brie. He *knew* where his road lay, despite his misgivings. He lifted a unicorn-shaped whistle hanging on a chain about his neck to his lips and blew it.

"Care to join me?" he asked his companion.

Yvonnel's eyes widened as she looked past Drizzt, and he knew that Andahar, his magical unicorn steed, was on the way. Sure enough, he turned to see the shining white creature, its ivory horn gleaming in the morning light, as it took its last few strides toward him, each magical step amplifying its size beyond the mere closure of distance.

"No, I will stay here. But take great care," Yvonnel warned, step-ping away. "You have walked this road before, and you may be dealing with demonic forces."

Drizzt climbed up on Andahar and nodded.

"I will await your return," Yvonnel promised, and Drizzt turned the steed and leaped away down the south road at a full gallop.

Behind him, Yvonnel sat down and began to prepare a spell of windwalking, for despite what she'd said, she *did* intend to go with Drizzt.

But he didn't need to know that.

HE SAT IN HIS OWN FILTH, BACK AGAINST A ROUGH NATU-ral wall, hands extended up above his head and chained to the stone. They fed him only once, stuffing moldy bread into his mouth and nearly drowning him with buckets of water.

That meal was on the first day of his captivity. Apparently the demons had come to believe that he wasn't worth much to them after all, and now were letting him starve.

He should have withered and died, he figured. Or maybe they were counting on him to stay near death. Perhaps his story of a wizard curs-ing him with long life because of those long-ago events in Citadel Felbarr was truer than he actually believed!

It didn't matter. Curse or not, one thing sustained Athrogate at that time: he had to find his beloved.

A flicker of distant light stung his eyes, and it took him a long while to open them. By that time, the torch was clear to see, as was the sturdy dwarf with yellow hair all braided into cornrows who was carrying it.

"So, dwarf, have you had enough?" asked his jailer, who appeared to be a dwarf woman with rather thin arms but very wide shoulders. But the accent and sophistication of her speech sounded very un-dwarfish.

"Enough? Me belly's growlin', so likely not."

"Very good," the jailer replied. "I do admire your courage in this hopeless time—although perhaps not so hopeless for you if you tell me what brought you here. Or rather, who sent you here. I know enough to know if you're lying, be warned."

"Bwahahaha!" Athrogate roared. "Ye think I'd be tellin' yerself the color o' the durned sky? Or the makin's of a halfling pie? Or a joke to make a baby cry? Or an answer to who, what, when, or why?"

"Clever."

"Truth, ye dog. Ye let me out o' these chains, get yerself the best weapons ye can find, and come at meself, and me bare hands'll show ye some more truth, eh?"

"I could hurt you."

"Better'n yerself have hurt me."

"Oh no, ugly creature, I could hurt you in ways you cannot imagine."

"Got meself a wild way of thinkin' o' things," Athrogate assured her.

The jailer stepped back, then conceded it all with a shrug. "Here, then, let us see," she said. She reached behind her back and tossed an object into Athrogate's lap.

Athrogate's eyes widened and he let out a wail of the deepest agony he had ever known.

"The pain has only begun," the jailer promised. She walked away, but Athrogate, staring at the object, wanting to throw it far aside and keep it in his view all at once, couldn't hear the dwarf woman over his own screaming.

Screaming at the severed head of Amber Gristle O'Maul o' the Adbar O'Mauls.

CHAPTER 21

The Widening Web

Z aknafein is working with Jarlaxle?" Matron Zhindia Melarn asked, shaking her head at the news Matron Shakti Hunzrin had just delivered. It was only for effect, though, as Zhindia had already come to understand that Jarlaxle's alliances on the surface were as much a part of the problem as the heretic Drizzt and his resurrected father. Even if Drizzt and Zaknafein were delivered to her, as she intended, that would not stop her from pursuing the wider web of Jarlaxle's blasphemous enterprise.

Shakti looked to her eldest daughter.

"It was Zaknafein Do'Urden, representing Jarlaxle, most forcefully," Charri Hunzrin assured the Melarni contingent, which included Matron Zhindia, First Priestess Kyrnill, House Wizard Iltztran, and Ardulrae Melarn, who was currently serving the city as the matron of scriptures at Arach-Tinilith.

And perhaps most notable here, Shakti Hunzrin knew, was the youngest member of the group, Ash'ala, the young daughter of First

Priestess Kyrnill. Ash'ala had once served House Melarn as the ambassador to their loose alliance with House Xorlarrin and Bregan D'aerthe. Indeed, all eyes fell over her then, but the young woman simply shrugged.

"I have not had any contact with Bregan D'aerthe since the fall of Q'Xorlarrin," she explained. Even referencing that fledgling drow city which had been overrun by King Bruenor's forces and was now known as Gauntlgrym, brought a tightness to Ash'ala's chest, for that had marked a clear drop in her station in House Melarn.

"Perhaps you now should speak with Jarlaxle," Matron Shakti Hunzrin offered.

"No," came the sharp and unexpected reply from Matron Zhindia, shaking her head resolutely.

"If they ally with Zaknafein and the heretic, they are enemies of Lolth," she spat. "By their own actions are they doomed."

"If you speak of Bregan D'aerthe, you speak of House Baenre," Ash'ala said, and then gasped, for she apparently hadn't meant to blurt out such dangerous thoughts.

"We shall see," a surprisingly calm Matron Zhindia answered. "Jarlaxle will learn the truth before him. Will he side with the glorious Spider Queen? Or will he side with his *iblith* friends? If he is worthy of our concern, the answer should be simple."

"Side with them in what?" Matron Shakti asked, her voice thick with wariness.

"Your recent mercantile adventures have brought chaos to the surface," Matron Zhindia explained. "And that is good. Now Jarlaxle, with Zaknafein—and, no doubt, that heretic Drizzt—has discovered the danger in the region, almost certainly, and so the lines will be drawn."

Zhindia tried not to laugh and tip her hand with her eagerness here. She couldn't believe how beautifully this had all come together, which of course only made her even more certain that her prayers had led her correctly. Not only had circumstances—and Lady Lolth—presented the opportunity for some ambitious matron to claim both the heretic and his father, who had been stolen from eternity; not only had the foolishness of Jarlaxle and of Matron Mother Baenre in allowing his alliances created a wonderful opportunity for a devout follower to correct an ongoing heresy; but now, so perfectly, an army of demons had been inserted into the very region, ready for that ambitious matron to take control.

Had Zhindia ever seen a more obvious sign? A demon army, delivered to her clandestinely by an unwitting ally and ready to sweep her to glorious victory.

"Those lines do not include Lolth," Zhindia conceded to the others, not wanting anyone to usurp her initiative in this increasingly obvious endeavor. She then quickly added, "Yet." Thus claiming ownership, something she meant to drive home posthaste. She flashed her always-awful smile around at the gathering, and bade them, "Follow."

Down the corridors of House Melarn, Matron Zhindia led her guests to a large circular chamber ringed by a walkway high above the floor. The other Melarni knew what to expect, and so they all watched the predictable gasps of Matron Shakti and her daughter when they peered over the railing.

For in the pit loomed a pair of spiderlike creatures, each with a body as large as an ox, supported by eight long legs. That in and of itself was not so spectacular in a city that sported even larger jade spiders, but the size alone wasn't the full story of these monstrous constructs. Jagged metal plates had been set along their backs, and the "hair" on their legs actually consisted of a multitude of metal blades.

Matron Zhindia called across the way to a pair of male guards, who immediately began turning cranks that opened a pair of large doors in the pit.

Out of one came an umber hulk, huge and powerful and fearless, with skin thicker than the heaviest armor a mountain giant might wear, and mandibles and claws strong enough to bore through solid stone. Never afraid, the beast charged at the nearest spider construct in full rage.

Out of the other opening came a band of ten minotaurs, the

formidable and cunning creatures falling into a defensive array immediately, lifting heavy axes.

Instead of charging, though, they followed the lead of the drow above them and watched the bull rush of the umber hulk.

The spider reared before the approaching monster. Four of its eight eyes began to sparkle and glow.

The umber hulk didn't slow, determined to fight. But then it was flying backward, blasted by a lightning strike from one of the eyes. Before the hulking monster even got off the floor, a cone of skin-cracking frost fell over it, stinging it so badly that it let out a howl that echoed deafeningly about the chamber. Then, stubbornly, the umber hulk was back up, and it stumbled forward, still ready to wage battle.

Except it wasn't actually a battle. Or rather, it was a battle in the same way a butcher might battle with a hog during slaughter. With little effort, the spider monster's four front legs whipped and battered the umber hulk, throwing it this way and that like a toy, disorienting it and putting it off balance.

The construct's giant mandibles cut it in half.

On the other side of the pit, the minotaurs shrank back, tightening their formation.

And that played right into the designs of the second construct as a dark beam flashed from one of its eyes, splashing through more than half its adversaries.

Five of those six beam-washed minotaurs turned to stone.

"I never promised that they would retrieve Zaknafein and Drizzt alive," Matron Zhindia said with a shrug.

"Retrieve?" Matron Shakti echoed. "These are *retrievers*? They are demon creatures!"

"Abyssal creations," Matron Zhindia corrected. "Golems. Single-minded and made to retrieve a single creature or person. But yes, most often employed by the great lords of the Abyss."

"How did you do this? This is—"

"The glory of Lolth," Matron Zhindia interrupted, keeping her business with Eskavidne to herself. "Why do you doubt me, Matron Shakti? Have you a crisis of faith?"

Shakti Hunzrin shrank back from those words. The Melarni were zealots in the cause of Lolth—so much so that their adherence to their principles above practicality had often hurt the standing of their house, and had created great reservations about them from all the other ruling houses of Menzoberranzan.

Before them right now was reason enough to distrust their fervor.

"You really hate them, don't you?" Charri Hunzrin dared to remark.

Matron Zhindia turned a wicked smile upon her.

"Jarlaxle and Drizzt," Charri explained. "They greatly wounded your family in their run through Menzoberranzan. Your daughter—"

"Speak not of her!" Matron Zhindia demanded, for her only daughter had indeed been taken from her, and murdered in a manner such that she could not be resurrected.

"I am surprised that you have but two monsters," Charri went on. "Yvonnel may be up there with Jarlaxle."

Matron Zhindia Melarn looked back to the pit, where the retrievers were tearing apart the remaining minotaurs, except for two, who were shot with, and fully engulfed by, reams of webbing. Each spiderlike construct then went to one of the captured targets, gathering its respective prey up to its belly as instructed.

"The retrievers will not go alone, I promise," Matron Zhindia said with a sneer. "House Melarn will go to war, an army of driders before us. We will bring ruin to the heretic's friends and will retrieve Drizzt and his father, stolen from Lolth's grasp in her eternal domain."

More than one of the gathered drow arched eyebrows at that proclamation.

"How many have said that before you?" Charri Hunzrin asked what many were thinking.

"How many have committed the resources I have?" came the rejoinder. "There is an army of demons already in place, awaiting us. All they need is direction.

"*I* am that direction."

More than one of the drow shuffled nervously at that remark, particularly as they looked down into the pit at the rare and horrible monsters.

At the perfect killing machines.

The constructs without weakness.

"GO WITH ALL SPEED TO INKERI MARGASTER," MATRON Shakti Hunzrin told her daughter Charri as soon as they were out of House Melarn. "Discern her designs regarding the dwarf king and other friends of Drizzt."

"And regarding Jarlaxle's band?"

"Do not yet prod her so, but yes, discern her designs most especially regarding Jarlaxle's band," Shakti agreed. She looked back at the now-distant structure of the zealot-filled House Melarn. "To battle Jarlaxle is to battle House Baenre, and that is something we do not yet desire."

"Matron Zhindia is convinced that Lolth stands with her," Charri pointed out.

"And we know that in this endeavor, should she go against Bregan D'aerthe, Matron Baenre will stand against her," Shakti was quick to reply. "We do not know the truth of Lolth's will in this matter, nor her level of interest, nor even any recompense she might deliver." She sighed and looked across the cavern to the Qu'ellarz'orl, where sat House Baenre. After the defeat of Demogorgon, Matron Mother Quenthel had truly solidified her alliances with most of the noble houses. Rarely in history had Menzoberranzan been so united behind the First House, and that First House, Shakti knew well, was so power-ful that it didn't even need any allies.

"But we do know," she continued, "what Matron Mother Baenre will do if she comes to believe that we are trying to be rid of Bregan D'aerthe." She sighed again and looked to her daughter. "Do you un-derstand?"

Charri Hunzrin nodded solemnly.

"Go to the Margaster with all speed," Shakti reiterated. "But with all caution."

"And if we learn that Matron Zhindia is correct?" Charri had to ask.

"Close no options, of course," Shakti instructed her. "We can al-ways return. We are on neither side, and on both, of course."

Charri Hunzrin bowed and ran off to find a wizard who could deliver her quickly to Waterdeep.

"I HATE THEM AS MUCH AS YOU DO," FIRST PRIESTESS KYRnill Melarn assured her matron. Theirs was not a typical drow familial relationship. Kyrnill had herself once been a matron, the ruler of House Kenafin. At that time, Zhindia had been matron of House Horlbar. Circumstances had forced the two houses to merge, for their relevance, if not their very survival, and in that agreement, Kyrnill had ceded the position of matron to Zhindia.

Of course, at that time, Kyrnill had expected that Zhindia would soon enough be murdered. The fact that she had escaped that web of intrigue intact had begun the rise of Zhindia Horlbar to a stature far beyond her position as matron of House Melarn, because her simple survival, against all odds, had marked her as Lolth-blessed. And it was difficult to go against one so favored by the Spider Queen.

Indeed, Zhindia had gained much in the decades since the merger. Most of all, with her cruelty and viciousness, invoking Lolth to dispense horrific punishments, she had inculcated fear into many within Menzoberranzan. Kyrnill could not lie to herself and say she didn't secretly hold such a fear . . . or pretend that she wouldn't want such respect as that. For now, though, she played her subservient role, looking to convince the matron of her allegiance.

Which Matron Zhindia did not seem to appreciate. "That is not true," she quietly answered.

"I was in the room with you," Kyrnill reminded her. She had been present during the attack on House Melarn by Jarlaxle, Drizzt, and their human associate Artemis Entreri. Six priestesses of House Melarn had been slain in that attack, though five were soon after resurrected through the power of Lolth. "My escape and your own are the only reason that the damage to House Melarn was not lasting and mortal."

Zhindia fixed her with a sober and stone-cold stare. "The favor of Lolth allowed us to reconstruct the house and bring back those murdered," she said, her voice flat and even and very near to sounding like a growl. "All but one."

From Zhindia's tone, Kyrnill understood that this conversation could quickly degenerate if she was not careful.

"You do not agree with my decision to join in the coming conflict on the surface," Matron Zhindia stated.

"You are the matron of House Melarn. It is not my place to agree or disagree. It is my place to obey."

"Grudgingly."

"Not so!" Kyrnill was quick to reply. "I have served you loyally for more than a century, my Matron Zhindia. We are not peers, nor rivals. You are my matron. I am your faithful servant."

"Truly?"

The way Zhindia asked had the hairs standing on the back of Kyrnill's neck. Zhindia was a fanatic, had always been a true zealot in the service of Lolth, or rather, in the service of whatever it was that she came to believe was Lolth's will. The problem with such fanatics, Kyrnill knew, was that the longer they survived, the more they became entrenched in their surety—whether it be about the fervor of their followers or the saltiness of their beef.

Each surety often brought the same level of consequence to the mundane and profound alike.

So while, eventually, the overly zealous fanatics would fail and fall, Kyrnill understood that the longer it took—in Zhindia's case, more than a century and counting—the greater the fall and the more people they would take down with them.

In the meantime, Kyrnill would continue to express her devotion in both word and act, and hope only that Matron Zhindia saw enough to not turn the zealotry on her.

CHAPTER 22

The Strength of Rage

He came over the rock to a six-foot drop and didn't hesitate, leaping onto the back of the creature below: a large and vicious hell hound. The canine beast howled as its back bent low under the weight, a force that would have broken the spine of a large dog or a wolf.

It did little damage to a beast as powerful as a hell hound.

It spun its head immediately, lightning fast, to expel its unwelcome rider—but Zaknafein's sword was already moving, and he had no intention of trying to make a mount of the demonic canine.

Now the hell hound yelped more loudly as the fine drow blade gashed into the side of its neck. The hound whipped its head to the other side, but again Zaknafein stayed ahead of the game, flipping his sword back up and over, catching it in both hands and plunging it down with all his strength into the back of the beast's neck, driving down, cracking bone.

The front paws splayed wide as the hell hound went down to the stone.

Up leaped Zaknafein, already spinning and drawing his whip, and in the same fluid motion snapped it into the face of the next nearest hound as it began to spring his way.

He scored a brutal hit, taking an eye from the beast, which stumbled aside and blew its fiery breath at the weapon master, though it was too far away then for the flames to hurt its target. A second crack of the whip drove it back farther, right into a barrage of expertly thrown daggers, jarring the hound, stabbing the hound.

Zaknafein brought his whip back in, winding it with easy expertise to replace it on his belt. He grasped the sword, standing straight up from the dead hell hound, and tore it free as he walked toward the second beast, which was squirming and spinning in pain.

He finished it with a perfect stab through the empty socket that used to contain its left eye.

"Two less," Jarlaxle said hopefully, coming around a nearby rock. He was adjusting his sleeve, moving it back down to cover a most interesting bracer he wore.

"Wherever did you find so many daggers?" Zaknafein asked, shaking his head to show that he was hardly surprised.

"So many?" Jarlaxle replied with a grin. "My friend, just a few. Just a few."

"Enough for a thousand more of these devil dogs?"

Jarlaxle shrugged. "Two less," he said again.

"Until one of the demons within the keep decides to bring two more in," Zaknafein replied. "We are up against an infinite army here, my friend."

"Not so. Their gating powers are limited."

"Except that they can gate in creatures who can gate in creatures!"

"Lesser demons cannot do that, and greater demons are, fortunately, rare. And we're not going to fight them all now, in any case."

"Then why did we come back?"

"Because I am almost certain that my associates are in there. I'll not leave them."

"These are demons, Jarlaxle." Zaknafein looked down at the dead hounds. "They don't make a habit of taking prisoners."

"There are more than demons at play here," Jarlaxle replied, and started back toward the coast with Zaknafein in tow. "Lord Neverember is connected to this, and he is no demon. An evil fool, perhaps, but most certainly human. A noble house of Waterdeep is part of this, too, and I doubt that all the dwarves of this Clan Stoneshaft have been possessed by the creatures within Charri Hunzrin's vile phylacteries."

"Those that weren't are likely dead, too."

Jarlaxle paused and cocked his head to cast a sidelong glance back at his companion. "I'd forgotten these fits of Zaknafein the Dour," he said, and started to laugh. But he stopped himself at his own reminder. In all the years since Zaknafein's death, had Jarlaxle remembered only the easy parts of the weapon master's personality, the fine blades and loyalty, the quick wit as sharp as those blades, the unrivaled courage?

It was easy to think kindly of one who was gone. But small memories started bubbling up, little moments when perhaps Zaknafein hadn't been the easiest companion to get along with. And once again, he was reminded of Artemis Entreri, and realized that was what made both men such important allies—they were complex beings who excelled at many things, but ultimately thought on their own. Reassured by having Zaknafein at his side, he pressed on.

"Have your mount ready in case we need a fast escape," Jarlaxle instructed, though he was certain that the ever-vigilant Zaknafein wouldn't need to be reminded.

As expected, Zaknafein didn't even respond, but Jarlaxle smiled a little when he saw some subtle movement near his friend's pouches.

They came back in sight of Thornhold Keep soon after, looking down from a different angle now, from a rocky bluff south of the dwarven stronghold that put them up high enough to see the top parapets of the place, even the dwarves walking the walls, torches in hand.

"Learn their patterns," Jarlaxle instructed.

"They are on their guard now," Zaknafein replied, pointing to a dwarf walking south on the front wall, turning the corner at precisely the same time as the dwarf walking west along the south wall turned right around the corner to the north. "Not sloppy."

"They'll grow bored soon enough. Guards always do. We've another four hours before daylight."

Zaknafein sighed.

"You would have me leave my associates in there?" Jarlaxle asked. "Would you have me leave if *you* were in there?"

Zaknafein cocked an eyebrow.

"If there was even a chance that you were alive?" Jarlaxle clarified, and Zaknafein chuckled. "Or is this simply your way of telling me that you warned me if we are again chased away?"

"Or is it warning of my curses if we can't get away?"

"I would be disappointed were it not so."

Zaknafein sighed again, but he didn't leave, and that's what Jarlaxle cared about right now.

So they crouched and they watched and they waited, and an hour passed, and then another. The eastern sky began to lighten ever so slightly, but to drow eyes it burned like a warning beacon.

Still the dwarves on the wall marched with great precision, keeping watch at all points. Had these been mere dwarves, and not (at least some) demons, Jarlaxle might have long ago made the attempt to get over the wall, but he was beginning to believe that they might have to wait until the next night for this clan to let down their guard enough for him and his partner to slip through.

He was counting the steps of the dwarf marching the southern expanse when Zaknafein nudged him, then directed his attention to the northeast. At first he saw nothing, but then he noted the approaching form, one he knew would soon enough be shining white under the morning sun.

"Your son," he murmured to Zaknafein.

Despite their secrecy, Zaknafein stood up, and that action, that simple movement that could have given their position away, revealed to Jarlaxle just how much this formidable weapon master, this supreme, often cold-blooded warrior, cared for Drizzt.

With their superb darkvision, the drow pair could now make out the rider on the thundering unicorn. Jarlaxle's eyes widened and Zaknafein gasped when Drizzt leaned low to the right-hand side of his

334 R. A. SALVATORE

mount, then, shockingly, dropped free, tumbling to the stone. He landed in a roll and kept rolling, so beautifully, until it brought him back to his feet, running full out behind the unicorn.

Every great stride of that magical steed took it farther and farther from Drizzt, but more importantly, every stride made the unicorn seem weirdly smaller, shrinking until in no time at all there was nothing left of the magical mount.

Nothing except for Drizzt, who continued his rush to the wall, darting about from stone to stone.

They watched him reach the eastern wall, about twenty paces to the right of the main door, and both blinked as if unable to comprehend the sight as the skilled ranger, now trained in the way of the Monastery of the Yellow Rose, went up that wall at full speed, hands and legs moving like the legs of a scrabbling spider.

He gained the parapet in short order and rolled right over, then disappeared from sight as if he had just jumped down the back side of the thirty-foot wall into the courtyard—which both could easily believe the case.

From somewhere beyond, a dwarf howled in protest, other guards took up the call, and all along the wall, the torches began to bob as the sentries ran to find the intruder.

Jarlaxle started to yell to Zaknafein that they should be quick to the wall, but before the first word had left his mouth, Zaknafein ran past him, already on his way.

"WHAT NOW? THEM DARK ELFS RETURN?" BRONKYN STONE-shaft asked the pair of agitated sentries when he saw them scrambling down from the walls into the keep courtyard. The clan leader was not in a good mood. Half his boys were possessed by demons, after all, and he was having a hard time trusting them.

And while that should have bothered him more than it did—he *had* made a deal with some monsters, after all—it was bringing him great wealth and potentially unimaginable power.

So he was willing to live with it.

"Might be," answered one, a young woman named Argamant, who was wearing a glabrezu pendant around her neck.

"Gwirkyn seen a shadow come over the wall," added Frenkyn, Bronkyn's favorite nephew, and one, by his demand, untouched by the possession necklaces.

"Gwirkyn's a lass with a lot o' imagination," Argamant noted.

"Aye, and we just seen two drow outside," Bronkyn reminded her.

"Firin' hot the girl's imaginin'!" said Argamant with a cruel laugh, but Bronkyn wasn't convinced and let her know it with a forceful shake of his yellow-haired head.

Bronkyn was about to argue, but a yell from inside the keep, followed by a roar like that of a hunting cat, filled the walls. That was soon followed by a demonic shriek, and any thoughts of further conversation were stolen from them. The three dwarves became two as Argamant transformed into a hulking glabrezu.

The other two were already in the keep when Argamant settled into her new form, but with her great strides, she caught up to them in the first room past the foyer.

All three watched in surprise as a feline, a huge black panther, sped past in the hallway beyond that foyer. Argamant leaped out of the room into the corridor and crashed into another demon, a huge fiend with a boar-like face and murderous tusks, a fat body, half giant and half warthog, with ridiculously small black feathered wings flapping behind.

As large as the glabrezu was, twelve feet tall, this demon, a nalfeshnee, was more than half again taller. Still, even with the two entangled and thrashing, Bronkyn and Frenkyn managed to rush out to take up the pursuit.

Through the maze of corridors and rooms they ran, always one step behind the elusive cat. Other dwarves joined in, other demons joined in, and that whole side of the keep shook under the thunderous pursuit, with doors being torn from their hinges and hurled aside, sometimes into the face of a fellow pursuer.

Lesser demons, the desiccated humanoid manes, ran into major demons, to be torn apart for getting in the way or simply because the vicious beasts needed to destroy something, anything. And all the while the panther moved just out of reach, until it seemed the dwarves had, at last, cornered it.

However, without stopping, through a window went the fleeing cat, and the pursuit rolled out into the courtyard, and shouts came down from all the walls.

And back in the corridor outside the small room, Argamant the glabrezu and the giant nalfeshnee continued their battle, caring not at all for the events beyond their mortal clash.

WE ARE FOUND!

Zaknafein's fingers waggled up to Jarlaxle, the two of them halfway up the keep's outer wall, wedged into a corner, and pressing in more tightly because of all the commotion just on the other side of the stone barrier.

Drizzt, Jarlaxle corrected.

Then move! Zaknafein demanded.

Trust in him! They are chasing, not fighting, Jarlaxle answered. He did begin to move, but slowly and carefully. Weightless from his levitation spell, the mercenary leader inched his way up the wall, pausing every few feet to listen carefully to the continuing commotion within.

"Damned big cat!" he heard at one point, a dwarven voice, and he nodded and smiled.

FROM THE SHADOWS DOWN THE WIDE CORRIDOR BEYOND the foyer, Drizzt watched the demonic battle, glabrezu against nalfeshnee, a pair of major fiends locked in vicious combat. The larger nalfeshnee carried lines of scars from the other monster's great pincers, but the resilient greater fiend was far from finished.

Indeed, even then the pig-faced behemoth waggled its arms, accepting yet another clawing strike from the glabrezu in order to cast a magical spell that filled the air with waves of unholy magic, slamming the glabrezu and stunning it.

The nalfeshnee lowered its massive shoulders and charged right into its opponent, bowling the glabrezu to the ground. Then it bent low and jumped, flapping its too-small wings furiously to bring its back all the way up to the thirty-foot ceiling, where it stopped the flapping and dropped from above, smashing against the prone demon.

Up it went again, to fall into another crushing blow, then a third time.

The glabrezu writhed and tried to stand, and when its crushed hips failed, it tried to roll out of the way instead, lifting its pincer arms to fend off the next attack.

But the nalfeshnee had obviously battled such fiends as this before, and coughed an evil laugh as it plummeted once again, accepting the sting of the pincers in exchange for the meteoric blow it landed on the chest of the glabrezu.

Even for a seasoned veteran like Drizzt, the sheer brutality of the giant demon proved jarring. He didn't look away, though, for he wanted to better understand the unbridled power of this monstrous beast, one he might soon be battling himself.

The glabrezu lay still after the next crash, and after inspecting the damage for a moment, the nalfeshnee just leaped up and began stomping on the helpless fiend's head, again and again.

Black smoke began to rise from the prone demon, telling Drizzt that it was destroyed and its essence already flying back to its lower planar home.

But no! Where the demon had been now lay a dwarf woman, groaning.

The nalfeshnee laughed again and kicked her aside, into the wall, then stormed away toward where the others had gone.

Drizzt watched the black smoke swirling all about the area, but not immediately dissipating. Instead, it wound, tightened, and dove into the throat of the dwarf!

But no, not the throat. Rather, into a necklace set with large gems. A phylactery.

Much more became clear to Drizzt then. He nodded as he thought of the Bloodstone Lands, the caves in Damara, and the succubus named Malcanthet.

He went to the fallen dwarf. She was alive, and didn't seem too badly injured—more stunned than anything. She flinched at the drow before her, looming as if he was going to finish the job.

Instead, he took her necklace and rushed back the other way.

Drizzt had been in this place before, twice: once to shelter from the rain, and the other time simply to scout the abandoned keep. He didn't remember the layout well, but enough to know where lay the dungeons, and so, he presumed, where he would find Athrogate and Amber. If they had survived.

Or likely, even if they had not.

He found the trapdoor to the lower level, a ladder lying beside it. First, he quietly dismissed Guenhwyvar, sending her home to the Astral Plane, knowing he might soon enough be recalling her and needing to be conscious of how much time she spent here. Then, slowly and carefully, he lifted the edge of the door just a bit to peek below. He saw no one in the room immediately beneath, but he heard dwarf voices not far away. Eschewing the ladder, he opened the trapdoor enough to slip through, caught a handhold to suspend him above the floor below, and, after a cursory glance at the nearby wall to ensure that he could get back up and open the trapdoor, he eased the wooden seal down once more.

Some ten feet off the ground, Drizzt swung toward the nearby wall and simply let go, safely and silently dropping to the floor.

He got his bearings. Two natural limestone corridors ran off this chamber, left and right, with the voices coming from the right, the west. He chose that path, figuring it would be easier to find any prisoners once he had caught the jailers.

He crept along the natural corridors, using the shadows of their uneven walls to his advantage. Soon the light of a fire spilled into the hallway, and the voices grew louder, coming from a small chamber just ahead.

To the floor went Drizzt, crawling silently the rest of the way.

Three dwarves sat around a cooking fire. The good news was that only one wore the baubles Drizzt expected of a demonic phylactery.

Drizzt hardly looked at that one, however, his eyes and his heart caught by the other two. For one wore a garment that he knew well: Athrogate's girdle, which granted him the strength of a mountain giant. The third of the group carried a mace, and not just any mace: a two-handed monster weapon with the name Skullcrusher.

The mace of Amber Gristle O'Maul of the Adbar O'Mauls.

Drizzt swallowed hard. Did the fact that the jailers carried these items mean that his friends were alive and imprisoned here?

Or did it mean the worst?

As his eyes adjusted to the harsh light of the fire, he noted that the passage continued directly across the small chamber, climbed just a bit, and seemed to widen and turn all about. Drizzt thought that he recognized that area, and if he remembered correctly, there were indeed cells in there, even if that just meant natural cubbies with shackles coming from the walls.

He took a better look at the jailers, noting a huge stone immediately beside the one wearing Athrogate's girdle. That didn't bode well, nor could Drizzt have any idea of what type of demon he might find himself facing from the one with the phylactery—and that particular dwarf had a huge two-headed war axe leaning against the wall behind her, one too large for her to wield properly in her natural form, surely. Yet none of it mattered, not really. With even the chance that his friends might be beyond and needing his help, his safety was the last thing on his mind.

But he did need to consider a different tactic than headlong attack.

He backed down the corridor, looking for a place where he might conceal himself.

Climbing up onto a natural shelf along one wall, he called out, "Elfs! Durned dark elfs! Ready yer arms! Stop 'em at the trapdoor!" in the best dwarven accent, tone, and dialect he could muster.

It didn't sound very convincing to him, and he winced more than once at his poor Bruenor impersonation. Nevertheless, he did hear commotion from back down the corridor.

"Went left, the wrong way!" he called. "Trap 'em! Trap 'em! Get a demon!"

He ducked in tight against the stone, and sure enough, two of the jailers came rushing up: the one with Amber's mace and the demon. And as that monstrosity passed below, Drizzt was glad of his choice to use deception instead of weapons. He wasn't well versed in whatever in the Nine Hells this thing was, but it certainly looked formidable: a hugely muscled green-skinned monster with goblin-like ears, great bat wings, and goat horns, wielding the massive axe with practiced ease. It ran hunched over but still passed only just below Drizzt's position, its horns close enough for him to grab.

"Went left, they yelled," the dwarf said when they passed Drizzt and neared the trapdoor.

The demon never slowed, rushing down the other tunnel, eager for a kill.

"Yeah, yerself goes," said the dwarf, shaking his head. "Meself'll just be waiting here, eh?"

Drizzt tapped him on the shoulder and he spun about. Eyes bulging when he saw the drow, the dwarf swept Skullcrusher across to swat the unexpected visitor aside.

But Drizzt fell flat to his belly, the mace sweeping overhead, then popped back up before the dwarf could reverse the stroke. He caught the dwarf's extended arm by the wrist and drove his other hand brutally hard against the elbow, pulling the wrist toward him as he struck. He heard the crack of bone and the dwarf groaned.

Drizzt lifted the arm and spun beneath it, coming around to drive his elbow right into the dwarf's face. Continuing his spin, he lifted his knee hard at just the right moment to drive it up between the dwarf's legs, lifting the fellow from the ground. The dwarf landed and lurched, weapon dropped, one hand going to his crotch, the other rising in defense.

But too late, as Drizzt had already pulled one of his scimitars and executed the fourth move of the routine, a downward right-hand cross, pommel leading, that caught the bending dwarf on the side of the jaw and sent him flying to the floor.

A quick look assured Drizzt that this one wouldn't be back in the fight any time soon, so he grabbed up Amber's mace and rushed back the other way. He slowed as he neared the room with the fire, peeking in from far enough to see the dwarf with Athrogate's girdle standing ready, huge rock in hand.

Drizzt crept up beside the door.

"'Ere now, Stinky," the jailer said. "That yerself, what?"

Drizzt summoned a globe of magical darkness just outside the door, so that its visually impenetrable veil bled into the room, nearly to the dwarf. Drizzt didn't hesitate, slipping in on his belly, moving to the side of the chamber.

"What, hey?" the dwarf said, and Drizzt peeked out of the globe, down low and to the side, and saw the diminutive fellow hoist the boulder high overhead.

He was still staring ahead nervously into the darkness globe when a drow hand slipped around his waist and deftly and quickly unlatched the girdle.

"Wha—?" the dwarf managed to say as his belt was yanked away, but only that before the boulder he held above his head collapsed his arms and cracked him in the head, bearing him to the ground beneath it.

Once again, though, Drizzt was already gone, out the other side of the chamber, moving fast through the myriad of alcoves and chambers beyond. He soon enough heard the sound of someone softly crying, and following that, came in sight of a bedraggled, beaten prisoner, a dwarf he knew well.

In the corridors he had left behind, though, Drizzt heard stirring. The return of the demon, probably, and by the sound of it, some of its friends!

He rushed to his own friend, who was sitting against the wall, arms shackled up high over his head. Drizzt started for the shackles, but stopped in horror when he glanced to the side.

There lay the severed head of another old companion, a dwarf who had accompanied him on his adventures for years.

"Oh, Athrogate," he whispered, his voice full of sympathy. This dwarf had finally found peace, had finally found love, and now . . .

"Eh?" Athrogate replied, barely opening his eyes—if he even could, with all the caked blood.

Knowing that time was running out, Drizzt knelt at the dwarf's side and put a waterskin to Athrogate's mouth, then splashed water all over the dwarf's face, trying to wipe away the blood. Athrogate coughed and shook his head, looking at Drizzt confusedly.

With one hand, Drizzt gave him more water. With the other, he looped Athrogate's belt about the dwarf's waist.

"Listen, friend, we've not much time," he explained, pulling the girdle tight and buckling it. Immediately, Athrogate began to growl, and moved as if to pull the chains.

"Hold," Drizzt bade him. "Not yet, my friend. They are coming. The ones who killed Amber are coming. Wait for them, until they are vulnerable."

Athrogate continued to stare at him blankly, but Drizzt was out of time, he knew, and so had to trust that the dwarf understood. He put a finger over his lips to call for silence, adjusted Athrogate's ragged shirt to mostly cover the girdle, then slunk off into the shadows. From a perch not far away, Drizzt watched the approach of the captors. He recognized the dwarf in front, the one who had become the demon, but was once again without its monstrous form. Behind her came a trio of other dwarves, two holding the poor fellow who had dropped a boulder on his own head, who was still lolling about in a daze. Behind them came a trio of hulking vulturelike demons Drizzt knew to be vrocks, formidable and vicious, with great clawed hands that could rake the skin off an umber hulk and powerful beaks that could split stone.

"Ye got a friend, do ye?" the lead dwarf asked Athrogate, walking right up and kicking the poor captive on the bottoms of his bare, whip-torn feet.

Athrogate opened one eye, enough to glare at his torturer. "Got lots," he managed to say, laboring with every word.

"Aye, ye got one who's come in," said the Stoneshaft dwarf. "Might that I'll be puttin' his head on yer lady friend's body, and hers on his! Now, ye tell me where yer friend might be and I'll kill him quick, eh?"

Athrogate half coughed, half snorted, but from the side, Drizzt nodded, noting the dwarf's fingers wrapping around the shackle chains.

"Hey, but his face's been wiped!" another of the dwarves then noted. "Ha!"

Up leaped Athrogate, arms wide, hands gripping those chains, knuckles whitening.

"Oh, but ye're to pa—" the lead dwarf said, or started to say, until Athrogate gave a gigantic tug on the chains, his belt supplying the necessary power. They were tightly bolted, but the stones of the wall proved less secure, the whole of it buckling behind him. Instinctively and defensively, not even realizing the scope of what he had done, Athrogate brought his right arm swinging across as the dwarf standing before him started to draw a sword.

A huge block of stone, fastened to the end of the shackle chain like the head of a mountain giant's flail, whacked the dwarf in the side and launched him flying into the wall. Now full of bloodlust, beyond pain, beyond hunger, beyond anything but hatred and the sight of his beloved Amber's head lying in the filth, Athrogate kept that arm up above his head, swinging the impromptu flail. He found a similar bludgeoning block attached to the left shackle, and wasted no time in putting that one into a complementary spin.

For a hundred years, Athrogate had wielded Cracker and Whacker. These impromptu flails were much larger and heavier, but the game was the same, and the dwarf went forward behind a maniacal laugh, swatting aside the two healthy dwarves next in line and running over the third as he fell to the ground, slowing only enough to stomp his bare foot on the fool's face.

In among the three demons he waded fearlessly, swinging wildly and scoring stunning hits. But these were five-hundred-pound monsters, and for every hit Athrogate gave, he took two, claws raking, digging the skin from his bones, sometimes so deeply as to scratch the bones as well.

Athrogate didn't seem to feel any of it. One vrock drove its beak at him from above his swing. The furious dwarf caught it in his other hand, clamping it tight, yanking it back and forth with such power that the demon had to open wide its vulture wings to maintain any semblance of balance.

No matter, though, for Athrogate's other hand came up and clamped about its bird neck. He tugged it in close and drove its head up the other way . . . and bit out the creature's throat. He flung the dying thing before him, driving the others away enough for him to get his flails spinning once more.

He heard the dwarves stirring behind him, soon to surround him, but he didn't care.

All he wanted was to inflict pain, to crush those who had done this to Amber.

THE TWO DWARVES STUMBLED TOGETHER, DIRECTLY BE-hind the rampaging Athrogate. They took up their weapons, unsteady and unsure.

Both grabbed at their hamstrings at the same time as a fine scimitar cut through each. Then there was suddenly another person between them, a drow elf, and even as they realized it, Drizzt snapped his hands out wide to either side with a stunning quickness, the pommels of his blades crashing into dwarven faces.

Off to the side of Athrogate went Drizzt, drawing one vrock with him. The furious creature clawed left, long arm sweeping down, but Drizzt hopped over the strike. Across came the right claw for the drow's shoulder, but a mighty weapon, a blade of two magics, that of Twinkle and that of Vidrinath, was up to block, and at just the right angle so that the vrock's own swing brought its arm hard against the fine edge.

Drizzt's other blade, his oldest weapon, stabbed hard into the monster's chest. The wound would not have proven mortal, surely, to this otherworldly being, and Drizzt thought it likely that such knowledge was why the stupid vrock had allowed the strike, thinking to counter by pecking Drizzt in the head.

However, Icingdeath was no normal blade, but a frostbrand, a weapon imbued with a magical hatred of fire. And of creatures birthed in fire.

Like demons.

The vrock's head came forward anyway as Icingdeath began to extinguish its life force, but that strike, too, was cleanly intercepted by the flat of Vidrinath, the weapon turning the beak aside just enough so that it skimmed past Drizzt's face. That near miss didn't shake Drizzt—he could have further deflected the beak if necessary. But he wanted his weapon in close, too close and too quick for the vrock to get its clawing hands back up. A subtle, sudden shift sent Vidrinath slicing across the creature's neck.

And Drizzt twisted Icingdeath, eating the creature's fiery heart.

The cavern shook then, violently, and a lump of blood and guts and feathers washed over Drizzt and his opponent. He turned as he skipped aside and saw Athrogate extracting one of his stone-block flails from the flattened form of a vrock. Growling, Athrogate started for the dwarves Drizzt had dropped, for they weren't yet dead.

"No time!" Drizzt yelled, and he grabbed the dwarf by the arm. He knew that it wouldn't have taken Athrogate more than a heartbeat for each kill, but he didn't want these dwarves dead. There were sinister forces at play here, he knew, and perhaps the taint on these fellows made them victims more than perpetrators. As it was, they had pretty grievous injuries, but they were no longer a threat, so if Drizzt could keep a little blood off his friend's hands, he had to try.

Athrogate seemed to hear his urgency, at least, and grabbing the rusty chains in bloody hands, he roared yet again, then ran out of the chamber and down the hall toward the distant fire. With Drizzt right behind him, the dwarf crashed right through the fire, kicking the logs aside, growling and snarling and roaring with every step, so wound into his rage that Drizzt was shocked he had managed to turn the fellow from the living dwarves.

Down to the trapdoor they went, and the poor dwarf Drizzt had initially dropped was just rising shakily back to his feet. He stumbled away down the far side of the corridor at their approach, but this time Drizzt couldn't stop his companion fast enough. On the Stoneshaft fellow in a few leaping strides, Athrogate grabbed him in both hands and flung him into the wall, where he crumpled again to the floor.

Athrogate lifted his foot to stomp the life out of the fellow, and Drizzt leaped at his friend, trying to body-block him aside.

He might as well have tried to move a mountain.

Down came Athrogate's foot, and the poor Stoneshaft fellow jerked and bounced under the violent impact.

Athrogate lifted his foot again, but this time Drizzt took a different approach, and kicked Athrogate's straightened leg in the back of the knee. The leg buckled, Athrogate stumbled, and Drizzt leaped upon him, bearing him down.

But Athrogate clamped his hands on the sides of Drizzt's head and pressed, and with such awful strength that Drizzt feared that his skull would implode.

"Your shackle . . . your . . . we have to get out of here," the drow stammered.

Athrogate roared and flung Drizzt backward, then hopped to his feet.

"I'll be killin' 'em all, and don't ye stop me!" the dwarf hollered, and moved to stomp the fallen Stoneshaft dwarf.

"With this, then!" Drizzt yelled, and pulled Skullcrusher off his back.

Athrogate's eyes widened and his knees went visibly weak.

Drizzt ran back the other way, back to the trapdoor, figuring he had to get Athrogate out of sight of the fallen fellow. To his relief, Athrogate came around the bend in pursuit almost immediately.

"That door!" Drizzt said, pointing up. "Many beyond it. Including those responsible for you being down here." He dropped the two-handed mace to the floor and went to Athrogate. Pulling a lock pick—another gift from his time at the Monastery of the Yellow Rose—from the cuff of his sleeve, he got to work on the rudimentary lock of the dwarf's shackle.

The chain fell free and Drizzt moved for the other one, but Athrogate jerked that arm away. "Oh, no ye don't," he said, taking up Amber's large mace in just his right hand and moving it about as if it weighed no more than a feather.

"Ye get me through that door, elf!" Athrogate said, as much a warning as a request, and in such a tone that Drizzt believed that if he didn't comply, the dwarf would heave him up into the air to splinter that door.

Scrambling deftly, Drizzt went up on the wall to the ledge just below the portal. Hearing noise beyond, he cautiously pressed up on the trapdoor, cracking it open, then closing it immediately. He turned down to Athrogate, who was hopping about anxiously, and put a finger to his pursed lips, then mouthed, *Many*.

Athrogate poked his finger emphatically at the door, then took up Amber's mace in the same hand as the improvised flail and hopped up, grabbing for the ledge Drizzt knelt upon but falling just short. He jumped again, this time swinging the heavy wall block up over the ledge.

Unable to prevent this action, Drizzt caught the dwarf's free hand to help him up, but then signaled for him to stay quiet.

No such luck.

No sooner had Athrogate gotten his feet under him on the ledge than he sprang once more for the door, bursting through it and grabbing the floor above, then tugging himself up to his waist.

Drizzt heard the reaction above and went to shove the dwarf, for there was no turning back then, but even as he grabbed Athrogate's feet, he was yanked off his balance and had to drop all the way back down to the floor. He managed to glance up just in time to see Athrogate caught in a great pincer and being hauled through.

A moment of indecision struck the drow. Athrogate was surely doomed, so was he to scramble up there and dive into the melee—and probable death—as well? A momentary thought told him to flee down the tunnels, hide, and sneak out later.

But no, that he could not do, so he went quickly to the ledge again, wincing at every roar and growl, whimper and crash above. He started through the open trapdoor, but fell low as something rushed over his head.

Again it flew past, and Drizzt struggled to make sense of it. On the third pass, he realized he was looking at the thick legs of a glabrezu demon being whirled around like a living Uthgardt throwing hammer!

The fourth rotation was different, though, with the whole demon passing overhead, flying back past the open trapdoor to crash into the wall behind.

With nothing spinning overhead anymore, Drizzt leaped through to the floor above. The demon was no threat, he realized immediately, for black smoke was already forming around the dead thing. And back the other way, dwarves and demons flew as Athrogate plowed through them, Skullcrusher and his flail blasting a trail like scythes through tall dead grass.

Little elation accompanied that sight for Drizzt, however, for Athrogate poured blood out of both sides from the deep gashes of the demon pincer. From farther down the hall, crossbows clicked, and Athrogate jerked, but then yelled and charged on.

"No, no, no," Drizzt said, drawing Taulmaril the Heartseeker from his magical belt buckle and setting an arrow to the longbow in the same movement.

Unfortunately, the archers in the corridor beyond Athrogate fled before Drizzt could get a clear shot, slamming a heavy door. Drizzt heard them drop a bar down behind the door, too, and for a moment he feared that the one exit route had been sealed. But Athrogate shouldered through it anyway, splintering the wood and launching the bent metal bar into the room beyond.

Drizzt rushed to keep up with the rampaging dwarf. All through the keep they scrambled and never once did Drizzt get shot—probably because all the bolts were slamming into Athrogate.

As they neared the outer doors, Drizzt skidded to a stop abruptly, seeing one fallen dwarf and recognizing her as the victim of the brutal nalfeshnee. She had played dead as Athrogate rushed past, and now was trying to lift herself to her hands and knees.

Drizzt replaced his bow in the belt buckle and ran to her. He caught her under one arm and hoisted her upright. "One sound, one bad move, and I kill you," he warned, drawing Icingdeath.

"I have freed you of the cursed necklace," he said to her. "When you are well, come to the east, to Bleeding Vines, and perhaps we will find a way to save your kin."

She just stared at him, as if in a daze, and he eased her back to the floor.

On Drizzt went, trying to catch back up to Athrogate, coming in sight of him just as he burst through the outer door and into the open courtyard.

Where a host of enemies waited.

CHAPTER 23

Diabolical Noose

I t would be discovered," Inkeri Margaster warned Charri Hunzrin when the drow trader suggested a demonic phylactery for Lord Neverember. "He is no minor player in this and is being watched closely by many rivals."

"Without that control, how will he be?" Charri asked.

"Compliant," Inkeri assured her. "Dagult Neverember cares only for Dagult Neverember. He will see the gain to himself and his precious Neverwinter City and so he will remain silent on the matter. He wishes nothing more than to have King Bruenor and his dwarves expelled from the land."

"He was called by many 'the protector,'" Charri reminded her. "How does one gain such a title if he is as you say?"

"Oh, Dagult did battle to save others. His title is well earned."

"Altruistic, yes?"

"Yes," Inkeri said, "and no, for he cares only for the glory that such actions give to him. Not all acts of charity are done to serve others, and not all acts of heroism are done for the benefit of others. Sure, they are grand words—charity, heroism, altruism—but the benefits of having these descriptions attached to oneself cannot be underestimated, and that's all he cares about. For dear Dagult, such glory is his greatest motivation."

Charri Hunzrin spent a few moments digesting that. The words Inkeri was describing were anathema to drow society—they didn't even have such words in their language, other than somewhat synonymous insults offered to fools who hurt themselves for the sake of others.

"Still," she argued, "surely Lord Neverember will fear that the noose will turn to him after it has so tightened about the realms of King Bruenor."

Inkeri Margaster laughed at that. "You give Lord Neverember too much credit, I fear, or perhaps not enough. Dear Dagult trusts my loyalty, and perhaps that is not displaced. He is a valuable ally and knows where the gold is buried. So much gold."

"You trust that he will not hinder you?"

She laughed again. "He will cover our movements as we tighten the noose about Gauntlgrym and render King Bruenor into the irrelevance he so richly deserves. By the time the other lords of Waterdeep even know of trouble in the Crags, the halfling town will be aflame and the dwarves will be caught in their filthy hole. And the Waterdeep lords will not understand what has caused it all—and almost assuredly won't care for more beyond their own bottom lines anyway."

"And in the ensuing chaos there, King Bruenor will be pressed from below," Charri Hunzrin said, voicing the rest of the plan. "His friends have made great enemies in Menzoberranzan, and they will arrive soon enough to bolster your efforts."

"Promises, so many promises," Inkeri Margaster said with a chuckle. "You ask me to take a great risk—and when all is going so well—yet you get to wait before taking action."

"Tighten the noose," Charri Hunzrin said, "and we will do our part."

"And *then* your Hunzrin warriors and priestesses will march beside us, all for the glory of Lolth?"

Charri hesitated and Inkeri laughed at her.

"So anxious to throw others into battle," Inkeri remarked.

"I had thought demons anxious for such chaos," Charri returned. "Do you not share your form with Barlgura?"

"Barlgura who serves Demogorgon," Inkeri confirmed, tapping her precious necklace, perhaps the most powerful of the phylacteries the Hunzrins had brought to the surface. "And, thus, is not particularly fond of the drow at this time, as he awaits his master's reconstitution in the swirl of the abyssal sludge."

"He is angry with *some* drow," Charri quickly corrected. "Draw the lines accordingly in your calculations, my friend."

"I am not your friend."

"My . . . client, then. Have I not served you well? Have I not brought unimagined power to House Margaster?"

"At what price, I wonder?" Inkeri mused.

"Besides," Charri said, rushing the conversation back to the topic at hand, "King Bruenor's closest ally is the heretical instrument who destroyed the material form of Demogorgon, along with those who facilitated that catastrophe. My allies are no friends of that group."

Inkeri Margaster assumed a coy pose, tap-tapping her long and delicate finger against her sharp chin and saying, "Hmm," as if she was intrigued but not convinced.

"Do you think you will find a better opportunity?" Charri asked. "Ever?"

"A measured strike," Inkeri agreed. "We will wound the halflings, perhaps mortally, and seal the tunnel connecting their village to King Bruenor's realm."

"And you will be better situated for it," Charri promised.

Inkeri laughed again, then conceded the point with a nod and turned away, moving back along the tunnel to the secret entrance that would take her to the wine cellars of House Margaster.

Charri moved off the other way, to the small secret chamber where a House Hunzrin wizard waited to magically teleport her back to Menzoberranzan. She nearly fell back out of the room as she stepped over the threshold of the concealed door, though, to find that the wizard was not alone.

He stood with Iltztran Melarn, and worse, Matron Zhindia sat on a magical disk of energy off to the side.

"You did well, priestess, but your hesitation was as transparent as your matron's cowardice," Matron Zhindia said, getting it right out in the open that she had magically eavesdropped on Charri's meeting with Inkeri.

Charri thought herself incredibly stupid at that moment. Why hadn't she erected defenses against such clairaudience?

"I don't blame Matron Shakti, nor will I punish her," Matron Zhindia went on, and Charri fell back a step, surprised that the matron of House Melarn would even suggest such a thing.

"That will be for Lolth to determine," Matron Zhindia explained.

As Charri continued to stare incredulously, the other woman began to laugh.

"It is such a beautiful thing, don't you see?" Matron Zhindia explained, her nostrils flaring, her eyes widening with excitement. "Look past simple events and view the longer perspective."

"What do you mean?" Charri dared to ask.

"Can you not understand? This is why I was not allowed to die at the hands of the heretics. This is the long play of Lolth."

Charri stumbled over a few words, not quite sure where to even begin. Matron Zhindia was not allowed to die? What did that even mean?

"I should have been killed in the assassinations rendered upon my house," Matron Zhindia explained, seeing the unasked question on Charri's face. "They had me dead, and yet I live. They murdered a number of my priestesses, and yet all but one are alive once again, by the grace of Lolth. Yes, my daughter is no more, but that, too—do you not see?—is the glorious Spider Queen's way of testing my devotion. And now she understands the truth of that and questions not my actions, and I have come to see the long play she has put in place."

"I do not . . . understand," Charri Hunzrin admitted.

"That does not surprise me. So listen well: Because of her inaction on the matter, the return of Zaknafein, the heretic's father, will bring down Matron Mother Baenre," Matron Zhindia was happy to explain.

"With my abyssal retrievers, also gifts of Lady Lolth, I will bring the stolen soul, Zaknafein, to Menzoberranzan to face his judgment. Aye, indeed, I will bring him to the City of Spiders, dead or in chains, and will gather his worthless son with him."

"That vendetta has been declared ended by Matron Mother Baenre," Charri offered.

"And she is wrong! Woefully wrong!"

"Lolth faced . . . Yvonnel is . . ."

"Another test of our devotion, and nothing more!" Matron Zhindia snapped, coming forward, and in doing so driving Charri backward. "When the truth is laid bare, when Zaknafein and Drizzt are captured and executed, or returned after final judgment, House Baenre's folly will become apparent! Such an obvious blunder will reveal the displeasure of Lolth against that fool Matron Mother Quenthel, and that will inspire our allies to rise against Baenre and finally be rid of that scourge house."

Charri was too stunned and too intimidated to respond. Her fingers moved reflexively, and she had to interrupt the signing before she impulsively and unwittingly replied her belief that Matron Zhindia was surely mad.

"You do not believe me," Matron Zhindia reasoned, and Charri began to consider defensive spells she might then enact to save herself.

But Zhindia Melarn remained quite composed and even relaxed back on her magical floating disk. "I do not blame you," she said calmly, "but you will see. You will understand the benefit of boldness when I deliver the stolen prize of Zaknafein and his son, and bring ruin to all that Drizzt has built on the surface. All that *Jarlaxle* has built on the surface.

"Yes, Matron Mother Quenthel will howl at that, will she not?" Matron Zhindia continued. "But for Matron Shakti Hunzrin, the fall of Bregan D'aerthe will prove a boon, yes? And you? You would like this, of course. You would like little more than to be rid of Bregan D'aerthe so that House Hunzrin becomes once more the undeniable leader of all trade beyond this cavern we call home."

"It is . . . ambitious," Charri stammered.

"As all things *should* be. Yet not so ambitious, I think. Rather, it is within our grasp—easily so!"

"How?"

"You have so much to learn. Weren't you just talking with that filthy human? How, you ask? Why, with a noble Waterdhavian house and a demon-poisoned clan of warrior dwarfs. Point them at those who did such harm. Loose their demons upon our enemies, and I will send my retrievers and driders among them!"

"I just told—"

"You need to make the point more directly!" Matron Zhindia demanded. "House Margaster should move all resources against them, and now! Not against just the foolish halflings, and not even just the halflings and Bruenor's kingdom."

"Against who? Jarlaxle?"

"Yes! It is time to destroy his abominable city. To destroy this infernal halfling town. And to let the demons trap King Bruenor in his hole. When he is imprisoned, with no friends, we can then let our monsters multiply with their abyssal gates, to bring ever more catastrophe to their sides, eventually filling the halls of Gauntlgrym thick with demon allies."

"Matron, these are *demons* we discuss, not devils. When their rage is let free, they will not be corralled."

Zhindia shrugged. "Then let them run free and lay waste. What do we care? They will eventually be defeated—the humans alone have too much power in this region. But by the time they turn the tide, the beasts given me by a handmaiden—yes, by Eskavidne herself—will have our prey, and Matron Mother Baenre will answer for her heresy!"

"I will speak with Matron Shak—" Charri started to say.

"You will return to Inkeri Margaster, at once," Matron Zhindia demanded, "or you will never return to Menzoberranzan to face your matron again."

Charri's eyes widened. "I am a high priestess . . ."

"You will be a dead high priestess," Matron Zhindia promised. Beside her, Iltztran Melarn glared at his counterpart, who held up his hands in surrender, wanting no part of the Melarni house wizard.

"View it this way, my dear Charri Hunzrin," Matron Zhindia explained. "Your matron would have House Hunzrin watch from afar, not wanting to invoke the wrath of Lolth or of Matron Mother Baenre. This is understandable—is not self-preservation the first tenet of the Spider Queen?"

Charri just stared.

"Self-preservation," Matron Zhindia repeated. "Keeping yourself alive, for how might you serve the Spider Queen if you forfeit your life over a foolish choice? And is not defying one who has promised your death if you do so an ultimately foolish choice?"

Charri managed to nod her head, just a bit.

"Then go now, child!" growled Matron Zhindia, who, in truth, was not much older than Charri Hunzrin. "The trebuchets are thick with fiery abyssal shot. Just tell them where to aim and make sure they pull the trigger!"

Charri Hunzrin didn't look back, nor did she hold any doubt whatsoever that her every word to Inkeri Margaster would again be heard quite clearly by the vicious Zhindia Melarn.

CHAPTER 24

Desperate Flight

They can't get through that," Jarlaxle lamented, looking down at the courtyard, which teemed with demons of all shapes and sizes and with dozens of dwarves all bunched together—likely more in fear of their own allies than of whatever was causing such a stir immediately within the keep, but still standing between Drizzt and freedom.

Zaknafein started forward over the parapet, but Jarlaxle caught him by the arm.

"You can't get through that, either!"

"I'll not watch my son die," Zaknafein said to him, and yanked his arm away.

"Half the damned Abyss is here!" Jarlaxle whispered harshly.

"*I'll not watch my son die.*"

Jarlaxle studied his companion's face, those eyes that did not blink, and the mercenary leader didn't even try to grab Zaknafein's arm again. This was the man who had willingly placed himself upon Matron Malice's sacrificial altar and accepted the thrust of her dagger into his heart for Drizzt's sake. This was the man who had, in undeath, resisted Zin-carla, perhaps the only one to ever resist the servitude of that spell, and had leaped into acid rather than strike out at Drizzt.

"Get your tornado toy out," Zaknafein said.

Jarlaxle shook his head. He had overtaxed the magical item and it had little, if anything, left to offer. But of course, he was Jarlaxle. He had other toys.

We need a plan, Jarlaxle's fingers signed.

I have one.

What?

Kill things, Zaknafein signaled back, and he moved along the wall toward the distant door to the keep itself. He paused and gasped, as did Jarlaxle, when that keep door blew open, exploded by a flying pig-like demon creature that flopped and squealed as it bounced through the waiting monsters, more than one of which kicked, bit, stabbed, or punched the battered thing.

Out behind the flying pig came a dwarf, wild-looking, snarling and screaming, swatting away everything nearby with a huge mace and spinning an even larger block of stone at the end of a rusty chain. Fearlessly, the fellow bore into the diabolical gathering.

A gigantic nalfeshnee swatted the dwarf off his feet, but he scrambled back up before the beast could stomp him. Leaping up, he ran through the demon's legs, biting the monster's thigh for good measure as he passed.

Out the other side, a glabrezu snapped its claws upon him, and he took the brutal hits willingly in exchange for planting that mace squarely into the demon's skull, crushing it to the ground. Extracting, swinging wildly, kicking and spinning, he got free of the tangle and rushed to an open spot—and there found three dwarves with leveled crossbows waiting for him.

DRIZZT TRIED TO KEEP UP WITH THE ROARING ATHROGATE, but the dwarf was simply knocking monsters aside without regard for the fact that they would recover and retake the chase.

Drizzt was more deliberate in his follow-ups, stabbing and crippling fiend and dwarf alike, then leaping past to pursue his friend. By the time he got near to the courtyard door it was open and hanging, and he visually followed the path of carnage to spot Athrogate, who even then launched a dwarf through the air at the end of his makeshift flail.

Athrogate stomped on a second dwarf, lying prone before him, then charged ahead, but skidded to a stop to swing out to his right, both hands on Skullcrusher, planting the weapon across the shoulders of a hell hound, splaying the beast's paws wide and flattening it to the ground.

"Oh, friend," Drizzt muttered at the sight of Athrogate, who had a crossbow bolt hanging from one cheek and two others sticking from his chest. Blood flowed freely down the dwarf's body, and although Drizzt knew it was the girdle that provided the strength, he was pretty sure Athrogate would be moving on rage alone should he lose that magical belt.

He didn't have much time to contemplate it, though, as a second hell hound breathed a cone of fire at the dwarf. Unsurprisingly, Athrogate kept running and kept roaring, now with flames dancing on his clothing.

"Guenhwyvar, I need you again!" Drizzt called, and he paused just long enough for the gray mist to begin to coalesce before charging out the door and into the fray.

Enemies came at the drow immediately, and from all angles. Swords, hammers, claws, beaks—even tail whips from a lizard-like demon—rained down on Drizzt before he had gone three strides from the door, the path closing fast between him and Athrogate.

He couldn't think of that, however, with the barrage upon him. He jumped, ducked, skipped, and worked his blades in a dizzying series of blocks and parries, fending, but ultimately retreating, step by step, back toward the door. He noted one large demon beginning to cast a magical spell, lightning crackling between its long clawed fingers. With no other options before him, Drizzt went back into the keep and dove aside, just before a tremendous bolt knocked the door from its hinges, launching it across the room and taking half the jamb with it.

Enemies poured in, and Drizzt assailed them from the side, always attacking the leading dwarf or demon so they couldn't encircle him.

He didn't need to hold them long, though, for as a pair of dwarves entered and faded off to the right, away from Drizzt, an uncoiled panther buried them beneath it, springing from them to leap into the chest of the vrock immediately trailing the duo.

Drizzt sent his blades into a spin and slid them away, pulling Taulmaril from his magical buckle. With Guenhwyvar holding the line and him shooting over her, he could get to Athrogate, he dared to believe.

But then he was scrambling again, falling away suddenly, for the wall beside him, the wall to the right of the door, was simply gone, vanished! In that single tumble, the agile drow had his bow away and his scimitars back in his hands, turning as he went over to face up to the large new opening, expecting a wave of enemies to simply bury him where he stood.

Only two came in at him, but it might as well have been a dozen! For these demons Drizzt knew well; indeed, he had defeated their namesake in the fight for Gauntlgrym. Nine feet tall, the naga-like creatures seemed half beautiful human woman, half serpent, with a tail that could deliver a poison sting and six arms, each wielding a weapon of great magical power. A dozen baubles and necklaces jingled on each as they advanced side by side, their expressions hateful.

Clearly they knew their prey as well as he did them.

They knew he was the drow who had defeated Marilith, the greatest of their kind.

"Hold the door!" Drizzt told Guenhwyvar, and the drow ranger went to secure the breached wall—breached by a passwall dweomer that wouldn't last for long, he hoped.

If he could just keep the demons in the line of that missing wall, when the spell expired and the stone returned . . .

He knew immediately that his efforts would fall short. He fell into his deepest warrior trance, giving himself over fully to his instincts, feeling, hearing, smelling the flow of battle, and just letting his primal self, this purest warrior he called the Hunter, take over. And now, with the added benefit of the balance and techniques he had learned from

Grandmaster Kane, he felt more capable and confident as a warrior than he had in his entire life.

But the mariliths could each strike seven ways, and these major demons knew each other well and worked brilliantly in tandem. For all the speed and beauty of his dance, Drizzt simply could not keep up.

He got hit. He got hit again. A tail stabbed him in the thigh just before he could drop that leg back, and he felt the burn of poison immediately.

"You will pay for the banishment of Marilith, Drizzt Do'Urden!" one of the six-armed demons said with a hiss.

On the pair came furiously, twelve weapons stabbing and slashing, driving the now-limping Drizzt backward.

Out of the corner of his eye he noticed another section of the wall go away, another hole appearing, and the thought to run out before it could crowd with enemies occurred to him, but only briefly before a massive fireball erupted over him and the mariliths.

HE HAD LOST WIDE PUDDLES OF BLOOD, HIS SKIN WAS TORN in a dozen places and more, and he could feel the metallic tips of two crossbow quarrels tearing at his insides and scraping against his ribs with every gasping breath. But Athrogate wouldn't slow, and he barreled on, sweeping with his makeshift flail, crushing skulls with the mace named for exactly that, leaving a wake of shattered enemies.

He heard the buzzing around him as he closed on yet another vrock, and so was not caught completely off his guard when he swept the wall-stone flail up high and found it caught by one of those horrid chasme demons. It tried to hoist him, and almost did, but the dwarf gave a mighty yank with his shackled arm, tugging the demon down to his level. There it turned to face him, prodding with its long proboscis.

Athrogate prodded, too, but with a powerful mace.

Skullcrusher knocked that insect appendage aside and splattered the bulbous face of the half-housefly, half-human abomination.

The flail fell free of the chasme's grasp as the demon flew back from Athrogate and bounced upon the ground.

Any relief or satisfaction the dwarf might have felt, however, lasted only an instant before the powerful beak of the vrock cracked him on the forehead and sent him flying backward and to his backside.

A gang of dwarves and demons leaped upon him to finish him, to crush him into the stone, and he had maybe seconds before he met his end.

"*Amber!*"

With that mighty howl Athrogate got his feet under him and stood once more, shrugging and swatting aside the attackers.

He couldn't see a thing for the blood that gushed down from his new wound in his forehead, but he didn't care.

"*Amber!*" he roared relentlessly, and he swung and darted this way and that, sometimes hitting, more often missing, and staggering with every off-balance step.

HE FELT THE COOL FLOOR BENEATH HIM AND SURRENDERED to the stone, his body relaxing so completely that he felt as if he were sinking into the earth below. He sent his consciousness there as well, instantly, knowing that any sudden jerks or twists against the biting flames of the fireball would lift him and make him more vulnerable.

Yet another of Grandmaster Kane's instructions saved Drizzt from serious injury, as the fireball barely touched him. His frostbrand scimitar would have minimized the flames, certainly, but this was a mighty blast, and still didn't even singe his clothing. Though he was pleased with himself for that one instant, he grimaced as he bounced right back up, hearing a howl of pain from poor Guenhwyvar off to his left. A cursory glance that way as he again engaged the mariliths made him wince all the more.

Guenhwyvar scrambled and thrashed wildly, driving a pair of demons back through the doorway. But the valiant panther, engulfed in flames, couldn't even see them, likely, and was contorting against the biting fires as much as at her foes! Drizzt knew he had to send her home to the Astral Plane, even in this desperate situation.

For the mariliths came on unbothered. They were creatures spawned in fire, creatures of fire, and they bathed in the fireball without the slightest bother.

Drizzt parried a flurry of blows from the creature on his left, then swung to the right to deflect a vicious stab from a short spear, and on that turn, he managed a glance, thinking to escape through the new hole.

But that hole was gone.

"Go home, Guen," he whispered, fully aware that he would soon be overrun from that direction, even if he somehow managed to hold off the fury of the two mariliths.

There was a finality in Drizzt's voice, thinking he'd never see his beloved panther friend again. He thought of his other friends, too, of Bruenor and Regis and Wulfgar, and of Jarlaxle, and mostly of Catti-brie and Zaknafein, wondering if his father would even bother to know Drizzt's son or daughter.

Yes, he thought of the child, his child, whom he'd never see.

"No!" Drizzt growled. He couldn't let that happen. He had to find a way past this.

Even with the Hunter, even with his training at the Monastery of the Yellow Rose, even with all the tricks and magic, his new sword of mighty combined enchantments, his deadly bow . . . even with all that, Drizzt had no chance of winning here.

But neither would he lose, he decided. He could not lose!

The tunnels . . . he had to escape into the tunnels behind him, down into the winding ways of the dungeons. He thought of poor Athrogate, but he couldn't see the black-bearded dwarf anymore, couldn't hear him yelling for Amber. Drizzt recognized that his friend was almost certainly already dead, and even if not, there was no way he could hope to get to Athrogate's side.

I rescued you, only to lead you to your death, he thought in a silent benediction.

And then he fought to make sure he didn't also die.

His blades worked in a blur, fending off the demons, and at the same time Drizzt flexed the muscles of his leg, seeking the poison, feeling it and rejecting it, pushing it back out through the wound, denying it deeper access.

He had to go, had to turn and flee at once . . .

But how?

He swept Vidrinath across, left to right, fully extended to buy him a bit of space from the mariliths. He meant to turn and run right behind that slash but was startled as the blade came across one way and a dark, somersaulting form came back the other way, just over it!

Before he could even register that, almost simultaneously, another form came from that same direction, an avian form that had Drizzt first thinking that another vrock demon had come in through that second hole.

But the creature ran behind him, not near him, and did not strike in its pass.

It all came together in Drizzt's sensibilities an eyeblink later, when he came to understand that the first tumbling dark form was Zaknafein, his father, who was now standing beside him, sword thrusting and whip snapping at the marilith on the left. He was bolstered by the fact that now they were two—but no, not two. *Three*, he realized when a line of magical daggers flew past him to strike at the sister demons!

And even three was wrong, because that blur of feathers belonged to a giant bird—not a vrock demon, but a huge diatryma summoned from the feather on Jarlaxle's hat. The magical pet met the charge of a vrock through the door where Guenhwyvar had been, their powerful beaks smashing together with a resounding crack.

It had all happened so fast, in a mere instant, but that distraction might have been the end of Drizzt had not Zaknafein worked his blade and whip so marvelously before his son, driving back the nearest marilith, and had not Jarlaxle sent those daggers flying from his magical bracer, which never seemed to run out of the missiles!

Working to recall the discipline of the Hunter, Drizzt tried to find a rhythm with Zaknafein, feeling the movements of the weapon master beside him, seeking a complementary style. And sure enough, they were soon fighting almost as one.

It all seemed so natural to him! To them both, he knew, as the harmony grew so quickly between their movements, as if the last two hundred years had not even passed, as if they were training side by side back in House Do'Urden in Menzoberranzan.

A lightning bolt shot through the door, and both the vrock and Jarlaxle's pet bird shrieked, but the vrock, unlike the bird, was not stunned or surprised, and used the distraction to drive its beak into the diatryma's skull, killing it instantly.

"Jarlaxle, the door!" Drizzt yelled, still working his blades defensively, fending off the press of the marilith barrage. He parried with short up-angled movements, his swords tapping, tapping, tapping until he saw an opening, then brought Icingdeath suddenly down and around, then up and over from the outside, then down again over the marilith's arms, forcing her to drop her upper limbs lower and fade back with a slither.

Not fast enough, though, as Zaknafein's whip snapped over Drizzt's descending arm, slashing across the demon's eyes and forcing her back still more.

"A passwall," Drizzt explained quietly. "Drive them into it." He glanced to the left, expecting a rush of monsters from that open door, but he shouldn't have doubted Jarlaxle. The mercenary leader's response came in the form of a flying glob of sticky green goo that slammed the vrock and threw it back to the threshold, catching the demon on the door jamb. A second glob followed, further sealing the door, though it surely wouldn't hold for long . . .

"Drive them!" Zaknafein said to Drizzt, pressing forward suddenly, an obvious move, as other monsters were trying to get in through the opening behind the twin mariliths. He cracked his whip three times in rapid succession to get both mariliths leaning back over their snake-like tails, then brought the whip expertly into a roll, setting it on his belt and drawing his second sword too quickly for the demon in front of him to take advantage of the exchange.

Now two swords and two scimitars rang out against the fury of a dozen demonic weapons, Drizzt and Zaknafein working as if they were one being. Drizzt stabbed Vidrinath out at the demon in front of his father, and when that marilith sent two blades out to parry, Zaknafein brought his right-hand sword across inside the demon's opening arms.

She got one of those arms out too wide for him to score a hit, but the weapon master's blade dug hard at the other forearm. The marilith howled in pain and her weapon dropped to the stone. Hardly slowing, Zaknafein brought both his blades down and under the predictable forward slash of the demon's two good weapon arms on that side, her left, and then came back across the other way, forcing backhand parries, turning her just a bit away from her partner.

At that same moment, Drizzt brought Vidrinath across with a mighty slash, not to score a hit but simply to force the marilith before him to follow the blade.

A full spin, with one step to the left as he came around, had Drizzt right beside Zaknafein, and had Drizzt's opponent, similarly turned, out and away from her partner.

Now the two drow warriors drove hard, side by side, forcing a retreat.

"It's a passwall dweomer!" Drizzt yelled to Jarlaxle.

"Well, why didn't you tell me that earlier?" came the mercenary leader's response from behind. Just a pair of heartbeats later came a better response: a wave of rippling magical energy that reminded Drizzt of the feeling he would experience on a beach when the tide rushed back out. The mariliths clearly recognized it, too, as they hissed and screeched and fell all over each other trying to get back out through the open wall. One even threw aside some weapons and grabbed a pair of lesser demons, yanking them back over her as if trying to block falling stones.

But these returning stones weren't falling. They simply *were*.

For where those stones had once been, the magical passwall had simply vanished them. Where those stones were missing, Jarlaxle's dweomer of dispelling magic had simply put them back.

And anything caught in that area of rematerializing stone was simply crushed to nothingness.

A pair of weapons clanged to the floor in front of the two warrior drow, one of those weapons still in the grasp of the hand of a now-severed arm. The end of a marilith's snakelike tail lay there as well, no longer attached but still dripping that nasty venom. And there, too, lay the severed upper halves of the lesser beings tossed back by one of the mariliths, quite destroyed.

Drizzt and Zaknafein fell back, panting. "Athrogate is . . . was out there!" Drizzt yelled.

"Ambergris?" Jarlaxle asked.

Drizzt shook his head.

"Then out there we must go," Jarlaxle decided. "Summon your mounts, both of you."

"We'll not get through that door," Drizzt observed, and indeed, the goo was giving way and it looked like a horde of monsters was about to burst into the room.

"We'll make our own door," Jarlaxle insisted with a tight smile, and he launched yet another glob of goo at the keep's portal, to hold it just a bit longer.

They summoned their mounts, and before Drizzt could question further, Jarlaxle walked his nightmare over to the other side of the room, near to where he and Zaknafein had entered the keep. In one hand he held that strange black cloth, which both Drizzt and Zaknafein knew well, and in the other a new toy. It seemed to be a short club or scepter, or perhaps a pennant, made of some black metal but covered in a cloth striped red and white.

"Be quick," he told his allies. "A straight run across the courtyard, for Athrogate and with him, to the front door!"

He threw that strange cloth-like disk at the wall, and it elongated and widened as it went, landing against the stone surface and creating an opening.

Zaknafein on his hell boar was first through, Drizzt close behind on Andahar, leaping out into the courtyard, into the swarm of surprised demons and dwarves—mostly the latter over at this side. Zaknafein seemed more intent on running them all down than on escaping, his wild mount jumping and throwing small fireballs, spitting out in all directions from its pounding hooves. Wholly without fear, the magical mount and its rider charged ahead, scattering enemies.

Drizzt spotted Athrogate off to the left, near the center of the courtyard. He started to yell to his friend, planning to alert his other two companions while putting up his bow at the same time to aid the dwarf from afar.

But the words stuck in his throat, and his bow lowered.

For Athrogate went up into the air, thrashing and screaming, spraying fountains of blood, caught in the grasp of a chasme demon, and so quick was its ascent that even if Drizzt had somehow managed to shoot the wretched demon off the dwarf from this distance, the fall would have likely doomed the already mortally wounded Athrogate.

"Ride on! Ride on!" he heard Jarlaxle implore from behind, and he glanced back to see the mercenary pulling the hole from the wall and tucking it away as he galloped his nightmare to catch up. Jarlaxle lifted that other item, tilted it away from his body, and did something—gave a command word, or pressed a hidden button, perhaps—and the flag unfurled. Except it wasn't a flag, but a circular shield of cloth, held wide and supported by a series of thin metal spokes. It wasn't fully flattened perpendicularly to the staff holding it, but still very round and quite wide, with a broad white stripe at its perimeter, a red stripe beside that, then a second white stripe, bordering a circle of red in the middle.

Jarlaxle brought it back over him, holding it in his right hand but angling it out to the left, toward the mass of enemies, including a contingent of dwarves leveling crossbows at the intruders. They fired as one, twenty quarrels speeding at Jarlaxle and a couple at Drizzt, and more from up ahead, flying in at Zaknafein.

Drizzt felt the sting of one across his chest, and expected more— and expected, too, that Jarlaxle and his nightmare would be struck a dozen times.

But Jarlaxle came galloping past, barely harmed, and Drizzt saw more than a dozen of the bolts stuck into his cloth shield! Even as Drizzt gaped at that strange sight, another quarrel flew ahead, aimed for Zaknafein, but it veered in the air, turned as if guided, and it too struck Jarlaxle's cloth barrier.

"What?" Drizzt gasped, running Andahar to pace the nightmare.

"Missile attractor," Jarlaxle replied. "Useful in the rain, too."

The absurdity of that statement was lost on Drizzt, though, as he looked ahead to his father, charging full speed for the closed outer gate, a hulking glabrezu demon blocking the way.

As he neared it, Zaknafein rolled off the back of his hell boar, hitting the ground but coming right back to his feet, swords in hand. The boar ran right between the glabrezu's long legs, smashing head-long into the door, splintering wood and knocking the thing from its hinges. And the distraction was just enough for Zaknafein, who leaped into the four-armed demon's reach, inside the bite of its pincer arms, his swords stabbing and slashing with brilliant accuracy.

"Aside!" Drizzt yelled, and Zaknafein dropped low under a clawing swipe, then leaped out to the left, just avoiding a snapping pincer.

The glabrezu started to turn to follow, and only then realized its doom as Andahar's long horn speared into its chest, driving it back-ward and out the door.

As the unicorn galloped along, Drizzt reached his hand out to the side to Zaknafein, who sheathed a sword, caught his son's hand, and swung up behind him with easy grace. Out they went, Andahar snort-ing and flailing its head, throwing the murdered demon aside.

Jarlaxle was then beside them, the hell boar up in front, snorting crazily and leading the way across the stones.

A fireball engulfed the trio, and a lightning bolt cut between them, stinging them all. But they held on and kept running.

And heard the buzzing behind them.

"Switch!" Drizzt said, and he lifted his right leg over Andahar, riding sidesaddle a couple of strides, then taking Zaknafein's left hand with his right, across his body.

Drizzt tucked Taulmaril in tight, then dropped to the ground, turning as he went, Zaknafein tugging to help the spin. Drizzt hit the ground and leaped right back up, throwing his left leg around and over Andahar's haunches.

Now sitting backward behind his father—one of Zaknafein's hands grabbing the back of his belt to help hold him in place—Drizzt lifted his bow. Out over the wall and down by the coast, he spotted the chasme holding Athrogate. The dwarf's makeshift flail swung up and then over the fly-like demon and seemed to catch its wings, for the thing faltered, its flight suddenly erratic, then nonexistent.

Drizzt winced as his friend and the demon fell from the sky, out of sight, to the rocks along the water's edge.

The ranger shook it off.

The time to grieve would come later.

He set an arrow and let fly—then another and another—many more in rapid succession, streaks of silvery lightning reaching out and high at the pursuing flight of chasmes.

Most of his shots missed, bouncing as he was on the speeding unicorn, but those that struck home took down the targeted demons, and the flight inevitably began to thin, and even with their aerial speed the chasme gained little ground on the thundering magical mounts.

Drizzt wanted to yell to his companions to turn about that they might try to find the fallen Athrogate. But as the surge of battle eased from his limbs and veins, the ranger realized he was hurt a lot worse than he had believed, with a crossbow quarrel stuck into his chest, several deep cuts along his sides from the mariliths, and a large lump of swelling in his leg from the sting of the poisoned tail.

Worse, he felt Zaknafein's hold slacken until his father slumped behind him, and only his quick reaction caught the weapon master before he simply tumbled from the unicorn. Wise Andahar began to slow.

Jarlaxle rushed back beside them. "Keep going!" he implored, and while they cantered on, Drizzt spun back around and Jarlaxle helped him set the unconscious Zaknafein across Andahar's strong shoulders.

Drizzt grabbed the unicorn's thick mane and kicked Andahar's flanks.

Indeed, they couldn't stop, for the chasmes were still there, though hanging back, and now a great pack of hell hounds was coming in pursuit.

So on they galloped, three drow on two magical mounts, led by a riderless hell boar.

They made the Trade Way and thundered along to the north, and the pursuit stayed hot long into the night. The trio didn't stop until the following morning, when they came to the light forest around the halfling town of Bleeding Vines.

EPILOGUE

Showithal Terdidy and Doregardo exchanged grim looks after Regis finished talking.

"So how are they?" asked Doregardo, the leader of the Grinning Ponies, halfling protectors of the Trade Way.

"Catti-brie thinks Drizzt should have died," Regis said. "She couldn't believe that he had somehow defeated the demon poison and hadn't bled to death. The tail spike got him inside the thigh, right in the bloody area."

The other two halflings nodded solemnly.

"He learned some tricks in Damara, it would seem," said Regis.

"Our Kneebreaker friends have told many stories of the monks of the Monastery of the Yellow Rose," Showithal explained, his voice rising in reverence when he spoke of the halfling legion that had come down from Damara to join the Grinning Ponies as defenders of Bleeding Vines. "I've heard such things as you describe."

"Zaknafein is worse," Regis went on. "He took many serious wounds."

"Oh, but if Drizzt is to lose his father aga—" Doregardo started to reply, but Regis shook his head.

"Catti-brie has him on the mend."

"And what of the fancy one?" asked Showithal with a sigh of relief.

"Jarlaxle?" Regis replied, chuckling. "Not a scratch. Never a scratch!"

"He's not natural, that one, even for a drow," said Doregardo. "A dangerous enemy."

"But a fine friend," Regis assured them, and the two soldiers nodded.

"Have you been to King Bruenor?" asked Doregardo.

"Both he and Jarlaxle have taken the loss of Athrogate and Amber Gristle O'Maul terribly. Drizzt, too. There's a lot of history between them, and they'll not soon be forgotten. Nor will the demons and dwarves that killed them."

"Hear, hear, to that," said Doregardo, and all raised their glasses in quiet salute.

"Fine, then—what's our move?" Showithal Terdidy asked.

"To Waterdeep, and to all the farms around," Regis explained. "Warn the folk and the lords of Waterdeep."

"Just south, then?"

"Luskan knows," Regis explained.

"What about Port Llast, and the farms north?" Doregardo asked.

"Jarlaxle will warn the areas north," Regis told him. "You've only twenty riders, and getting word to Waterdeep is most important, as well as most delicate. Avoid passing through the region around Neverwinter City at all costs. Lord Neverember is not to be trusted, nor are any working for him. I will go so far as to say that he is the biggest problem here."

"We're to tell that to the lords of Waterdeep?" Doregardo asked.

"No!" Regis replied immediately. "That's why this is so delicate, and why we'll entrust it only to you and yours. We can't accuse a noted and powerful Waterdhavian lord like Dagult Neverember on just the evidence we've found so far. And how would we know the full extent of his alliances in any case? He is allied with House Margaster, that much we know. But beyond that, it is wise to assume he has other powerful friends in Waterdeep.

"No," he went on, "we'll keep the conversation to the demons that have taken root in Thornhold, and rally the legions of Waterdeep to help us destroy that threat."

"You've told us of demons in Neverwinter City and Neverwinter Wood, as well," Showithal reminded him. "You would have us make no mention of that?"

"In time," Regis advised. "We start with Thornhold, then circle out to Neverwinter City. When we have the full confidence of the lords of Waterdeep and have ascertained the whole conspiracy, we will speak to them of House Margaster and, in time, of Lord Neverember and his money washing."

The two riders looked at each other again and nodded. "As you wish, Spider Parrafin," Doregardo said. "We set out for Waterdeep with the morning's first light."

Regis nodded his appreciation. He knew that his friends had a long and difficult road ahead of them.

He knew that *all* the folk of the north had a long and difficult road ahead of them.

BREVINDON MARGASTER STOOD AT THE PROW OF THE CAR-rack *White Seal,* the lead ship in the pirate flotilla, sailing north on the southern winds as spring took hold along the Sword Coast. A hundred ships followed, sloops and caravels, carracks and even a pair of longboats, including one oared by giant refugee firbolgs from the Moonshae Isles.

More than two thousand men, women, giantkind, goblinkin—even a crew of gnolls—rode these winds right behind him, eager for plunder.

The young nobleman grinned. This great armada had been hired for a fraction of the vast Margaster fortune, and less than the price of any mercenaries Brevindon had ever heard of, so eager were they for new plunder in the north, above Waterdeep.

And so eager to reclaim Luskan from the secret powers behind the rise of High Captain Kurth.

I told you, said the voice in Brevindon's head, the voice of the demon residing in the phylactery he wore about his neck.

"You did," the man admitted. "And know that House Margaster and Lord Neverember will not forget it."

You know what I want.

"Yes, Asbeel."

Have they fashioned my—our sword?

Brevindon glanced back to starboard, far aft, to a heavy carrack and the smoke that poured from her raised bridge.

"They work on it," he told the demon. "Large and twisted and jagged."

And the gem I gave you? The adamantine, too?

"Yes, of course," he assured his visitor. "All is being done in accordance with the guide you helped me pen."

Too large for you, my host. But when I am free, you will learn the power of that blade! the cambion promised.

"WE'VE A BIGGER PROBLEM THAN LORD NEVEREMBER, I fear," Jarlaxle told King Bruenor, in the dwarf's private quarters deep within Gauntlgrym. Beside the dwarf, his two queens, Fist and Fury, grumbled about revenge for the death of Amber Gristle O'Maul, who had become a dear friend to them.

"Mayhap, but I've been wantin' that one's head for a long time," Bruenor replied, not seeming to hear Jarlaxle.

"Demons," the rogue tried.

"Fought 'em afore."

"Indeed, but in such numbers?" asked the drow. "I have not seen so many demons in one place outside of the Underdark or the Abyss itself. And among them are major fiends, who can open gates to the lower planes and bring forth more minions still."

Bruenor cocked his head and looked at the drow sidelong. "Guess I'm not surprised," he muttered.

"Surprised?"

"That ye been to the Abyss. Searching for a vacation home, were ye?"

That brought a smile to Jarlaxle's face, but it didn't last. "We must act quickly, or their numbers will multiply," the drow warned.

"I've gates o' me own!" Bruenor replied.

"And I fear you will need them, good dwarf," Jarlaxle said. "All of them."

"Waterdeep won't sit back," said Bruenor. "The whole o' the north's in danger, and last I looked, demons ain't much caring what or who they're murderin' and eatin'!"

"We know not who in the city is allied with us and who with Lord Neverember," Jarlaxle admitted, offering a shrug, almost in apology.

Bruenor surely understood. Yes, the lords of Waterdeep might now tolerate demons in the lands about their grand city, but they weren't overly fond of drow elves controlling Luskan, either. Nor of the magical Hosttower being raised from the rubble, led by a former archmage of Menzoberranzan!

Bruenor's known friendship with Jarlaxle had not helped him enlist many allies in his running feud with Lord Dagult Neverember, who was, after all, a lord of Waterdeep himself. Indeed, in the months of Gauntlgrym's renewal, Bruenor had been quite surprised to discover how isolated he and his clan had become from the area's powers. He figured relations would improve now that the magical teleportation gates were working and goods from Mithral Hall, Citadel Adbar, and Citadel Felbarr would soon be flowing through Gauntlgrym, to say nothing of the weapons being fashioned by expert blacksmiths at Bruenor's primordial-fired forge.

But that was still in the future, and the demons were in the present. And the past . . .

Well, the past always lingered, and old habits—and prejudices— died hard.

"I want to kill them as much as you do," Jarlaxle offered then. "Athrogate was not only your friend."

"Aye," Bruenor admitted. "Nor Amber, I know. To be certain, I'm still not knowing how much I should trust ye, elf, on the little matters, particularly when coin or magic's in the pot, eh? But when the fight's started, I'm glad ye're on me side."

Jarlaxle bowed and tipped his hat.

"And what help from the Hosttower?" Bruenor asked. "Them wizards shouldn't much like demons that ain't their own to play with."

"Those wizards who are about will aid us, I am sure. And we will need them, I am just as sure."

Bruenor wanted to counter that with some words about Jarlaxle never really seeing the wrath of Clan Battlehammer unleashed. He held the thought private, though, fearing that his voice wouldn't be so convincing. Athrogate was gone. Amber Gristle O'Maul o' the Adbar O'Mauls was gone. And his friends had just limped home with severe wounds to tell him that news.

He expected that Clan Battlehammer was about to find the fight of their lives, probably even beyond the catastrophe of the War of the Silver Marches.

He would soon enough learn that he was underestimating his enemies.

"IT WILL GET WORSE," ASH'ALA MELARN SAID TO KIMMURIEL Oblodra, her parting words as the psionicist became insubstantial and drifted through the wall of the Underdark corridor where they had secretly met.

A large part of Ash'ala wanted to go with him. Her prospects in Menzoberranzan were not good. She had been the ambassador of her house to both Bregan D'aerthe and House Xorlarrin, but now House Xorlarrin was no more, or would soon be again, but in the place of fallen House Do'Urden, and at the sufferance of and alliance with House Baenre. House Melarn, which had openly attacked House Do'Urden, was no more in the favor of the Xorlarrins, and particularly not with the Baenres!

And the Baenres were also the great protectors of Bregan D'aerthe.

Where did that leave Ash'ala? She was the third daughter of the first priestess, Kyrnill. Once, her prospects were grand, for Kyrnill was then Matron Kyrnill Kenafin. But Zhindia Horlbar was now their matron; her grip had never been tighter, and Kyrnill's place had never been less important. Or less stable. If Kyrnill fell, her daughters would find themselves at Zhindia's mercy.

And Zhindia, Ash'ala understood, was not possessed of that particular quality.

She almost called back to the departing psionicist, to beg him to take her with him to join with Jarlaxle. She did not, though, mostly because she knew that Kimmuriel would not do it. She was more important to Bregan D'aerthe where she was, seated beside the powers of House Melarn, than she could be as just another member of the mercenary band.

So she sighed instead and made her way back to the city and House Melarn. She was barely through the front gates when a sentry informed her that the matron was looking for her regarding an urgent matter. She rushed through the house, a bit concerned, and found Matron Zhindia in her private quarters, sitting in a comfortable chair beside First Priestess Kyrnill.

"I was told you would see me," she said, bowing respectfully. "I have gained a bit more information about the plans of Matron Zeerith Xorlar—"

"Have you?" Matron Zhindia interrupted, seeming quite amused, which of course had the hairs on the back of Ash'ala's neck standing up. Her fears became a horrible reality a moment later when a quartet of guards, including the house wizard, came through a side door with a floating disk, upon which lay Kimmuriel Oblodra, shackled to the disk by strands of energy across the wrists, ankles, waist, and neck!

One more shackle, a living shackle, by far the most horrific and gruesome, held the psionicist captive, for coming in behind the disk was an illithid, two of its octopus-like tentacles up Kimmuriel's nose.

"My matron—" Ash'ala began.

"Do not even bother to speak," Matron Zhindia interrupted. "We know it all, and if there is more to be learned, my mind flayer friend there will simply take it from you." She motioned to the open door, and more drow entered the room, Ash'ala's fellow priestesses of House Melarn. They surrounded her and led her into a different room, and the young woman's knees went weak indeed when she came to that destination.

It was a small chamber, with only a single item within: a large metal tub filled with water. An armrest extended from each side of the basin, complete with straps and culminating in pillywinks.

"No, no, no," Ash'ala begged, and the strength left her legs. Her sisters caught her before she hit the ground, though, and stripped her naked as they held her up.

Then they dragged her into the tub and strapped her arms down to either side.

Matron Zhindia and Ash'ala's mother had entered the room by this point, and Zhindia looked to Kyrnill and motioned, saying, "You should apply the thumbscrews, First Priestess, to show your devotion to Lolth above your family."

Ash'ala could see the pain on her mother's face as she screwed down the poor girl's fingers, but with that pain came, too, a measure of outrage that stupid Ash'ala had ever put her in this position.

Thus, when Kyrnill tightened down the vise, she offered no mercy, crushing Ash'ala's fingers under its brutal press.

While that was transpiring, others began to paint Ash'ala's face and neck with rothé milk and honey, a sweet and gooey mixture.

They all stepped back, leaving Ash'ala sobbing when Matron Zhindia leaned over to stare into her face.

"Fear not, child, for you'll be fed well," she said. "And I will bring the flies to you personally."

Ash'ala began to beg and to wail, to thrash and tug against the straps holding her arms fast.

But Zhindia just laughed and twisted down one of the pillywinks to elicit a scream of absolute agony.

"Fetch the illithid, that it can extract all we need from this one's mind," Matron Zhindia ordered one of the others, and she quickly turned back to Ash'ala, and gave the thumbscrews another agonizing turn.

"Pain tells you that you are alive, child," she purred in sobbing Ash'ala's ear. "That is a good thing. You see, I want you to enjoy the many meals we will feed to you. I want you alive when the flies are feasting on the milk and honey. I want you alive when you are lying in this tub of your own excrement. I want you alive when the maggots hatch in the filthy tub all about you, that you can feel every bite and every squirm over the days as they devour you."

HE COULDN'T OPEN HIS EYES, BUT HE HEARD A SOUND, DIS-tantly, and soon understood it to be a voice. He knew the language, but not well.

"You grant me spells of healing! Why?" the speaker said in a me-lodic voice, a beautiful voice, he thought. "These are your enemies! Is your highest quality that of unpredictability?"

He didn't understand the next words. They were in the same language, he guessed from the inflections and consonant sounds, but seemed more ancient, somehow.

Then he felt the warmth as a wave of healing washed through him, aimed at his lower arm—and only then did the broken fellow realize the acute pain in that area.

"I betrayed you!" the voice said, ending in a laugh that seemed helpless.

He managed to crack open one eye, hardly focusing, and saw a beautiful drow woman standing over him. He tried to speak her name, or who he thought her to be, but could find no breath behind the word to speak it audibly.

"I stole Zaknafein from eternity to deliver him to the heretic who denied you, and yet you grant me spells!" she said, shaking her head, her thick white hair flying about. "And you grant me spells of healing for these, your enemies!"

"What're ye about?" Athrogate managed to ask.

She looked down at him with purple eyes.

"Rest easy. You should be dead. You were on the edge of the grave."

He couldn't have resisted that suggestion if he wanted to, for despite the healing she had given to him, from whatever god, he couldn't deny a great weariness, one bordering on death indeed.

ACKNOWLEDGMENTS

I'd be remiss if I didn't mention three groups of people who worked hard and long to make my return to Drizzt and the Realms a reality.

First, to Paul Lucas, my agent, and to the rest of the folks at Janklow and Nesbit. When I went to Paul with the idea of approaching Wizards of the Coast, he put the outlines of the deal together and roared ahead. Over the months, as every new *t* needed crossing and every new *i* needed dotting, Paul stayed right on it, remaining positive, keeping me calm.

Second, for nearly twenty years, I worked with Wizards of the Coast (and ten more before that with TSR). These people weren't just my coworkers and editors; they became my friends. So, to Liz Schuh and the gang at Wizards of the Coast, and to the team at Hasbro, you have my sincerest gratitude. You worked outside the box, went to places you'd never gone before, and most of all, put your trust in me. The respect is mutual, I assure you.

And to David Pomerico and the folks at HarperCollins, once again, crossing *t*'s and dotting *i*'s as the days, weeks, and months rolled by, taking on every challenge for such a project with patience and a desire to get it done.

Because that was the thing about this nearly yearlong journey: we all wanted to find a way to make it happen.

So we did.

ABOUT THE AUTHOR

Thirty years ago, R. A. Salvatore created the character of Drizzt Do'Urden, the dark elf who has withstood the test of time to stand today as an icon in the fantasy genre. With his work in the Forgotten Realms, the Crimson Shadow, the DemonWars Saga, and other series, Salvatore has sold more than thirty million books worldwide and has appeared on the *New York Times* bestseller list more than two dozen times. He considers writing to be his personal journey, but still, he's quite pleased that so many are walking the road beside him! R.A. lives in Massachusetts with his wife, Diane, and their three dogs, Ivan, Pikel, and Dexter. He still plays softball for his team, Clan Battlehammer, and enjoys his weekly *DemonWars: Reformation* RPG game.

Salvatore can be found on Facebook at https://www.facebook.com /RA-Salvatore-54142479810/, on Twitter at @r_a_salvatore, and at RASalvaStore.com.